There's a new br
Debra Webb's t
pulse-rai

The Equalisers

Three exciting romances from favourite author
Debra Webb

The Equalisers

DEBRA WEBB

First published in Great Britain 2012
by Mills & Boon, an imprint of Harlequin (UK) Limited,
Eton House, 18-24 Paradise Road, Richmond, Surrey TW9 1SR

THE EQUALISERS © by Harlequin Enterprises II B.V./S.à.r.l 2012

A Soldier's Oath, Hostage Situation and Colby vs Colby were first published in Great Britain by Harlequin (UK) Limited.

A Soldier's Oath © Debra Webb 2007
Hostage Situation © Debra Webb 2007
Colby vs Colby © Debra Webb 2007

ISBN: 978 0 263 89704 3
ebook ISBN: 978 1 408 97071 3

05-1012

Printed and bound in Spain
by Blackprint CPI, Barcelona

A SOLDIER'S OATH

BY
DEBRA WEBB

Debra Webb was born in Scottsboro, Alabama, to parents who taught her that anything is possible if you want it badly enough. She began writing at age nine. Eventually, she met and married the man of her dreams, and then tried various occupations, including selling vacuum cleaners, working in a factory, a daycare centre, a hospital and a department store. When her husband joined the military, they moved to Berlin and Debra became a secretary in the commanding general's office. By 1985 they were back in the States, and finally moved to Tennessee, to a small town where everyone knows everyone else. With the support of her husband and two beautiful daughters, Debra took up writing again, looking to mystery and movies for inspiration. In 1998, her dream of writing for a living came true. You can write to Debra at PO Box 64, Huntland, Tennessee 37345, USA, or visit her website at www.debrawebb.com to find out exciting news about her next book.

This book is dedicated to all the fans of the Colby Agency. Thank you for your faithfulness to this series. Please enjoy the first in this new trilogy revolving around Jim Colby, Victoria's son.

Chapter One

Friday, February 18
St. Louis, Missouri

Willow Harris shifted the car into Park and turned off the engine. She drew in a slow, deep breath and ordered herself to remain calm.

This particular part of the east side of St. Louis wasn't exactly the kind of place a woman wanted to find herself in at dusk, but she had no choice.

He'd called.

She'd had to come, no matter the time of day or night. The man she'd driven here to see didn't keep the usual business hours.

Before getting out of the car she said one last prayer. *Please, God, let the news be good.* She wasn't sure she could take any more bad news.

Eight months.

She'd been fighting to get her son back for eight long months. An eternity. Hurt welled up inside her at the idea that she'd missed his second birthday. Just last week. She'd missed so much already. All those evolving toddler moments. Precious changes that no mother should miss.

Nothing would bring those moments back.

Closing her eyes, she forced the painful thoughts away. She had to be strong. She would never be able to bring her baby home again if she couldn't hold herself together better than this.

"Whatever it takes," she murmured as she opened her eyes and firmed her resolve. No weakness, no fear. "I will do *whatever it takes*."

Willow emerged from her car and headed for the office of Davenport Investigations. She'd been here several times before. But this time was different. This time she would be given an update on the man who'd actually managed to get close enough to send back pictures of her son.

No one had gotten that close before.

Anticipation fluttered in her chest.

She couldn't wait to see the pictures of her baby.

Eight endless months had passed since she'd last seen him.

She hadn't been able to hold him…to kiss his sweet little head. Maybe if she were really lucky, this man would be able to reunite her with her precious child.

After numerous failures he could be the one.

The bell over the door jingled as she entered the

suite of offices that sat tucked between a dry cleaning service and a small chain drug store, both of which had long ago gone out of business. The small waiting room was empty and absolutely silent as usual. Not once during her four previous visits had she encountered another client. Mr. Davenport explained that he carefully arranged appointments to ensure complete privacy. As much as she understood that need, walking into his office alone this close to dark made her a little uneasy.

Whatever it takes, she reminded herself.

She passed two upholstered chairs flanking an end table, the magazine-cluttered top highlighted by the dim glow showering down from a ceramic lamp. No desk, no chair, no telephone and, evidently, no receptionist. Just a space-challenged room designed for waiting.

Since she'd timed her arrival to the minute— experience had taught her not to bother coming early—she strode up to the door that led into Davenport's private office and knocked. He should be waiting for her to show up about now.

"Come in, Ms. Harris," he called through the closed door.

Willow moistened her lips, took another deep breath and entered his office.

He sat behind his massive wooden desk, didn't bother standing as he gestured for her to have a seat. She'd wondered at his lack of social etiquette at first, but the hope that he could help her had overridden any second thoughts. Desperation had a way of doing that.

His desk, credenza and file cabinets were clear of clutter as if he'd taken care to lock away every single scrap of paper that might reveal information regarding one of his clients. However lacking in decorum he might be, he was definitely discreet.

"You have good news?" she asked as she settled into the lone chair on her side of his desk. "And the pictures?" Hope bloomed in her chest at the mere idea of seeing her baby, even if only in covertly snapped photos.

He tossed an envelope in her direction. "I received these day before yesterday."

Willow didn't ask why he hadn't let her know about the pictures before today. Nor did she inquire as to why he avoided giving her an answer as to whether or not he had good news. He most likely had his reasons for doling out information in the way he did, reasons she probably wouldn't want to know. That was something else she'd learned about this man, he didn't like prying questions unless he was the one doing the asking. Her fingers trembled as she opened the envelope and took out the digital prints. Her heart thumped hard and tears burned in her eyes.

Ata.

Her baby.

He looked so big…so different. Two years old. And

she'd missed that special day. The need to hold him was suddenly so intense that she could scarcely breathe.

How could the man she'd thought she loved, the man she'd trusted and married, have done this to her? Somewhere in the back of her mind a voice taunted her, reminding her that she should have listened to her parents. They would tell her that this was the price she paid for getting in bed with the devil. Her stomach knotted violently and she pushed the painful thoughts away.

Yes, she'd made a mistake. But surely God would not consider taking her child from her reasonable punishment for an innocent error in judgment. She refused to believe as her parents did. If that made her evil, then so be it.

Clearing her mind of the ugly past that represented her dysfunctional childhood, she shuffled through picture after picture, her heart bursting with equal measures of joy and sadness. Ata playing on the balcony outside her former husband's home. Her baby's face pressed against the glass of a car window. Him toddling around her ex-husband's mother in the market.

Davenport's man had gotten very close.

Close enough to reach out and touch her baby.

She held the pictures against her chest and lifted her gaze to the waiting investigator. "How soon does he think he can make a move?"

This was the moment she had waited for—prayed for—night after night for so very long.

"We have a problem, Ms. Harris."

Her heart dropped, landing somewhere in the vicinity of her stomach.

Raymond Davenport was not a man she could even hope to read or assess in any way. His expression remained as impassive, as utterly devoid of emotion as a lamp post. But something in his tone, the subtlest note of defeat or disappointment had dread crushing against her vital organs and seeping deep into her bones.

"I don't understand." There couldn't be a problem. Not now. They were so close. "You said your man had gotten close to my son." She held out the pictures. "The proof is right here. What could go wrong?"

"We've had no further contact since I received the photos."

Fear, stark and brutal, roared through her, ruptured the thin membrane of hope. She instinctively knew that this was very bad news.

"On an extremely sensitive job like this one," Davenport went on, "when you lose contact for more than twenty-four hours that usually means only one thing…*trouble*."

She didn't want to hear this. Dear God, she did not want to hear this. It couldn't be true…*please don't let it be true*.

Davenport leaned forward, propped his hands on his desk. The hard-earned experience and cool distance usually in his eyes were overshadowed by something softer, something very much like sympathy. "Ms. Harris, I understand how badly you want to get your boy back. Believe me. I have two sons of my own and grandkids. Every day you have to wait is pure hell, but…"

She wanted to speak up…to tell him not to say more. She didn't want to hear what she knew was coming. But she couldn't force the words from her lips.

"…yours is not the first case like this I've worked. The culture we're dealing with in this situation is completely different. Winning by legal means is impossible, you've learned that the hard way. Stealing the child back is usually the only option for a parent faced with these circumstances."

He paused, and in that moment Willow recognized with slowly building horror that, in this man's opinion, all hope was lost…again.

Before she could protest his unspoken assessment, he continued, "That said, your position is different in yet another way. Your ex-husband and his family are…unique."

In this instance *unique* was just another word for untouchable. The al-Shimmari family was *connected,* socially and politically. Immense wealth added to their power. The Kuwaiti authorities wouldn't dare cross the family.

"Are you saying I should give up hope?" She wouldn't. Never. Never. She would keep looking until she found someone who could help her. If not this man, then someone else. Nothing he could say would change her mind.

"I'm saying, Ms. Harris," he offered quietly, far too quietly for such a brusque man, "that you're looking for a miracle and you're not going to find it. Your ex-husband will order the execution of anyone who gets close to the child. If my man is dead—and I suspect he is—then *no one* is going to be able to get close enough to get your son back."

With a strength she couldn't fathom the source of, Willow restrained the tears that threatened. "Thank you, Mr. Davenport." She stood. "I assume the pictures are mine to keep." How she said this without her voice wobbling she couldn't imagine.

He nodded. "Of course."

She squared her shoulders in an effort to hold onto her disintegrating composure a moment longer. "You'll send me a final bill?"

"Let's call it even, Ms. Harris." He pushed out of his chair and stood, another first in her presence. "You take care of yourself now."

Somehow she pivoted on her heel and walked out of his office. She didn't recall crossing the sidewalk or even getting into her car. Awareness of time and place didn't connect again until she was driving away, the pictures of her son spread across the passenger seat.

Choosing Davenport had obviously been a mistake. She tightened her grip on the steering wheel.

Of course it had been. If he'd lived up to his renowned reputation, she would not be leaving empty-handed. This was nothing more than a minor setback. She would find a new private investigator. A better one. Someone who could get the job done without any excuses. She would start her search for someone more qualified right now. This minute.

...you're looking for a miracle and you're not going to find it.

She blinked back the emotion brimming on her lashes. No. Dammit. He was wrong. She was not looking for a miracle. She didn't need a miracle. All she needed was a man cunning enough and fearless enough to get the job done.

Chicago, Illinois
Same Day

JAMES COLBY, Jr., Jim to the handful of people close to him, waited several minutes before he entered the bar.

It had been a long time since he'd gone into an establishment like this. Maybe not long enough, he mused as he took a long look around. Places like this represented his old life...a life that, thankfully, no longer existed.

The room was dimly lit, the cigarette smoke thick in the air despite the current regulations on smoking in public places. A scattering of tables stood between him and the bar that snaked its way around the length and width of two walls. Few of the stools were occupied and even fewer of the tables. Then again, at 6:15 p.m. it was still fairly early. The crowd, if there was to be one, likely crawled out of the woodwork later in the night.

But Jim wasn't looking for a crowd. Actually, the fewer patrons the better for his purposes. He seriously doubted that the man he'd come to see would hang around once the place got busy. All the more reason to stop wasting time and to get this done.

Spencer Anders sat on the stool farthest from the entrance, his back to the wall. He'd watched Jim enter the bar. He watched now as he approached.

Some three yards from his position was an emergency exit. Jim supposed Anders could use that egress for a hasty retreat if he wasn't in the mood for company. But he didn't. He sat there and continued to observe the man closing in on his position.

Jim strode across the room and took a seat a couple of stools this side of the other man. No need to crowd him.

"Spencer Anders?"

Anders downed the last swallow of his bourbon. "That's right."

"My name is Jim Colby. I have a proposition for you."

"Well, Jim Colby—" Anders placed his empty glass on the bar "—you've been misinformed as to my status." He stood and tossed a couple of bills on the bar to cover his tab. "I'm not looking for any propositions."

Jim kept his smile to himself. He didn't want to tick the guy off, but neither did he want to let him get away. "I heard you were looking for steady employment."

"Really? Who're you?" Anders challenged, "an employment service representative?"

Chicago's population amounted to about four million people. Finding one former army major who didn't want to be found would have taken some time and initiative under normal circumstances. Since tracking Anders to this place, his regular hangout since arriving in Chicago three months prior, hadn't been that difficult, Jim had to assume he wanted to be found despite his get-lost attitude. Anders had taken a room in a nearby motel that served more as a halfway house than anything one might find in a travel guide. He accepted temporary jobs that required only hard labor and no real sense of purpose. He never stayed on long enough to make friends. So far as Jim could see, he spent most of his time making enemies.

"A mutual friend mentioned you were in town seeking a new career direction."

This got ex-Major Anders's attention. For the past two years his MO appeared to include moving on once he'd worn out his welcome. Whether he actually tried to pull his life together after settling in each new location was unknown, but the end result was always the same.

"You must have me confused with someone else, Mr. Colby." He allowed his gaze to zero in fully on Jim's so that there was no misunderstanding as to the finality of his words. "I don't have any friends."

Spencer Anders would have walked away then and there with no further discussion, Jim decided, if he hadn't played the ace up his sleeve.

"Lucas Camp tells me you're the best in covert and low-visibility operations."

Anders hesitated. For three beats Jim wasn't sure if he would turn around or if he would just walk on out. But then he executed an about-face and moved back to the stool he'd vacated.

When Anders's gaze rested on Jim's once more, he said, "I've never worked directly for or with Mr. Camp. I'm surprised he even knows my name. The way I heard it he's retired now."

That was true.

"What's your connection to him?" Anders wanted to know.

Jim had expected that one.

"He married Victoria Colby, my mother."

Anders's eyes narrowed, but not with suspicion. "You're from the Colby Agency?" The name appeared to connect fully for him then.

Jim wasn't surprised that the man recognized his mother's name or that of her agency. The Colby Agency was one of the top private investigations agencies in the country. A man with a background like Anders would consider P.I. firms when searching for employment. In his case, however, that same background prevented him from applying to most.

"I'm not here representing the Colby Agency."

The anticipation that had tapered Anders's focus vanished. "I'm certain you're a busy man, Mr. Colby. Why don't we cut through all the crap and get straight to the point?"

Jim liked this guy already. "I've recently opened my own firm, Mr. Anders. You have the training I'm looking for as well as extensive experience in the Middle East. Considering current events and the Middle East's ongoing status as a hot spot politically as well as economically, I need that kind of experience on my team. I have a vacancy and I'd like you to fill it."

Anders motioned for the bartender to refill his empty tumbler. "You drinking anything?" he said to Jim.

Jim shook his head. That he wasn't even momentarily tempted gave him great satisfaction. That Anders would offer suggested interest in his proposition.

The bartender sidled over and splashed a couple of fingers of bourbon into the other man's empty glass. When he'd moved out of earshot to take care of the next customer, Anders said, "Why open another P.I. firm? You have a problem working for your mother?"

Jim got those questions often, especially from the investigators at the Colby Agency. He would have

been welcome there by all on staff. Victoria Colby-
Camp had expected Jim to take over one day. But he
had other plans. No…not plans…needs. He needed
to do this. And that need had nothing to do with any
inability to work with or for his mother.

"What I have in mind doesn't fit the mold, Mr.
Anders. I'm afraid my mother would be startled at
some of the methods I might choose to utilize."

Still visibly skeptical, Anders sipped his drink before
suggesting, "Perhaps Mr. Camp didn't completely fill
you in on my less-than-desirable work history."

Jim resisted the impulse to argue that if he wanted
to compare histories he would gladly give him a run
for his money on who had the ugliest past. But he
would save that for another time.

"I'm aware of the circumstances surrounding the
way you separated from military service if that's
what you mean." And it was, of course. Spencer
Anders had a stellar record other than that final nasty
smudge. Discounting, of course, a number of misde-
meanor disorderly conducts in public establishments
very much like this one since leaving the military.

The suspicion Jim had expected to see earlier made
its appearance at that point. He understood. Most prospective employers would be put off by the idea of a
general military discharge. It wasn't quite a dishon-
orable discharge, but it carried an equally unattractive
stigma. But Jim knew something most didn't, Spencer
Anders had been railroaded by a superior officer.

The fact that his betrayal couldn't be proven beyond a shadow of a doubt was the reason he'd been charged with the lesser offences of insubordination and conduct unbecoming of an officer rather than being shipped off to spend a life sentence in a military prison. Those seemingly lesser charges had carried a stiff, humiliating penance of their own. Anders had been stripped of rank, all the way down to a first lieutenant, and then generally discharged when he opted to resign rather than accept the charges and grovel as expected.

Then again, to a man like Anders, being labeled a traitor to his country was pretty much a life sentence in itself.

"Then I have to question just what sort of firm you plan to operate, Mr. Colby."

Jim appreciated his frankness.

"Did your source also tell you," Anders went on before Jim could respond to his last statement, "about my difficulties since leaving military service?"

Spencer Anders had separated from the U.S. Army two years ago. Since then he'd spent most of his time in dives not unlike this one, attempting to obliterate the past; only the towns changed. His blood alcohol level lingered above the legal limit more often than not, Jim would wager. He also recognized the strategy. Been there, done that. But booze wasn't the answer to Anders's problems. Telling him so wouldn't help. This was something he had to come to terms with on his own.

"As long as you stay sober on the job, I don't care what you do in your free time." Jim, of all people, understood what made a man like Anders turn to the bottle for a solace found no other place. The bad habit was taken up for a single, unhealthy reason and would be dumped for the same. He wouldn't need any twelve-step program, all he needed was his self-worth back.

That would come in time given the right circumstances.

Anders finished off the bourbon. "Just because I was forced out of the army doesn't mean I'm interested in a life of anything beyond the occasional barroom brawl. Believe it or not, high crimes aren't my style."

Jim almost laughed at that. "There are times," he admitted, "when working within the law won't get the job done. But I'm not talking about breaking the law for the sake of breaking it, Mr. Anders. I'm only talking about going slightly beyond it and perhaps ignoring some aspects of it when the need arises."

"Well, good luck to you, Mr. Colby. As much as I appreciate the offer, I'm not sure I'm the man you're looking for."

Jim took a business card from his coat pocket and laid it on the bar. "Call me if you change your mind. The doors open Monday morning, and I'd like you there when that happens."

He didn't wait for a response.

As he drove away, Jim wondered how long it

would take the man to decide he needed a second chance badly enough to risk failure and betrayal.

Jim knew firsthand how hard it was to meet that particular challenge and the expectations that went along with treading out onto that shaky limb. Sometimes the fear of failure was the scariest part of all.

He thought about his wife and baby girl. There wasn't a day that passed that Jim didn't consider whether or not he could be the man, the husband and father, those two needed him to be.

Was starting his own venture part of that whole I-don't-want-to-fail scenario? With his own business he would set the rules, answering only to himself. No one else would be holding a preconceived measurement or standard of success against his every endeavor.

The thought had crossed his mind, more than once if he admitted the truth.

Just a little baggage of his own he had to carry around until he got past it.

Jim drove to the South Loop and took the exit that led to his new suite of offices. The old brownstone needed some renovation but nothing he couldn't handle in time.

After parking in the back alley, he unlocked the rear entrance and flipped on the lights. He should have gone home. Tasha would be wondering if he planned to make every night a late night. But he'd wanted to check the answering machine before going home. He'd made a few calls this afternoon, and he hoped to get some timely responses.

He made his way to the front room that was now a lobby, turning on lights as he went. When he was halfway up the stairs to the second floor the doorbell buzzed; someone was at the door.

His first thought was that Tasha had come to drag him home, but bringing Jamie out in the blustery February weather wasn't his wife's technique. She'd call and order him to get home.

Could be his first customer. He had hung up a shingle of sorts today.

Or, if he was lucky, it would be Anders to come to say he'd thought about Jim's offer and wanted the job.

A grin slid across Jim's face as he opened the door and identified his visitor. None of the above.

"Mom." He leaned against the door frame and crossed his arms over his chest. "Come to see what I've done with the place?"

Victoria Colby-Camp returned his smile. "I'm sure you haven't had time to do that much. But you'll get it done."

That she believed in him so completely no matter how many times he missed the mark or fell down as he tried to turn his life around still surprised him. She was a hell of a mom for a guy who'd gone as low as it was humanly possible to go.

He glanced past her. "Where's your other half?"

Victoria rarely went anywhere without Lucas unless he was out of town and she had no other choice. The two were inseparable.

"He's keeping your lovely wife and our grand-daughter company while dinner gets cold."

Dinner. Oh, man. He'd forgotten. Dammit.

"Just let me check my voice mail and lock up and I'm on my way."

"I'll ride along with you," she offered. "Lucas can bring me by to pick up my car later."

Jim let the smile nudging at his lips do what it would. He'd never been big on smiles, but these days the women in his life knew how to draw them out of him. His mother knew him all too well. If she didn't ensure he got going he would get distracted and end up hanging around another hour.

"Sure. Gimme a sec."

He bounded up the stairs and into his office. The second floor would serve as his private office and a conference room. The lobby, other offices, and a small kitchen-turned-employee-lounge would take up the downstairs space. Assuming he ever had any employees. Monday morning he would interview receptionist candidates. He had three applicants so far.

The blinking red light on his answering machine signaled that he had at least one message.

Anticipation roiled through him as he pressed the button. He waited through the announcement that he had two new messages. The first was from Renee

Vaughn, a former assistant district attorney from Atlanta. They had spoken by phone yesterday. She was interested in a position at his firm. He was definitely interested in her.

"Mr. Colby," her voice rang out with the strength only a real fighter possessed, "this is Renee Vaughn. I've decided to fly in for a face-to-face before I make a final decision. I'm hoping two-thirty on Monday will work for you. Call my cell if anything comes up." She rattled off the number and the call ended.

"One down and two to go," Jim murmured. His goal was to start out with three associates. He hesitated to call them investigators. The work they would do here wouldn't always involve investigating, at least not in the usual sense.

"Mr. Colby, this is Spencer Anders," floated from the answering machine next. The noise in the background told him Spencer had still been at the bar when he called. At least he'd called.

Jim resisted the urge to shout "yes!"

"I've been thinking about your offer and I'd like to talk to you again. I'll come by your office Monday morning about nine…if you're still interested…. We'll go from there and see what happens."

His trepidation was crystal-clear, but Jim had no doubts. Anders was exactly the kind of associate he wanted on his team. He'd have to thank Lucas for tipping him off to the guy's availability. That Anders had reacted so quickly, if not decisively, indicated an underlying desire to get his life back on track.

A big load off his shoulders, Jim headed down to rendezvous with Victoria. This news gave him something to celebrate at the family dinner tonight.

"Ready?" Victoria asked as he joined her in the soon-to-be lobby.

"I am now." He followed his mother out the front door and locked up.

"I see you've officially hung your shingle."

This was a kind of running joke between them now that he'd actually started classes at the University of Chicago last semester. Taking only one or two classes at a time, completion of the program would require years and years. He was prepared to accept the wait. No matter how long it took he wanted to obtain his law degree. The goal meant a lot to him and even though his mother would never say so, he knew that accomplishment would mean a lot to her as well. She insisted that he was perfect just as he was, but then, she was his mother. His wife was extremely pleased as well.

Jim glanced up at the brand-new sign he'd hung next to the front entrance. Pride welled in his chest. He had made this happen, with a lot of support from the people he loved. "Yep, it's official now."

The Equalizers were about to open for business.

Chapter Two

Spencer Anders remained in his car for an additional twenty minutes. He'd made up his mind. The hesitation was unnecessary, but here he sat. Nine-fifteen. He'd told Colby he'd be in around nine.

Why the hell had he done that? The impulse had hit him less than half an hour after Colby had walked out of the joint that had been Spencer's second home since he'd arrived in the Windy City. He used the pay phone at the end of the bar and made the call.

What the hell had he been thinking?

That he had to get his life back? That somehow, things had to start making sense again before he lost himself completely?

Yes to both of the above.

Spencer moistened his lips and fought back the craving for a drink. One didn't go with the other. If he was going to make this work he had to keep his head together.

He could do it.

He banished the nagging voice that tried to tell him otherwise.

"No going backward," he muttered. This was his chance to go forward again. He couldn't screw it up.

Spencer climbed out of the car. He glanced first left then right before crossing the street. He didn't know that much about Jim Colby, but he did know the Colby Agency's esteemed reputation.

He didn't fully understand Jim's decision to start his own firm rather than working at his mother's prestigious agency, but he did trust Lucas Camp.

The name reverberated through him. He'd never actually met the man, but he knew the name, and that was more than sufficient. Five years was a long time. The mission was one of those unwinnable situations where no one was going to walk away satisfied. Still, the mission was crucial. There had been only two members of Spencer's team left by the time a special unit was brought in to attempt a rescue.

Mission Recovery.

Spencer had never heard of the unit. Some black-ops organization loosely attached to the CIA, he'd learned later. Lucas Camp had been the deputy director.

Lucas Camp's unit had saved Spencer's life and the lives of his two remaining team members. If this gig panned out, Spencer would owe Lucas Camp for saving his hide yet a second time.

Maybe he would get the opportunity to thank him in person. Spencer had no idea how the hell Lucas Camp knew he was in Chicago. No, wait. That wasn't true. Camp had been, probably still was, even if only in an advisory capacity, attached to the CIA. Getting intimate information about the Pope himself wouldn't be a problem for a man like him.

Spencer had to admit, having anyone vouch for him these days was a plus. Maybe the whole world didn't see him as a traitor.

That same old fury started to burn deep in his gut. He suppressed the triggered feelings. Thinking about the past would be detrimental to the present, not to mention the future. He had to make a clean break.

That time was now.

He paused at the door to consider the sign. The Equalizers. Interesting moniker. He considered what Colby had told him in their brief meeting. His target client base was those whose troubles couldn't be resolved so easily within the boundaries of the law. He wondered what would make a man like Jim Colby veer that close to criminal activity. From what Spencer knew, the Colby Agency had an impeccable reputation, one respected by clients and law enforcement alike. What made the one and only son of the owner of that esteemed agency different?

Secrets of his own, Spencer surmised. Maybe he

and Colby had something in common—a history best left in the past.

Spencer braced himself and reached for the door. Now or never. This was his chance to start over. He couldn't let it get away. He owed it to himself.

Taking into account the fact that he would otherwise have died five years ago, he owed it to Lucas Camp. He just hoped like hell that he had still had it in him to live up to the man's recommendation.

A new kind of enthusiasm kindled inside him. Jim Colby had told him that his mother was now married to Lucas Camp. If Lucas had recommended him, that meant he wanted Spencer working with Jim. So, he could look at this from the standpoint that not only would he be doing himself a favor by getting his life back together, he'd also be doing Camp a favor. A bit of a stretch, but, hey, it wasn't completely implausible.

Not only was it plausible, the concept served as plenty of motivation for doing this right.

Inside the brownstone, the lobby area was deserted. A desk and a couple of chairs. No receptionist or waiting clients. The decorating reminded him of most military offices, unremarkable and rather drab. Not a problem. After graduating college he'd spent ten years in the army he'd loved. Drab was a preferred color.

Tension rippled through him and Spencer drew in a deep breath before ordering himself to stay calm.

He already knew Colby wanted him on his team. The rest would be nothing more than technicalities. This wasn't an interview, it was a negotiation.

The smell of fresh-brewed coffee wafted from somewhere down the hall. Spencer had about decided to head that way when Jim Colby appeared.

"Right on time." He raised his steaming cup. "Coffee?"

"Coffee would be good." Spencer had already downed three cups but he could definitely use another. The caffeine helped him battle the need for additional fortification. What he now had to consider forbidden fortification.

"Follow me."

Colby led the way to a small kitchen that Spencer presumed would serve as an employee lounge. Refrigerator, microwave, sink and a couple of cabinets. His would-be employer passed him a brimming mug.

"Thanks." The coffee tasted as good as it smelled.

"My office is upstairs."

Spencer nodded and followed Colby to the second floor. Though the brownstone's decor hadn't been updated in a couple of decades, the architecture made it comfortable and interesting in a classic sort of way. The location wasn't one of the most desired in the city, but the neighborhood appeared in the early stages of revitalization. A year or two from now and the streets would be teeming with thriving businesses and highly sought-after lofts. Colby's selection of the location was probably a strategic one.

A sleek wooden desk and leather chair, along with a couple of upholstered chairs for clients, were already stationed in Colby's office. Unpacked boxes of office equipment as well as supplies were scattered about, along with the necessary filing cabinets. Looked as if the boss was well on his way to settling in.

"I'm still getting organized," Colby said as he took the chair behind his desk. "I'll be interviewing receptionists this morning. I hope we'll have someone to answer the phone by lunchtime."

We. Anticipation spiked before Spencer could stop the possibly premature reaction. "What's your current body count?" Might as well get a handle on the personnel arrangement and chain of command before he made any kind of commitment beyond this impulsive appearance.

"So far, two. Me," Colby said with a pointed look at him, "and you."

His answer surprised Spencer. So he really was getting in on the ground floor of a new venture. "What's your operational plan?" Learning the exact nature of what he was getting into here was the first order of business. He wasn't about to be caught off guard again in this lifetime.

"I hope to hire at least three associates."

Associates. Not investigators. This nudged Spencer's curiosity.

"What types of cases do you plan to take on?" The answer to this question was key in many ways. The clientele at any firm was the primary factor in how the firm was judged by others. Though he seriously doubted that Lucas Camp would recommend him for a position within a firm that wasn't on the up and up, Spencer hadn't missed the look in Jim Colby's eyes when he'd talked about helping those whose troubles went beyond the law's boundaries.

"Pretty much whatever walks through the door." Colby set his coffee aside. "In the beginning it may be necessary to take cases we'll choose not to take later on. Right now our primary objective is to get our name out there. To let people know we've set up shop. This business thrives on word of mouth more so than any other means."

Made sense. "What's the plan on case authority? Will you expect to be kept in the loop on all decisions relative to a case once it's assigned?"

"When we take on a client, I'll make a decision as to who is the best man for the job. If it's your case, I'll expect you to lay out a plan of action and then keep me up to speed on how it's coming along. Otherwise, the ultimate moment-to-moment decisions are yours to make."

Spencer nodded. Sounded fair to him. "What about salary?" Since Colby's business was just getting off the ground he wondered how lucrative a proposition this could possibly be.

"We'll all be working for the same base salary, including me," Jim explained. "Whatever profits we net, we'll split evenly among the associates."

Now there was an answer he hadn't expected. "Like a partnership?" Surely that wasn't what he meant. No firm allowed the new hires to start out as equal partners.

"Exactly. We'll all share the burden of cost and we'll all share the bounty."

Once he'd absorbed that surprising response, Spencer moved on to his next question. "Do you have other associates in mind already?"

"I'll be interviewing a candidate this afternoon. If I'm lucky, she'll be coming on board also."

A woman. Spencer had wondered about that as well.

"Renee Vaughn," Jim went on. "She's a former assistant district attorney from Atlanta."

At one time Spencer had considered a law degree. He'd gotten his bachelor's degree in political science, but he'd opted for the military instead of law school. Maybe that had been his first mistake.

"I have an office set up for you," Jim said, dragging Spencer from his unproductive thoughts. "If you're prepared to get started this morning, I'd like you to work up a history for me. Cover your basic skills, any specialized training and the locations where you've worked or been assigned. I'll keep a file like this on all associates for use in determining what cases each is best suited for."

Made sense.

Spencer stood. "Show me the way and I'll get right on it."

Accepting his statement as a yes, Jim nodded. "All right then."

The associates' offices were located on the first floor along the corridor just past the lounge. There were four small offices and a room Jim indicated would be a supply room. At the end of the corridor was the building's rear exit that led into an alley that would serve as a personnel parking area.

As the first associate hired, Spencer got his pick of the offices. He opted for the one on the left side of the hall next to the lounge since it had a window with a view of the neighborhood park across the street.

When the first receptionist candidate arrived for her interview Jim left him to get started on a detailed work history. Typically, that came first, in the form of a résumé, but this situation appeared to be hardly typical.

Maybe that was the reason Spencer felt at home for the first time in more than two years. He'd learned that he couldn't count on anything typical or run-of-the-mill. The everyday was no longer reliable.

Do not go down that road.

All he had to do was keep his eyes forward. No looking back. There was no undoing the past, no matter how wrong. His military career was over. Period. He had an opportunity for something new here. He had to keep that goal in mind if he was to have a future. At the rate he'd been going that prospect had grown pretty dim of late. But that was behind him now.

No looking back.

1:00 p.m.

WILLOW HARRIS sat in her rental car for over half an hour. Most of that time was spent attempting to work up the nerve to make the first move. It wasn't that she was afraid for her safety. The neighborhood wasn't that great, but it wasn't any worse than the one in East St. Louis where her former P.I.'s office was located.

Waiting…working up her courage, she did a lot of that lately. In the beginning sheer adrenaline had driven her, overriding any second thoughts or hesitancy. She'd pushed and pushed and searched and searched without the first consideration for her safety or anything else.

But it was different now.

Another anxiety stalked her like a ruthless killer in the dark.

Fear.

The fear of dashed hope. Each time she moved on to a new investigator her anticipation of finally getting her son back renewed…only to be sucked completely out of her when failure crashed down upon her shoulders all over again.

She'd spent all weekend attempting to locate someone who might be able to help her. Her gaze focused on the street in front of her car. The story had been basically the same with each agency she'd called.

I'm very sorry, Ms. Harris, but that's a case we don't feel comfortable taking on.

Just when she'd been ready to give up, the last guy she'd called—a low-rent one-man operation she'd almost skipped over in her online Yellow Pages search—had told her about a rumor he'd heard. A new shop was opening up in Chicago. There was a buzz going around that this one would be different from all the others.

So here she was, in Chicago sitting outside a place that might very well be her last hope.

The Equalizers.

Her low-rent P.I. had waxed on about how this place planned to take covert investigations to the next level. The Equalizers would accept the less desirable or riskier jobs that no one else wanted to touch.

Since the firm had only just opened, Willow couldn't be sure if the plan to take on any and all cases was out of necessity or not, but she was here.

She was desperate.

Her savings and investments were dwindling fast. This place might very well prove her final hope in more ways than one. There wouldn't be enough money to hire anyone new if this one failed.

An ache twisted through her, making her want to curl up into a ball of defeat. No. She had to be strong.

The only way she would ever get her son back was if she didn't give up, if she tried harder.

Determination rushed through her on the tail of a burst of adrenaline when Davenport's words echoed in her brain. Maybe she *was* looking for a miracle. Who said there was anything wrong with that? Miracles manifested themselves in many ways. She'd been taught that concept her whole life. That was one part of her upbringing she needed to hang onto.

Willow got out of the car and strode across the street to the entrance of the brownstone designated as number 129. The painted wooden sign hanging next to the door announced the name of the business in bold strokes.

The Equalizers.

Well, she would just see if the firm could live up to its fledgling reputation.

Acting before she could think of another reason to waver, she opened the door and went inside. The sudden warmth reminded her that she'd gotten cold sitting in her car with the engine turned off for all that time. A winter chill had blasted the midwest last night, causing major delays in several airports. Thank goodness Midland hadn't been one of them. Once she'd made up her mind to come, she would have done so even if she'd had to walk.

A receptionist sat behind an L-shaped desk. Her back was turned to the door while she typed away at her computer. Several chairs and accompanying tables bordered the room. Magazines were fanned across the top of one of the tables. No plants or goldfish tanks. No heavy stench of cigarette smoke as she'd encountered in many of the agencies she'd visited. Just empty and quiet, like Davenport's office had been, except for the receptionist's busy fingers on the keyboard.

The decorating scheme left something to be desired, but the place was neat and clean. She could appreciate that after the last couple of places she'd visited in the past forty-eight hours.

Since the receptionist didn't make the usual overture though she'd surely heard the door close, Willow stepped closer to her desk and spoke up. "My name is Willow Harris. I'm here to see the man in charge." She purposely left off the phrase *if he's available*. She'd come too far to accept any kind of excuse. The idea that he could be out of town banded around her chest and squeezed. Booking the first available flight and rushing here might have been a mistake, but she'd had no choice.

Her situation wouldn't wait. She'd waited too long already.

Please let him be here.

Rather than offer a customary greeting, the receptionist frowned as she gave Willow a thorough once-over with assessing brown eyes. She appeared less than pleased at being interrupted from whatever she'd been doing on the computer. Maybe she wasn't

the receptionist at all. She could be one of the investigators who had decided to use this computer for one
reason or the other.

"Is he in?" Willow prompted after another
awkward moment elapsed. And here she had thought
she'd already seen the most bizarre and unprofes-
sional this business had to offer.

"How do you know the person in charge isn't a
woman?" The woman tucked a handful of sandy-
brown hair behind one ear and gave Willow a
pointed look.

Too taken aback to be embarrassed, Willow struggled a moment to come up with an appropriate
response. "Well…who *is* in charge?" Maybe this
woman didn't work here at all.

"Mr. Jim Colby," the woman behind the desk said
with a smile that wasn't really a smile, more a
fleeting tick. "Do you have an appointment?"

Willow looked around the small reception area.
There was no one else there. Unless Mr. Colby
already had a client in his office or was expecting one
momentarily, she didn't see the point in the question.
But then she remembered the discreet way Davenport had operated.

"No," she admitted. "I don't have an appointment.
I flew in from St. Louis this morning in hopes that
Mr. Colby could make some time for me."

"Calling first would have been smarter."

Willow reminded herself that she needed to get

past this woman and to the man in charge. Giving her any advice on how a proper receptionist conducted herself might not be conducive to making that happen.

The truth was the woman was right. But Willow managed to keep her voice calm. "I know. I apologize for just showing up like this, but the matter is urgent."

The receptionist, who didn't wear a name badge or have a name plate on her desk and who looked utterly unimpressed, smiled another of those unsmiles. "I'm new here. I'll have to check his calendar first." She flipped through the calendar taking up space on the oak desktop next to the telephone. Not a single page she previewed had anything at all written on it.

"He appears to be free," the receptionist announced. "Just have a seat, Ms. Harris, and I'll find out if he can see you today." She gestured to a chair.

Willow settled into a chair and tried to slow her mind's frantic churning. Exhaustion simply wasn't an adequate description of just how tired she felt. It was, however, the only word she could think of at the moment. This man—Jim Colby—had to help her.

The receptionist buzzed her boss on the intercom, using the handset to keep his end of the conversation private. A couple of pauses and yes sirs, and then she placed the handset back in its cradle.

"Up the stairs and the first door on the left."

Evidently that was a yes to the question of whether or not he was available. Willow offered a polite smile, deserved or not. "Thank you."

The woman didn't say anything, not even a "You're welcome." She swiveled in her chair and resumed her work at the computer. Mr. Colby needed to seriously consider public relations classes for his receptionist.

The desperation clawing at Willow's heart was the only thing that kept her from walking out, considering the vibes she'd gotten so far. If she'd wasted the money coming here…if she'd made a mistake…

She blocked the thoughts. Stay focused. There hadn't been any other choice. This was her last hope.

A man she presumed to be Jim Colby waited in the doorway of an office in the upstairs corridor.

"Ms. Harris." He thrust out his hand. "I'm Jim Colby."

She placed her hand in his and he gave it a firm shake. "Thank you for seeing me, Mr. Colby."

"Can I get you some coffee or water?" He directed her into his office as he made the offer.

Expansive oak desk, a credenza and lots of file cabinets along with numerous unpacked boxes took up most of the floor space in the office. Mr. Colby had, literally, just set up shop. "Ah…no, thank you," she abruptly remembered to say in answer to his question. Though she appreciated that he appeared determined to be polite, getting right down to business was her priority at the moment. She sat down in one of the upholstered chairs and waited for him to do the same on the other side of his desk.

He studied her a moment, intense blue eyes looking right through her as if she were an open book published in easy-to-read large print. His assessment, however, appeared far less suspicious than that of his receptionist.

"What can I do for you, Ms. Harris?"

This was the hard part. How did she adequately relay the volatility and urgency of her situation as concisely as possible?

"It all started four years ago," she began, without allowing the gut-wrenching memories that attempted to bob to the surface to do so. She'd learned long ago not to revisit that past. It was too hard to maintain her sanity otherwise. "I was traveling on business in Kuwait. I met a man and we had a…sort of whirlwind romance. We married only a few days later."

She didn't see any reason to give him the trivial details of her lapse into stupidity. She'd relived those days over and over again already in an attempt to pinpoint something—anything—that should have served as a warning to her. So far she'd found nothing.

"Two years ago we had a child, a boy."

Something in his expression changed when she said *boy*. She already knew what he was thinking. A boy was a far more prized asset than a girl, even in a country as liberal and progressive as the State of Kuwait, making her quest a far more difficult one.

"Eight months ago I realized I couldn't live the

way my husband wanted me to for a moment longer."
It was not nearly as simple as that, but she knew from
experience that he would ask questions until he had
all the information he needed. No need to go into the
gory details until she knew whether he intended to
take her case or not. "I decided that a divorce was the
only option. I could return to my home in the States
and put those years in the Middle East behind me."

"But your ex didn't want you to take his son out
of the country."

Before she could stop the onslaught, memories
from that day swarmed inside her head, making her
want to cry. She blinked back the emotions. This
might be her last chance. She couldn't screw it up.

"Not only did he not want me to take him out of
Kuwait, he wanted me to go and he never wanted me
to see my child again." How could she have lived
with him for nearly three years and not noticed how
little he actually cared for her? She'd gotten a crash
course those last few months.

Focus, Willow. No drifting.

Jim Colby waited for her to continue. She licked
her lips, swallowed at the emotion pressing at the
back of her throat and said the rest. "He had me
exported out of the country like black-market cargo.
He left me at an airport in California with no ID at
all. He took everything to ensure I couldn't immediately return. Then he filed for divorce and claimed I
had deserted him as well as our son."

"The Kuwaiti legal system ruled in his favor, of course."

She nodded, unsure of her voice now. Images of her little boy kept swimming in front of her eyes.

"When was the last time you saw your son, Ms. Harris?"

"Eight months, one week and two days ago." She could give him the actual hour, but she'd given enough.

"Why seek professional help now? After so many months? Did your attorney give you reason to believe your situation could be worked out some other way?"

He cut right to the chase. She liked that. Hope glimmered inside her.

"I started with the legal system. But I soon figured out that I wasn't going to make this happen through legal channels. My lawyer was pretty up-front about that. Then I started hiring private investigators in an attempt to find someone who could help me."

"How many P.I.s have you hired during the past few months?"

She wanted to tell him that information was irrelevant. But he was right to ask. He couldn't operate unless he had all the pertinent facts. Going through half a dozen P.I.s had taught her that.

"Six."

He was number seven if she didn't count the low-rent guy who had given her the free advice about coming here.

If the number surprised him he didn't let on. But

she wasn't so sure she would be able to read anything in those blue eyes anyway. If she'd thought Davenport was unreadable, this guy had it down to a science.

"What is it you want me to do for you, Ms. Harris?"

Not only could she not read his eyes, his voice gave away absolutely nothing.

She clutched the arms of her chair, braced herself for an uphill battle. "I just want my son back, Mr. Colby. I don't care how you have to do it. I want him back."

"You're certain he's still alive and living in Kuwait?"

The question, uttered with such frankness, tore at her heart. But at least it wasn't a no. That meant he was considering her request.

"Yes, I'm positive."

Now would come the part that would change his mind.

"Tell me about your ex-husband. Is he the kind of man who would go to extreme measures to keep what he believed belonged to him? What kind of personal security, if any, does he maintain?"

Ice slid through her veins. This was where he would insert the "no."

"My ex-husband will do anything to keep his son." She thought of Davenport's man and a new wave of terror washed over her. She had to tell that part to Colby. "Including possibly hurting anyone who gets in his way. He has a heavy security detail." Davenport had used those terms when describing her husband's personal security.

Please, God, she prayed, *don't let this man be afraid to take her case.*

The strangest thing happened then. Mr. Colby smiled. Not the wide, ear-to-ear kind of charming smile to set her at ease. Not at all. This quirk of his lips was one-sided, almost daring. She hadn't noticed the scar on his cheek until then. The scar had her looking closer…noting the harsh planes and angles of his face. He looked hard…brutal maybe. Fear trickled through her. Whatever it takes, she reminded herself.

"Sounds like your ex-husband needs a lesson in proper parenting. Not to worry, Ms. Harris, I know how to handle men like him."

She blinked, took a breath to banish the trepidation that had started to build. Had she misunderstood?

"Does this mean you're taking my case?"

"I'm not only taking your case, Ms. Harris, I'm going to get your son back for you."

Chapter Three

6:20 p.m.

Over three hours.

Willow had left Jim Colby's office at three o'clock. He'd promised to call as soon as he was prepared to brief her on his strategy for recovering her son.

She'd checked into a motel close by. She'd been waiting ever since.

Her cell phone lay on the bedside table, the charging icon blinking. She'd almost forgotten to plug it in. That would have been bad. That portable device had become her lifeline in the past few months. She never knew when the P.I. currently working her case would need to reach her, so she'd kept the thing turned on 24/7.

She thought about Jim Colby and his insistence that he would ensure she got her son back. That was definitely a first. She'd had several ambitious P.I.s claim they could handle her case upon initial acceptance, but not one had looked her dead in the eye and stated unequivocally that he would get the job done.

A blend of hope and uncertainty twisted in her chest. Could Jim Colby really do this?

Who was this man who would dare to make such a promise?

Before coming to Chicago she had looked up what she could about him on the Internet, but most of the stuff that had popped up on her search was actually about his mother and her private investigations agency. His past appeared to have fallen beneath the radar somehow. Whether that was good or bad she hadn't decided just yet.

But if he could get her son back she didn't care what lay behind that slightly marred, flinty face. Who he was didn't really matter. All that mattered was whether or not he could do what he said he could do.

She wanted desperately to cling to that hope, but she needed to know more before she let herself believe fully in this man. However prestigious his mother's reputation, he was an unknown and unproven entity.

God, she was so tired. She'd barely slept last night. As much as she wanted to crash and sleep for hours, she couldn't do that until she had some indication of what would happen next.

…you're looking for a miracle…

Maybe Davenport had been right. Maybe she *was* looking for a miracle. She'd certainly had the kind recounted in the Bible told to her over and over again as a child, but did real miracles actually happen anymore? And the next question was, had she found that miracle, if it really did exist, in the Equalizers?

A knock on the door of her motel room had her practically jumping out of her skin.

Housekeeping? Surely not at this hour. No one knew she was in Chicago. Not that she had anyone. Even her folks had disowned her when she married someone they considered a terrorist. That had been the kinder of the names they had given him.

Evidently they had been right after all. Certainly *devil* came to her mind whenever she thought of her ex these days.

A second knock jerked her back from the preoccupation that total exhaustion allowed to creep up on her so easily and at the least likely moments.

She stood. Smoothed a hand over her skirt and walked as quietly as she could to the door. Pressing her eye to the peephole she resisted the urge to draw away in surprise or fear or possibly both as her brain registered the stranger standing on the other side of the door.

Male. Thirty or thirty-two maybe.

Tall, strong-looking.

Uneasiness coursed through her veins.

This had to be a mistake. He had to have stopped at the wrong room.

Should she say something? But then he'd know she was in here...alone. Why hadn't she bought pepper spray months ago? Coming here like this—doing all she'd done over the past eight months—was more than enough reason to be concerned with protecting herself.

The trouble was she hadn't been thinking about anyone except her son. Dumb, Willow. What good would she be to her son if she got herself killed?

"Ms. Harris?"

Willow took a big step back from the door.

How could this stranger know her name?

"Ms. Harris, my name is Spencer Anders. Jim Colby sent me to discuss your case."

She allowed herself to breathe. Jim Colby. Okay. But why would he send someone to her motel? Had she even told Mr. Colby where she'd be staying?

For a moment she couldn't think, then she remembered. Yes, she'd left word. She'd called the receptionist and provided the name and address of the motel where she could be reached. After her experience with the receptionist, Willow hadn't been sure whether Mr. Colby would get the message or not. Evidently he had.

She stepped to the door once more. "Do you have identification?" She cleared her throat, annoyed at the tremble in her voice. New concerns immediately started to surface. Why wasn't Mr. Colby handling her case himself? He was the one to insist he could get her son back. Was this his way of copping out? If his man failed would Colby be off the hook for making such a claim so hastily?

Willow closed her eyes and fought the vertigo of fear and confusion. She had to stop this. She had to focus.

She opened her eyes and watched through the tiny hole as the man who had identified himself as Spencer Anders reached into his hip pocket and withdrew a wallet. When he held a Louisiana driver's license up for her to see she confirmed that his name was indeed Spencer Anders.

"Why do you have a Louisiana driver's license?" Relevant or not she wanted to know. Louisiana was an awfully long way from Illinois. If he was a licensed P.I. in Illinois, wouldn't he need to be a resident of this state? Too many questions that just didn't matter. She was borrowing trouble and putting off the inevitable.

"I'm new to Chicago." He slid the license back into his wallet, then tucked the wallet into his pocket once more. "Look, Ms. Harris, if you're uncomfortable speaking to me in your room, I'll wait for you in the coffee shop down the block."

Maybe she should call Jim Colby and confirm that he'd sent this man.

"We've worked out the strategy for recovering your son," Anders said, drawing her attention back to him. "If you're still interested in hearing the details, I'll be waiting in the coffee shop. Take a left at the motel entrance and you can't miss it."

…recovering your son…

Willow wrenched the door open when he started to walk away. "Wait."

He hesitated a moment before turning to face her. A new trickle of trepidation slithered down her spine. Stop it, she ordered. This man was here to help her. Getting off on the wrong foot wouldn't be productive.

He faced her and only then did she actually look at him closely enough to absorb the details. Dark hair, really dark. Gray eyes. Tired eyes. His expression wasn't precisely grim, but the lines and angles of his face spoke of having seen more unpleasantness than any one human was built to take. Just like his employer.

His height, six-one at least, put her off just a little. At five-two, she found that almost everyone was taller than her. Perhaps it was the broad shoulders that went along with the towering height, coupled with the grim face that unsettled her just a little. No, she decided, it was the eyes. Somber. Weary. The eyes looked way older than the thirty-one or -two he appeared to be. And yet there was a keen alertness staring out at her from those solemn depths.

What she saw or didn't see was of no consequence. He was here. He had a plan. That was the whole point…the only point.

"Come in." She squared her shoulders and told herself to get past the hesitation. All this attempting to read between the lines was making her paranoid. She'd never met Davenport's man, the one who'd probably lost his life while getting close to her son. For all she knew he might have been far more intimidating than this man.

Willow moved away from the door to allow Anders entrance. After coming inside he closed the door, but remained standing directly in front of it.

Taking a deep, steadying breath, she opened the conversation. The next move was clearly hers. "Thank you for coming, Mr. Anders." That was a mega understatement, but it would suffice. She could thank him properly when he'd gotten her son back.

"I have a few questions for you, Ms. Harris." He reached into an interior pocket of his leather jacket. "The information you provided was helpful, but I need more details to round out our strategy."

Jim Colby had asked her to make a list of the events that had led up to her decision to ask for a divorce from her husband, as well as anything she could think of related to him or his family that might be useful in the coming task. She'd spent an hour coming up with as many details as she could call to mind. Mr. Colby had obviously passed her list along to Mr. Anders.

Might as well get comfortable. If this went anything like her interviews with previous investigators, it would take some time.

"Please." She indicated the chair next to the small table positioned in front of the window. "Sit." She perched on the edge of the bed and tugged at the hem of her skirt to ensure it stayed close to her knees where it belonged. She cleared her mind of any static prompted by worry or anxiety as she clasped her hands in her lap and waited for him to begin. Listening carefully was essential in understanding the details.

As he took the seat she'd offered, she focused on the man in an effort to get a fix on him. First, she considered the way he dressed. The leather bomber jacket was brown and had the worn appearance of being a favorite. The blue jeans were equally faded and obviously a favored wardrobe selection as well. The black V-neck sweater he wore beneath the jacket was layered on top of a white T-shirt, both of which looked new. If she had to assess him solely on his overall appearance she would conclude that he was a nice man with a lot of painful history.

Willow abruptly wondered if he came to the same conclusion about her. Nice, with a heavy load of hurt slung around her neck like a millstone.

"Did you sign any kind of legal documents when you married Mr. al-Shimmari? A prenuptial agreement or other binding arrangement? Anything at all besides a marriage license?"

Willow regarded his question carefully before shaking her head. There had been essentially no paperwork involved. "Nothing. I know it sounds strange now, but we really were in love. Or, at least, I was. I had no money, other than my salary and a few small investments, and he didn't appear worried that I would attempt to steal any of his." She'd already been down this road with her attorney during the divorce proceedings. There was nothing to be gained by rehashing it, but she kept that to herself. She needed to give this man a chance.

"Did he or his family pressure you to convert to the ways of Islam?"

A frown tugged at her forehead, the tension somehow reaching all the way to the base of her skull. This was one she hadn't been asked before. "No. Not really. It was suggested a couple of times, but he knew I wasn't going to convert when we married. We talked about that. He didn't have a problem with my decision."

Spencer Anders leaned forward and braced his elbows on his knees. "Ms. Harris, do you know if your ex-husband was Sunni or Shia?"

She wasn't sure where he was going with this. "Sunni." His hands kept distracting her. They hung between his spread thighs, relaxed but infinitely dangerous-looking. A person's hands said a lot about them. She'd always been fascinated by hands. She blinked, forced her eyes to meet his and her brain to get back on track. "Why?"

Those gray eyes searched hers as if he needed to be sure she didn't already know the answer he was about to give her. What was it he thought he knew that she didn't? Apprehension started its dreaded rise once more.

"According to the laws of his country and his religion, he could marry you without consequence. He could have children with you and retain full custody in the event you divorced—under one condition."

She'd learned about that law the hard way. Her attorney hadn't been able to find any exceptions or conditions. "What condition?" If what he was about to tell her impacted his ability to help her get her son back…maybe she didn't want to know.

"That you didn't convert. A non-Muslim woman cannot be granted custody of any child, girl or boy, when divorcing a Muslim man. You didn't need a pre-nup because as a non-Muslim you weren't entitled to any property or money. That's the law, Ms. Harris. You never had a leg to stand on."

He was right. This part was definitely no surprise to her. "I found that out too late." She should have been smarter. But she'd been in love. The idea that Khaled had urged her to retain her own beliefs for underhanded purposes sent fury roaring through her even now. He'd insisted that he was perfectly happy without her bothering with conversion. She'd considered his understanding an act of love and trust. Lies. All of it. His assurances had all been for one thing alone—to guarantee he couldn't lose any children they might have.

There was just one thing about the way the marriage ended that didn't sit right with that scenario. Her attorney hadn't been able to give her an answer to that question. "Since the law protected his right to custody, why ship me out of the country so secretively?" He'd kidnapped her off the street and sent her to L.A. with two of his goons. They'd left her there, with no money and no ID. It had been a nightmare. Why had he bothered? Was the act meant to humiliate her? To frighten her? That he'd later denied it only added insult to injury.

"To justify his claims of desertion," Anders offered as if that answer should be crystal-clear. "Though you had no right to custody, you could have challenged the divorce as long as he had no legal grounds against you. Dumping you back on American soil made you look like the bad guy and gave him exactly what he needed—legal grounds to support his accusations and sympathy."

Anders was right. Why hadn't she thought of that? She'd been duped from the beginning, but this last was the ultimate betrayal. He'd charmed and seduced her, then tied her hands with sweet words of understanding.

How stupid and blind she'd been.

"So what do we do?" She appreciated that he had been able to clear up that question when her attorney hadn't been able to, but she needed more. She needed this man to lay out a plan that would ensure her son's safe return to her.

The sooner the better.

For one long beat she held her breath. Whether it was the cool distance she saw in his eyes or the apprehension compounding inside her, overriding her momentary burst of anger, she was afraid to breathe. She needed him to say he could make this happen.

"I have more questions related to your ex-husband's family and living arrangements as well as his financial dealings. It's essential that I have as much information as you can give me before walking into this situation. Information is power, Ms. Harris. The more I have, the better prepared I am to accomplish my mission."

"You'll be going to Kuwait, not Mr. Colby?" That she sounded disappointed was not lost on him. She hoped that wouldn't prove a strike against her, but she was a little disappointed. Jim Colby had been so sure he could get her son back. Was this man capable of the same promise?

"I'll be handling your case," Anders verified. To his credit he kept any resentment at her question out of his voice as well as his expression.

She'd let her feelings be known, no point beating around the bush about her bottom line. "Can you make the same guarantee Mr. Colby made?" She needed his reassurance. More than he could possibly fathom. This was far too important for her to be dancing around the issue.

Spencer wasn't sure he should answer this woman's question the way he would prefer. Jim Colby had put him in an awkward position. Yes, Spencer was relatively certain he could make this happen. He'd spent a decade in covert operations and a good deal of that time in the Middle East. He knew how to get in, accomplish his mission and get out. Not a problem.

But this wasn't as cut-and-dried as a military operation. And it damned sure wasn't black or white.

This was a child. A small boy, whose life and future hung in the balance.

As good as Spencer was, and he was very good at his job, stuff happened. A stray gunshot, unexpected extra manpower in a standoff—way more variables than he had time to contemplate could come into play. It wasn't as simple as going in, nabbing the child and getting out.

Khaled al-Shimmari wasn't just your run-of-the-mill Middle-Eastern rich guy. The man had connections, major connections. His family was extremely powerful, more so, Spencer felt certain, than this lady suspected. He didn't see any reason to go into that with her just now.

There was one glaring detail in particular he planned to keep to himself for the moment: the fact that her ex was suspected of supporting terrorism. Spencer had logged into certain FBI files with the help of the new receptionist Jim had hired. She might not have much personality, but she could hack into anything. That skill could be very useful and at the same time extremely dangerous. But that was Colby's problem, not Spencer's.

Willow Harris stared at him expectantly. She wanted an answer to her question. Yes or no. He understood what she was looking for.

"I can tell you that I have extensive experience in

the Middle East. I'm former military and my unit specialized in hostage retrieval. I have a perfect record, no failures whatsoever." He hoped that answered her question without actually answering it. Being evasive wasn't his intent, but he couldn't make her the promise she wanted. Not in good faith anyway. Colby had put him in a hell of a position. Spencer wondered if his new employer really had that much confidence in him or if he was simply that desperate for business.

With her hands wrung together in her lap, she bit her bottom lip and analyzed his response for a moment. He took advantage of that time to do a little analyzing of his own. She was young. Twenty-eight according to his research. She had a degree in marketing with an emphasis on foreign trading. She'd been recruited right out of college with a firm that catered to Middle-Eastern investors.

Willow Harris had no criminal record, not even a parking ticket. She'd graduated college with honors and appeared to be very conservative in behavior and dress. Her navy skirt went all the way to her knees. The white button-up blouse was buttoned all the way up. Silky blond hair fell around her shoulders. She was pretty and clearly too naive for her own good. Those big green eyes watched him now as if he were the only man on earth who could save her from a fate worse than death.

Poor kid. That bastard al-Shimmari had taken total

advantage of her. Spencer had a bad feeling about just who al-Shimmari really was. The fact that he was on the FBI watch list might very well be only the tip of the iceberg.

He had his doubts as to whether this case was as straightforward as it appeared from a distance.

She inhaled a big breath, unintentionally drawing his attention to her lips. Nice lips. Soft, full. Spencer snapped his gaze to hers and gave himself a swift mental kick for being an idiot.

"Your military history is impressive, Mr. Anders." She licked those distracting lips and seemed to struggle with her next words. "Can you…will you tell me why you're no longer in the military? I mean, you look too young to be retired and I…well, I was wondering why a man like you would walk away from such an impressive career."

Not as naive as he'd presumed, apparently. He considered lying to her. He was relatively certain she wouldn't want to hear the truth. But she'd been lied to enough already. Six P.I.s in as many months. Nope. This lady deserved the whole truth.

"My superior officer accused me of being a traitor."

Her pupils flared with surprise.

No turning back now. "He claimed that I sold information about an operation to the enemy. Since he couldn't prove it, I wasn't court-martialed to the degree he'd hoped. There were, however, other lesser charges backed up by supposed eye witnesses. In the end I was charged with insubordination and behavior unbecoming an officer. I was demoted and given the opportunity to start over. I opted not to."

That was the condensed version. It was also all she would get from him.

Even those few sentences had bitterness and fury churning in his gut.

She blinked rapidly, concealing her initial reaction. "Oh."

He knew better than to expect her to be anything other than shocked or appalled, maybe both. And yet he expected more somehow. He was sick and tired of people judging him wrongly for getting screwed by a ranking officer. He hadn't done anything wrong.

But she couldn't know that.

She would only understand one thing: her newest hope for getting her son back had been labeled a possible traitor to his country by the United States Army. That had to be a little scary.

"Well." She cleared her throat delicately and sat up a little straighter, but didn't look directly at him. "Were you...? A traitor...I mean?"

The anger and bitterness rushed out of him in a choked laugh. He had to hand it to the lady, she was original. Instead of ending the meeting and ushering him out, she flat-out asked what was on her mind.

"No. I wasn't a traitor. I just got on the bad side of the wrong jerk, the man who happened to be my commanding officer. He used me as a scapegoat when he couldn't find the real traitor." Spencer had always wondered if his superior had been the real traitor…if the whole setup had been about some sort of vengeance since Spencer had outshone him numerous times. He supposed he would never know.

Willow Harris's expression brightened as she let out an audible sigh. "Good. Now that we have that out of the way, when do we leave?"

"We?" Dread kicked into high gear. This was not a tactic he'd anticipated. Jim Colby certainly hadn't mentioned her desire to be involved with the operation.

She folded her arms over her chest and set her chin to a challenging tilt. "I've decided that this time I want to be involved. Ata is my child. Maybe that was my mistake all along. I should be a part of the operation."

No way that would work. "I'm afraid your presence would only complicate matters, Ms. Harris. You don't have the proper training—"

"This is not negotiable, Mr. Anders." She stared straight into his eyes, hers stone-cold determined. "I will be right there beside you every step of the way, otherwise I'll have to take my business elsewhere."

The last gave Spencer pause. Jim Colby would not be pleased if he screwed this up. He had accepted this case, and he wanted it done. ASAP. He damn sure couldn't expect to stay in business by turning clients away. This job was Spencer's chance to really start over. To build a new life with an employer who seemed to trust him implicitly.

If he tossed away this opportunity…would another one that offered the same come his way?

Not likely.

His hands shook. He could sure use a drink right about now. But that wouldn't solve the problem. Jim Colby was counting on him. Spencer was counting on *himself*.

And this lady—his full attention settled on Willow Harris—was counting on him. She wanted her child back. She deserved her child back.

Spencer pushed aside all the reasons he would be out of his mind to move forward under these terms. "You understand, Ms. Harris, that this mission will be dangerous?" He wanted all the cards on the table. No misconceptions or misunderstandings. "Your presence could actually jeopardize my ability to react as swiftly as I may need to, in effect jeopardizing the whole operation."

The delicate muscles of her long slender throat worked hard as she summoned a response. "I understand the danger. I'm fully prepared to take the risk."

Was she? he wondered. She'd lived in Kuwait for three years or a little better. Did she really comprehend how bad it could be without the support and approval of her ex-husband? He doubted it.

"Just one more question." This one would be the deal-breaker.

Her gaze locked with his. He didn't miss the determination there or the underlying fear. She might want him to believe that she wasn't afraid, but she was. She was very afraid. As she should be.

"If I have to make a choice between saving you or saving the child, I will save the child." He allowed the ramifications of those words to sink in a second or two before he continued. "Are you prepared to die knowing that your death possibly equates to a forfeit?"

Three, four, then five beats passed.

"Yes."

So much for his scare tactics. "In that case," he relented, "we'll begin preparations tomorrow."

Chapter Four

Tuesday, February 22

Spencer spread the map of Kuwait City over his desk and considered his strategy. The major streets ran in east-west rings starting with 1st Ring Road in the heart of the city all the way to 6th Ring near the airport. North-south streets intersected the rings. The al-Shimmari estate sprawled in the Suilhibikat area wedged between 2nd Ring Road and 3rd. This was where most of the wealthy Kuwaiti families resided.

The al-Shimmari residence was twenty thousand square feet protected by towering security walls as well as armed guards. According to his mother, the boy, Ata, was never out of sight of the grandmother, who was extremely possessive, or at least one personal-security guard.

The ex-husband, Khaled, had high-level government connections. Which meant Spencer couldn't risk entering the country accompanied by Ms.

Willow Harris. Before she would have time to clear customs Khaled would know she was in-country.

That one was a no-brainer.

Spencer had been surprised at the kind of connections Jim Colby himself had right here in Chicago. Fake papers for Willow Harris and her son had been as easy to get as filling a prescription at a local pharmacy. The quality of the passports and driver's license was remarkable. He wasn't the slightest bit worried about her papers being flagged, here or there.

What did worry the hell out of him was *her*. His mission would involve getting as close to the target as possible without being noticed by the enemy. He had no doubt that, if given a careful block of instruction, he could count on her full cooperation in whatever capacity he deemed operationally necessary. His primary concern, however, was whether or not she would be able to maintain any sort of objectivity, much less keep a handle on her emotions. Seeing her child again for the first time after so many months would take an immediate toll.

He didn't know her, other than what he'd seen and heard so far, but there was no reason for him to believe that she would behave any differently than any other mother thrust into a situation such as this.

Human emotion had no place in a covert operation.

He had been trained to set aside all emotion and to focus on attaining the target. Willow had no training whatsoever other than in how to negotiate and maneuver stocks and bonds. She was ill-prepared for this operation and, unfortunately, he hadn't come up with a legitimate reason to change her mind about full participation. He had spoken with Jim Colby regarding his reservations about her involvement. Jim had left the ball in his court.

If Spencer didn't think he could accomplish the mission with her in tow, then he could pass with Jim's blessings. Willow Harris would simply have to go elsewhere for help in retrieving her son.

That was the thing, though. Spencer was reasonably sure he could accomplish the mission either way. It was those pesky variables that troubled him. If his or someone else's timing was off, if there were unexpected changes in location or the body count of the enemy…any one of a hundred different scenarios could alter a single reaction, resulting in devastating consequences.

He didn't want to get this woman injured or killed. He'd watched his team members slaughtered on that mission five years ago and he had no desire to go through an encore performance.

Every time he'd thought about telling Willow Harris that he just couldn't take the risk, he remembered the haunting pain in her eyes. The elemental need to hold her child in her arms again. No one should have to go through that kind of agony, especially not alone.

When it came to variables there were plenty, it

seemed, in Willow's personal life, the circumstances with her child aside. She appeared to be completely on her own with no support network. Yet her mother and father, according to his research, were still alive. She drifted from job to job, sticking mainly with temporary agencies for any kind of work for which she possessed the qualifications. She lived in the kind of apartments most people would consider barely a cut above the slums. Evidently most of what she'd earned and/or saved had gone into the pockets of one P.I. after the other. She'd forked over the firm's required retainer fee without blinking an eye. Yet the motel she'd selected was one whose clientele rented more often by the hour than the night.

From all accounts she had sacrificed a great deal in hopes of getting her son back.

Spencer scrubbed his hand over his jaw. Man, he couldn't allow feelings of sympathy to sneak up on him like that. He was real sorry for her troubles, but sympathy, no matter how well-placed, led to trouble. He'd learned that the hard way. He could not—would not—get personally involved on this case or any other.

He had a fresh start here, he wasn't about to let anything or anyone screw it up. He had a job to do, end of story. Feeling sorry for a client wouldn't get the job done. He had to remember that. Allowing emotions to slip in would lead him straight back to his old buddy…booze. No vulnerabilities. If he permitted a single chink in his armor of determination he'd live to regret it.

The intercom on his desk buzzed, followed by the receptionist's voice. "Spencer, your two o'clock is here."

Willow Harris.

He'd told her to come in around two. He'd known it would take most of the morning to pull together the necessary documentation. Next he would lay out his plan for her approval. Moving forward with actual travel plans would be foolhardy prior to getting her on board with his change of identity strategy.

"Thanks, Connie. Send her on back."

"Fine," the receptionist huffed before disconnecting.

Spencer shook his head. He didn't quite get this one. Connie Gardener was extremely intelligent and intensely focused. She was a definite asset when it came to research and planning. But the lady had no people skills. None whatsoever. She'd just as soon tell you to drop dead as to say good morning, depending upon her mood. And that predilection extended to the boss as well as to Spencer or the mailman or anyone else who stuck his or her head through the door. Somehow, Connie just didn't get that she was a receptionist at this firm. Being receptive and polite was part of her job.

Spencer supposed Jim Colby saw beyond her prickly personality to the definite asset beneath. As long as she didn't actually run off any clients, Spencer didn't have a problem with her. Considering most of their clients would likely be as desperate for help as Willow Harris, he doubted even a snarky receptionist would keep those in need away. He had to assume Colby had some reason Spencer didn't know about for hiring and keeping the woman in spite of her lack of tact.

Willow Harris appeared at his open door just then, dragging his attention back to the more pressing problem at hand. She wore another skirt today, this one pink. The hem brushed her knees the same as yesterday's navy one had. Despite the conservative length of the skirt, the straight, slightly narrow fit flattered her petite figure. A pink sweater and sensible brown flats completed her wardrobe. She looked nice if not trendy.

"Good morning, Ms. Harris."

Her lips tilted in the expected expression of politeness, but the smile didn't reach her eyes. "Mr. Anders."

"Have a seat." He indicated the chair in front of his desk. "I was about to get a refill." He picked up his coffee cup. "Would you like a cup? Or maybe a soft drink?"

"Coffee would be nice. Thank you." She took a seat, careful to tug her skirt down as far as it would go before primly crossing her legs.

"I'll be right back." He paused at his door and studied her a moment. With her back to him, he could do so without rousing her suspicion or her questions.

She shifted in her seat a couple of times before she appeared to get comfortable. Her hands trembled once, twice, as she attempted to figure out what to do with them.

As calm as she wanted to appear, she was nervous.

About whether or not he could get the job done? he wondered, doubt creeping in despite his best efforts.

Or was her apprehension related to returning to Kuwait and possibly having to face her former husband?

Spencer turned, his movements soundless, and headed for the small employee lounge. Her apprehension would have to be addressed before they moved forward. He would need to know exactly how she felt and why she felt that way. *She* needed to think long and hard about whether or not she could really handle the coming emotional storm. Nothing about this mission was going to be easy.

"Anders, do you have a moment?"

Spencer turned from the coffeepot at the sound of Jim Colby's voice. His new boss and partner came into the lounge accompanied by a female. Thirty-two, thirty-three. Elegant business suit. Dark hair pulled away from her face, not a single strand out of place.

The prosecutor. What was her name? Oh, yeah. Renee Vaughn. From Atlanta. Colby had mentioned her. She'd come by for an interview yesterday, but Spencer had missed her.

"Sure." Spencer sat his coffee cup aside.

"This is Renee Vaughn from Atlanta. She's joining our team." To the lady, he said, "Anders is former military—Special Forces."

Vaughn thrust out her hand. "It's a pleasure, Mr. Anders."

Spencer gave her hand a shake. She had a firm grip and a definite no-nonsense air about her. "Good to have you on board, Ms. Vaughn."

"Mr. Colby!" Connie shouted unceremoniously. "You've got a call on line one!"

Jim Colby excused himself, leaving Spencer and the newest associate to fill the abrupt silence.

Vaughn jerked her head toward the door. "What's your take on the receptionist?" The humor sparkling in her eyes tipped Spencer off to her amusement with Connie's unrestrained brashness.

"She's one of kind, that's for sure."

"Definitely," Vaughn agreed. "But I hear she's a former computer security analyst. Spent time in federal prison for hacking."

That certainly explained a few things. "Really?" Spencer filled his coffee cup. "I hadn't heard the prison part." Maybe he and Connie had more in common than he'd first imagined.

"She mentioned it to me as soon as I arrived for my interview yesterday. Maybe because I'm a former district attorney. I'm not sure if she thought I should be impressed or was simply warning me." Vaughn shrugged her designer-clad shoulders. "I'll assume both for the moment." Her gaze settled fully on Spencer then. "What about you, Anders?" she asked. "Got any skeletons in your closet?"

"I'll tell you what I do have, Ms. Vaughn," he offered as he reached for a second cup and filled it. "A client waiting in my office. Help yourself to the coffee."

"I'd tell you to call me Renee," she said, reaching for a cup of her own, "but I haven't been called by my first name since law school. You can drop the Ms. though. Vaughn is fine."

"I'll remember that." He didn't wait around for her to ask any more questions. He told himself that he wasn't ashamed of his past; he just didn't want to talk about it with a virtual stranger. But that was probably more lie than truth.

Back in his office, he pushed the door closed with his foot, then passed the cup in his right hand to his client. "Watch out, it's hot." His oversight hit him then. "Will you need cream or sugar?"

"Black is fine." She took the cup, cradled it in both hands as if she needed the warmth more than the caffeine. "Thanks."

Spencer took his seat and prepared to launch into the details of the mission strategy he'd developed.

"When do we leave?" she asked before he'd even begun. "I don't want to wait any longer than absolutely necessary. I've wasted too much time already."

"I understand." He gulped a mouthful of coffee, ignored the burn, and braced for an argument. "I've had to make a few adjustments to our travel plans in order to avoid tipping off the enemy as to our arrival."

Those wide green eyes searched his, too much recent disappointment setting her on instant edge. "What kind of adjustments?"

"Your ex-husband is well-connected. I don't want to risk his being tipped off about our arrival." He picked up the passports he'd had made and passed them across the desk for her perusal. "In order to head off that possibility, I thought we could travel as a couple."

"Lana Anders?" She looked from the passports to him. "How did you get these pictures?"

The underlying suspicion in her voice wasn't unexpected. "You left a copy of your driver's license and the most recent photo you had of your son for your file." The guy who'd made the new passports was a true artist. The absolute best Spencer had seen. Not that he'd associated with that many forgers in the past, but a man couldn't work covert operations without rubbing shoulders with the underbelly from time to time. "The pictures were altered subtly, that's why you didn't immediately recognize them."

She stared at the passports and new driver's license for a moment or two longer. "They look authentic."

"I don't think we'll have a problem getting through the checkpoints."

Her continued hesitation had just about convinced him that she would balk at crossing this particular legal line, but then she surprised him.

"I'm glad you had the foresight to take this step." She placed the passports and license back on his desk. "You're right. He probably has me on some sort of watch list to ensure he gets a call if I show up in his country again. I should have thought of that."

He contemplated explaining to her that it was his job to weigh all the possibilities, that he'd been trained for that very purpose, but that wasn't necessary. When she'd had time to think about it, she would realize that rationale without him having to tell her. Right now he very much needed her to believe he regarded her as capable. Destroying her self-confidence any further would not be conducive to a good working relationship, a relationship he hoped wouldn't prove to be a fatal mistake for one or both of them.

"We'll be traveling on business," he went on, laying out the rest of the plan for her. "Real estate. We have a client who hired us to scout out office space in Kuwait. I've booked a hotel already. I opted for something outside the main tourist areas in order to keep our profile as low as possible."

"How soon can we leave?"

"Tomorrow morning. There's a short layover in Amsterdam, but that's actually going to tie in nicely with our cover profile. I've arranged an appointment in Amsterdam to view a commercial property. We'll need all the credibility we can manage since we don't have time to set the profiles as fully as I'd prefer."

Willow wasn't sure she understood exactly what

he meant when he said "set" the profiles, but since he was the expert on this kind of thing, she'd let him make the rules. The idea of pretending to be his wife had initially put her off, then she'd realized he was right. Definitely. That he was thinking two or more steps ahead inspired her confidence. Since this might very well be her last hope, at least until she could save up more money, she wanted the effort to be worthy.

No, what she wanted was for the effort to be successful. She wanted to escape Kuwait with her son. Once they were back in this country her attorney would take the appropriate measures to protect her and Ata from her ex-husband. Unfortunately, no matter that the American courts had ruled in her favor from the beginning, if she didn't have Ata in her custody there was nothing she could do. Extradition didn't apply to stolen children. This was the only way.

"Do you have any packing instructions?" She knew how to dress for life in Kuwait, but she didn't have any idea the fashion essentials for covert maneuvers.

"You'll need rubber-soled shoes. Sneakers will do. Dark clothing for night wear and something along the lines of khakis for daytime. Modest attire, as I'm sure you know. Our main objective is to blend in wherever we are, whatever the hour."

She got it. And he was right about the modesty thing, not that the concept would ever be a problem for her, she'd been raised far too strictly even to consider otherwise. Still, a woman in Kuwait was expected to be covered. The less skin revealed the better. Long sleeves, long hemlines, high necklines. Even though the western influence had changed the way some women opted to dress, many, especially the male hierarchy, did not approve of this choice. The only way to ensure she drew no unnecessary attention was to follow the old-school rules.

What she really wanted to know more about was this man's plan for stealing her son away from her ex and his obsessed mother. "What's your game plan once we've arrived? I mean…" She didn't want to sound dumb or impatient. The investigators she'd hired previously had kept their methods to themselves. Not asking enough questions might or might not have been a mistake, either way she didn't intend to take the risk this time. She needed to stay on top of every move. "Do you already have an idea of how you want to approach my son?"

Those gray eyes studied her for what felt like half a lifetime before he spoke. She couldn't decide if he was weighing just how much to tell her or if he simply wanted to gauge her readiness for moving forward.

"The first day we'll acclimate and do the tourist gig to make ourselves look legit. Then we'll set up surveillance and wait for the right opportunity." He lifted those massive shoulders in a noncommittal shrug. "Or we'll create an opportunity of our own."

He sounded so confident, so casual, as if he did this sort of thing every day. She wanted desperately to believe it would be so easy. But a part of her was scared to death that she would gamble on this last-ditch effort and fail, leaving her with nothing.

Not even hope.

This was the moment. Dread knotted in her chest. She'd wrestled all night with the question of whether she should tell him about the last P.I.'s investigator. She'd intended to tell Jim Colby on their first meeting and she'd actually hinted at it, but she hadn't come right out with what she knew. Part of her was scared to death this man would opt not to go through with his plan if he understood the full risk. He might see this as information he had needed before agreeing to move forward with her case and use her omission as grounds to pull out.

Anxiety tightened like a noose around her throat.

No matter how she weighed it, justified it or pretended the truth away, he deserved to know that truth. As desperately as she wanted her son home with her, she could not bring herself to allow him to go forward blind.

"There's one other thing I should probably tell you." She drew in a much-needed breath and reminded herself that she had no choice. "The last P.I. I hired, Mr. Davenport, sent a man to find my son and bring him back home to me." Willow moistened her lips and prayed that she wasn't about to make a major mistake. "He got very close. Close enough to take pictures of my baby in a number of settings and situations. I can't believe just how close he managed to get."

Those gray eyes continued to peer right through hers, as if he could see into her deepest, darkest thoughts. He asked, "Did this man learn anything that might be useful to our operation? I was under the impression none of the other investigators had accomplished anything of real value."

The realization that his deep voice contained an edge that hadn't been there before filled her with dread. If he changed his mind or decided he couldn't trust her…she just didn't know what she would do then.

"None of the others were able even to get close…except for the last one. If he discovered anything useful, Mr. Davenport didn't pass the information along to me." Don't stop now. Just do it. Say what had to be said. "Davenport did say that he had lost contact with the man he sent in—the one who got the pictures. He believes the man may have been taken prisoner or murdered by my ex-husband or a member of his personal security."

There, she'd said it.

She waited for Anders's response, her heart flailing behind her sternum so she could scarcely draw in enough air. Please don't let him back out now. Not now. They had to do this. She had to get to her baby, had to bring him home.

"This operation comes with major risks, Ms. Harris. Risks are a part of my job. But what you've just told me is all the more reason for you to stay right here while I go do what has to be done."

Relief rushed along her nerve endings, making her feel unsteady. He hadn't changed his mind about moving forward. Thank God. "I can't do that, Mr. Anders. I have to go with you. I have to help get my baby back." No risk was too great to her. She had to make him understand that.

He didn't argue the point, which surprised her. Instead, with the help of the receptionist, Connie, he took care of the necessary travel reservations. He went over a few more details with her, and then she left to return to her motel and pack. She would meet him at his office the next morning at seven for one final briefing with Mr. Colby before they headed to the airport.

Then they would get started.

She couldn't wait.

No matter what happened, she had to do all within her power to get her son back. Some part of her had the almost overwhelming feeling that if she didn't get him back now she might never see him again.

The feeling ate at her a little more each day.

She surveyed the single suitcase she'd finished packing. Several changes of clothes and the essential toiletries, nothing frivolous. She didn't dare take a picture of her son, other than the one hidden in her wallet. Even if her purse had to be searched, she felt comfortable that the picture wouldn't be discovered the way she had it hidden. Anders would carry her son's passport.

Exhausted, she plopped down on the bed next to her suitcase. She really should get some sleep. It wasn't that late. She glanced at the clock radio on the table by the bed. Nine-fifteen. But she hadn't slept well the night before and she needed to be fresh in the morning. Starting tomorrow she had to be in tip-top condition. No distractions, fatigue included. She thought about the sleeping pills the doctor had prescribed, but the hangover and dulled senses the morning after weren't worth it. She'd just have to try getting some sleep the old-fashioned way.

Shouting in the room next door made her jump. She pressed her hand to her chest and stared at the wall that separated her room from the one next door. A man's voice sounded angry, a woman's pleading. Whatever was going on, nothing about it conveyed pleasantness.

Maybe she should call the desk and complain. Like that would do any good. The desk clerks she'd encountered so far looked about as interested in their work as fence posts.

A loud crash accompanied by the sound of breaking pottery, the table lamp, she surmised, launched her into action. She'd just reached for the phone when a rap on her door paralyzed her.

It wouldn't be the people next door since she

could still hear them shouting. It was too late for someone from the Equalizers to be dropping by…wasn't it?

Standing there in the middle of the room wouldn't answer the question. She moved quietly to the door and checked the peephole.

Spencer Anders waited on the other side.

She had to admit, considering the ruckus next door, she was relieved to see him. After sliding the chain free of its catch, she opened the door.

It wasn't until she came face-to-face with him that the possibility that he'd arrived bearing bad news formulated in her sleep-deprived head.

"Have our plans changed?" She tried to steel herself for what might be coming, but there wasn't any way to adequately prepare. She wasn't sure she could handle bad news. Not now, after she'd gotten this close. She was packed, the tickets had been purchased.

"May I come in?"

In her experience when a person avoided answering a direct question then there was a problem. Her heart started to pound in anticipation of the worst.

"Sure." She managed to back up and open the door wider. "Is there a problem?"

He closed the door behind him, leaving her with nothing to hold onto. Whether it was the look on her face or the trembling that had started along her limbs, he appeared to comprehend her mounting hysteria.

"There's no problem. We're right on schedule."

She might have exhaled some of the tension just then if the ranting in the other room hadn't chosen that exact moment to explode all over again.

"Excuse me."

Spencer Anders pivoted, opened the door and walked back outside.

Confused, Willow followed as far as the door.

He turned and held up a hand for her to stop. "Stay there."

As ordered, she didn't move. Several seconds passed before she realized that she didn't have to stand here like this just because he said so. By then his banging on the door next to hers had silenced the shouting in the other room and startled her so that she couldn't think to move anyway.

What was he doing?

The neighboring door burst open. "What the hell do you want?" the man towering in the open doorway demanded.

"I'd like to speak with the lady in the room," Anders said, his tone utterly calm and oddly genial.

"She's busy right now," the lanky, mean-looking guy glaring at Anders snapped. "Unless you're a cop, I'd advise you to get lost."

Sobbing from inside the room made Willow's chest tighten.

"I'd like to do that, buddy," Anders offered, "but you see, I have a problem with jerks like you."

His next move happened so fast Willow would

have missed it entirely if she hadn't been watching so closely. He slammed the guy square in the jaw with his fist. The jerk dropped to the floor without so much as a grunt.

"You okay, ma'am?"

Willow blinked, and in that fraction of a second, Anders was attending to the woman who'd rushed past the fallen jerk and straight into her savior's arms. By the time the cops had arrived, Anders had ordered Willow back into the room and closed the door.

She peeked past the curtains and watched him comfort the woman as the police took away her boyfriend or John or whatever he was. Nearly a half hour later the cops, as well as the jerk and the woman were gone.

Willow jumped away from the window when Anders knocked on her door even though she'd watched him walk right up and rap his knuckles there.

"I apologize for keeping you waiting," he said as soon as he'd stepped back into her room.

Her brain kept telling her to say that she understood, but her lips wouldn't form the words.

That intense gray gaze settled on hers once more. "I wanted to give you one last chance to change your mind about going with me to Kuwait. I'm not sure you fully comprehend the magnitude of the danger we may very well encounter."

She should have anticipated that he would attempt to dissuade her again, but somehow she hadn't.

"I'm going, Mr. Anders. Nothing you can say will change my mind."

She stared right back at him with all the defiance she could muster in her current state of teetering between total exhaustion and absolute confusion as to what she'd just witnessed with the couple next door. Unfortunately, her body betrayed her and attempted to tremble beneath his continued visual assessment. Dammit, she should be stronger than that.

"In that case, I won't waste my time or yours." He reached for the door once more. "I'll see you in the morning, Ms. Harris. Try to get some sleep."

Then he left. No more questions or warnings, nothing. He just walked right out as if her answer had been all he needed to move forward.

Willow locked the door and slid the chain back into place. She measured how he'd stepped in to rescue the woman next door against how easily he'd accepted her answer and gone on his way.

A paradox, she decided. One she wasn't sure she possessed the wherewithal to decipher.

Whatever he was or wasn't, she sincerely hoped he could follow through with his promise to get her son back. She needed him to be able to do that.

Right or wrong, her son was all that mattered to her just now.

Call it mother's intuition, but every instinct was screaming at her that time was running out fast. Very fast.

Chapter Five

Spencer watched Willow Harris sleep. She had fought the need for hours before finally surrendering. Then she'd curled up in the window seat next to him. He was glad she'd given in. This might be her last chance to get any decent sleep until the mission was over.

Another hour and they would land at the airport in Kuwait City. He'd spent most of the travel time asking questions about the way she'd met al-Shimmari. The story went like most others with a similar ending. Girl meets boy, girl falls in love with boy. Boy uses wealth and power to take advantage of girl who has not a clue how the cultural differences will eventually impact her life.

The adage *love is blind* was too damned true.

The story got somewhat muddy during the last year she spent in Kuwait. No matter how he'd phrased the questions or from what angle he had approached the subject, she'd found a way to dodge being completely forthcoming about that timeframe.

He didn't understand her reasons for holding back. As badly as she wanted to regain custody of her son he had to assume that she would share any possible information even if only remotely relevant. That assumption would lead him to figure that nothing about that final year was significant. However, there was a strong probability that she couldn't see past the emotional wall she'd built to protect herself from those final months of her marriage. She could be holding back information that would prove useful without even knowing it. That was the part that worried him.

Of course he couldn't be certain that anything about her marriage, other than the clash of cultures, was pertinent to the current situation, but he had a feeling.

After a decade of diving into covert operations in various settings and under a wide array of conditions, he'd learned to trust his gut implicitly. His instincts had only let him down once.

Spencer leaned back deep into the seat, allowing his thoughts to wander back just over two years— something he rarely permitted. The mission had been as uncomplicated as they came, get in, retrieve the hostages and get out. He and his team had done it a hundred times before.

But that last time something had gone wrong. The

hostages were already dead when the team arrived. Spencer had taken the fall for the intelligence leak that had led to the deaths of the hostages.

He hadn't been able to prove his innocence, but neither had the military investigators assigned to the case been able to prove his guilt.

As far as he was concerned there was only one man to blame for what happened. Colonel Calvin Richards. Richards was retired now, but he'd managed to destroy Spencer's career before taking that retirement.

Bitterness burned through Spencer. This was why he didn't let himself think about that particular part of his past. His fingers tightened on the arms of his seat. He hadn't deserved that kind of end to his career. Prior to the incident two years ago he'd been touted a hero. He'd never wanted the attention that went along with being labeled a hero, but he sure as hell hadn't expected to be called a traitor.

"Would you like something to drink, sir?"

The flight attendant smiled down at him, ready to provide whatever refreshment he required. The answer to her question was no. He told himself to utter the single-syllable word but the thought of having a drink—just one—was almost overpowering. One drink would likely do the trick. He could relax…let go the tension now twisting his gut.

The other passengers seated around him in first class had been served already. Beer, wine, cocktails, bourbon. It would be so easy. Having a drink once they landed in Kuwait would be near impossible since alcohol was illegal.

Sweat beaded on his forehead. He wished he could work up the courage to just say no.

"I'll take a soda."

Willow's voice jerked his gaze in her direction. She sat up a little straighter in her seat and gazed expectantly at the flight attendant. He hadn't realized she'd awakened, much less moved.

"Nothing for you, sir?" the attendant prompted one last time.

"I'll have the same as the lady." That his voice was practically a croak made him even angrier, this time at himself for being weak as well as a fool.

"I'll be right back with your drinks." The attendant continued down the aisle.

"I can't believe I slept so long." Willow stretched her arms and torso, the motion as sleek and languid as a cat's, the soft moan accompanying those movements sounding as satisfied as a contented purr.

"You were tired." It was the only response he could dredge up from his preoccupied brain at the moment. He shifted his attention from her, careful not to focus on the alcoholic beverages being enjoyed by the other passengers, and gave himself a mental kick.

The attendant returned with their complimentary drinks. Spencer allowed the fizz of the soda to sit on his tongue before swallowing. He would not let his need to fortify himself screw up this operation. His mind was made up. The two years not withstanding, wallowing in self-pity had never been his style.

This was his opportunity to get his act together. He would not let defeat suck him in again. Willow Harris was counting on him.

Her little boy was counting on him as well, though he didn't know it yet and might not appreciate it for years to come. The next couple of days would determine the course the boy's young life took. Would he be raised as an American with his mother's influence affecting his daily life? Or would his future lie in a different world with a man who very well could be associated with terrorists?

To Spencer's way of thinking, under normal circumstances both parents should be involved with the rearing of a child. But, if there was even an iota of truth to the rumor that al-Shimmari had ties to terrorists, the man had no right to shape the life of his child.

Proving al-Shimmari's ties to illegal activities was not Spencer's job. His focus was reuniting the boy with his mother. He would, in fact, be attempting to steal the child and to smuggle him out of the country with a fake passport. If they were caught, they would face stiff penalties, including jail time.

It was common practice in these cases for one parent or the other to attempt to regain control over their child's destiny. In this case, the key was to have the child on American soil and in the care of the mother in order to claim jurisdiction for legal purposes. On his own ground, that was exactly what Willow's ex-husband had done. He, in turn, would fully anticipate that she would retaliate in kind. Unfortunately none of her previous investigators had been successful.

Spencer considered that at least one man may have died in his attempt. This gave him all the more reason to believe that al-Shimmari might not be on the up and up.

Whether he was or not made no difference to Spencer. It did, however, greatly influence the lengths the man would likely be willing to go to in order to protect his continued possession of the child. Possession was extremely important to maintaining legal custody. The American courts generally ruled in favor of the American parent. Willow had, in fact, gained a court order granting her temporary custody months ago. The Kuwaiti courts had chosen to ignore that order. No surprise there.

"I brought along a khimar to wear. I didn't know if you would think it was necessary, but I'm leaning toward that extra layer of precaution."

Spencer wrestled his attention back to the present. "I brought one as well. I planned to suggest that you wear it to ensure as much invisibility as possible." He'd hoped she wouldn't have a problem wearing the scarf. Though it wasn't necessary as a western visitor, any steps they could take to ensure she wasn't identified by anyone from al-Shimmari's circle of family, friends or business associates would be a good thing. He hadn't brought it up before in an attempt to avoid giving her anything else to worry about. He'd felt certain she would agree to the last minute suggestion.

Maybe he'd underestimated her determination to cooperate.

"Funny," she said quietly, "I never wore them before."

She didn't look at him as she said this, instead she stared out the window at the passing clouds or maybe nothing in particular.

"An act of defiance?" Was this how the marriage had started off? Or had her husband at first permitted her to cling to her western ways?

"Our relationship was different in the beginning." Her gaze shifted to the back of the seat in front of her as she spoke. "There was mutual respect. His mother didn't like that he allowed me to be American, but he seemed perfectly happy with the *me* he'd married."

"When did things change?" They'd covered some of how things started to deteriorate, but maybe if he persisted along these lines she would delve into those final months. He settled his half-empty glass on the tray and waited for her to go on with her story.

"After Ata's birth." She held her soda in both hands as if she feared a sudden bout of turbulence would catch her off guard. "It was as if he grew ashamed of me. The pressure to stay home and out of the public eye was at first subtle, but then I started to feel like a prisoner. God knows that fortress he calls a residence is more like a prison than a home."

She placed her drink on the tray above her lap, but didn't let go of the glass. "Everything about Ata became an issue. I wasn't holding him right. I wasn't feeding him properly. Half the time Khaled's mother was in charge of Ata's care. They just pushed me aside and did things their way, as if I had no say in the matter."

That couldn't have gone over very well. "How did you put a stop to that?"

For the first time since the conversation began she looked him square in the eye. "I pitched a fit. For a while things were better."

"But that didn't last long."

She shook her head. "Then my ex-husband found business to occupy my time." She leaned her head back against the seat. "To keep me away from our son as much as possible. I didn't recognize the tactic at first. I was so happy to be involved with my husband's pursuits I didn't see the hidden agenda."

This was the first he'd heard of her being involved with any of al-Shimmari's work. "What exactly did you do for the family business?"

She traced the droplets of water forming on her glass. "Since my training was in trading stocks and evaluating investment potential, he pretended to want my advice on his financial portfolio."

If Spencer had been surprised before, he was outright shocked now. Why would a man like al-Shimmari allow her access to his financial records? Sure, she'd been educated in finances, but she wasn't a seasoned pro by any means. "What do you mean he pretended to want your advice?"

She shook her head slowly from side to side. "God, I was such a fool."

Spencer didn't rush her, he just let her talk. He sensed that what she had to say next would prove key to new and vital information about al-Shimmari.

"The entire portfolio I'd evaluated for hours and hours, days really, was a hoax. What he allowed me access to was nothing more than a fake set of financial records created specifically for my entertainment."

Tension roiled through Spencer. "What tipped you off?"

"We were in his office at home. I was pointing out a problem I'd discovered when he was called out of the room for a moment. His computer screen was open to what I thought was the same data system I accessed from my own small office. So I sat down at his desk to print out a page I'd somehow failed to print. The differences in his database and the one I was permitted to access were glaringly obvious."

Spencer's tension escalated to a new level. "Did he catch you at his computer?"

She laughed, the sound dry and wholly lacking in amusement. "He didn't have to catch me. I confronted him about the differences." Another laugh choked out of her. "I was totally convinced that someone was keeping a second set of books, so to speak, in order to skim his finances. It never entered my mind that he was the guilty party."

Spencer could imagine what happened next. None of it good.

"He was furious," she went on. "He accused me of making up the data he claimed didn't exist. I was never allowed even to speak of his work or his finances again. Two months later I broached the subject of a trial separation. I'd gotten so frustrated with the way his mother kept Ata away from me and with his indifference I was ready to take drastic action." Her attention turned back to the window. "I thought maybe if I shocked him with that news that maybe he would turn back into the man I'd married. I had no idea that he'd already made plans of his own. A few days later I found myself in LAX with no ID or money."

Spencer touched her arm, the one closest to him. "Those months must have been very difficult for you." Being so far from home with no support network, surrounded by people who didn't want her, had to have been a nightmare.

She looked up at him, her green eyes filled with that haunted look that tugged at his emotions. "The hard part came when they wouldn't let me see my son again." She grabbed his shirtsleeve when he would have moved his hand away. "You have to get my son back for me, Mr. Anders. I can't keep living this way." She blinked back the tears that filled her eyes. "I dream about him, only to wake up and realize that I'm alone. Do you know how that feels? To be completely alone? So alone that nothing matters to you anymore?"

A single tear trekked down her cheek and he couldn't resist touching her again. He swiped the tear away with the pad of his thumb. No one should have to go through this kind of hell. She loved her child. She only wanted the things any mother would want. The man she'd loved and trusted had taken that away from her.

"I'll get your son back." He didn't answer the other question. "No matter what else happens, I will see that you get your son back."

The crackle of electricity between them startled him at first. But he couldn't draw his hand away from her sweet face. She needed him. No one had needed him in so long. More than that…he needed her just a little.

The sound of the flight attendant's voice over the speaker system shattered the moment. "…Seatbelts should be fastened and trays should be placed in their upright position in preparation for landing…" Another of the flight attendants hurried along the aisle to reclaim empty refreshment containers and any other trash from the passengers.

Willow kept her gaze straight ahead as the plane

started to descend. He had wanted to ask her if she'd found anything in al-Shimmari's finances that sent up a red flag for her. Obviously there was something her ex-husband had wanted to hide from her. Or maybe he just hadn't wanted her to know the true extent of his assets. But why bother to hide those? As a non-Muslim she had no rights to his holdings. If he hadn't gotten so caught up in touching her he might have asked the question.

Later, when they'd gotten to the hotel maybe he'd ask her to elaborate on what she'd found. For now, they had to concentrate on getting through customs and the airport without incident. Operations of this nature were best accomplished one step at a time.

When the plane bumped along the tarmac, Willow felt her tension start to climb once more. She'd spent the past forty-eight hours bracing for this moment and still she felt ill-prepared for what was to come.

What if Khaled learned that she was here?

What if one of his many spies saw her?

She chewed her lip and fought the panic. He wouldn't find her. Mr. Anders had taken care of a passport under an alias. She would wear the khimar. Khaled would not know she was in the country. She and Ata would be gone before he suspected she was up to anything. He surely thought he'd foiled her attempts to retrieve her son when he captured or murdered Mr. Davenport's man.

If she and Spencer succeeded, Khaled would retaliate, but she'd just have to cross that bridge when she came to it.

This was the only way.

Willow resisted the urge to look at the man next to her. There were other things she wanted to tell him. But she couldn't. She'd sworn never to tell. If she breathed a word of what she knew, Khaled would not rest until she was dead. If she were dead there was nothing she could do for Ata. His well-being was first and foremost in her mind.

Nothing else mattered.

Nothing.

Khaled's business dealings were not her problem. There were government agencies responsible for catching men like him. She couldn't be that kind of martyr. Not when her son's life hung in the balance.

She knew exactly what would happen if she told Spencer Anders or Jim Colby what she knew. They would do the same thing any of the others she'd hired would have done had they learned her secret: go straight to the FBI.

As much as she loved her country…as much as she longed to do what her brain told her was the right thing, her heart wouldn't let her do anything that would jeopardize her child's safety.

Khaled had told her what he would do if she ever told a soul. The fact that he hadn't simply killed her had been surprise enough. At first, she had been so happy that he hadn't executed her on the spot, that she had stupidly thought maybe he still loved her. But he hadn't, not the way a man was meant to love a woman in any event.

So, she'd had to muddle through alone. Her family had disowned her. She had no friends. The few she'd had before moving to Kuwait had gone on with their lives. There was no one to help her except this stranger she'd hired with the last of her savings.

She could say or do nothing that would alienate him in any way. He could never know she was keeping such a horrible secret. He was ex-military. He would not understand her reasoning.

Every step had to be carefully planned. Every word cautiously chosen.

When the seatbelt light had gone out and the flight attendant announced that they could deplane, Spencer stood and stepped back for her to exit before him. Willow dragged the khimar from her purse and wrapped it around her hair as she moved down the aisle. She had lightened her hair just a little and she'd lost some weight. She had to believe that no one would recognize her. Otherwise she might just have a nervous breakdown before they got out of the airport.

As they walked along the corridor that would take them into the terminal, Spencer moved closer, but he didn't touch her. Apparently he understood that acts of affection or touching in general were not well-perceived in this country. His apparent knowledge of the country prevented any awkwardness.

God really had been looking out for her when he'd led her to the Equalizers.

Her heart started to pound harder when they moved into the crowded terminal. She tried not to scan the crowd. She wanted to look like any other arriving visitor. If she appeared suspicious or apprehensive someone might notice.

As they approached customs, she found herself holding her breath. If they made it through this security checkpoint, they would be home free.

Several other passengers lined up in front of them.

Anders leaned down. "We'll be fine," he whispered softly.

She prayed he was right.

Working hard not to study the faces of the customs officers, she rested her gaze anywhere but on the activities going on directly in front of her.

Stay calm, she told herself over and over.

There is no reason for anyone to be suspicious. Her papers were in order. She had nothing in her possession that would raise questions.

Five more minutes and this part would be over.

One of the officers motioned for her and Anders to move forward. It was their turn.

She walked slowly up to the counter and placed her purse and small carry-on bag there. Somehow a smile tilted the corners of her mouth.

"State your business in our country."

Anders answered in spite of the fact that the man

looked at Willow when he asked the question. "We're appraising real estate for one of my clients." He smiled down at Willow before turning his attention back to the man. "And doing a little vacationing."

How could he sound so calm and cool?

The officer continued to review their passports and belongings. Willow noted nothing even remotely familiar about him. He looked to be in his forties. Medium height and weight with a bit of gray in his dark hair. His tone was brusque when he spoke, but that was typical.

Just when she'd decided she could relax marginally, the officer motioned for another man to join him at the counter. He passed Willow's passport to his associate. Her heart lunged into her throat.

The second man, who wore a similar uniform to the first, looked at Willow and said, "Madam, you will need to come with me."

Chapter Six

Willow knew what it was to be afraid. She'd been afraid many times in the past year, but not once had she been as terrified as she was at that moment.

"Is something wrong?"

She looked from the customs officer waiting for her to follow him to the man next to her who'd asked the question, his tone clearly impatient.

"Whatever the problem," Anders added firmly, "you'll need to explain it to me as well as my wife."

Willow held her breath, prayed there was merely a misunderstanding.

"There is no problem, sir," the officer assured him. "We select individuals at random for questioning. This is a security measure that is perfectly legal and of only minor inconvenience, I assure you."

Anders nodded. "Fine, but I insist on being present. Do you have a law against that?"

"No, sir. This way, please."

The wave of relief that rushed over her made

Willow sway ever so slightly. She did not want to do this alone.

Anders placed his hand at the small of her back and guided her in the direction the officer had already taken. "Don't worry," he murmured, "this won't take long."

Her entire being gravitated toward him and the protection he offered. It had been so long since anyone had protected her in any way. She hadn't realized how badly she'd needed someone to take care of her until that moment.

The interview room was small. It reminded Willow of the rooms where suspects were taken in the television cop shows. Anders sat next to her at the small table. The officer took a seat on the opposite side.

"You stated that you are in Kuwait on business." This the officer said to Anders.

"Yes," Anders responded. "I'm an international Realtor. I have a client who is interested in office space here. I've contacted a local agent." He reached into his pocket and removed a business card and offered it to the officer. "He'll be showing me a couple of spaces later this morning. I'm sure he'll be happy to verify that for you if you find it necessary to call."

It was the middle of the night. Willow didn't know who Anders's contact was, but surely he was in bed.

"Have you been to Kuwait before?"

There was no doubt as to whom this question was directed. The officer's gaze bored straight into hers.

"No." She tried to swallow the emotion tightening in her throat. "This is my first visit." Anders had instructed her on what she should say if the subject came up. She hadn't expected it to come up only minutes after her arrival in the country.

"You've been here before."

That too-familiar fear paralyzed her for two beats before the officer turned his attention to Anders.

"Have you not?" he pressed.

"Yes," Anders confirmed. "Several times."

Another uniformed man entered the room. He deposited Willow's purse and carry-on bag onto the table. He placed Anders's briefcase there as well.

The officer handed both passports to Anders. "I hope your visit is productive and enjoyable."

Willow's heart rate didn't return to normal until they had exited the terminal and picked up the rental car. As much as she wanted to close her eyes and block the memories bombarding her, she couldn't. She couldn't ignore the details of the place she had called home for three years or the incident that had just occurred, reminding her that this was not America.

"Are you okay?"

She inhaled deeply and let the breath out to clear her head. "I'm fine." It was a lie, but she didn't need him feeling sorry for her. She needed to be strong. She needed to focus on getting her son back. The memories, the fear, all of it would do nothing but distract her.

After a few miles of silence, he said, "Just so you know, that little intimidation episode back there might have had more to do with me than some random selection."

The lights of Kuwait City in the distance held her attention for a moment before she turned to the driver. "Why do you say that?"

"I'm ex-military. I was in and out of this territory dozens of times. My name might have triggered a security check."

"If you knew that was a possibility, why didn't you use an alias?" Spencer Anders appeared far too smart to make a misstep that glaringly obvious.

"I wanted them to associate you with me. Any suspicions will be on me, not you."

"Oh." Wow. Another one of his protective measures. She couldn't help being surprised all over again at having someone take steps to shelter her. "Thank you."

He didn't say more so Willow opted not to. Instead she focused on surveying the city. The lights were gorgeous, but she knew from experience that the true beauty of Kuwait City could only be seen by day. A heady mix of market bazaars and gleaming skyscrapers along a glistening coast. The mosques and souks and other sandy traces of bygone Bedouin days awaited the wanderings of tourists. No matter how much emotional stress she'd endured here she knew that beyond the glitzy opulence lay a deep sense of traditional values and warm Arabic hospitality.

She had loved this city with its diversity of people and richness of culture. It was only the man who'd brought her here that she despised. They wouldn't pass his residence en route to the hotel. Like the other wealthy residents, his massive villa lay in the Suilhibikat area closer to the heart of the city. Kuwait boasted the wealthiest population in the world; thankfully most were kind and generous people.

The situation Willow found herself in now was her own mistake. If she hadn't let love blind her four years ago she might have taken the time to consider the laws that could possibly come into play in her future. But she hadn't dreamed things would go wrong and that the child she hadn't known she would have would become a pawn in the ugly battle.

REGISTERING at the hotel at 2:00 a.m. took little time since there wasn't a line of arriving patrons. Spencer tipped the bellhop generously and closed the door behind him. When he turned around he found Willow standing in the middle of the room staring at the bed.

"There's only one bed."

True. "Remember, we're traveling as husband and wife. Our cover needs to appear realistic."

His reminder didn't erase the frown from her face, but she did seem to relax fractionally.

"It's a big bed," he added with a sweep of his hand to indicate the king-size width.

The frown eased into more of a neutral line. "It is big."

At least that was settled.

"Did you want to use the shower first?" After the long hours of travel, he was definitely ready for a shower.

She waved him off. "You go ahead. I'll…" Her shoulders lifted and fell. "…unpack a few things."

At past two in the morning he wasn't about to argue. He waited until he'd gotten inside the bathroom with the door closed before he stripped. It felt good to peel off the clothes wrinkled by too many hours sitting on a plane or in an airport.

He turned on the water and gathered the complimentary soap and shampoo and a towel before climbing beneath the hot spray. Closing his eyes, he just stood there for a couple of minutes and let his body absorb the heavenly heat.

When he'd managed to prod his brain back into action he started the cleansing routine, but a part of his mind kept going back to those tension-filled minutes at the airport.

There was every reason for Willow to be apprehensive about running into her ex-husband or someone he knew. He understood that her previous investigator had given her additional reason to believe her ex might be dangerous. But al-Shimmari hadn't killed her when he had the chance. He could have located her at any time during the past few months if harming her had been his intention. Not that Spencer was giving him any credit at all. He wasn't. The guy was on a federal watch list. He was most likely damned dangerous to the world at large, but not necessarily to any one particular individual, like his ex-wife.

Apprehension and anxiety Spencer had expected. Absolute terror he had not. The idea that being recognized had scared her that badly made him wonder if there was more she wasn't telling him. Had something happened between her and her ex that she hadn't divulged? Had she seen or heard something that gave her reason to suspect he might want to harm her if she returned?

That still didn't explain why al-Shimmari hadn't simply tracked her down and taken care of her if she had seen or heard something he didn't want her to know.

She'd been more forthcoming those last couple of hours on the plane than she had been since they'd met. Maybe she would reveal more as she came to trust that he truly was on her side. He understood that she had been let down many times before coming to him. Her trust wouldn't be easily gained. Unfortunately, time was their enemy.

When he'd pulled on fresh boxers and jeans he cleaned up after himself. He found Willow sleeping soundly on the far edge of the bed. She'd slipped off her shoes, but otherwise she was fully dressed. He pulled the cover up around her and then climbed into bed on the other side, as close to the edge as possible.

A big part of gaining her trust would include respecting her feelings. He sensed that no one had worried about her feelings in a long time. From what he could see so far, she was so accustomed to being alone that she was startled when he came to her rescue in any capacity.

No one should ever feel that alone.

He remembered what she'd said on the plane about being alone. That was the part that bothered him the most. It wasn't right. Not right at all.

He pushed away the thoughts. Ordered himself to sleep. Tomorrow, later today actually, he would need to make contact with his "real-estate" connection. There were things he needed. Things he couldn't have brought along in his luggage or in his carry-on bag.

Whether Khaled al-Shimmari was actually connected with one or more terrorist cells, whether he was capable of murder or not, Spencer had every intention of approaching this situation as if he and his security personnel were lethal as well as hostile.

Being fully armed would be his first step.

Thursday, February 24

WILLOW INHALED deeply. Her lungs filled with warm air, her senses vibrated with the scent of something earthy and delicious. She wanted to open her eyes, but that place between asleep and awake wouldn't let her go. It felt so good. She hadn't slept this well in so very long.

She snuggled deeper into the covers, hugged her pillow more closely.

Warm…smooth…hard.

Willow's mind shifted toward the awake zone. Slowly, she opened her eyes and let the room around her move into focus.

Hotel.

Kuwait.

Spencer Anders.

The sound of her breath catching echoed in the room.

"Morning."

The deep, thick sound of his voice vibrated up from his chest. She knew this because her cheek was pressed to that smooth, warm flesh. She felt the rumble.

Her initial thought was to roll away from him as quickly as possible, but his arm was around her, draped along the length of her back.

She couldn't lie here like this. What would he think?

"Good morning." She scooted away from his inviting body, noting thankfully that he lifted his arm out of her way without any awkwardness. Now if she could only unwrap herself from the cover she would make a mad dash for the bathroom.

But that wasn't going to be easy. Somehow she'd wound herself in the sheets all the way from her edge of the bed until she'd nestled against his muscled torso. The room was cool. Maybe her body had instinctively sought out the heat. And then generated a little of its own, she admittedly self-consciously.

Enough of this. She had to get up.

As if he'd picked up on her discomfort, he dropped his feet to the floor and disappeared into the bathroom. But not before she'd gotten a full view of that broad chest and those sculpted abs. Even his back looked strong and toned.

She put her hands over her face and groaned.

He had to think she was totally pathetic.

Not that she cared what he thought of her personally. She drew her hands away from her face and glared at the ceiling. None of this was personal. She had hired him to get her son back. He didn't have to like her or even respect her. He only had to do what she'd paid him to do.

If only she could maintain that sense of logic.

Kicking off the twisted covers, she managed to scramble out of bed. Her clothes were as twisted as the covers, so she righted them before sifting through her suitcase to pick out something to wear today.

Khaki slacks and a white long-sleeved pullover and sneakers.

The bathroom door opened and he emerged.

She hurried past him, careful not to make eye contact, and closed herself in the bathroom. A shower would help. She was a little off-kilter this morning. Jet lag. She just needed to regain her bearings and she'd be fine.

Truth was she hadn't woken up with a man next to her in nearly a year. Waking up next to a man to whom she wasn't married was even more unusual.

But that was her hang-up. She had plenty.

Spencer ordered room service and made a quick call to his contact. They would meet in an hour at one of the available commercial properties in the city. Touring a couple of office buildings would confirm his cover. If anyone had decided to keep an eye on him, this would back up Spencer's reasons for visiting the peaceful state of Kuwait. Meetings with a couple of random agents in the city wouldn't hurt.

When the light rap came at the door, he checked the peephole and established that it was room service. He opened the door and watched as the waiter rolled the cart into the room. He signed the check and locked the door once the waiter had gone.

The coffee smelled great. He needed caffeine. Lots of it. Though he doubted any amount of caffeine would erase the feel of Willow nestled snugly against him. The heat from her body had awakened urges he'd thought long dead. Not so, evidently. Too bad the timing was seriously off.

HE'D HAD his second cup of coffee by the time she reappeared dressed for the day.

"There's fruit and sweet rolls." Since he couldn't be sure what Willow would like, he'd gone with the safest bet. "And coffee."

She dove into the fruit before having her first cup of coffee.

Watching her eat so ravenously reminded him that she'd skipped dinner on the plane last night. He'd assumed she was too upset to eat. She was bent on making up for it now it seemed. Her lips closed around a strawberry and he couldn't help but stare.

He now knew something personal about Willow Harris the woman, not Willow Harris the ex-wife and mother. She loved strawberries. The way she closed her eyes and relished the burst of flavor on her tongue spoke volumes about just how much she loved the lush red berries.

She opened her eyes and her cheeks turned pink. "Sorry. I get a little carried away sometimes."

He sipped his coffee and tried to act nonchalantly. "I'm the same way about coffee."

She'd left her hair down. Even in the plain white pullover and khakis she looked soft and feminine, elegant somehow. Maybe it was because she was so tiny and her clothes, though conservative, fit so well.

At five-two, she couldn't weigh more than ninety pounds. And even though he recognized that her clothes weren't designer, more like bargain super center, they looked tailor-made for her figure.

Like her, he'd dressed casually. Jeans and a pullover sweater with a casual sports jacket. Though the temperature was probably in the mid-sixties, it could drop unexpectedly. Especially if it rained. No matter what the weather did, the jacket would serve another purpose as well. Weapons were illegal in this country. Carrying one required certain precautions on his part, concealment being top priority.

Willow stopped eating long enough to ask, "Did I hear you making an appointment with someone?"

He grabbed a sweet roll. "We're meeting my real-estate contact at ten-thirty. We'll look at a couple of properties today and get the lay of the land. I made a couple of other calls to local agents as well."

She poured a cup of coffee and sipped it thoughtfully before voicing her next question. "When can we drive by the house?"

She wanted a glimpse of her son. He certainly understood that. But moving too hastily could prove a mistake.

"We'll do some driving around in that area later this evening, maybe just before dark."

"Today's Thursday, the family may be out to dinner as a group tonight. Getting close to the house probably won't be difficult."

The Kuwaiti work week was generally Saturday through Wednesday. Thursday was considered a sort of family night. The next two days were holy days, not to mention a national holiday, Hala February.

"As long as we maintain an appropriate distance, I think we'll be okay," he warned, not wanting her to get her hopes up too high. Just because they drove by didn't mean she would get to see her son.

"I understand."

He wondered if she did.

She devoured another strawberry. The act made his gut clench. He had to get a handle on these unusually strong feelings of attraction and protectiveness. Certainly he intended to protect her, but he realized already that he was having difficulty maintaining objectivity.

Not good.

Recognizing the problem was the first step, he reminded himself. Just like at Alcoholics Anonymous. Not that he'd attended enough of those sessions to know what came next, but he did know that pinpointing the problem was essential in correcting it.

Funny, he realized abruptly, he hadn't thought about alcohol since that tense moment on the plane. Not that it would have done him any good. The only way to get an alcoholic drink in Kuwait was to go to a private, very illegal, party. Still, he felt some sense of relief at not waking up to the urge to pour himself a drink.

He hoped the change for the better was about getting his life back together with this career endeavor. But he had a feeling it had more to do with his distraction with his client than anything else.

And that was definitely not good. At all.

"Whenever you're ready, we'll get going." Getting his head screwed back on straight would be a hell of a lot easier outside the intimacy of this room—away from the bed they'd shared last night. No matter that nothing had happened. Waking up to her cuddled up against him had been more than enough to inspire his too-vivid imagination.

Evidently, while he'd overindulged in alcohol since exiting his military life, he'd neglected his physical needs. Now he was paying the price of having gone too long without sexual release.

She grabbed the scarf and quickly wrapped it around her head to cover her hair and neck. "Okay. I'm ready."

He shouldn't have let her come.

The realization slammed into him like an unexpected mortar round.

She was afraid. She was vulnerable. He'd allowed her to come to this country where being a woman could be a handicap under far too many circumstances.

Protecting her might very well be impossible when push came to shove.

He'd warned her about that.

Unfortunately he was the one who hadn't fully

heeded the warning, because right now he felt completely obsessed with keeping her safe. And that compulsive need jeopardized the mission overall.

All signs of objectivity had vanished the instant he'd seen the sheer terror in her eyes back at that airport.

He had no choice.

He had to keep her safe.

Or die trying.

Chapter Seven

11:00 a.m.

"You do not want to get caught on the street or anywhere else in Kuwait with these weapons."

Spencer surveyed the array of handguns his contact had to offer. A Beretta .9mm, a .40 Glock, as well as your garden variety .32s and .38s. Various ammo clips and silencers. Night-vision goggles and binoculars.

The night-vision goggles would be nice, but he was on a budget here. With that in mind, he reached for the Beretta and the .32.

His contact pushed several clips and a box of bullets across the table. "That should set you up."

Spencer paid him in cash, American currency.

"You know how to contact me if you need anything else."

Spencer tucked the Beretta in his waistband at the small of his back. The .32 he dropped into his jacket pocket. "We won't be here long enough to require anything else."

Though Patrick Bach had always been a reliable contact for most any sort of special needs any time day or night Spencer had called on him in the past, there was always risk involved in a transaction as illegal as this one. Those in the trade didn't always play by the same rules transaction after transaction. The rules changed based on the buyers and the quantity of money they were willing to spend.

Spencer had worked operations when he'd been forced to rely on his own methods for survival, including arming himself on the local black market. Bach hadn't once let him down. But there was always a first time.

As Bach packed up his wares, he glanced at Willow then he grinned and said to Spencer, "I didn't realize you'd separated from the military and gotten yourself an actual wife, Anders. I guess this is one way to keep domestic life blissful."

Spencer had instructed Willow to remain on the far side of the room and to refrain from speaking to Bach. So far she'd done so. Since he hadn't introduced her to the man, he had to assume Bach was fishing. It also meant that his arrival in-country had hit the underground grapevine. Nothing he hadn't expected.

Spencer picked up the ammo and dropped it into his pocket. "I didn't realize you'd gotten so curious about the personal lives of your customers, Bach."

Spencer didn't offer the first glimmer of amusement in response to the jab at humor.

Bach held up both hands in the universal gesture of surrender. "Just making conversation, man. Just making conversation."

Spencer leaned closer to him and smirked. "Besides, you know a guy like me never really goes back to civilian life."

A knowing grin spread across Bach's face. "Right." The devious glint in his eyes told Spencer the sly bastard had taken the comment exactly the way he'd intended.

If Bach leaked that Spencer was in-country doing illegal business related to his former career that was so much the better.

To her credit, Willow had the submissive female act down pat. Even in the elevator ride back to the lobby she stayed in Spencer's shadow. This posturing kept Bach from getting a good look at her face as they exited the building.

The fewer details he was able to pass along, in the event he was so inclined, the better. Taking every possible precaution to protect her would be in the best interests of them both.

Willow kept her gaze lowered as Anders shook hands in closure with his contact. She'd worked extra hard not to look at the man during the meeting. Even now, as she climbed into the passenger seat of the SUV Anders had rented, she didn't look up.

Once shielded behind the tinted windows of the vehicle, she surveyed Damascus Street. She could just make out the stripes of the painted water-storage tanks in the distance. Beyond that, if they were to drive in that direction, they would come upon the park and then the industrial area. She and Khaled had picnicked in that park…before. She'd never been allowed to take her son there. Khaled had rigidly dictated where and when she could take her son from the residence.

She'd wondered what he was afraid of. Asking had proven a monumental mistake. He'd lashed out at her, making her feel incompetent and untrustworthy when it came to caring for their son.

Eventually she'd learned the truth. Khaled had made so many enemies he feared their retaliation against his family, especially his only child.

Goosebumps spilled over her skin. Her son was not safe as long as he was associated with her ex-husband and his evil deeds. Somehow she had to get him out of this country. She had to find a way to ensure Khaled was never allowed custody of her child again.

Not even for a day.

On some level she felt remorse that her son would not be able to know this side of his heritage. She could try and teach him the Islamic values, but it wouldn't be the same. That was the saddest part in all this. Ensuring his safety and having him in her life equated to tearing him from the land of his birth. It was the only way.

She couldn't trust any member of her ex-husband's circle, especially not his mother. Massouma was totally fixated on every detail involving her only son's child. Once Willow took Ata away, he could never return or she would be right back at square one.

Coming to terms with that finality hadn't been easy. She'd lived in this land for three years. Her respect for these people went as deep as the oil wells that paraded through the desert beyond the suburbs of the city. But nothing or no one was as important to her as her son.

"It isn't easy being back."

Anders's comment tugged her from the depressing thoughts. The words were a statement rather than a question.

"There's a level where I feel torn," she admitted, surprised even as she said the words. "I shouldn't. I know I shouldn't. But I do."

She didn't know precisely how, but somehow he understood how she felt. Maybe because he'd spent so much time in the Middle East during his military career, or perhaps simply because he had been betrayed himself. Did he have any idea how much his appreciation for her feelings meant to her?

That he'd managed to draw her in so deeply, so quickly, was a little scary. Still, she couldn't deny enjoying the feeling of being protected.

"I'm glad Mr. Colby asked you to take this case." It was the best way she knew to thank him for his perceptiveness and compassion.

The stall in traffic allowed him to look at her for several seconds before moving forward once more. "I hope you don't change your mind before we're finished."

He held her gaze an extra beat, but the blare of horns prodded his attention back to the traffic.

Willow told herself to look away. It didn't do any good. She kept staring at his profile long after he'd looked away. She recalled the way she'd felt that morning when she'd awakened next to him. Even before that, she'd slept like the dead for the first time in months.

He made her feel safe.

It was crazy. She scarcely knew him.

That he'd separated from the military in such an egregious manner should have put her off…should have her unsettled about his trustworthiness. Yet, she trusted him completely…felt fully protected in his presence.

He had stood up for the woman, a complete stranger, in the motel room next to hers. It had been so long since she'd seen an act of chivalry so impressive and selfless that maybe she was overreacting. Then again, she hadn't had sex in more than a year. As embarrassing as that fact was, she wasn't actually ashamed of it. She'd slept with one man in college, another after settling into her job following graduation, both had been relationships versus casual sex. Her next partner after that had been her husband.

She'd never had casual sex in her life.

Part of that was a direct result of her strict upbringing. There were times when that not-particularly-pleasant upbringing had come in handy. For instance, when she'd taken up residence in Kuwait, dressing and behaving conservatively had come naturally to her. She'd been almost thankful for her parents's ironfisted child-rearing methods. But then those same methods had ingrained in her a willingness to trust the man she'd married when she shouldn't have. She'd blindly gone into that relationship and followed all his edicts without once questioning anything until it was way too late.

Not that she blamed her parents for her mess. She didn't. This was a tragedy of her own making. Still, they were not totally free of guilt here. She'd learned the hard way that lying in one's self-made *hard* bed was not the only option. Even now she could hear her father's voice echoing that sentiment, *You made your bed, you'll have to lie in it.*

The muscles in her face tightened, making her jaw clench at the old hurt. No. You didn't have to simply lie in it. There were things a woman could do, should do, when her husband mistreated her, physically or mentally.

If she'd only realized sooner what kind of man

Khaled was, she might have escaped with her son before he'd suspected her disillusionment or her plans.

That wasn't really true. If she'd suspected something wasn't right she would have gone to him and asked, assuming he had been falsely accused, just as she did when she'd discovered the discrepancy in his finances. There was no getting around the fact that she had simply been naive. And in love.

Big mistake.

Her attention shifted back to the driver, the man she respected so much despite knowing him for a period of time more accurately measured in hours than in days. Was she making the same kind of mistake all over again?

She'd watched the way he handled that illegal business with the guns. Did she really have any reason to trust him? Sure, he seemed to sympathize with her, seemed compassionate toward people in general, but did that make him a good guy deep down where it counted?

Stop it.

They were here. He was doing his job so far. She had to stop overanalyzing every single thing. She could not afford to be distracted. Her actions could very well distract him. Allowing that to happen would jeopardize what they were here to do.

Time to get her act together and focus.

Time to behave like a mature woman who had learned her lesson about trusting the wrong man. The compromise was simple. She should appreciate Spencer Anders for his seeming compassion and empathy as well as his obvious skill at doing what had to be done in this situation and environment. All the while, she most definitely should understand that his ability to get the job done did not make him a good person.

Somehow she had to learn to separate her feelings. Respect didn't necessarily have to equate to trust or…anything else. Like the feelings of attraction she had experienced lying next to him that morning.

She was a woman, she had needs. Those needs could not be permitted to get tangled up with the heat of the moment. Recognizing the problem was the key to moving forward productively.

She definitely recognized the problem. If she were really lucky, he didn't. Knowing that he knew she was even remotely attracted to him would just be too humiliating.

"Our next stop is the building on the left at the coming intersection. We're a little early." He checked his wristwatch. "Ten minutes. We'll park and wait in the car."

"Is the person you're meeting at this location an actual real-estate agent?" Anders had told her that the last guy worked on the fringes of the business as a cover for his real job—selling weapons in a country that had banned the personal ownership of weapons years ago. She had known men like that existed in

Kuwait when she'd lived here—as did those who sold alcohol illegally. There was a whole underground of illegal activities here just as there was any place else.

This was, however, the first time she'd had direct dealings with the folks who carried out those prohibited trades.

"This one's for real. I picked his agency from the listing in the local paper and called to make the appointment this morning." He parked the SUV in a narrow alley between what appeared to be two office buildings. When he'd shut off the engine he turned to her. "There's one more after this for cover purposes, and then we'll drift into tourist mode."

There was such intensity in his eyes, such determination. How could she not believe he would make this happen? She'd watched men like him in the movies, read about them in books. A hero. Every instinct told her this man was exactly that.

She had to believe.

"Oh, yeah, you mentioned that earlier."

For the first time since arriving at the airport and having that customs officer scare ten years off her life, she felt confident again.

Jim Colby had promised her.

The man he'd chosen for her case would make it happen. She believed that with all her heart.

Believing was something she was really good at most of the time. Her childhood had included a deeply entrenched certainty that without faith all was lost. She'd never once failed to have enough faith. Even when objectivity would have served her better, she'd stuck by the idea that faith would get her through whatever life tossed in her path.

Maybe that was how she'd survived when she'd feared her ex-husband might simply kill her to silence her. It would have been relatively easy in this society. Women certainly weren't the ones front and center in the mainstream. Without any other family ties here, if she'd gone missing hardly anyone would have noticed, much less asked about her.

Anders opened her door, dragging her from the disturbing speculation. She hadn't even realized he'd gotten out.

She climbed out of the SUV and followed him to the front entrance, admiring the architecture and scattered palm trees along the street as she went. There wasn't a lot of landscaping to brag about in Kuwait, but the immaculate care taken of the city was noteworthy, as was a good deal of the architecture. An art gallery across the street nudged at her curiosity. There was a time when she wouldn't have missed a gallery of any kind, even one that catered to the really bizarre alternative art she didn't particularly care for. She loved studying the work others did with their hands.

Did that make her a hands girl?

She glanced down at the right hand of the man next to her. She'd noticed his before. Nice hands. Big, but not rough-looking. Well-formed with long, blunt-tipped fingers. Not the artist type, but the capable kind made for touching a woman in ways she could only imagine.

Jerking her gaze front and center, she railed at herself for being so foolish. She'd gone off on a very inappropriate tangent there. Probably just her mind attempting to find ways to decompress. Distraction wasn't a problem, as long as she didn't obsess about any part of him she would be fine.

Right?

Right.

Okay, now she was answering herself.

Not good.

Anders signed in at the reception desk in the lobby. She waited near the cluster of chairs and potted palm trees. The ceiling soared high, allowing for a wall of windows that invited the sun to pour into the lobby. She wouldn't want the job of working the reception desk in the summer. The air conditioning might keep the room at a tolerable temperature, but there was no way to escape the harsh glare of the summer sun in this part of the world. It could be brutal.

As Anders approached her, she decided making a quick trip to the ladies' room before the real-estate agent arrived might be in order.

The sign for the restrooms as well as the elevators held a prominent position on the wall well behind and beyond the reception desk that dominated the front of the lobby.

"I'm going to the ladies' room. I'll be right back."

He glanced around the deserted lobby. "I'd feel better seeing you to the door."

There was no need to be embarrassed. He was right.

"Whatever you think is best." She headed for the designated corridor.

He stayed in step right beside her. When she reached the door, he hesitated. "Maybe I should check it out first."

"Anders, I'll be fine." She looked back in the direction they'd come. "You should wait for your appointment. You'll still be able to see this door from the waiting area."

He glanced back to confirm her assertion. "All right." That intense gaze landed back on hers. "But make it fast. I won't relax until you're back in my line of vision."

She pushed through the door, leaving him staring after her.

For a couple of moments she stood on the other side of the door wondering if he'd walked back to the waiting area or if he'd opted to hang around until she emerged once more.

She didn't remember the last time anyone had worried so about her. That he did it with such care made her feel warm inside.

Shaking her head at just how pathetic she was,

Willow moved toward the stalls. The restroom was pretty much like one found back home. The American influence in Kuwait couldn't be ignored even when it came to toilets.

When she'd relieved herself and washed up, she considered her reflection a moment. At twenty-eight she still looked young, but she felt old inside. She'd stopped feeling young and vibrant ages ago.

Willow tugged the scarf from her hair and ran her fingers through the long, blond length. She'd thought about cutting it several times, but something always got in the way. Or maybe she was afraid to change much of anything for fear her baby wouldn't recognize her.

Would he even remember her?

Pain arced sharply inside her. What would she do if he didn't? He would cry for his father…people would notice. How could they hope to get through customs and back on a plane if her child screamed the entire time?

What if attempting to steal him was a mistake?

Willow closed her eyes and fought back the emotions churning wildly inside her.

She was doing the right thing.

She knew it. She believed it with her whole heart.

Faith. Where was her faith?

Anders was waiting for her. The real-estate agent might have arrived already. She shouldn't be in here worrying about an issue that hadn't come up yet.

Taking extra care, she wrapped the khimar around her hair and neck. A few blond strands peeked past the scarf, a vivid contrast to the black silk. Her cheeks were flushed and her lips red from biting and licking them repeatedly. She needed Chap Stick.

No, what she needed was to relax.

Stay calm.

Get this done.

Summoning her wayward courage she moved to the door and pulled it open. Anders still waited near the potted palms and seating area. Evidently the other man hadn't arrived yet.

With a deep breath she emerged into the lobby and headed straight for Anders. He watched her from the moment she stepped beyond the door. That he continued to look directly at her when she stopped in front of him made her a little giddy.

Dumb. So dumb.

What was wrong with her?

She was going way overboard with this whole big-strong-protector thing. Yes, he was supposed to protect her, but that was his job. It wasn't like he was doing it because he was attracted to her or had some vested personal interest in her. Other than the case.

"He should be here any minute now."

The moment felt oddly awkward. "Good."

He looked away then, as if he felt the awkwardness too.

She stared at the floor, the plants, pretty much anything but him. Then she busied herself watching the man behind the reception desk answer the phone.

No matter that she wasn't looking at Anders. No matter that he probably wasn't even looking at her, she could feel him. It wasn't that general awareness of someone's presence…this was a pull of some sort. A feeling of nearness that overwhelmed all else.

She closed her eyes and fought the vertigo effect the unexpected sensations had on her. Jet lag, she told herself. Her emotions were oversensitive. That was all it could be. Sleep deprivation played tricks on one's mind. She knew this firsthand.

There was no reason to let this silly reaction get out of hand. She opened her eyes and surveyed the lobby in every direction except the one in which he stood. She wished the real estate man would hurry.

"You seem nervous."

The deep, husky quality of his voice shouldn't have made her shiver, but it did. Dammit.

Frustration surged. "I'm fine." She flashed him a glance that relayed that frustration. "I just want this part over with."

"I understand."

The empathy in his eyes backed up his words.

Why did he have to do that? She needed him to be that unyielding, distant man she'd met that first night.

"How could you?"

He flinched as if the words had stung somehow.

She refused to feel bad about it.

"You're right. I can't imagine how this must feel."

Why hadn't he stopped at *You're right?*

Movement at the front entrance dragged her attention there in hopes that the real-estate agent had arrived and they could get past this strained moment.

"Is that him?" she asked, hoping to avert his focus from her.

Anders turned to look at the man who'd walked up to the reception desk.

She watched as well. Something about the way the man signed the guest registry was vaguely and strangely familiar to her.

Willow stared hard at the man as he placed the pen on the desk and chatted with the clerk. The way he handled his briefcase…his mannerisms as he spoke… Somehow she recognized his body language.

She studied his profile as he produced identification for the clerk as Anders had been required to do. Then he withdrew a cell phone from his jacket pocket as if he'd received a call. He turned his back briefly to take the call.

The way the man moved…the profile…

"Oh, God."

Anders wheeled toward her, searched her face. "What's wrong?"

Fear exploded in her chest.

Impossible.

She had to be wrong.

But she wasn't.

"I know that man."

Chapter Eight

Spencer knew his first moment of sheer panic.

It was a wholly unfamiliar sensation.

He kicked it aside.

"Go back into the ladies' room." He looked directly into her eyes, noted the terror there, refused to let it affect him. "I'll make excuses for you. Stay there until I come back for you."

She didn't answer. Didn't move.

"Do you understand?"

The stridently muttered demand appeared to snap her into action.

"Okay."

She headed for the ladies' room without a backward glance or a second's hesitation.

Spencer shifted his attention to the man who had just picked up his briefcase and turned to head in his direction.

In an instant Spencer had cleared his mind of all else and stepped into character. He started forward, outstretched his hand at just the right moment to meet the other man's. "Spencer Anders."

"Yuri Avnery."

Spencer gave Avnery's hand a firm shake. "I'm looking forward to seeing the space. The location is excellent. Exactly what my client is looking for."

Avnery nodded. "Very good." He gestured toward the bank of elevators. "Shall we?"

Spencer relaxed marginally. "How long has the space been on the market?"

Avnery provided a few details regarding the previous business tenant. Spencer put on an attentive face, but his mind was on Willow and whether or not leaving her alone in the ladies' room was a good move.

Not that he'd had a choice.

When they'd boarded the elevator, Avnery asked, "Your wife decided not to accompany you after all?"

Spencer's alert status moved back into the red zone. Avnery knew the answer to that question. He'd assuredly seen Willow standing near Spencer, not to mention her name had been on the register.

"I'm afraid my wife got bored and decided to visit the gallery across the street."

He recognized that the man had in all likelihood noted her hasty retreat to the ladies' room. That shouldn't actually set off any warning bells.

Spencer hoped like hell he'd only gotten a look at her back. Even a glimpse of her profile might eventually trigger some kind of recollection if, in fact, Willow did know him.

Damn.

There were hundreds of real-estate agents in this city. How the hell had he managed to select one she'd run into before? If he believed in karma, he'd be worried. But there was no reason to believe there was a problem just yet.

"That's too bad," Avnery said. "I was looking forward to meeting her."

The interest in his eyes was undeniable. Maybe a little too interested.

"It's not often," he added, "that my clients bring along their wives for input."

Definitely too much interest. Spencer's instincts went on point. "I'm sure my wife would love to think that she had some say in the matter, but I'm afraid she's here for the shopping and sightseeing."

Avnery nodded, a smirk hovering just beneath his perfectly composed professional veneer. "I find that the female perspective is not often conducive to constructive business."

Spencer would just bet he did. Men like Avnery considered women good for nothing more than sexual and domestic slavery. He was reasonably sure this guy was Israeli. Maybe he'd been raised in Kuwait or Saudi Arabia. Whatever the case, his perspective on how women should be treated was definitely skewed.

That was the thing about men like Avnery, they

needed a female in submission to feel more like a man. He didn't have to know this guy personally to understand that his feelings had nothing to do with religion or tradition.

He could only assume that if Willow knew this man he was somehow associated with al-Shimmari, which explained everything about his attitude. He would also assume for the moment that his interest in Spencer's companion was more related to his warped view of women than the possibility that he'd somehow recognized Willow.

Avnery gave Spencer the grand tour of the suite of offices that made up the third floor of the building. He pretended to be impressed. But mostly he was worried about the woman hiding in the restroom downstairs.

He was supposed to protect Willow Harris.

They'd barely arrived in-country and already he'd made a strategic error.

Maybe all the booze had stolen his edge.

The idea that Willow might have to pay the price for his two-year layover in hell twisted like concertina wire in his gut.

WILLOW WORKED hard to slow her breathing.

She'd almost lost control there for a minute.

How did she know that man?

She'd definitely met him before. The way he moved. That harsh profile, long, wide nose…jutting chin.

Think!

Okay, calm down.

Pushing off the bathroom door, she started to pace in front of the line of stalls.

Black hair. Maybe five-eight or nine. Medium build.

She rubbed at her forehead as if that would help. It didn't. The familiarity was there. She knew him. But how?

If she knew his name…maybe that would help her remember.

Willow stopped in mid-step. Surely his name would trigger the right synapse.

Before reason had kicked in she'd made it to the door.

Anders had told her to stay in here until he came back for her.

But what if he was in danger?

What if this was a setup?

Khaled might have found out she was here with Anders and sent that man in place of the real estate man they were supposed to meet. No, that couldn't be right. Anders had contacted this guy. Hadn't he?

This was ridiculous!

She couldn't hide in this restroom like this.

Going out there and getting this guy's name was the right thing to do. Then she would know for sure. She refused to be a coward.

Willow pulled the door open before she could change her mind. The lobby remained empty. The typical workweek ran from Sunday through Wednesday, there wouldn't be that much business going on today.

That was to her benefit.

Taking care to restrain her stride, she made the nerve-wracking journey to the reception desk. The man behind the counter looked up, but he didn't ask if he could help her.

"My husband is viewing the suite of offices on the third floor. I thought I might visit the gallery across the street."

The man stared, didn't even blink.

Keep going. "Would you mind taking a message for my husband so he knows where I am when he comes down?"

"One moment."

While he rounded up a pen and paper, she covertly read the final two names on the register. Spencer Anders. Yuri Avnery.

The name didn't ring a bell.

"At the gallery across the street?" the clerk confirmed.

She nodded. "I'll be waiting there."

"I will see that he receives your message."

Willow thanked him and turned to face the front entrance. It wasn't like she could *not* go now. She'd told the clerk she was going. It had been the only way she could think of to get a look at the register. Maybe if she'd had time to plan an excuse she would have come up with something better.

It didn't matter now. She had to go.

Anders would probably yell at her.

But keeping their cover intact was too important to screw it up with a misstep this trivial.

She could do this.

It wasn't a big deal.

All she had to do was walk out the door and across the street. There was little traffic on the street and even fewer pedestrians. The chances of running into anyone she knew from before were about the same as winning the lottery.

Maybe a little less than that, but the basic concept was the same.

Concentrating on making her decision happen, she put one foot in front of the other. No looking back. No hesitating. Just do it.

She exited the building and didn't stop until she'd reached the street. When the unexpected surge in traffic passed, she crossed the street.

It wasn't until she'd gotten inside the door of the gallery that she could breathe again.

Thank God.

The shop owner glanced up at the tinkle of the bell and announced, *"Aa-salaam-aleikum!"* Peace be with you.

"Aleikum salaam," popped out of her mouth before she'd considered the repercussions of responding at all. Would the typical American tourist know to say this traditional Muslim greeting? Possibly. It

was on the Internet. Everything was on the Internet these days.

Besides, she'd said it. There was no taking it back now.

Stop being paranoid, she railed silently. She hadn't been here in nearly a year. She had never been in this gallery. Kuwait was a bustling city. It wasn't like she had to worry about running into someone from her past life around every corner. She hadn't even known that many people.

She might not even know the man with Anders right now. Anxiety and panic could be playing tricks with her mind.

So she did what all Americans were famous for doing when traveling, she browsed and made all kinds of comments to herself as well as the shop owner and she even gasped from time to time at the lovely artwork. Willow felt certain the man was rolling his eyes behind her back.

Paintings, sculpture, pottery. She studied each piece in painstaking detail, anything to keep her mind focused on something other than the man across the street.

Eventually his name intruded.

Yuri Avnery.

She called his image to mind. What precisely was so familiar about him?

The way he moved for sure.

His whole profile? She couldn't be sure.

Try harder.

Still nothing specific bobbed to the surface of that murky lake of memories. Maybe she'd suppressed so much of that past that she'd lost some details.

But she did know him, she decided after further consideration.

She was almost positive.

The bell over the door jingled and her head came up. Tension roared through her with the force of a freight train barreling down its track. She peeked around the piece she currently studied.

Three women, garbed in traditional Islamic dress, full *hijab,* whispered among each other as they hurried over to the wall where the oil paintings were displayed.

Willow let a whoosh of tension rush past her lips. She really did need to get a grip here. If she walked around acting like this someone would notice. Calling attention to herself was not the thing to do.

Okay. If she couldn't remember the guy she should start a process of elimination. First, she resurrected the long-buried images of the household staff along with the names of each man in her husband's domestic employ.

Nope. He hadn't been someone she'd run into in the house on a regular basis. Not that she'd actually thought he was. She would surely have remembered someone she saw every day.

She thought of the people she saw from time to time at the various shops she'd frequented. Not the grocery clerk. Not the postman. Not the drycleaner. Not at the pediatrician's office.

Then she moved on to her husband's business associates. Not that she saw any of them that often, but she did on rare occasions. Those would be far harder to recall.

The trio of women moved to the metal sculptures next. The gaze of the one who appeared to be the leader of the group abruptly bumped into Willow's. Willow smiled before she could suppress the impulse. The other woman quickly looked away.

God, she had to remember the rules of etiquette. No staring. No prolonged direct eye contact. No smiling. No…

Yuri Avnery's profile suddenly loomed in her head. Only it wasn't the image she'd captured in the lobby across the street. He wore white robes…not the business suit he'd been wearing as he'd signed in fifteen or twenty minutes ago. Long white robes and the headdress, the *ghutra*. A shimmery gold over-cloak had embellished the pure white.

There were a lot of people at the event she recalled, all dressed in the very finest traditional garb. Tables. Waiters. Her husband…

Her breath evaporated in her lungs.

Oh, God.

She remembered him. Only his name hadn't been Yuri Avnery…Abdulatif something. She couldn't remember the last name.

He was her ex-husband's hatchet man. She'd only met him that once, but she remembered Khaled referring to him in just that way. She had assumed he'd meant that he was the man who got rid of the excess in his businesses. You know, the kind of man who came in and cut the fat…job layoffs, pink slips. Stuff like that.

But her husband hadn't meant that at all. Khaled had laughed at her later when she'd suggested as much.

The moment replayed over and over in her mind. The way her husband had looked at the man…the way he'd laughed when he made the statement about what the man did for him.

He was a hatchet man all right, but he didn't cut excess employees…he got rid of problems.

Like Spencer Anders.

Willow was at the front window of the gallery before she'd realized she'd moved.

She stared up at the third floor of the office building across the street.

If she was right…God, she prayed she wasn't…the man up there with Anders was an assassin.

"DOES THIS suite of offices satisfy your needs then?"

Spencer followed Avnery along the corridor that led back to the third-floor lobby that served the suite of offices.

"I have another location to preview this afternoon, but this is very much in line with my client's interests."

Avnery paused at the wall of windows that overlooked the street. "Quite a pleasant view," he suggested with a wave of his arm.

Spencer took his time strolling over to join him. So far the meeting had gone off without a glitch. Still, Willow had been certain she knew this man. It wasn't impossible that she knew him in his capacity as a real-estate agent. Her ex-husband might have sought his expertise at one time or another. Or perhaps they'd met at a social function. No matter, Spencer's instincts were nagging at him.

Something about this man was not right.

"I may want to come back and take some digital shots of the place," Spencer commented. "Unless you have photos or maybe a virtual tour on your Web site." He watched the man carefully now that he wasn't following him around from room to room. At one time he'd been particularly good at spotting a liar. "Your secretary mentioned a Web site." He hadn't actually spoken to this man when he'd made the call this morning.

Avnery nodded. "Of course. I believe you'll find everything there that your client requires."

His response was slightly stilted…the least bit hesitant. Spencer's tension escalated to the next level. "Can you spell out any unusual legalities involved with an American tenant?"

Avnery glanced down at the street. "Ah-ha. Your lovely wife appears to have grown bored with the gallery as well."

Spencer's attention rocketed to the gallery across the street. Willow stood in the floor-to-ceiling plate glass window staring up at this building…it felt almost as if she were looking directly at him.

"I am confident she won't be bored for long."

A long white limousine lurched to a stop in front of the gallery.

Spencer went for his weapon.

"Don't move, Mr. Anders. I would most assuredly dislike having to kill you here. I'm certain the carpet would be ruined and my friend Avnery would be upset with me."

Spencer turned slowly to face the imposter. The silenced end of a .9mm Ruger was aimed directly at his chest. His fingers itched to go for his own weapon.

"I am quite the excellent shot. You might want to consider that before you make a move for your weapon."

Spencer raised his hands in the air. "I'll take your word for that, Avnery."

The other man smirked. "I'm certain you know my name is not Avnery, but that is most irrelevant. Let's move to the elevator, Mr. Anders. Your next appointment will be your last, I'm afraid, but it is a command performance."

"Then let's not keep the man waiting." Spencer executed an about-face, giving his back to the man with the gun. That was, clearly, his only choice. And maybe if he kept him off guard he wouldn't remember to check to see if Spencer was armed.

"One moment, Mr. Anders."

No such luck. Spencer stopped.

Oh, well, that left him with only one option.

Avnery or whoever the hell he was patted his left side first since it was his left hand that was free. It was in the pivotal instant when he switched his weapon from his right hand to his left that Spencer made his move.

He twisted one-eighty, slammed against the man's right shoulder with his full body weight.

The silencer hissed. A pop followed.

Spencer shoved the man's left arm upward as they went down together.

They hit the floor.

Another hiss and pop.

Spencer had a good thirty pounds and six inches of height on the guy, but the other man was strong.

Enough with this.

Spencer drew back and jammed the heel of his right hand beneath the guy's chin. His head snapped upward. A final hiss and pop erupted from the weapon clenched in his hand. A violent twist of his head and the fight was over.

Spencer scrambled to his feet and ran for the stairwell.

He buttoned his jacket on the way down. Ran a hand through his hair to ensure he didn't look as if he'd just been in a fight. No need to tip off the clerk any sooner than necessary.

At the door to the lobby, he paused long enough to catch his breath. He opened the door a crack and scanned the area.

Two men hustled through the front entrance and spoke in Arabic to the man behind the desk. Spencer didn't catch everything that was said, but he got that they were looking for him.

If those men were from the limo, he had to assume that the vehicle was still out there and that meant Willow would still be close by as well.

When the two men headed for the elevator, Spencer opened the door a little wider to watch them board.

The elevator doors glided closed. He counted to three and exited the stairwell.

Barely suppressing the need to break into a run, he strode across the lobby.

"Mr. Anders!"

Spencer ignored the clerk.

He didn't have to look back to know the man would attempt to contact the men headed to the third floor.

They'd have to catch him if they wanted him.

He burst out onto the sidewalk.

Two things were immediately clear: the limo was still parked in front of the gallery and Willow was no longer standing at the shop window.

He ignored the blaring horns as he dashed across the street.

The limo windows were too dark to see inside, but the driver's seat beyond the windshield was empty.

That meant that any other occupants besides the ones who'd gone after him were likely inside the gallery.

Withdrawing the Beretta, he burst through the shop door. It wasn't like they couldn't see him coming. But he couldn't *not* go in...Willow was in there.

Other than the whoosh of the door closing behind him the shop appeared dead silent.

No signs of a struggle.

No milling customers.

Nothing.

He moved deeper into the gallery, around sculptures, beyond complicated displays of smaller pieces of artwork comprised of various mediums.

As he moved past the counter, a muzzle rammed into the back of his head.

"Mr. Anders."

Spencer froze. He analyzed the voice. Male. Western...almost.

"I've been waiting for you."

Three more men stepped out of the shadows of the farthest recesses of the gallery, weapons trained on one target...Spencer.

The man who'd spoken moved in closer behind Spencer. "Before you die," he said, his words uttered softly now as if he were speaking for Spencer's ears only, "I have only one question."

He jammed the barrel of his weapon harder into Spencer's skull. "Where is my wife?"

Chapter Nine

He'd found them.

Willow's heart sank a little more as she watched Khaled and his men force Spencer Anders into the waiting limousine. Someone from the airport or the hotel had to have tipped him off, had to have been monitoring Anders's calls from the hotel.

The vehicle pulled away from the curb. Two black cars, windows heavily tinted, moved into place, one in front of the limo, the other behind it. Her ex-husband's security detail.

She shivered.

Her next thought made her sinking heart shudder painfully.

Spencer Anders was as good as dead.

"Where would you go?"

Willow sucked in an anxious breath and wrestled her attention from the caravan disappearing in the distance to the woman speaking to her.

"Where would you go?" the woman repeated.

Three sets of eyes watched her from above dark veils, anticipating her answer. Though she didn't know their names, nor they hers, all in the car understood what had just happened.

What did she do now? She was unarmed. It wasn't as if she could try to stop Khaled and his men.

Jim Colby.

She needed Jim Colby.

Willow looked directly at the driver, infusing her expression with all the hope she could summon. "If you would be kind enough to take me back to my hotel, I would appreciate it." Willow gave the name of the hotel where she and Anders had spent the night. Her things were there and the telephone in the room would allow her to call the United States.

The woman behind the wheel, the one who appeared to be the leader of the group, nodded and turned her attention forward. The others watched in silence as their friend merged into the growing traffic.

Willow understood what they were all thinking. Her presence in this car could get them arrested...or worse.

The woman driving, the most outspoken of the group and the one who'd taken charge at that pivotal moment, had more than likely saved Willow's life.

She blinked back the tears that burned in her eyes.

When she'd realized who the man pretending to be a real-estate agent actually was, she'd rushed to the front of the shop. She'd seen Khaled's limo coming...she had known he was coming for her.

Since the shop owner had been preoccupied with a customer, Willow had gone for her only option: the rear entrance of the gallery.

The three women she'd noticed entering the shop a few minutes earlier had watched her flight. One of the women, the one driving now, had followed Willow outside and offered her assistance.

For the first five or so seconds Willow hadn't been sure what she should do. She'd almost been afraid to trust these strangers. But desperation had driven her. Anders would die and the hope of ever seeing her son again was fading fast.

She'd had no choice.

Moving as quickly as they dared without drawing unnecessary attention, the women had led her down the back alley for a considerable distance. Then they had slipped between two buildings and moved back to the street well beyond where the limo and its entourage were parked. Surrounding her in a wall of black, the women ushered Willow to the car. They'd stayed out of view there until Khaled and his men had driven away.

Willow couldn't be sure why these women had decided to help her, but she was immensely grateful.

Keeping low in the backseat, she couldn't help turning to look from time to time to ensure they weren't being followed.

"No one is following," the driver said, evidently noting Willow's furtive glances out the rear window.

Willow told herself to relax. She wouldn't be able to think rationally if she didn't calm down.

Slow, deep breaths.

Jim Colby would know what to do.

But could he do anything in time to save Anders?

Willow's chest tightened.

Probably not.

This was her fault. Her desperation was already responsible for one missing investigator. She should have stopped when Davenport had warned her of his suspicions about his missing investigator.

But her heart just wouldn't allow her to let go of the hope that she would get her baby back.

The name of the street they had just passed snapped Willow back to the present. Wait. This wasn't right. The driver had missed the turn for the hotel.

A new rush of worry ascended upon her.

What if these women weren't helping her…what if they were taking her to her ex-husband's home? There were rewards for people who showed extraordinary respect for the rich and powerful.

Stop.

Don't jump to conclusions right away. There could be a logical reason for choosing a different route than the one Willow knew. Right now she had every reason to believe these women were helping her. With that in mind she waited until they reached the next intersection to see if the driver was simply taking a different route.

Definitely not.

"We've passed the hotel," she said aloud, trying hard not to sound accusatory or nervous.

"The authorities may be looking for you." The driver glanced in the rearview mirror as she said this. "You should be properly prepared."

The woman sitting next to Willow in the backseat touched her arm. "You look like an American."

The realization that she wore a white blouse and khaki slacks bulldozed its way into Willow's awareness.

The women were right.

She would be easy to spot dressed like this. The man posing as the real-estate agent and the clerk at the desk of the building they had visited had probably given descriptions of her attire. Why hadn't she thought of that?

Willow placed her hand on that of the woman next to her. "Thank you." She met the driver's gaze in the rearview mirror then. "I don't know why you're taking this risk, but I'm sincerely grateful."

"If we do not help each other, then who will help us?" the driver said bluntly.

Truer words had never been spoken.

Obviously things were changing in this intensely male-dominated society. Slowly, very slowly, but they were happening.

The home they visited briefly belonged to the driver. Willow learned that the three women had been best friends since childhood. They used every opportunity to encourage other women to stand up for themselves as well as others in order to facilitate change.

Food and drink were offered, but Willow couldn't accept the hospitality since every minute she wasted might be Anders's last. Not to mention that the longer she stayed in the company of these generous ladies, the more risk she brought to them.

Once at the hotel Willow said good-bye to the good Samaritans who had rescued her from certain death. With their help she was now clothed in full traditional dress, from black veil to long black *abaya* and no-nonsense black shoes. She'd pinned her shoulder-length blond hair back as tightly as possible to ensure no telling strands slipped loose.

Careful to scan the hotel lobby as she went, she moved toward the bank of elevators. Half a dozen arriving guests were crowded around the check-in desk. Two others had moved on to the elevators.

Despite being fully camouflaged, Willow found herself holding her breath as she waited for one of the elevator cars to arrive. She kept her gaze appropriately lowered so as not to make accidental contact with the other guests standing close by. There were so many rules for public conduct…failure to adhere to even one would attract attention.

The elevator doors slid open, offering entrance and sending a surge of relief gushing through her. She followed the other guests into the waiting elevator car and then selected the floor above the one where her room was located. Since she had no way of knowing what might be waiting for her at the room registered to Mr. and Mrs. Spencer Anders, she needed to take precautions.

The floor she'd selected was the first stop. She emerged from the elevator and moved down the corridor toward the stairwell exit, thankful that she didn't run into any other guests.

At the exit to the stairs, she listened a moment in an attempt to hear anyone in the stairwell. Sounded quiet. She pushed through the door and listened again. Still quiet. Moving as noiselessly as she could, she hurried down the one flight.

Bracing for the worst, she cautiously eased the door open and peeked into the corridor. What she saw had her swiftly drawing back into the shelter of the stairwell. The urge to run quivered along her limbs.

Suppressing the flight impulse, she leaned against the wall next to the door. She had to think. Think! Forcing herself to recount the details, she analyzed what she'd seen. The door to their room stood open. Men in uniforms that she recognized as the local authorities were moving in and out of the room. She'd seen at least five in the fraction of a second that she'd dared to look.

What did she do now?

If she couldn't get to their room she couldn't call.

Sure she had her purse, but no working cell phone.

She had a small amount of cash and a credit card, but she couldn't use the credit card without having it traced right back to where she'd used it.

Going back to the airport with the return ticket in her purse wouldn't help. The moment she presented her passport she would be taken into custody. Not that leaving was actually even an option.

The bottom line was she was unarmed…and unprepared for a situation like this.

She had to call Jim Colby.

Waiting for the authorities to finish their work and clear out was out of the question. Anders would be dead well before then…if he wasn't already.

She had to do something.

If she'd asked to use the telephone in the home of the woman who had helped her escape the gallery the call might have led the authorities back to her and her friends. No way could she have done that. Acts of defiance were not tolerated, especially those carried out by women.

But she had to do something.

There had to be a way for her to do this.

If she didn't figure out something fast it would be too late.

Willow closed her eyes and fought the defeat sucking at her. She wanted so badly to get her baby back. To escape the reach of her devil of an ex-husband.

Right now it felt exactly as if she had failed already. Failed her child and herself.

Maybe it was already too late and she'd been too blind to see it.

Davenport could have been right, and she'd refused to accept it.

What if she was looking for a miracle?

And what if she wasn't going to find it?

Chicago
Friday, February 25, 8:15 a.m.

"CONNIE, have you heard anything from Anders?" Jim hesitated in front of his receptionist's desk. "He was supposed to call with an update last night."

Connie looked up over the rim of her coffee mug. "Technically, I don't start to work until eight-thirty, but the answer to your question is no."

She promptly returned her attention to the newspaper.

Jim wondered if she thought her prickly attitude would keep the world around her at a distance. The MO was classic. Don't let anyone close and you won't lose your focus and you damned sure won't get hurt, betrayed or otherwise screwed.

There was a thing or two he could tell the lady about keeping the world at a distance, but that would have to wait. At the moment he had bigger problems to deal with, like where the hell his associate was and just how much trouble he might be in.

When a guy was halfway around the world in a

country that didn't necessarily play by the same rules as his home base, and he went missing, the best course of action was to call an expert.

Jim knew only one man who could reach out and touch just about anybody, just about anywhere.

Lucas Camp.

"Put Anders through if he calls," he said to his quirky receptionist.

Connie glanced at her watch. "Yeah, okay."

As Jim started up the stairs, she called after him, "Don't forget you've got that new guy, Sam Johnson, coming in at nine."

Surprised that she would bother to remind him without him specifically asking her to do so, Jim tossed her a thank-you and decided that maybe she would grasp the concept of teamwork after all.

He double-timed it up the stairs and put in a call to Lucas. If he was in town he would be at the Colby Agency with Victoria by now.

Mildred, Victoria's secretary, patched him straight through to Lucas.

"What can I do for you, Jim?" Lucas asked in lieu of a greeting. "Victoria had an early staff meeting, but I'm manning her office."

Jim smiled at how this powerful man catered to the woman he loved. "Actually it's you I want to talk to." He grabbed a pen and pad in case he needed to take down any names or numbers.

"Shoot."

"I sent Spencer Anders on his first case and there may be a problem."

A brief hesitation preceded, "He's had a rough go with the bottle. We discussed that issue if you'll recall. I was sure he wouldn't let you down."

The depth of disappointment in Lucas's voice gave away just how badly he wanted things to work out for Spencer Anders.

"No, it's not that kind of problem," Jim assured. "I'm concerned I may have underestimated the need for a two-man team on this one."

"I see." The sound of movement rasped across the line as if Lucas were gathering pad and pen as well. "Give me the details." The disappointment had morphed into brutal determination. No one messed with Lucas Camp or his people.

Jim quickly explained the child-custody battle between Willow Harris and her ex-husband. "When Anders didn't call in last night I knew he'd run into trouble."

"I have a couple of contacts in the area I can reach out to," Lucas offered. "Let me make some calls and I'll get back to you."

"Thanks, Lucas."

Jim asked the other man to say hello to his mother for him, then he dropped the handset back into its cradle. Had he made a mistake sending Anders on a case like this as a first assignment? He could have gone himself, but he didn't have the geographical or cultural experience necessary to consider himself the best man for the job.

Spencer Anders had the experience.

He also had some hefty baggage. Jim would have recognized Anders's love affair with things eighty-proof or better even had Lucas not warned him. Jim noted the signs with the same ease as a well-trained physician observing the symptoms of an everyday illness.

But he'd also comprehended that Spencer Anders had the courage and grit necessary to set all else aside in order to accomplish his mission. Jim had done that himself many times in the past.

No. It wasn't Anders's preoccupation with booze that worried Jim right now, it was his enemy—Khaled al-Shimmari.

Jim's intercom buzzed and he picked up, hoping like hell it would be Connie informing him that Anders was on the line. "Yeah."

"Sam Johnson is here. I sent him up."

Not Anders, but an appointment he definitely looked forward to. "Thanks, Connie." Jim hung up the phone and stood as his appointment arrived at his door.

"Jim Colby." Jim extended his hand as Johnson reached his desk.

Johnson gave Jim's hand one quick but firm shake. "Sam Johnson."

"I'm glad you've decided to join the Equalizers."

Jim gestured to the chair on the other side of his desk, before settling into his own.

Sam Johnson was a forensics scientist by training even if he was currently employed as an orderly at a local hospital. He'd grown up, gotten educated and worked in Los Angeles County until one year ago. Like Jim and the rest of the new staff at the Equalizers, things had abruptly changed for Johnson and his life hadn't been the same since.

His visitor glanced around Jim's office. "Looks like you're getting settled."

Jim had visited Johnson at the hospital, but this was Sam's first time at the office. The way-over-qualified orderly had read the ad in the classifieds and called to inquire, but then he hadn't shown up for his initial interview. After doing some research on the guy Jim had decided to take the necessary initiative.

Jim surveyed his office as Johnson had. At least the boxes had been unpacked and discarded. More organizing would come later. "We're getting there."

Johnson's gaze met his once more, the hesitation there impossible to miss. "You mentioned two other associates."

Jim nodded. "Spencer Anders, former military, and Renee Vaughn, former district attorney. I'll introduce you to Vaughn after we've had a chance to talk, but Anders is out of the country on a case."

"I'm gonna say this right up front." Johnson leaned forward slightly, all signs of hesitation gone from his expression. "I come with major issues attached. You might live to regret your decision."

Jim relaxed more fully into his chair in hopes of setting the other man at ease. "I'm aware that there were rumors related to your resignation from your position at L.A.'s premier crime-scene investigation unit."

Unlike most employers, Jim wasn't hung up on the past. If a candidate had the right training and a desire to get the job done, that was what counted. Coming onboard with the Equalizers was a fresh start, a clean slate. History was just that, *history*.

"The case is cold, but it isn't closed," Johnson warned. "There are a couple of homicide detectives who will always be convinced I executed those scumbags. I can't guarantee they might not dig up some new evidence and decide to reopen the investigation and show up at your door one of these days. The potential to get ugly is there. You should know that."

"Let's get one thing straight." Jim propped his forearms on his desk and leaned forward to match the other man's stance. "Three lowlifes brutally and re-peatedly raped then murdered your fiancée right in front of you. Personally, I don't care how they died. They got what they deserved. If you took the law into your own hands, then that's between you and whoever you pray to when times get tough. This position is yours if you want it. We start our business relationship today, no looking back, no questions about the past."

Johnson's gaze held his in a long, blatant moment of assessment. "Forgive my bluntness, Mr. Colby. But you're either a very gullible man or you were misinformed as to the manner of death in the three homicides for which I am still the only person of interest. In fact, there's some question as to the sanity of a man who would commit such heinous crimes, cloaked in vengeance or not." He drew in a deep breath. "If you need some time to reconsider your offer I won't be offended or even surprised."

Jim felt his lips spread into an outright grin. The reaction was still a little startling. "Johnson, I'm beginning to wonder if you really want this position."

The glimpse of desperation in the other man's eyes before he banished it was answer enough. "I'm here," he said, his tone trenchant, "because I want the position. I just want to make sure you understand what you're getting in the deal."

"Then we don't have a problem, Johnson, because I can assure you that you haven't done *anything* that would surprise me." He turned on the intimidation factor in his gaze to underscore what he was about to say. "And I can guarantee you that some of the things I've done would scare the hell out of you and your two detective friends out in L.A."

Jim wasn't sure whether Sam Johnson was relieved or startled, either way, the man didn't offer any more protests against his employment. With that hurdle out of the way, Jim showed him to his office on the first floor.

Only one other office remained once Johnson was settled, but Jim wouldn't fill that one right away. He hoped, at some point when their daughter was older, that his wife would come to work with him, if only for a few hours a week.

He missed her now that he worked away from home.

He needed her close…if only for a little while each workday.

Jim returned to his own office on the second floor and stared out the front window that overlooked the park across the street. Life was definitely harder for some people than it was others. Too many people didn't understand that concept, resulting in far too many negative labels.

Every single person he had hired had been labeled, maybe wrongly, maybe not. Traitor, hacker, murderer, incompetent…none of which was any better or worse than the labels he'd amassed. The question was, did these individuals get tossed away for their mistakes, real or imagined, or offered a second chance to rise above the challenges fate had thrown at them? And he wasn't talking about some conditional opportunity based on whether or not they measured up to somebody's idealistic image of good or bad.

No, not at all.

The only condition of employment at the Equalizers was very simple—can you get the job done?

Jim's vision was the same when it came to the kinds of cases he intended to take. He wanted the ones no one else would touch. Not easy, not glamorous, *desperate*.

He wanted to be the place people came when they had nowhere else to go.

That was the job he wanted to do.

No, not wanted, *needed*.

The thought ushered his attention back to this morning's primary problem.

Where the hell was Spencer Anders?

If he'd gotten himself killed already, Jim was going to be seriously disappointed. He'd expected the guy to last longer than twenty-four hours.

The real worry, though, was Willow Harris. If Anders was in trouble, where did that leave Willow and her child?

Chapter Ten

Kuwait
8:26 p.m.

Spencer lay on a cold hard floor.

As hard as the stone floor was, the coolness felt good against his aching muscles.

He wasn't sure where the hell he was right now. He'd awakened to this darkness, and so far he hadn't been able to work up the nerve to move.

Moving was going to hurt.

Bad.

They'd ripped off his shirt to make sure he felt the full impact of the torture. First they'd used him for a punching bag and then had come the electric shock treatments. His failure to cave as expected at that point was when his new friends had gotten really annoyed.

He'd refused to give them what they wanted. Eventually he'd lost consciousness.

He could imagine that a cloud of disappointment

had descended around that time. No one trained in the art of torture wanted to report to his superior that he'd failed. Oh, yeah, Spencer would wager that the lack of results had gone over like a lead balloon. He wished he could have seen that part.

But his body had had enough and subsequently had shut down. His military training had included all the techniques for enduring and suppressing the natural responses to torture tactics.

The fact that al-Shimmari had no idea where Willow was had kept Spencer motivated during the torture.

She'd gotten away.

He didn't know how, but she had evidently recognized the danger quickly enough to get out of the gallery before her ex-husband's men descended upon her position.

However, there were two obvious problems with the current scenario. One, he couldn't be sure how long she would last on her own before al-Shimmari got his hands on her. Two, she was no closer to getting her child back.

Spencer had to escape.

If he'd been more on top of his game he would have thought of that earlier.

A laugh choked past his busted lip.

All he had to do was get up and he'd get that done. Yeah, right.

Spencer rolled onto his side and held his breath

until the agony associated with moving diminished. When he could breathe again he pushed up on all fours.

This slow, painful process continued until he was upright. They'd taken his shoes, he realized as the cold of the stone pervaded the bottom of his bare feet.

No shoes, no shirt. He couldn't exactly wander the streets dressed like this.

He'd worry about that when he got out of here.

Since it was pitch-dark in here, his first step would be to determine where the door was and if there was a window. He flattened his palms on the wall and started the methodical search around the room.

He discovered the door on the second wall he inspected. It felt warmer than the floor. Wood, he decided. Traditional door handle. He moved on to the next two walls.

No window. Not that he'd actually expected one. Locking him in here with a possible escape route would have been far too stupid of his captors.

There would be at least one guard outside the door. Spencer's continued containment would not be left to chance. He doubted that they planned to keep him for the long term. However long he'd been lying here unconscious was likely a mere break to give him time to pull it together before another torture session.

He knew the routine.

The process would be repeated until one of three things happened. He broke and gave up Willow's location—which he didn't actually have—some of al-Shimmari's' men captured Willow, or until he died.

None of the above options worked for Spencer.

If Willow had managed to evade capture until now, he needed to see that she continued to stay free. Only one scenario for accomplishing that…get the hell out of here and find her.

Spencer leaned close to the door and listened for any sound on the other side.

Voices…at least two…slowly became more distinct.

Someone was coming.

He backed away from the door.

A muffled conversation outside the room kept his attention for the next thirty seconds or so. The men were discussing the need to move the prisoner.

No…not move. Get rid of the prisoner.

His Arabic was a little rusty.

The metal on metal clink of the lock disengaging sent tension rippling through him. The urge for fight or flight erupted in his gut.

He relaxed his muscles, loosened his fingers from the fists they had formed.

The best action right now was no action. He couldn't presume a line of defense until he evaluated the enemy. The one thing he could count on was that any act of aggression on his part would be met with lethal force at this point. They'd obviously decided they'd gotten all they were going to get from him.

Or they'd captured Willow.

Fury burned deep inside him. If that was the case, his priority would be to get her out of here.

An overhead light hummed to life. Spencer blinked to adjust his vision. The same kind of peephole installed in exterior doors and used for identifying visitors had been added to the only access to the room. Whoever was on the other side of the door would be evaluating the threat he represented. He worked hard to look vulnerable. Shoulders slumped, head down.

The door opened. "Against the wall!"

Spencer backed into the wall. Careful to keep his head lowered, he eyed the man who'd entered the room. One of his torture-wielding buddies. Mid-thirties. Medium build. A coward without a gun in his hand.

But he did have a gun. And there were others still outside, one, possibly two. Probably the same three stooges who'd worked him over before. Cowards or not, the odds were stacked against him.

"You are not such a lucky man, Mr. Anders." The long white *dishdasha* that fell to his ankles like a robe and the traditional headdress just didn't mesh with the sinister glare in his dark eyes. He strode straight up to Spencer and surveyed his face as if he wanted to remember every detail. He made a tsking sound. "Not so lucky at all."

Spencer told himself not to respond, but he'd always had a stubborn streak. He lifted his gaze to meet the other man's. "How's that?"

"If you had been lucky you would have died the first time we stopped your heart. But you refused to die." Smiling, he lifted the gun so that he could press the muzzle to Spencer's forehead. "I'm afraid we have no more time for games. My friends believe you have nothing more to share, but I suspect differently. Where is the woman?"

"I told you, I don't know."

The cold steel bored deeper into his skull. "One last chance, Mr. Anders. Where is she?"

"It's a rush, you know."

Those black, beady eyes sparked with fury. "What is this you speak of?"

Spencer allowed one corner of his mouth to hitch upward. "The blast of adrenaline when your heart starts to beat again. You suck in that life-saving breath of air and—*bam!*—the heart bucks back into motion. It's like a drug, the euphoria overwhelms all else for about ten seconds."

"There will be no euphoria this time, Mr. Anders."

"You know what? You're right."

"Yes, I am—"

Before the man could finish his statement, Spencer slammed the heel of his hand into his throat.

Twisting away from the gun a split second before it discharged, Spencer lost his balance. The blast from the weapon echoed in the room, drowning out the sound of his grunt as he slammed into the hard floor.

Spencer grabbed the man's weapon and rolled to

face the door just in time to take down the next guy who burst into the room.

That left one more.

Spencer scrambled to his feet and flattened against the wall next to the door to wait for enemy number three to make an appearance.

The quickly diminishing sound of hurried footsteps told him the third guy had gone for back-up.

Bracing for battle, Spencer slipped through the open door. The larger room beyond was clear.

There were two corridors leading out of the adjoining room, as well as a staircase leading to a higher floor. Since he couldn't be sure which of the corridors the last man had taken, he opted for the stairs.

His senses on point, he moved up the stairs. As he reached the landing of the next floor, he heard the scramble of footsteps and the frantic voices below.

The cavalry had arrived.

He surveyed the hall that ran east and west of the landing he'd reached. Doors lined either side of the corridor in both directions. All closed. A massive window claimed the wall space on the landing. Spencer moved to the window and looked out over the parking area and portico that dominated the front of the grand villa belonging to the al-Shimmari family.

A half dozen vehicles lined the elegant parking area including the limo that had brought him here.

The shouted orders below signaled that the search had begun.

They would expect him to make a run for it.

That was exactly what he wanted them to think.

He chose the west end of the hall and moved to the first door on his left. He listened at the door for a few seconds before opening it. A bathroom. Not exactly a prime hiding place.

The pounding in his chest accelerated as the noise downstairs cranked up another notch.

He reached for the next door, this one on the right.

Time ran out on him just then.

The thud of footsteps on the main stairs at the other end of the hall warned he was about to have company.

Spencer opened the second door and went inside without looking or hesitating first. No time to worry about what lay on the other side.

He flinched as the latch clicked into place.

Doors flew open and banged against walls at the other end of the hall. Time to find a hiding place or climb out a window.

Spencer turned to take in the room he'd entered and came to a dead stall.

Bedroom.

A child's bedroom.

His gaze settled on the sleeping form in the middle of the small bed.

The dim glow from the table lamp next to the bed provided enough illumination for him to recognize the boy's dark hair.

Willow Harris's son.

The din in the hall jerked his attention toward the door. He had to hide.

The lever on the door moved.

Too late.

Spencer stepped behind the door at the same instant that it opened.

A man entered the room, his breath heaving in and out of his lungs as if he'd run two or three miles before bounding up the stairs. He walked around the room, opened then closed the closet door. Eventually he took care to move quietly back into the hall, closing the bedroom door behind him.

Spencer resisted the need to release a sigh of relief.

Not yet.

The exchange that took place in the hall right outside the child's room filled Spencer with dread and left him with extremely limited options.

Though the boy's room was deemed clear, one of the men was ordered to stand guard outside the room. Spencer recognized the voice of the man who gave the order.

Khaled al-Shimmari.

The door abruptly opened once more.

Spencer held his breath all over again.

He couldn't see a damned thing save for the door in his face but he could hear. Someone walked across the room, paused a moment, then crossed back to the door. Spencer turned his head toward the crack where the hinges of the door attached to the jamb.

A glimpse of the man who exited the room told him that Khaled al-Shimmari himself had entered the room to check on his sleeping child.

The door closed.

Another man was ordered to remain at the door, bringing the count to two.

It was the oldest trick in the book on Spencer's part. Hide in the last place the enemy would expect. Too bad he couldn't take credit for the strategy.

He'd stumbled upon the boy's room and gotten trapped here. Either God didn't trust him to get this done on his own or he was one lucky SOB.

Now, if he was really lucky, the kid wouldn't wake up anytime soon.

Spencer shoved the weapon into the waistband of his trousers. The bright side to this was he'd come to Kuwait to find the boy and here he was.

The not-so-bright side was the fact that they were stuck in this room.

Sweat beaded on his forehead. It had been a while since he'd had to hatch up an escape plan from an in-escapable situation. The question of whether or not he could still do it weighed heavily on his mind.

For the first time since he'd made a move to give his friends downstairs the slip his body reminded him that he'd been seriously abused tonight.

He shuddered at the memory of his heart being brought to a stop at least twice and then jolted back into action, before he'd passed out. His trousers were still a little damp from where they'd hosed him down before starting the shock treatments.

He hated that crap.

Shaking off the distracting thoughts, he moved quietly across the spacious room to the window to get a look at what lay outside.

To his surprise the window wasn't a window. French doors opened onto a balcony or terrace that overlooked the lavish and well-lit pool below.

Spencer shook his head. A pool in the middle of the desert. The al-Shimmaris had it all. Too bad the family patriarch had sullied the family name with his nasty business dealings.

Khaled's father had died four years ago. As the only son, Khaled had taken over the family. Seemed strange to Spencer now that he'd married so quickly after his father's death.

Unless creating an heir was the point.

Maybe he'd never intended to keep Willow as a wife. Marrying a non-Muslim woman certainly ensured that he didn't have to worry about sharing the family wealth…or the custody of his only child.

Willow Harris might very well have been set up from the beginning.

The perfect egg donor and surrogate for a single heir.

Spencer cleared the thoughts from his head. He had to figure out a way to get out of here. Obsessing over what had or hadn't happened between Willow and her ex would splinter his attention.

He looked back at the child sleeping soundly in his bed.

Getting out of here with the boy might be impossible, but he had nothing to lose by trying.

Except his life and if he didn't succeed in getting out of here he'd lose that anyway.

Spencer eased back to the door that connected the room to the hall and listened. The search of the second floor had apparently been completed. His enemy probably presumed that he'd made a run for it, which meant they would be searching the grounds as well as the rest of the house more thoroughly.

He moved back to the double doors leading to the balcony and peeked past the edge of the curtain. That it was dark outside would prove useful once he got off the property. The way the property was lit up right now it could have been broad daylight.

What he needed was clothes, preferably something to help him blend in, and then all he would require was a major distraction to facilitate his escape.

He almost laughed at that.

No big deal. Yeah, right. He'd always firmly believed in just one kind of miracle—the ones he created himself.

First things first.

Blending in.

Time to take a risk and hope like hell that no one monitoring the security system would notice that an exterior door was opened.

Spencer disengaged the lock on the handle and opened one side of the double doors. He surveyed the balcony before easing out the door. Trying to keep the lock quiet, he pulled it closed behind him.

Pressed against the stone wall next to the doors, he assessed the milling about around the pool and extensive courtyard area. All attention appeared to be focused on the search of the grounds. Al-Shimmari had himself a mini army out there from what Spencer could see.

Oh, yeah, he was definitely going to need a distraction to get out of here.

Keeping close to the wall and in the narrow shadow of the house created by the massive outdoor lighting, he sidestepped to the next set of doors. He was about to reach for what he hoped would be the entrance to another bedroom when the curtain hanging on the door shifted.

Spencer flattened against the wall.

A woman, her gray hair uncovered, peered past the drawn curtain.

He couldn't be sure if she'd been sleeping and the ruckus had disturbed her or if she'd sensed his presence outside her room.

Sweat bled from his pores as he braced for her to open the door and step out to get a better look at the business taking place below.

To his surprise the curtain fell back into place.

Spencer watched the lever on the door, expecting it to move.

But it didn't.

He relaxed marginally.

Okay. If the room to the left of the child's room was his grandmother's, maybe the one to the right was the father's.

Spencer turned his attention in that direction.

Only one way to find out.

If he remembered correctly, Willow had told him that the kid's room was on the opposite side of the house. Had his father and grandmother felt safer with him between them considering Willow's attempts to get him back?

Putting the boy in a room with access to the balcony seemed pretty shortsighted in Spencer's opinion.

Worked for him though.

One small step at a time, he eased past the boy's room and to the next set of doors. He kept his breathing slow and even, kept his back pressed next to the wall.

He listened intently for a few seconds, didn't hear anything. Time to go for it.

He reached for the lever on the door and hoped no one had retired to this room.

One fraction at a time he lowered the lever until the latch released with a click that made his muscles jerk.

At least it wasn't locked.

With painstaking slowness, he ushered the door inward. The room lay in total darkness.

Inside, he closed the door behind him, then stood

very still to let his senses filter the atmosphere for the presence of another human being.

As his eyes adjusted to the near-total darkness he could make out the various furnishings positioned around the space. The bed was empty. Good.

He started toward one of the doors in search of a closet, but the white object lying across the bed lured his attention back there. A *dishdasha*, or what looked like one. Spencer pulled it on. The robelike covering fell all the way to his feet. All he needed now were shoes.

Moving soundlessly, he found the closet and switched on the light inside. A row of shoes provided ample selection for his needs. He slid his feet, first his right, then his left, into a pair. He reached to turn out the light but then decided a head covering could be useful if he managed to get off the property. He grabbed a white *ghutra* and turned off the light.

Before heading back to the balcony, he paused at the door leading to the hall and listened long enough to pick up on any activity. Still quiet.

That wouldn't last much longer.

Soon they would come to the conclusion that he'd either gotten away or was still somewhere in the house.

He didn't want to be around if and when they came to the latter conclusion.

The only question now was whether or not he attempted to take the boy with him.

Using the child as a hostage would no doubt facilitate his escape, but he refused to go that route. Too much risk to the child.

Seconds later, dressed in his stolen garments, he returned to the balcony and made his way back to the boy's room. The child still slept soundly. Could he count on not waking him when he lifted him from that warm bed?

Spencer considered the balcony outside. At either end a massive staircase led down to the lavish courtyard with its sparkling pool.

If he timed his move just right, when the main thrust of the search moved indoors once more, he might—might—be able to get down those stairs with the child without getting shot.

Big fat if.

If the child didn't wake up. *If* the usual exterior guards were distracted by the search. *If* the grandmother didn't decide to come outside.

Spencer stared down at the sleeping child. Could he take that chance?

Could he not? He might not be able to get this close again.

The sudden urge for a drink slammed into him full-throttle. He shook with the force of it.

Just one drink. If he could have just one he might get through this.

His hands started to shake hard. His breathing grew ragged. One drink would give him the edge he needed.

Otherwise he couldn't hope to succeed.

He knew his limits. Hell, he'd spent the last two years learning what a failure he was. The very people who had depended upon him in the military considered him a traitor.

What had he been thinking taking this job? What had Jim Colby been thinking? Spencer was a has-been. He had no right pretending he could do this anymore.

Shouting in the hall outside the room jerked his gaze toward the door.

The search was resuming full force...*inside* the house.

Time was up.

He had to move now or lose any possible window of opportunity.

But could he do it?

Fury at his own weakness hardened inside him. One thing was certain, he damn sure couldn't do it standing around here feeling sorry for himself.

Spencer opened the door onto the balcony and took a quick look. Still clear.

Determination surged. This was the reason he'd come to Kuwait. Willow Harris was counting on him. He would not let her down.

He threw back the covers and scooped the sleeping child into his arms. The slight feel of the child's weight made him tremble. His life was now literally in Spencer's hands.

Failure was not an option.

Spencer pivoted and moved quickly out of the room.

If he survived getting off the property, all he had to do was find Willow.

Chapter Eleven

Willow sat in the taxi.

She stared at the compound that was Khaled's home.

If she didn't do this, Spencer would die. If he wasn't dead already.

The last few hours were one huge blur of trying to find a way to get in touch with Jim Colby. When she'd finally worked up the nerve to steal a cellular phone from a tourist it had been too late. Jim Colby had been out of his office.

She'd considered going to the American Embassy or to the authorities, but either option would have been a mistake. Her ex-husband was too powerful. Not to mention that she was here via an illegal passport. The embassy would try to help, but their hands would be tied where Ata was concerned. The red tape would have gotten in the way of them helping Spencer in time. She couldn't risk that they would insist on holding her since her passport was a fake.

"This is your stop, yes?"

Willow's attention snapped to the driver. He'd waited patiently for her to make up her mind to get out. She cleared her throat. "Yes." Digging into her purse she withdrew the last of her cash and handed it to the driver for the fare. "Thank you."

She reached to open the door and the man's voice stopped her. "You are sure this is where you want to get out?"

As impatient to be on his way as the man was, he obviously recognized her anxiety. She met his gaze in the rearview mirror, concern radiated from his eyes.

"Yes, this is the place."

Willow looked away before she could lose her nerve. She got out of the taxi and closed the door.

Staring at the gate that led into the fortress, she reminded herself that her son was in there. If she got to see him just once, maybe dying wouldn't be so bad.

But then what would happen to him?

There was nothing wrong with being raised in this culture. Most of the people here were good people. It was the secrets she knew about her husband that made her fear for her child's well-being.

Men like Khaled drew hatred. Her son would always be in the line of fire. He would never be safe here.

Willow squared her shoulders and walked to the gate.

The guard, one she didn't know, on the other side stared hatefully at her through the bars. "What do you want?" He looked her up and down as if she were an object to despise.

She reached up and pulled down the dark hood of the *abaya,* revealing her blond hair. "Tell Khaled that his ex-wife is here for her son."

The guard's eyes widened. He might not recognize her but her request had certainly told him who she was. He jerked the radio off his belt and spoke quickly, too quickly for her to understand his frantic words.

Mere seconds later the gate opened and she was hauled inside.

Evidently the word that Khaled's former wife had arrived spread like wildfire. As two guards escorted her to the house, people, Khaled's personal army, seemed to line up to watch her long somber march to the house.

The massive double doors on the front of the house stood open. Khaled waited just inside, his dark gaze burning into her even from a dozen yards away.

As she was ushered across the threshold, her ex-husband shouted an order for his army to resume its search, then he turned that furious expression toward her. "You know where to take her," he said to the guards.

Willow's heart butted against her sternum.

She would not get to see her son. The disappointment dragged her heart to her feet. How could the man she'd once thought she loved be so cruel?

The guards took her to Khaled's private office. She

was left inside alone, but she wouldn't be really alone. The guards would remain stationed outside the door.

The flare of something like a flashlight past the windows and door leading into the courtyard snagged her attention. What in the world was going on out there?

She walked to the window and pushed the curtain aside. People swarmed like bees. All the exterior lights were on and numerous large, handheld lights were being used to search for something.

The idea that she might be able to escape into that mayhem had no sooner crossed her mind than the guard taking up a position outside the French doors captured her attention.

She should have known that her former husband would cover that avenue as well. She'd tried to run away too many times in the past. He knew all her tricks.

The sound of the door opening behind her drew her around to face the man to whom she had once been married.

"You are a fool." He ground out the words as if speaking to her left a bitter taste on his tongue.

She folded her arms over her chest and took a couple of steps in his direction. "It isn't the first time I've been a fool."

Fury flashed in those dark eyes that used to make her swoon with just a look. "I warned you what would happen if you ever returned."

He had. And for a long time that warning had

worked. She had stayed in America, leaving the work of attempting to retrieve her child to hired professionals. But no more. Ata was her son. She had wasted too much time already. She had been wrong not to come before.

"I've come for my son," she said bluntly. No use pretending. He knew why she was here. "If you let me take him, I will keep my mouth shut." She stared straight into those cruel eyes. "If you don't, then my attorney will send a letter detailing everything I know about you to the American government."

Her threat fell on deaf ears. Khaled laughed so hard he lost his breath. Fear snaked around her chest and squeezed until her lungs felt ready to explode.

When he'd stopped laughing, he glared at her. "I am not afraid of your attorney or your government. I gave you the opportunity to live because you are the mother to my son. I did not want to have to one day tell my son that killing his mother had been necessary." He took a step in her direction. She held her ground. "All you had to do was stay away. But you could not. You kept sending your hirelings. And now here you are, threatening me. How dare you!"

She refused to surrender to the fear. "I want to see my son." Surely he wouldn't deny her that. Whether he allowed her to walk out of here again or not, surely basic human compassion would force him to honor her request.

"No." He took two more steps, bringing him directly into her personal space. To her credit, she didn't flinch. "You have left me no choice. You will die just like your friend."

Oh, God. She was too late. Anders was dead. Hurt ripped at her heart. She had done this…she had cost him his life.

Desperation seared through her veins. She lifted her eyes to his and clutched at one final straw. "I know you love me, Khaled. Otherwise you would have killed me when I discovered some of your secrets. You let me live because you loved me. You still love me." She searched his eyes in hopes of finding a single glimmer of compassion. Maybe it wouldn't work but it was worth a try.

"Yes," he admitted softly. "I do love you. But not enough," he added cruelly.

The door burst open and Khaled wheeled around to face the intrusion. "What is it?"

The guard looked terrified.

Willow sidestepped her ex to get a better look at the other man.

"Did you find him?" Khaled demanded.

Find him? Willow stared up at her ex and realization dawned. He was talking about Anders. He had to be. Hope bloomed in her chest. Maybe he wasn't dead. *Please, God, don't let him be dead.*

The guard's shoulders slumped even further. "No, we did not find him. He has disappeared."

"Then what do you want?" The demand was a vicious roar.

"It is your son, sir."

Terror gripped Willow's heart.

"What about my son?" Khaled grabbed her by the arm as if he suspected whatever he was about to hear was somehow her doing.

"He…he is missing."

SPENCER LEANED AGAINST the back of the small house and caught his breath.

Lady Luck had to be shining on him big-time. He'd thought for sure he would be nailed trying to get the boy out of the compound. Instead, he'd encountered practically no resistance.

He'd made it down to the courtyard, then hesitated behind a clump of palm trees to get his bearings. The men searching the property for him had all moved to the front of the house for some reason. Damned strange.

Never one to look a gift horse in the mouth, he'd headed for the back of the property since the front was clearly out of the question. He'd found a smaller gate with only one guard. Perfect.

The guard had been preoccupied with determining what was going on up front. He hadn't seen or heard Spencer coming.

One well-placed blow and the guy was down for the count.

Once he'd escaped the compound, the next obstacle had been staying out of sight on the street. People would notice a man running with a child in his arms.

He'd had to weave around and between residences, staying in the shadows as much as possible.

The strategy had worked...so far.

He needed a telephone. Since Willow was still out there somewhere he had to assume she would attempt to contact the office. If Spencer were damned lucky a single phone call would complete this mission.

The boy had roused once. Evidently the darkness and the *ghutra* had prevented him from seeing Spencer's face. The child had squirmed around for a bit then he'd nestled against Spencer's chest as if he'd felt right at home.

Knowing it shouldn't have been that easy, Spencer had racked his brain for an answer. Then he'd known. The *dishdasha* he'd taken from Khaled's room had apparently been worn before. It had been on the bed. Maybe it was a sleeping garment. Whatever the case, the other man's scent must have lingered on the garment. Since the child hadn't been able to see who was carrying him, the familiar scent must have kept him calm.

Spencer hoped that wasn't where his luck would end.

He had to have a phone.

So far, each house he'd checked had been occupied.

Except this one.

He pushed off the wall and moved to the rear entrance. He was pretty sure no one was home here. There was no car. The house was dark. He had to take the risk. He needed a phone.

There was no time to waste.

He'd checked the exterior of the home for signs of an alarm system. He'd found no indication there was one. Since both doors and all the ground-floor windows were locked, he would need to break in.

Bracing the child against his left shoulder and keeping that arm snugly around him, Spencer used a well-placed kick to force the side door open.

Two more slams against the wood were required before the door burst inward.

He stepped inside and listened beyond the sound of his own breathing.

Silence.

He was relatively certain that if anyone had been at home they couldn't have missed his entrance.

After closing the door, he went in search of a telephone. He found one in the hall. After turning on a table lamp, he entered the necessary numbers and waited for the call to go through.

It was nearly midnight, that meant about three in the afternoon in Chicago. Colby should be in his office. If he was out, Connie would just have to get him on his cell phone and do the talking for Spencer.

Spencer sat down in the closest chair. He peered down at the boy nestled against his chest. Willow had missed her child so desperately. She would be thrilled to have him in her arms again. The idea that he would be able to give that to her made Spencer feel a sense of pride and confidence he hadn't felt in a very long time.

Made him feel other things as well. Things he had no right to feel. Willow Harris sure as hell didn't need a guy like him. She was far too good for him. But that truth didn't keep him from wanting her.

Connie's voice echoed in his ears. As impatient and unfriendly as her tone was, he felt himself smile at the welcome sound.

"Connie, it's Spencer Anders. I need to speak to Jim Colby. It's urgent."

"Spencer? Is that really you? We thought you were dead. You've had us all worried sick."

Spencer heaved a sigh. "I thought I was dead too, but I'm not." His body reminded him that he might have a fractured rib and he definitely had a number of contusions and abrasions. "I'm in a hurry, Connie, patch me through to Colby."

"All right, all right. Don't be so pushy. I'm putting you through."

Spencer leaned his head against the wall behind the chair. God he was tired. But he was alive. And he had the boy. All he had to do now was find Willow and give her son to her.

"Anders, you okay?"

Jim Colby.

"Yeah. I'm okay. I escaped the al-Shimmari residence about an hour ago." He licked his lips and let the new burst of pride well in his chest. "I've got the kid."

The accolades he'd expected didn't come.

Silence echoed across the line.

Wasn't this supposed to be good news?

"We have a problem, Anders."

Damn.

Spencer tried to keep his sense of humor about him. "You mean besides the fact that we're going to need a covert extraction to get out of this country?"

"Willow called here about three hours ago. She'd managed to get her hands on a phone. We traced it back to an American tourist visiting Kuwait for the Hala festival. The guy had reported the phone stolen."

Spencer knew that the bad news was coming. "Where is she?" Dread started its ominous creep through his veins.

"I'd stepped out of the office so I didn't get to speak to her personally. But Connie did. Willow told Connie that you had been taken prisoner by al-Shimmari."

"Where was she when she called?" Panic tightened in Spencer's throat. If she'd called in three hours ago, where the hell was she now? "Did Connie tell her to stay out of sight?" If she had laid low somewhere, he could go to her now and turn her son over to her.

That thought had hope cutting through all the dread and worry.

"We don't know. She didn't say. Listen, Anders,

she was worried about you. She told Connie that she was going to find a way to help you."

The memory of all those people who were supposed to be searching for him moving to the front of the al-Shimmari property zoomed into too-vivid focus.

"Oh, hell." Spencer closed his eyes and fought the images that attempted to flash before his eyes next.

Willow had been the distraction he'd needed.

She had surrendered herself, drawing everyone's attention to her.

His eyes snapped open and he sat up straighter. "I know where she is."

"You think she's turned herself in to al-Shimmari?"

Hearing the words out loud sharpened the pain twisting inside him. "Yeah, I'm sure of it."

The soft protests of the small boy sleeping in his arms reminded Spencer that he would need more than a distraction this time. He'd need a miracle.

"Lucas Camp has contacts there," Colby said. "I've got him working on this. Give me your location and someone will come for you and the child. Let us get the two of you to safety and then we'll rescue Willow."

No way. "I'm not going anywhere without her."

"I understand how you feel, Anders, but think about how Willow would feel. She would want you to ensure her son was safe first. You know that."

As much as Spencer didn't want to admit it, Colby was right. Willow would want him to do whatever necessary to protect her son first and foremost.

"All right. Get me some backup." Spencer gave his location. "As soon as someone is here to take care of the boy, I'm going after her."

"If you go back in there before we have measures in place," Colby warned, "we might not be able to help you, Anders. You need to stand down until I give you the go-ahead."

"I'll take my chances."

Spencer hung up the phone. He didn't want to argue with his new boss. Every moment they argued was another wasted.

He needed someone here to take custody of the boy. Now.

After that, he could handle what came next.

It was Khaled al-Shimmari who needed to worry.

Chapter Twelve

Tears spilled past her lashes and joy trembled through her as Willow stood in the doorway of her son's room.

Spencer Anders had succeeded.

He had escaped with her child.

Thank God.

Khaled whirled from his son's bed and flew at her like a madman. "Where is he?"

Willow tried to hold back the smile, but she simply couldn't do it. "I have no idea."

Khaled's fingers clenched around her throat and he slammed her into the door frame. "Tell me where he has taken my son!"

She gasped for breath, but even the fear of death could not diminish her elation at knowing her son was away from his father and this family.

Khaled put his face closer to hers. "If you do not tell me the truth I will kill you now."

"I…don't..know," she managed to choke out.

"Khal!"

The hold on Willow's throat loosened ever so slightly as her ex-husband glared toward the feminine voice that had spoken. "This is none of your business, woman! Go to your room!"

Khaled's mother, Massouma, didn't back off. She would not be bossed around by her son within the walls of their home. In public perhaps, but not here. Willow remembered well just how much power the woman wielded.

"Let her go."

The cold fury in Massouma's voice made Willow shiver. As much as she appreciated the relief of having Khaled's hand fall away from her throat, Willow knew that this woman was no ally to her.

"He will not leave Kuwait," Khaled threatened, his fury burning a hole through Willow once more. "Your friend will die and so will you." His fingers clenched into fists at his sides as if to punctuate his promise.

"If you kill her now," his mother inserted coldly, "you will have no leverage with this thief who took your son." She inclined her head and stared with pure hatred in her eyes at Willow. "You can kill her later. If you had taken care of her months ago as I suggested, you would not be facing this problem now." Massouma turned more fully toward her son and tugged her dark cloak higher on her shoulders. "I am going to bed now," she announced as if the subject of murder had not been broached. "I will expect you to have resolved this matter by the time I rise."

No wonder Khaled had no heart, his mother was a monster. Willow had known the woman was cruel and obsessive, but she'd never imagined just how evil and merciless she could be. Thank God Spencer had gotten her son out of here. She did not want these evil people raising her child. They were a disgrace to their country and their faith.

Khaled grabbed Willow by the hair. "Come with me."

She struggled to keep up with his furious strides, especially when he descended the stairs. She fell more than once. Each time he jerked her upright, almost tearing the hair from her scalp.

She knew where he was taking her…to the room he used for interrogating those he presumed to be enemies.

If he got her down there…she wouldn't have a chance of escaping.

She had to think of something.

A diversion.

Anything to give herself a chance, however slim, of getting away.

"Wait."

He stopped at the bottom of the stairs. "Tell me where my son is and I will end your life quickly. No pain or suffering. You have my word."

How kind. And God knew just how much his word meant to her. "Giving you the location won't help."

He jerked her face up to his, almost snapping her neck. "Where is he?" he growled from between clenched teeth.

Willow wet her lips and prayed she would be strong enough to do this. "If the man who took Ata doesn't see me he won't show at all. I have to be the one to meet him. That was the deal we made."

"This is not acceptable."

Khaled started dragging her forward once more.

"You can be close by," she assured him between groans of pain. "He just can't see you. He has to believe I came alone." Please, God, let this work.

He halted, glaring down at her once more. "Where is this meeting to take place?"

God, please don't let him see the lie in her eyes. "First, you have to promise me that you'll do this the way I tell you."

"I don't have to promise you anything!" he screamed at her, his whole body shaking with the force of it.

Willow shuddered. "Please, Khal." She hadn't called him by that familiar name in two years. "If you don't listen to me, he'll disappear and neither of us will ever see Ata again. You don't know this man. He's…" *Everything you're not,* she bit back. "He's done this before. He warned me that if I didn't make it he would sell our son to the highest bidder to recoup the money I'm supposed to pay him." She hated lying, but she had no choice.

For the first time since this had begun she saw fear

in her ex-husband's eyes. Of all people, he knew how vicious his enemies were. Any one of them would pay dearly to get their hands on his son.

His fingers unknotted from her hair. She stumbled before regaining her balance. "If you are lying, I will slowly, very slowly, peel every inch of skin from your body *before* I kill you."

"I'm telling the truth," she lied some more. "He's waiting for me right now. I wasn't supposed to come here like this." Might as well try to gain a few more points. She blinked rapidly, prompted her eyes to tear. "I got worried that I'd made a mistake. I decided to come here and warn you, but it was too late."

She hadn't realized until now what a good liar she'd turned into. Marrying the wrong man had forever changed the landscape of her life. If her prayers were answered, this monster would not get the chance to ruin her son's life.

"You expect me to believe that you still have feelings for me?" His disgust was answer enough as to whether or not he had any for her.

Not that she cared. She'd long ago lost any fondness for this man.

"I just want our son to be happy, Khal." This much was true. "He needs both of us."

For one fleeting instant his face softened. But the instant was gone in a heartbeat. "You will never again be his mother. You are not fit to be his mother, nor are you fit to be my wife."

She looked away to prevent him seeing the anger she felt blazing in her eyes. He was the one who wasn't fit, but now was not the time to debate that issue.

When she'd regained control and adopted a contrite expression, she urged, "Let me go to him before it's too late."

"Where?"

"Remember," she worked up the courage to say, "he can't know you and your men are there or he won't show. He has to think it's me alone."

"Where?" he demanded.

"The park where we used to picnic." He would know the one. "Near the painted water tanks off Damascus Road." At one time it had been their favorite place to go. How could she have been such a fool? She'd really thought he loved her. Now she would pay the ultimate price for her naiveté. That she could live with…as long as her son didn't have to pay for her mistakes.

Khaled manacled her arm savagely. "We will do this your way…for the moment."

She nodded her understanding.

He issued the necessary orders to his men as they exited the house. At the limo, she hesitated.

"I can't show up in your limo," she protested. "It's not that far…I could walk."

The murderous glare he pointed at her made her shiver in spite of her best efforts to appear strong.

"And let you make a run for it? I think not." He ordered one of his men to call a taxi.

She wasn't surprised that he would willingly do so. No taxi driver in the city was going to risk infuriating the al-Shimmari family. The driver would do exactly as Khaled ordered.

A few minutes later the taxi had arrived. Khaled instructed the man exactly what he was to do. He was not to allow Willow to get out of the car until she reached the park. She was not to make any calls on the driver's cellular phone. The driver was to take her straight to the park and then he was to go away and never speak of this event again.

Willow felt sorry for the poor taxi driver. He looked terrified. She could definitely relate.

Well, as long as her son was safe, she could live— or die as the case might be—with that.

As she climbed into the taxi she said a final prayer for her son and for Spencer Anders.

God speed, she beseeched. As long as they were anywhere but here they would be safe.

That really was all that mattered.

SPENCER HAD PARKED on a side street that allowed a good visual of Khaled al-Shimmari's front gate. He'd watched in confusion as those gates opened to allow a taxi entrance.

Why would a taxi be ordered at this time of night considering what was going on?

Instinct nudged at Spencer that all hell was about to break loose.

Once Lucas's people had arrived to take the boy, Spencer had laid out a strategy. He had been provided with ammo for the weapon he'd taken from the guard who'd tried to kill him. He'd been dropped off at his rented SUV with an international cell phone and any tools he might need. Spencer had easily hotwired the vehicle, but disabling the steering-lock mechanism had been a little more difficult. Nothing he hadn't done before.

Lucas's people had offered to supply him with a vehicle, but if he was caught, he didn't want al-Shimmari to know he had backup.

With the SUV usable, he'd driven here to wait. Lucas had insisted he would provide a diversion of some sort. Spencer could only guess at what he had in mind. Maybe a visit from some local government official. A command performance with a terrorist contact. Something to get al-Shimmari out of his house.

Two of Lucas's friends were out there somewhere watching and ready to step in if the need arose. Spencer sensed that the four men and one woman he'd met tonight were some sort of special ops unit, but he'd known better than to ask questions. The woman and two of the men had taken the boy to a safe place. The kid had cried once he'd awakened fully, but he would be okay. The woman appeared to know how to handle a frightened child.

The boy would definitely be a hell of a lot better off with anyone other than his heartless father.

Then had come the hard part.

Waiting.

Spencer kept thinking about how much pain Willow had endured at the hands of this lowlife scumbag. She hadn't suspected for a moment what she was getting herself into when she'd met this jerk.

He'd used her for his own purposes and then he'd gotten rid of her.

Spencer had to admit that maybe the man had cared for her on some level. After all, simply killing her when he'd shipped her back to the U.S. would have made his life a lot less complicated.

He'd had a reason for allowing her to live and since Spencer couldn't come up with any other reason, it had to be love—or some facsimile thereof. Spencer had his doubts as to whether or not the man was capable of the real thing. More likely she had been like a prized possession that he hated to lose.

"And maybe you're obsessing," he muttered.

Whatever the bastard's reasons for allowing Willow Harris to live, Spencer was glad. She deserved to be happy. She deserved to have her son back…and to be loved the right way.

That definitely left him out of the pool of candidates. He was so screwed up he couldn't be counted on for much, certainly not commitment. This job was about as committed as he could get.

Spencer scrubbed a hand over his unshaven face. Even managing to get the job done appeared to be a bit of a stretch for him.

But he refused to give up.

Willow Harris was counting on him.

Jim Colby was counting on him.

Evidently the only person not counting on him was *him*.

The gate opened once more and the taxi exited.

"What the hell?"

Spencer strained to see if there was a passenger.

Oh, yeah, there was definitely a passenger.

He couldn't tell if the passenger was male or female.

The gate closed as the taxi pulled away.

Spencer tapped his fingers on the steering wheel. Should he continue to sit here or should he follow the taxi?

Damn.

He reached for the gearshift to slide the vehicle into Drive, but movement at the gate drew his attention.

The gate yawned open once more.

Spencer gripped the steering wheel with both hands as he watched for a vehicle to exit the property.

A black SUV pulled out onto the street and headed in the same direction as the taxi.

Then the big white limo glided through the open gate.

"Bingo."

Another black SUV followed the limo from the

property. Spencer waited a few seconds before he shifted into Drive and took that same route.

Lucas's people would follow as well, he figured. Only he doubted he or al-Shimmari would see them. These people were good. Damn good.

The streets of Kuwait were quiet. Most of the homes and all of the shops he passed were dark. People were asleep in their beds with no idea that something sinister was taking place right outside their windows.

Spencer thought of that little boy he'd carried for miles tonight. He couldn't let that child down, he decided. The boy would need his mother. Somehow Spencer had to see that Willow made it through this night.

He'd never held a child like that.

Not even once. He had a couple of nieces and nephews, but he'd always been gone during family holidays. The few times he'd visited home in the past five years, the kids had stayed clear of him. His sisters had insisted they were just afraid of strangers. His sisters were probably right. Spencer had been, still was, a stranger to what was left of his family.

His folks had died a long time ago. His sisters were the only family he had left and he didn't bother to give them the time of day very often.

That was a shame.

He should have done better.

He wondered how Willow's folks would feel if

they realized what she'd been through while they were busy pretending she didn't exist. Someone should tell them that she deserved better.

Funny, he mused, how reflective a man got when he knew he was in all probability going to die.

Self-pity wasn't Spencer's style.

Better men than him had died for a lot less.

But he would be damned if he would go down without a fight.

Or without taking al-Shimmari with him.

That might just make it worthwhile.

The limo and the two SUVs took an abrupt right, but the taxi continued on.

Spencer lay back.

Did he follow the limo or the taxi?

His gut told him to stick with the taxi.

Let Lucas's people stay on the limo.

Spencer had always gone with his gut and it had only let him down that once. Even if that time had been devastating, it was hard to beat those odds.

Giving the taxi plenty of space, he followed its lead.

The driver pulled over at the park near the two massive water tanks.

Spencer parked a safe distance away.

He decided not to wait for the next move.

Ensuring the interior light was in the off position, he opened his door and eased out of the vehicle. No one had emerged from the taxi just yet.

There wasn't much in the way of streetlights in the

area. Spencer used the darkness to his full advantage. He took a position next to a cluster of palm trees.

His fingers wrapped around the butt of the weapon protruding from his waistband.

A sense of calm fell over him and he recognized it for what it was.

He was ready.

To do what had to be done…or die trying.

Chapter Thirteen

Willow scooted to the edge of the seat and prayed her words wouldn't fall on deaf ears. "Please, sir, I know you're afraid—"

"Get out of my taxi," he ordered without looking at her.

Khaled had given him strict orders. To deviate would be to sign his own death warrant. She understood why he wanted no part in this.

Still, she needed his help.

It wouldn't take Khaled long to discover that she had lied. When he realized that Spencer Anders was not coming, he would kill her.

She would do anything—anything—to protect her son but every fiber of her being resisted the idea of surrendering to certain death. She wanted to see her son again. Wanted to hold him…to watch him grow up. To be there for him.

"You must get out now," the man repeated. "I

cannot help you." As firm as his words were she heard the quiver of regret as well.

He probably had family too. She couldn't ask him to sacrifice his life…his family. "I know." But when he drove away she would be left alone with no possible help. Unwilling to give up yet, she went on, "If you could just call the authorities as you drive away and let them know that you noticed trouble in the park."

"I cannot! Please! Get out!"

"He's going to kill me," Willow pleaded. "Just call the authorities, that's all I ask."

The driver said nothing.

Willow had done all she could. He would either call the authorities or he wouldn't.

She was wasting time. If she got out now, she might have a chance at running.

As she opened her door she hesitated. "Thank you. I know you'd like to help." She couldn't hold this against the driver. This was her mess. He was an innocent bystander. She'd made the choices that got her here. Pushing him to do something that would get him or someone in his family hurt was wrong.

Willow got out of the taxi. The vehicle sped away the instant the door thudded to a close.

She drew in a deep breath and surveyed the park. She struggled to retrieve her memories of the area. Which way should she run? What was close by? There was an industrial area somewhere beyond this point. But she wasn't sure she could make it that far before she was caught.

Headlights switched on in a vehicle just down the street. The blinding glare made her feel exactly like a deer trapped in the hypnotic beam of an oncoming car.

Willow's heart surged into her throat.

Had Khaled already figured out that she was lying?

Or was this some other threat?

Panic crushing against her chest, she turned all the way around to see if his limo was coming yet.

The unknown vehicle rolled toward her.

She had to run.

Dragging in a big breath, she took off, deeper into the park.

"Willow!"

She couldn't slow down or he would catch up with her.

"Willow! Wait!"

Her brain caught up with her frantic race. She knew that voice.

Willow skidded to a stop and turned around.

Spencer?

If he was here…where was her son?

She started running again, only this time she ran toward the vehicle…toward Spencer's voice.

He met her halfway. "God, you're all right."

She didn't understand. "Where's Ata?" Surely someone else hadn't taken him. Pure terror roared through her.

"He's safe. Come on." He grabbed her hand and moved back toward the SUV. "We have to get out of here."

Willow kept looking around expecting to see Khaled pop from behind a palm tree or one of the water tanks.

Then she saw the headlights. Three sets.

"It's him." Her legs stopped moving. She couldn't take another step.

The limo and its accompanying SUVs screeched to a halt between their position and the vehicle Spencer had abandoned to come after her.

"This way!"

He ran the other way, pulling her along behind him.

"There's no place to go," she argued. Didn't he see? It was over. They had lost.

At least her son was safe.

For now...but what would happen tomorrow or the day after that?

She lagged behind the man pulling at her.

Spencer stopped abruptly. She slammed into his back.

"Listen to me." He grabbed her by the shoulders and gave her a little shake. "This isn't over. We haven't lost yet. Now stop fighting me and *run!*"

He was right, she realized with a burst of adrenaline.

The sound of doors thudding to a close behind them triggered another explosion of adrenaline deep in her chest.

She grabbed Spencer's hand and ran like hell.

A bullet whizzed past her ear and the panic rocketed once more.

Spencer took charge of the forward momentum, zigzagging to make them a more difficult target for their pursuers.

The tromping behind them grew louder. Spencer knew the enemy was gaining. He was already dragging Willow. There was no going any faster.

But he had to try. Both their lives depended upon evading the enemy for as long as possible.

To her credit, she worked hard to keep up.

There were lights in the distance. He hoped that meant houses or something they could use to put a buffer between them and the enemy.

More shots flew.

Two or more weapons, he estimated.

"They're shooting at us again," Willow cried.

Spencer wasn't so sure.

He pulled her behind the next clump of palm trees. "We need to assess what's going on back there."

Al-Shimmari and his men didn't appear to be coming any closer. Lucas's men had obviously shown up.

"What's happening?"

She was afraid. Spencer put his arm around her shoulders. She was trembling. "Sounds like Jim Colby came through with that backup we needed." He didn't take the time to explain that the help actually came from Jim's stepfather, Lucas Camp.

Willow wilted in his arms. He held her close to his chest for a moment. As much as he'd like to stay just like this for a little while longer, he recognized it might not be safe.

"We should keep moving just in case."

She wiped her eyes and nodded. "You're right."

"We'll work our way back to my SUV, taking a wide path around the trouble." The exchange of gunfire had fizzed out. He hoped that meant Lucas's men had neutralized the threat.

Recalling that Kuwait was still finding landmines from the Iraqi invasion years back, he slowed their progress, and took care where they walked.

As they reached the SUV, his instincts started to nag him. He hadn't heard any gunfire in the last couple of minutes, but he hadn't heard anything else either.

Something didn't feel right.

He opened the passenger-side door. "We should get out of here." Lucas's men could take care of themselves. His top priority had to be getting Willow to safety.

The thud of a vehicle door slamming wrenched Willow's attention toward the limo. Someone was still in the limo?

"Get in," Spencer ordered. "Get in and drive to the embassy. I'll be there soon."

"But I—"

"Do it!" He felt certain that without the sticky

politics of having her son with her, she would be well protected at the embassy.

A figure moved around to the front of the limo. Spencer leveled his weapon and took aim.

A woman.

He hesitated.

Big mistake.

The shot exploded from the woman's weapon. He felt the sting sear through his chest.

He started to squeeze off a round, but something stopped him. His fingers wouldn't obey the order his brain kept giving.

"Spencer!"

He blinked, couldn't wrap his mind around what was happening.

"Spencer, come on!"

Willow was tugging him toward the vehicle.

"Did you really expect it to be this easy?"

Willow ignored the woman. She kept pulling at Spencer, trying to get him to safety. She didn't need the aid of the moonlight or even to look to recognize the woman who had spoken.

Khaled's mother, Massouma.

"Why're you doing this?" Tears spilled down Willow's cheeks. She couldn't get Spencer to take another step. "Hurry," she murmured. "Please, Spencer."

He tried to do as she asked, but he only succeeded in falling to his knees.

She attempted to pull him back to his feet. Her hand landed on something warm and damp.

"Oh, God."

He was bleeding.

The shot had hit him in the chest. Panic showered down on her like acid rain, scalding her skin and stilling her heart.

"I knew better than to depend upon my son to take care of this situation," the cold-hearted woman said as she stopped only a few feet from where Willow huddled close to Spencer. "He has a soft spot for you that has proven his undoing." Massouma waved the gun in Willow's face. "Now, where is my grandson?"

Willow couldn't think.

Spencer was bleeding profusely.

She had to do something.

"Where is he?" Massouma demanded.

"I don't know where Ata is," she snarled at the woman who was as much a devil as her son. "If this man dies, we'll never know where he is." She added that last part in hopes the woman would call for help.

She should have known better.

"I wanted you dead months ago," the matriarch of the al-Shimmari family announced proudly. "The upcoming negotiations are far too important to risk any interference or problems. These people do not tolerate mistakes."

"Please," Willow begged. "Help me." Spencer was dying. Couldn't she see that?

"You were his only mistake. The fool fell in love with you and married you before I could stop him."

Why did Massouma keep talking about this? They were wasting time. Spencer needed help now. He was bleeding to death. His frantic gasps for breath were ripping Willow's heart right out of her chest. She had to do something.

His right hand was trapped between their thighs. Somehow he pushed against her leg with that hand.

Then she realized why.

The gun.

He still had the gun in that hand.

"You're wrong," she argued with the woman to distract her. "He never loved me. He just wanted to create an heir."

Willow slid her hand between her and Spencer and inched her fingers over the butt of the weapon as he released it.

"You think he couldn't have had his choice of women?" Khaled's mother laughed haughtily. "He wanted you. He was so stupid."

She kept saying *was*. Did she assume he was dead?

"Why don't we ask Khal?" Willow suggested as she moved her hand and the weapon forward slightly in preparation for some sort of action. God, she hoped she could do this. She'd never fired a weapon in her life.

"We cannot ask him, he's dead."

Shock radiated through Willow. "What? You can't know that. He could still be out—"

"His men went into the park, not Khal. I tried to explain to him how stupid he had been. He was jeopardizing everything, but he would not listen. So I killed him myself before he could further embarrass my husband's name. Not to worry, my dear. My grandson will be trained properly. He will never show this kind of weakness."

Spencer was dying right in front of Willow and this crazy woman just kept talking.

"We have to help this man or we'll never be able to find Ata," Willow urged, her voice pleading.

The long pause that followed sent a new wave of desperation washing over Willow. Spencer was running out of time.

"Get him to his feet and we'll take him for medical attention," Massouma instructed. "Then I will have my grandson back."

Willow didn't argue. She got to her feet and leaned toward Spencer as if she were going to pull him to his feet. Instead, she thrust out her hand, pointing the gun at Massouma.

Willow didn't hesitate. She fired.

A single moment of distraction had done the trick. Massouma's assumption that Willow intended to cooperate had been *her* undoing.

A startled expression on her face, the woman stumbled backwards. The gun in her hand fell from her useless fingers. She crumpled to the ground next to it.

The sudden silence was deafening.

A guttural sound whispered from Spencer's throat.

Willow had to stop the bleeding.

She had to do something.

Ushering him down onto his back, she placed her hand over the wound and attempted to staunch the loss of blood.

What did she do now?

Where was that backup he'd told her about?

"Please!" she screamed as loudly as she could. "I need help! Somebody help me!"

Chapter Fourteen

Saturday, February 26
9:10 a.m.
American Embassy, Kuwait

Willow couldn't stop wringing her hands together. She was exhausted and she wanted two things: to see her son and to hear news about Spencer's condition.

Spencer. She didn't even remember when she'd decided to start calling him by his first name. It had just happened naturally.

The doctors had stabilized him as best they could at Amiri Hospital, but then he'd been airlifted to a regional trauma center for surgery.

His condition had been listed as critical.

Fear flared in her chest. She had prayed and prayed that he would be okay. That she would get a chance to thank him.

She closed her eyes and let go a heavy breath. She wanted to do more than thank him. She wanted to tell him how she'd felt things for him that she had feared she would never again feel.

Right now, prayer was the only thing she could do for him.

She'd spent several hours in the custody of the authorities. They had finally released her to the embassy's representative. She'd made her statement as to the events that had taken place since her arrival in Kuwait. She was pretty sure she would still be in custody if it weren't for a man named Thomas Casey.

Casey had explained that Lucas Camp, Jim Colby's stepfather, had contacted him regarding Willow's situation. It was Casey's team of specialists who had jumped in to help her and Spencer. She remembered there were two men, but Spencer had been bleeding to death in her arms and there hadn't been time for formal introductions.

Once she'd been released by the authorities, Casey had taken her to the hotel where she and Spencer had stayed that first night. She'd showered and changed and then she'd come here.

Casey had promised that he would see that she was reunited with her son. And he'd also promised to keep her updated on Spencer's condition.

So far neither had happened.

She was trying to be patient. Food and drink had been offered, but she had no appetite. She did, however, appreciate being clean. Having her little boy see her with blood all over her would have been bad.

It was still difficult for her to believe that her ex-husband and his mother were both dead. She squeezed her eyes shut and blocked the image of her pulling that trigger. She'd never shot anyone before. She'd never even fired a weapon before.

But she'd had no choice.

If she hadn't pulled that trigger she and Spencer would both be dead right now. Her son would have ended up with that woman. Massouma had talked of some kind of negotiations with dangerous men who didn't tolerate mistakes. Willow felt certain this was why her instincts had been prodding her to act quickly to get her son back.

Willow opened her eyes. She'd done the right thing killing the woman.

No question.

A soft knock on the door drew her head up. Her breath caught at the idea that this might be Casey bringing her son to her.

She was on her feet when the door opened.

Thomas Casey entered the room. But he was alone. Disappointment sent the anticipation draining out of her.

"Where's Ata?" She held her breath, needing to hear good news.

"He's here," Casey assured her. "I wanted to speak with you a moment first."

Fear shattered inside her again. "Do you have an update on Spencer's condition?"

"He's out of surgery now and holding his own. It's

still too early to forecast a full recovery, but the doctors are optimistic."

Thank God.

Her relief trembled through her. She was so tired, she didn't know how she was still standing.

"Thank you for keeping me posted. May I see my son now?"

"Of course." Casey gestured for her to sit down. "Let's talk about your travel arrangements."

Somehow Willow managed to sit without taking her eyes off the man who appeared hesitant to tell her some portion of whatever he had to say. "Is everything okay?"

He smiled patiently. "Everything's fine."

He really did have kind eyes. For a man who looked as if he could take on the most intimidating opponent, he really was nice, with broad shoulders and a heavily muscled build. He appeared extremely fit and capable. She would never be able to thank him and his team of specialists enough.

"You haven't seen your son in over eight months, is that correct?"

Willow nodded. Worry that he'd been hurt during that time and she didn't know suddenly plagued her. "Is he okay?"

"We had a local doctor give him a thorough onceover just to be sure, and he's perfectly healthy."

Then why didn't he bring her baby to her?

"I need to make sure you understand that he may not recognize you."

The idea was one she had already considered, but hearing it out loud sent denial rushing through her. "I'm his mother. He'll recognize me."

"Of course he will, but it may take some time. I just don't want you to be alarmed if he appears afraid of you. I've been involved in a couple of reunions of this nature. I want you to be prepared."

He was right. Her son had only been sixteen months old the last time she'd seen him. For a sixteen-month-old, eight months was half his life. He might not recognize her right away.

Anguish ripped through her.

Stop it. That was selfish. She had to be patient.

This was not her son's fault. The last thing he would need with all the coming changes in his life was her overreacting.

"I understand, Mr. Casey. Thank you for helping me to brace for the possibility."

"I've made arrangements for the two of you to return to the United States on a flight this afternoon. If that's acceptable to you."

She started to object. To say that she needed to see Spencer first. But she wasn't family. If he was still in the ICU, she wouldn't be able to see him.

Right now, her son had to be her top priority.

"I appreciate that. Would someone be able to keep me posted on Spencer's condition?"

"Jim Colby will be receiving updates twice daily."

Okay, that would work. She could call Mr. Colby's office.

Casey pushed to his feet. "I'll go get your son now."

Anticipation soared. "Thank you," she offered. "Thank you for everything."

"I'm glad we could help, Ms. Harris."

Casey left the room and barely a minute later he was back with her baby in tow.

Willow worked hard at keeping her tears at bay. "Hey, sweet boy," she whispered. She'd called him sweet boy all the time…before.

Ata resisted at first, but eventually he came to her.

Careful of how tightly she hugged him, she inhaled his baby scent. He had grown so much. He was beautiful.

Her chest filled to the bursting point with joy.

She had her baby back.

No one would ever take him from her again.

She would keep him safe.

Her baby soon became fascinated with her hair. She laughed and cried in spite of her best efforts not to become too emotional.

She was alive. Her baby was alive.

And they were going home.

Monday, March 21, 10:20 a.m.
Chicago

SPENCER REVIEWED the case file for the assignment Jim Colby had just given him. It would be his first since his surgery.

It wasn't a field case, just one that required research that could be done from his desk. Spencer would be on desk duty for at least another month.

Colby wanted to ensure he was in top physical form before putting him back on field duty.

He couldn't think about his surgery or the bullet he'd taken without thinking of *her*.

Willow had called every single day to check on him, but she hadn't once asked to speak with him. He could have called her, he supposed. But he'd wanted her to make the first move…if she wanted to make a move.

That was the thing. He knew how he felt. He wanted to get to know her better. He was pretty sure she'd felt something for him. But her feelings might have been prompted by the stress of the situation or simply by the need to hang on to someone.

He just didn't know.

She wasn't that far from here. St. Louis was within driving distance. But she had her son to take care of. She was likely busy getting her life back together.

As he was, he told himself.

But he missed her.

He kept thinking of how soft her skin had felt. Of how much he'd enjoyed waking up next to her that one morning.

More than anything he wanted to make her happy.

He could do it. He was certain of that now. He'd given up the booze. Period. He'd made a number of decisions about his life. He wanted to make his position at the Equalizers one that people would be talking about instead of his past. He wanted to buy a house.

He wanted a lot of things, but mostly he wanted her in his life. And he wanted her son too.

The intercom on his desk buzzed. He picked up. "Anders."

"Spencer, there's someone here to see you. She doesn't have an appointment."

She. Hope foolishly sprouted.

"Is this about a case?" It might not be her. No point in getting all excited for nothing.

"Of course it's about a case," Connie snipped. "This is a firm that takes cases."

Spencer couldn't help smiling. Their receptionist was definitely one of a kind. "Send her on back, Connie."

He didn't question why a new client would ask to see him versus going to Colby. Maybe the boss was out this morning.

Spencer stood in preparation for meeting the client.

Willow Harris appeared at his door.

She smiled and he lost his breath as well as his ability to speak. Even his knees went a little weak.

"You're looking good, Mr. Anders."

Mr. Anders. Not Spencer.

"Thank you." He didn't know how he managed the words around the huge lump in his throat, but somehow he did. "You look pretty great yourself." She did. The pale-green dress looked cool and fresh and highlighted her lovely green eyes. The hem of it fell all the way to her knees as usual, but he loved that about her. She looked…really great. "How's Ata?"

"He's doing wonderfully. It's like we were never apart." She glanced around his office as if she wasn't sure what to say next. When her gaze collided with his once more, she said, "I was in town and I wanted to drop by and thank you for what you did for me and my son."

Ah. So that was why she was here. "Thanks aren't necessary." He couldn't bring himself to say he'd only been doing his job. "Have a seat." He indicated the chair in front of his desk.

"Actually." She wet her lips; his gaze followed the movement with far too much interest. "I was hoping you could take an early lunch. I'm buying."

She looked so sweet, so sweet and so nervous.

He shouldn't read too much into her offer, but he just couldn't help himself.

"To thank me?" he suggested. The suspense was killing him. He had to know.

Her expression turned serious. "Partly." She took a big breath. "Mostly I wanted the opportunity to talk to you about where we go from here. I mean, I thought we might…have dinner or go to a movie sometime."

Obviously reading his confusion, she added, "I decided to move to Chicago. I had a job interview this morning. I got the job. I'm going to check out apartments this afternoon."

He couldn't take it anymore. "There's one still available in my building." In fact, the apartment was right across the hall from his. Jim Colby had recommended the building. "It's a great place."

"That sounds promising. So, are we on for lunch?"

Damn. He'd forgotten she asked him to lunch. "Yeah. Sure." He moved around to the front of his desk. Just standing this close made him ache with need. "But I can't let you buy."

She frowned. "Why not?"

He lifted his shoulders in a shrug. "Conflict of interest."

"But my case is closed."

He had to touch her. He reached up, slid the pad of his thumb over her soft cheek. The need to touch more of her was almost overwhelming.

"You're right," he surrendered. "You can buy…as long," he murmured, "as I get to kiss you right now."

"I thought you'd never take the hint."

He didn't want to rush this. He wanted to enjoy every nuance of looking at her…of touching her.

First he plunged his fingers into her hair. He tilted her face up to his and he got lost in those beautiful eyes. Before he could snap out of the mind-blowing trance, she tiptoed and pressed her lips to his.

The kiss was soft and sweet, and at the same time hot and needy. He wanted so much more, but that would have to wait. He intended to take his time every step of the way. No rushing. No mistakes.

She and her son deserved the absolute best he could give. He intended to start with his heart.

Jim Colby checked his schedule. Since he had no appointments for the next couple of hours he intended to go home and have lunch with his wife. And if their daughter took her nap on time, perhaps lunch would develop into other satisfying activities.

He stood and started for his door. He hesitated at his window and watched a moment as Spencer Anders and Willow Harris crossed the street hand in hand. Jim smiled. He was glad to see those two connect. She'd called him at least twice every day to check on Spencer. It was about time the two stopped beating around the bush and got it together.

His own life was definitely coming together now. His three associates were onboard. The receptionist he had chosen was warming up to her work.

The Equalizers were off and running.

As their reputation built and word got around, business would boom.

For now, he was happy with the small cases they'd gotten. The bigger ones, like Willow Harris's, would come. He had exactly the right associates, not to mention a few handy connections, to handle anything that came their way.

The intercom buzzed. Jim turned back to his desk and pressed the speaker-phone button. "Yeah."

"Jim, there's a guy on the line who says he needs to speak with you. He said it was urgent."

"Thanks, Connie. I'll take it."

Jim pressed the button for line one and picked up the receiver. Urgent was exactly the kind of case he was prepared to take on.

He looked forward to the challenge.

Maybe this call would be the next big case that only the Equalizers could handle.

* * * * *

HOSTAGE SITUATION

BY
DEBRA WEBB

This book is dedicated to Sean Mackiewicz.
Thank you for all you do.

Chapter One

"Stop the car!"

Renee Vaughn shoved a fistful of cash at the taxi driver and scrambled out of the car. She sucked in deep, ragged gulps of air…still unable to get enough oxygen into her lungs. Her body shook with the news that had chilled her to the bone.

It's not right.

The judicial system had failed.

She had failed.

The execution would not be stayed.

At midnight, an innocent man would die, and there was nothing she could do to help him.

Nausea roiled in her stomach. She took the few steps across the sidewalk to brace herself against the nearest building. She closed her eyes and tried to block the painful memories churning in her head.

She was a murderer.

The sounds of evening's rush-hour traffic filtered through the haze of emotions, ushering back time and place. Renee forced her eyes open and blinked to focus.

She'd been down this road already. This wasn't her problem any more. She should go home, put it out of her mind. She'd been taken off the case two years ago. Her former client's new attorney had taken out a restraining order to ensure she kept her distance.

There was every reason for her to forget…to put the whole damned mess behind her.

But she couldn't. The man sitting on death row awaiting execution was her brother. She knew the truth, or at least part of it, and he would not allow her to stop this. No one would listen to her.

The wind whipped around her, urging her to move…to pull herself together. She glanced around to get her bearings. Madison Street. She could walk home from here. Her place wasn't more than ten blocks away. Her legs still felt a little unsteady, but she'd be okay just as soon as the initial shock wore off.

Her gaze landed on St. Peter's. Of all places for her to decide she needed out of the confines of the taxi. Before the thought could completely evolve in her brain, she was walking through the door. She couldn't remember the last time she'd been in church. Or the last time she'd prayed, for that matter.

Her mind in a chaotic battle of emotion against reason, she moved up the aisle between the rows of pews, her movements on autopilot. She approached the chapel at the back of the church and knelt in front of the icon. She lit a single candle, offered a silent prayer for the innocent man who would die a few hours from now. It would take a miracle to save her brother now and, as an attorney and former prosecutor, she knew better than to believe in miracles. Her chest constricted and a flood of tears pressed against the backs of her eyes.

Her mistake. No matter what anyone said, she knew where the fault lay.

She didn't have to be present in Huntsville, Texas, to imagine the scene. A crowd would be gathered already. Newspaper and television journalists from across the state. Protesters, those for and against the death penalty, with their signs and chants. The family members of victims, anticipating the moment when a convicted killer would finally pay the price for his crimes.

Renee rose from the kneeler and slumped onto the front pew and sat there for a while, thankful for the anonymity and silence in the empty church. She should go home. In another hour, the church would be filled with parishioners attending Mass. But somehow she couldn't find the strength to haul herself up and walk out the door. Instead, she sat there and stared at the flame. Reaching up with a shaky hand, she ruthlessly brushed back the lone tear that managed to escape her stronghold.

"Damn it," she muttered, then immediately railed at herself for the slip.

Why should she punish herself for the actions of others? Her brother had caused this. She had tried to stop it once she knew the truth, but he had not allowed her to do the right thing. That was masochistic. She had promised herself that with this new move, she would not permit the past to take over her life again. If only someone would tell that to her foolish emotions.

A hand settled on her shoulder. Startled, she glanced up to find Jim Colby standing in the aisle. "You trying to beat the rush?" he asked.

She straightened, cleared her throat. Having him appear here was about as unexpected as finding herself at this church. He moved around her and lowered himself onto the pew scarcely an arm's length away. How could he sneak up on her so effortlessly? When had she so completely lost her edge? She blinked back the new burning tears. She would not let him see this kind of fragility. This display of weakness was not who she was. She had to get back on track.

"Ensures the best seat in the house," she said, playing along and forcing a tight smile. Don't think about it anymore. There is nothing you can do. Focus on now. What was Jim doing here? She wouldn't have taken him for a guy who bothered with Mass. Even so, that wouldn't be his reason for showing up like this. Her new boss was not a happenstance kind of guy. He was focused, intense, deliberate.

Jim smiled that slow, half tilt that she'd come to associate with him. She got the distinct impression that smiling was not typical of him, though he seemed to like to do it more and more as time went by. She'd been working for Jim Colby for a couple of months now. He was different—edgy, almost dangerous. Case in point: those penetrating blue eyes. Eyes that kept folks on their toes in his presence. Not that she was intimidated by her boss, but on some instinctive level she understood that he was not a man to be taken lightly.

"How'd you know I was here?" The idea that he would have followed her from the office didn't seem plausible.

"The mechanic dropped off your car."

Her car? She deflated a little more. How could she have forgotten about that? "Oh...I—" She gave her head a shake. "I was supposed to call to see if it would be ready." The mechanic had picked up her car at the office that morning with a simple instruction: call before leaving for the day to see if it's ready. But then, that had been before she'd got the news that the stay of execution had been denied.

Don't think about it.

"Since you hadn't made it home and weren't answering your cell, I called the cab company. Dispatcher said the driver dropped you off here. I thought I'd come give you a ride back to the office to pick up your car."

Her cell...it was on Silent. She nodded her understanding, still a little rattled. "I appreciate that." She had a feeling there was more to this than just letting her know her car was ready.

As if she'd voiced the thought aloud, his gaze locked with hers. "We have a new client. The job's going to require a somewhat dicey field assignment. At least a few days on location." He studied her for a moment, then added, "I was thinking you might be right for this one, if you feel you're ready."

Renee sat up straighter. She'd been waiting for this opportunity. She moistened her lips, swallowed at the emotion still hovering in the back of her throat. "I'm ready." No way was she going to let the past mess this up. The call she'd received less than one hour ago echoed unnervingly, but she pushed it away. Her brother's mistakes and decisions weren't her problem anymore…hadn't been in two years. She couldn't change what was going to happen…no matter how wrong. *He* had seen to that.

"I know you've been anticipating your first field assignment," Colby said.

Admittedly, running background checks and following up on cheating spouses was not how she'd seen things going at her new job. Still, paying one's dues was not a new concept to her. "I'm confident the past couple of months aren't an accurate measure of what's to come." Despite having changed jobs twice in the past two years, even she had her limits on how low she would take her career expectations.

"This one may be a little tricky."

Their gazes met. Anticipation hummed inside her.

"Tricky?" She tried to glean something from his expression, but it was impossible. Jim Colby was far too good at camouflaging whatever was on his mind.

"There could be complicating factors."

Complicating factors? She didn't have a problem with complications. In fact, she had more of a problem with a lack of them; it gave her too much free time to allow the past to invade her present. She tamped down the ache that instantly attempted to intrude. If Jim was worried about her ability to defend herself, he shouldn't be. She'd faced physical threat in the past and she'd learned from it. A comprehensive self-defense class should be mandatory for all attorneys and prosecutors.

"What kind of complicating factors?" she ventured.

"This one means you'd have to take on a whole new identity and deliberately mislead a man in order to lure his only brother into a trap."

Her curiosity spiked, sending a surge of adrenaline roaring through her veins. She'd been looking for just this sort of case. Something out of the ordinary. Something exciting…dangerous. The last startled her just a little. Would living on the edge help her put the past more firmly behind her? Make her trust herself again?

Only one way to find out.

"When do I start?"

He studied her, his eyes searching hers for some glimpse of uncertainty or maybe hesitation. She

allowed none. She knew betrayal and deceit intimately. Using that painfully gained knowledge to
get the job done wouldn't be a problem. If someone
innocent got hurt…who cared, right? As long as the
job got done and the case got closed…the end justified the means.

"It may be necessary for you to, let's just say, get
very close to the target," he countered. "Are you sure
you can do that, Vaughn? I'm certain that kind of deception wasn't one of your electives at that fancy law
school you attended."

She did the smiling this time. "You're right. It
wasn't. I had to learn that part the hard way. Now,
when do I start?"

"Now."

Perfect.

He went on, "You can look over the file tonight
and we'll get started on your cover profile first thing
in the morning." He pushed to his feet. "That way
you can catch an afternoon flight and jump right in."

"Do we have photos? Background histories?"
Renee stood, genuflected and fell into step next to
him as he moved down the long center aisle.

"Photos, histories. We have it all. Our client
came prepared."

"Excellent." That would speed up the process. If
he wanted her on a plane in less than twenty-four
hours, getting up to speed ASAP would be essential.

As Renee climbed into Jim's car, she checked her

cell phone. Two missed calls and one voice mail. One of the calls was from Jim. The second had her heart thumping as she listened to the accompanying voice mail. The first three words of the message had her sagging against the seat with relief in spite of her determination not to care.

The governor called.

The stay of execution had been granted.

Renee stared out at the busy street surrounded by the eclectic architecture that set the city of Chicago apart from any other on the globe.

This was good news.

And just like that, the past nudged its way back into her life, starting the cycle of obsession and denial all over again.

Key Largo
Wednesday, May 2, 2:00 p.m.

"IT'S A FORTRESS."

A fortress. Yes. Renee studied the three-story home through binoculars from her position aboard the *Salty Dog*, a for-hire touring vessel. The two-acre estate of which her guide spoke was located on a desirable shore with not one, but two magnificent vessels—a speed boat and an enviable-sized yacht—moored at the private dock. The residence reminded her more of a compound than a home. Not exactly the sort of place one expected to find a self-professed starving artist. Though his work was well known in the southeastern region, he was no Picasso.

"Concrete walls. High-tech security system." Her guide pushed up his Miami Dolphins cap and scratched his head. "A nightmare, logistically speaking, if you're planning an unexpected *visit*."

Renee lowered the binoculars and slid her sunglasses back into place. She'd spun quite a tale to explain her need to do this type of surveillance. Thankfully, her guide had accepted her bitter story of betrayal and hadn't asked any more questions. At least her past experience had allowed her to sound genuine. "I don't see any security personnel." It was possible a bodyguard or guards were inside, but one would think guards would do routine rounds of the property. Maybe the security system was so state-of-the-art that walk-arounds weren't necessary.

"He doesn't have any bodyguards. At least not that anyone has ever spotted." Henry Napier shot her a look that suggested he was as befuddled by the idea as she. "No one can figure out that part. He drives a Maserati GranSport that cost six figures. That's new, by the way. So's the yacht." He gestured to the property that could easily be showcased in the glitziest of lifestyle magazines. "With all that you'd think he would be afraid to go to sleep at night without at least one bodyguard, but, apparently, he isn't."

Typically a man of such means would have personal security. But the man who lived in that house was no typical homeowner. She turned her attention back to the estate worth at least five million. Paul Reyes was the younger brother of Victor Reyes, a drug lord whose own compound was so carefully protected that only his closest confidants knew its location somewhere in Mexico. The concept that Paul lived so openly and clearly unprotected just didn't fit with the facts known about his older brother.

"This is as close as I can take you," Napier said. "City regulations. The rich folks don't like us getting too close. You still have another hour left on your tour. You want to just sit here?"

Renee didn't answer right away. She was too focused on the idea of the man beyond those well-fortified walls. Her target, Paul Reyes. Quiet, withdrawn, a mystery. That was pretty much all anyone knew about him, other than the artwork he sold through a local gallery. She'd stopped this morning at the gallery and looked at his work up close and in person. He was good, no question.

What made this man the polar opposite of his older brother? By all reports, Victor was cruel and vengeful. He had achieved his fame and fortune by taking advantage of the weaknesses of others. He didn't care who was hurt or what damage he caused to society as a whole. He cared only for himself. No one—not a single law enforcement agency—had ever come close to taking him down.

The client, Darla Stewart, who had hired the Equalizers, was the sister of a murdered New Orleans narcotics detective. Victor Reyes was responsible for her brother's death. The police and even the DEA had failed to get this guy for using New Orleans, among other seaside cities, as ports of entry for the evil he spread. When Stewart's brother, Detective Chris Nelson, had made stopping Reyes his personal quest, he'd been squashed and pushed aside like a pesky fly.

Desperate to bring her brother's killer to justice, Stewart had sought out the one man her brother had insisted he trusted in all this, DEA Agent Joseph Gates. According to Gates, he had a solid case built against Reyes for his drug crimes, but Mexico refused to acknowledge his existence, which rendered the extradition request invalid. According to the Mexican authorities, they didn't even know Victor Reyes, much less where he lived. That was possible, but it was far more probable that law enforcement south of the border had been paid off. Money could buy most anything, especially in a country such as Mexico, where poverty prevailed among the masses.

For Renee, the assignment was simple. She would use Paul Reyes as bait for luring his older brother onto American soil. Agent Gates and the DEA would take things from there. Until then, the agent's hands were tied. The DEA had spent endless resources monitoring the movements of Victor's brother here in Florida, his single connection to the U.S., with absolutely no results. With numerous other cases popping up every day, resources were already too thin. Reyes, until he appeared on American soil or the Mexican government changed its mind about extradition, was no longer a priority. Darla Stewart had been devastated when the Reyes case was put on a back burner by the DEA. With no other options, she had gone to the Equalizers for help. Agent Gates had promised to help in spite of his orders to refocus his energy, but ultimately there was nothing he could do until Victor Reyes entered his jurisdiction. All Renee had to do was make that happen.

Sounded like a piece of cake. But there was a hitch. The setup had to be legit as much as possible. Since Paul Reyes surely wouldn't be game for cooperating, then the trickery used to gain his unwitting assistance had to be on the up-and-up. Gates didn't want any snares to serve as reason to have his case torn apart by a team of legal eagles. Renee understood exactly how the legal system worked and how it could be twisted to serve an incomprehensible purpose. She had always won her cases. Even when she should have lost. She'd been set up by someone she trusted. That wouldn't happen again in this lifetime.

Though she had an understanding of sorts with Jim Colby, and she respected him, she would never totally let down her guard to him or anyone else. Complete trust was out of the question. She wouldn't be going there again. Hell, she didn't even trust herself beyond a certain degree, so how could she possibly trust anyone else? She'd trusted her former boss and mentor and he'd let her down.

She pushed the troubling thoughts away. No rehashing the bitter lessons of the past.

"Thanks, Mr. Napier. We can go back now. I've seen enough."

The old man nodded as he prepared to turn the vessel about. After her arrival late yesterday, she'd been told that Napier was the man to go to for the lowdown on island residents. Napier was a Key Largo native. He loved retelling island lore and made it his mission to keep up on the most famous and/or infamous residents. Judging by his weathered skin, the man had spent most of his life floating about these waters spying on those who made the exotic locale home. She had not been in the least disappointed by her guide.

The sun and wind and water made her feel more alive than she had in a very long while, she realized as they journeyed back to the dock lined with touring vessels. Or maybe it was the case. Working undercover like this was a first for her. Most of her time in her former career had been spent in an office or library doing research and prep work with witnesses, or in the courtroom arguing her case. This was definitely a change for the better. It felt far more purposeful.

It gave her the opportunity to be someone else.

She'd left her uptight—as her Equalizers colleague Sam Johnson called them—business suits in

Chicago. For this assignment, her first actual field-work, she'd chosen to dress as the natives did. Casual and sexy. She had the figure for it; she'd simply never had the desire. A conservative mentality had gone along with her previous career, at least on a personal level. She'd been anything but reserved in the courtroom.

She'd been good, damn it. She just hadn't been smart enough to see what was coming that one time.

Again, she ordered the memories away.

Back on shore, she generously compensated her guide and climbed into her rental car. She drove directly to her hotel. The cool air inside her room was a much-appreciated respite from the Florida heat. She turned on a light and retrieved her file from its hiding place inside the ventilation return in her room.

She considered the picture of the Reyes brothers. Victor was thirty-eight, with dark hair and eyes. If she were casting a thriller with a drug lord as the villain, he would definitely fit the bill. As handsome as he was, there was an air of menace about him. Partly posture, but mainly the way he looked directly into the camera seemingly daring anyone to cross him. She'd seen his kind before, usually stationed at the defendant's bench.

Paul, on the other hand, appeared quiet and utterly calm, harmless. Though he had been blessed with those same dark good looks, there was a serenity about him that spoke of intelligence and patience. Just two years younger than his brother, the two were, according to the reports she'd read, vastly different. Victor lived by the old rules, where women were nothing more than chattels and anything less than absolute loyalty from his followers was punishable by death. Conversely, Paul lived a quiet, reclusive life with hardly any contact with others.

The brothers had parted ways nearly a decade ago when Paul reportedly got fed up with his brother's evil deeds and came to live full-time in the United States. Be that as it may, the family blood money, in Renee's opinion, had to have purchased the lavish estate where he lived. As good as his artwork was, Paul hadn't made the leap into mainstream popularity yet.

Renee put the file away and dressed for the next step in her plan. Cream-colored slacks, a matching silk blouse and strappy but practical sandals. In her purse, she had the owner's card from the gallery she'd visited that morning. As far as she could tell, Paul rarely ventured from his estate for anything other than, in very rare instances, a gallery opening or a showing of his work. Even a large showing was no guarantee the artist would be in attendance.

That left her only one option—go to him.

She took the .22 from the box of long-stemmed roses that had been delivered by Jim Colby's contact here in Key Largo. After strapping on the ankle holster, she snugged the weapon into position. If she was lucky, she wouldn't have to use it; but if the past was any indication, luck wouldn't be anywhere around when she needed it most.

6:00 p.m.

OCEAN BOULEVARD was, as the name suggested, flanked by gorgeous sapphire water and dotted by enormous mansions. Near the end of the boulevard, where the most magnificent of the homes reigned over much larger portions of land, Renee pulled up in front of the massive iron gates of the residence belonging to Paul Reyes. She inhaled a deep, fortifying breath. Time to do this for real. She powered her window down, pressed the call button on the speaker box and then waited. Even her heart seemed to stand still as the seconds ticked by in silence.

"Yes?"

Paul Reyes. Although she had never heard his voice, the single word convinced her that it was him. The deep, velvety richness of the timbre matched the dark eyes and the quiet intensity of his face. Or maybe she just wanted it to be him, since she found the vaguely accented sound quite pleasing.

"Mr. Reyes?" She had to be sure. Her anticipation of plunging into her first case might very well be playing havoc with her reason.

"Please state your name and business."

She looked toward the camera positioned on the wall next to the gate before saying, "My name is

Renee Parsons. Mallory Rogers from the Rogers-Hall Gallery suggested I come to you in person with my intriguing proposal." Then she smiled, the most seductive one in her limited repertoire. Looking stern and purposeful was her most frequently utilized expression.

Renee held her breath now and hoped like hell her plan would work. If he called Mallory Rogers before he allowed Renee inside, she would be in trouble.

The grind of metal jolting into movement hauled her attention to the gates. Her heart jerked back into a frantic pace on the heels of an adrenaline dump. He was going to allow her in.

Anticipation roaring through her like a freight train, she took her foot off the brake pedal, and the vehicle rolled through the entrance which now yawned open. The driveway cut through a lush lawn and ended in a circular parking patio embellished by a massive center fountain.

With the vehicle in Park, she cut the engine and emerged. The air was thick and the heat hadn't subsided with the sun's descent. Before closing the door, she reached back inside and grabbed her purse and draped it over her shoulder. Inside her bag she carried a tiny listening device. Barely the size of a quarter, all she had to do was leave it in a strategic spot and she would be able to monitor his conversations in that room. Highly illegal, but a part of the way things were done in her new career.

Knowledge was power and since information on this man and his brother was seriously limited, getting what she needed this way was crucial. She had to learn all she could and burrow in as deeply as possible. Taking any and all appropriate steps to speed up the process, without being too hasty, was absolutely essential to the proper outcome.

She strolled across the lovely flagstone parking patio and up the steps that led to the front entrance. She took her time, made each step as sensual as possible as she surveyed the gorgeous property. He would be watching, and he needed to believe that she deeply appreciated beauty. Staying in character was another key element.

A wide covered portico ran the length of the house in front. She hadn't been able to see this side of the grand mansion from the water, but it definitely lived up to her expectations. She pressed the doorbell and settled her attention on the lush potted plants on either side of the towering double doors. Not a single detail had been overlooked when planning this Mediterranean-style property. All had been designed to be pleasing to the eye and equally welcoming to all the other senses.

The door opened and she found herself holding her breath all over again.

Paul Reyes stood in the open doorway. Cool linen slacks and shirt designed in pure white contrasted sharply with his smooth, dark skin. "Ms.

Rogers has no recall of recommending that anyone pay me an unannounced visit. Do you care to amend your reason for showing up at my door, Ms. Parsons?"

Oh, hell, she was made. But she was here. Might as well give it her best effort. She thrust out her hand. "It's a pleasure to meet you, Mr. Reyes."

He looked at her hand, then her. Fortunately, propriety appeared to prevent him from ignoring her gesture. He closed his hand around hers and gave it a shake. His was soft but firm. Dark brown eyes assessed her closely, the slightest hint of suspicion lingering there.

"What is it you desire of me, Ms. Parsons?" he asked as he released her hand. "Your bold determination has intrigued me."

He was intrigued. That was a start. "I'm from L.A., Mr. Reyes, and my gallery would really love to show your work. From what I've learned so far, you don't show outside Key Largo, though your work sells in several neighboring states. That's such a terrible waste of your potential. I felt the need for a face-to-face meeting any way I could get it in order to plead my case. We want Paul Reyes to become a household name on the West Coast. We can make that happen."

Jim Colby had provided a cover for her with a gallery owner friend in the Los Angeles area. That cover profile was her one ace in the hole. If it didn't work, she was on her own.

For several seconds, Paul Reyes appeared to consider her explanation carefully. There was no way to read what he was thinking, but at least he hadn't closed the door in her face.

"Do you have any credentials to prove you are who you say you are?"

Relief almost made her smile. "Certainly." She withdrew her fake California driver's license and a business card from the gallery on Melrose, each sporting the name Renee Parsons. She passed both to him for his scrutiny. She doubted anyone outside a trained professional would recognize the license was a fake, and the card was real. The owner in L.A. had overnighted a number of things to the hotel in Key Largo to help with Renee's cover.

"I have a contract proposal if you have the time to review our plan for your incredible work." The proposal, also provided by the L.A. gallery owner, she carried on a BlackBerry in her bag. "We're willing to work with you in whatever capacity you feel comfortable. We're impressed, Mr. Reyes. We want you." This part was true. Once Jim had shown the gallery in L.A. some digital images of Paul's work, they had shown interest.

"All right, Ms. Parsons." He handed her license and card back to her. "Since you've come all this way, you have half an hour. Convince me that I should consider your gallery's offer more seriously and we might be able to do business."

Half an hour. It was more than she'd hoped for.
He opened the door wider in invitation.
She was in.

Chapter Two

If Renee had thought the exterior of the house was well appointed, the interior was nothing short of lavish. Cool, sleek marble and cypress floors and soaring ceilings. From where she stood in the entry hall, she could see straight through to the endless blue of the ocean beyond a wall of towering French doors.

The floating staircase in the entry hall was at once grand and utterly modern. Somewhere inside the house the windows stood open, filling the air with the ocean's lightly salted breeze. It seemed strange to her that he would allow open windows, much less the unobstructed view from the rear of his house. Then she remembered that she hadn't been able to see in from the outside. Obviously the windows were equipped with a special tint or screening. And if the security system was half as state-of-the-art as she suspected, he likely wasn't worried about an unexpected intrusion, either.

After all, this was Paul. His brother Victor was the one who had to watch his back so closely.

"This way," he said, drawing her attention back to him. Their gazes met briefly before he turned to lead her deeper into the luxurious home.

Renee reminded herself to keep an eye on the man when her attention wanted to revel in the exquisite details around her. Evidently his artistic talent extended to his taste in design. Either that, or he'd hired himself one hell of a great interior designer.

They took a right at the grand entrance to the great room with its compelling ocean view. This side corridor provided access to several doors; he chose the second on the right—a library. The room was far too richly adorned to be called a home office. The wall of book-filled shelves lent credence to the idea of a library.

He paused in the middle of the room, looked at her and then at the purse she carried. "You mentioned a proposal," he reminded, his tone openly dubious.

"Oh, yes." She fished the BlackBerry from her purse. "It's quite an extensive proposal." She glanced around the room, her gaze landing on the computer on his desk. "I can download it if that would be more convenient." She held her breath, hoped he would go for her suggestion.

The three-second pause that followed had her heart missing a beat.

At last he swept a hand in the direction of the desk. "Be my guest."

Able to breathe again, she moved across the room to his sleek desk. She sat down, retrieved the portable cable from her purse and used it to connect her BlackBerry to his hard drive. A minute later, she had downloaded the proposal. The proposal was legitimate, but imbedded within its program was an interface that would allow her to remotely access his computer from her BlackBerry. Any files stored there might provide valuable information on his brother Victor; then again, they could very well offer nothing at all. She hoped like hell his security software wouldn't recognize the bug and work to disable it before she could accomplish her mission.

Sam Johnson, the newest associate at the Equalizers, had brought the software with him from L.A. One of the scientists he'd worked with had been a computer buff and had designed the basically invisible intruding interface to check up on what his girlfriend was doing on the Net while he worked the nightshift at the state forensics lab. He had suspected an online romance. He'd found out far more than he'd wanted to know.

"Here we go." She pushed out of his chair and gestured to the screen where the proposal portion of the program had opened to reveal the first eye-catching page. She needed him impressed.

He searched her face long enough to make her

nervous. Surely he couldn't know already that she was there under false pretenses. She hadn't made any mistakes. As nervous as she felt, on the outside she appeared calm. She wore what she considered her courtroom face.

"You must forgive my manners," he said suddenly as if he'd been lost in thought for a moment. "I so rarely have guests that I sometimes forget what is expected. Would you care for refreshments, Ms. Parsons?"

Relief rushed along her limbs. "Call me Renee," she urged before manufacturing a friendly smile. "A drink would be great." This was a move in the right direction. She needed him to feel comfortable in her presence. If only she could manage the same. The tension had ebbed a fraction, but it still had her on edge. Maybe that went with the territory.

"Why don't we attend to our thirst before we review your proposal?"

The idea that putting the proposal on his computer might have made him somewhat suspicious crossed her mind but she'd just have to play this out and see what happened. That her fingers had gone ice cold was not good. In the courtroom, she had gone in with guns blazing and had never once let the competition see her sweat. To a great extent, she was out of her element here. Her reactions weren't going to be her usual controlled responses. That was to be expected, she reminded herself. As long as she didn't let him see her fear, there was no need to stress.

Paul Reyes led the way down the corridor, beyond the entry hall to the sprawling kitchen that claimed a sizeable chunk of the downstairs floor space on the front side of the house. Gleaming stainless steel appliances maintained the modern edge, but lots of granite and tumbled marble infused an organic element. The limestone floor and wall-to-wall windows, along with the simple furnishings, ensured a casual elegance. With a deftness born of repetition, her host prepared a blend of fresh juices and garnished the concoction with sprigs of mint.

He offered a stemmed glass to her. "Far more healthy than wine."

"Thank you." She accepted the glass and sipped the blend, careful not to show her surprise at his non-alcoholic choice. "I suppose you work out, as well." He certainly looked fit. She told herself she hadn't really noticed, that making the comment was about laying the groundwork for a common physical connection, but that was only part truth. Paul Reyes was a handsome man with a deep, silky voice and just enough of an accent to make him inordinately sexy. And the body—well, there was one for the covers of the hottest magazines. She imagined that the man would look damn good in most anything or nothing at all. Getting close to him wouldn't be a chore.

"Staying fit is imperative to my image," he insisted with a blatant survey of her, from her pink toenails to her unrestrained hair. "The mind and body must be in agreement. Don't you agree?"

The way he looked at her set her further on edge. It shouldn't have. She needed him to be attracted to her. That was the point of the scoop-necked blouse and the form-fitting, low-slung slacks. But that predatory gleam in his eyes was more than she'd bargained for this early in the game. Or maybe she just hadn't expected that kind of overt reaction from a man so withdrawn in almost every other respect.

"Oh yes," she stammered. "I heartily agree."

He smiled, obviously enjoying her discomfort. "Are you one of the Los Angeles gallery's regular buyers?" he inquired. "This is what you do?"

"Actually," she heaved a beleaguered sigh and launched her well-planned story, "no. I was asked to approach you personally because I'm such a huge fan of your work. The owner is hoping my passion will prove persuasive enough to close the deal. I hate to come off as a starstruck fan, but that's exactly what I am."

If her answer moved him in any way, he kept it hidden well. Those dark eyes remained steady on her until the need to shift with uneasiness was nearly overwhelming. She held her ground, refused to allow him to see that he made her far too nervous. This was her new career. She refused to fail.

"Passion is a very powerful tool, *Renee*. In my line

of work, it is critical to all involved. One should never be ashamed of passion."

Beyond the idea of how much she liked the way he said her name, his answer brushed her senses the wrong way. Gave her pause.

My line of work.

Perhaps it was simply a matter of communication differences. After all, English was not his first language. Semantics, she argued. No need to send her suspicion radar to the next level over the way he used a couple of words. She was overanalyzing. Being nervous made her do that. Once she relaxed more fully into her role, she would be fine.

"Shall we get back to the proposal?" she prompted, needing her strict agenda to get her back on track. Her success in the courtroom was rooted, first and foremost, on extensive preparation. She needed to treat this assignment along those same lines until she hit her stride with the whole "getting comfortable" part.

He placed his half-empty glass on the island's sleek granite counter. She did the same. This time they walked side by side as they retraced the route to his library. The sun had sunk deep on the horizon, melting into a golden blanket over the vast blue ocean and offering a spectacular panorama.

The idea that drug money may have contributed to this magnificent residence caused the muscles in her jaw to tighten. But this man was not a part of that, she reminded herself. It didn't mean that he hadn't accepted money or gifts from his evil sibling, but he was innocent of his brother's crimes. If anyone should feel guilty, it was her, but she did not. The end justified the means. That was her new motto. She intended to use him to lure his death-dealing brother into a trap. Despite the break in the relationship with his only sibling, biology dictated a bond that assuredly went deep. He might hate what his brother did, but to plot his sibling's downfall was another concept altogether, one toward which he might very well be disinclined. The only way to most reasonably assure his cooperation was to mislead him. She'd already lied to him repeatedly and would several times more before this first meeting was over. Paul Reyes would have no fond memories of her when this was over.

"As you can see," she said as she moved through the first section of the presentation, "our gallery would display your ability to capture the essence of the sand and water and sky to its fullest advantage. Southern California isn't unlike the Keys, in more ways than perhaps you realize. Your work would fit in very nicely, would bring a fresh perspective to our gallery's already outstanding offerings. We have an international clientele, more so than you'll find here, no disrespect to the local talent or trade."

"Please," he made a sweeping motion toward the computer screen with one hand, "go on."

Renee couldn't determine if he was intrigued yet,

but she still had his full attention and that was something. As the final slide in the proposal was displayed on the screen, she made the next move. "I know you'll need some time to think over all of this. Perhaps we could have dinner tomorrow evening." She lifted one shoulder in the barest of shrugs. "Discuss any questions you might have in a more relaxed, nonbusiness rendezvous."

His hesitation was expected. As a recluse, he would have no desire to leave his sanctuary. However, the invitation needed to be standard. The average person wouldn't know all that she did about him. The slightest misstep could give away her true agenda.

"That's an excellent idea, Renee." He glanced at the computer screen one last time. "I'll review your proposal more thoroughly and make my final decision. I would prefer, however," his gaze connected with hers once more, "to have our next rendezvous here. I assume that will be acceptable to you?"

Exactly the answer she had hoped for. "Of course." Now for the finishing touch. "I'll be in town for the next few days. My schedule is completely at your disposal, Mr. Reyes."

"Paul," he suggested for the first time since her arrival.

She smiled, held his gaze a beat. "Paul." This she said with a breathy quality that caused his pupils to flare and the corners of his mouth to lift slightly. The

idea that she might be better at this than she'd anticipated gave her confidence a major boost.

The tension crackled ever so slightly as he blatantly assessed her for a second time, taking his slow,
sweet time. "Seven," he said, breaking the spell,
"would that work for you?"

"Seven definitely works for me." She reached for
her bag. "I look forward to discussing our future
working relationship and seeing more of your paintings." Her expression turned visibly hopeful with the
last.

"That can certainly be arranged." He placed his
hand at the small of her back as he guided her to the
hall and toward the front door. "My studio provides
a great deal of inspiration." He paused as they
reached the entry hall and looked directly at her. "At
times, however, I find myself in need of additional
stimulation. A beautiful woman can be extremely
stirring to a man's blood."

Now they were getting somewhere, it seemed. "I
can't wait to see your studio."

The smile slid back into place. "You will receive
the grand tour, I assure you."

A definite click followed by a roaring sound,
similar to that of several garage doors closing simultaneously, jerked his attention back toward the
interior of the house. Renee followed his gaze.

Barriers slowly closed down over the windows,
blocking the magnificent view. Had a hurricane

warning triggered the house's security system? The metal-on-metal action of locks being set in motion hauled her attention back to the front door.

What the hell was happening?

"Renee." Reyes swiveled to face her. "Something is wrong. You must run! Now!"

He reached for the door, but it was locked. He tugged at it frantically.

Her pulse shot into warp speed. "The security system," she urged, "can you shut it down?" Apparently the system had gone into some sort of automatic secure mode.

Reaching for the keypad next to the door he fairly shouted, "I do not understand this." He jabbed buttons to no avail. "This has never happened before."

Footfalls on the floor behind them had her wheeling around. Two men. Large. Threatening. She dropped into a crouch, her attention riveted on the two men advancing as she grabbed for her weapon.

"Don't move!" the first man barked, his weapon leveled on her.

With no desire to get killed, she pushed her hands up and slowly rose to her full height once more.

"Who are you?" Reyes demanded. "What do you want?"

"You," the second man snapped as he moved in close enough to press the barrel of his .9 millimeter against Reyes's forehead.

As Renee attempted to position herself between

the two men in an effort to protect Reyes, an arm
went around her neck. Something like a mask closed
over her mouth and nose. She fought the strong arms
manacling her. Her lungs burning, she gasped for air.

Then her vision narrowed until there was nothing.

Her body stopped fighting and went limp.

Merida, Mexico
Same Day 6:50 p.m.

HIS EYES HAD CLOSED, the lids far too heavy to
restrain. Staying awake was no longer possible. The
weariness had overtaken him quickly this night. Too
many sleepless ones had come and gone. He needed
to rest…but if he slipped too deeply into that welcoming oblivion, he might not hear the enemy's arrival.

He needed to stay awake. Yet he was so very tired.
For days that had become weeks, he had fought the
temptation, had struggled to survive on stolen moments of mere dozing. He could trust no one.

How much longer could he be held prisoner this
way?

What purpose did his brother hope to serve with
his actions? None of this made sense. He had long
ago taken leave of his brother's company. Refused
to be a part of his love of spreading pain and death.

The click of the lock jerked his head up and his
eyes wide open.

It could be the devil…come to finish the job at

last. Part of him would be glad to have this nightmare over. This moment had been coming for years. He should have seen that. No one would be left to bear witness to his rottenness. Escaping the reality of their strained relationship had been merely a dream. One could not deny evil when it thrived in his very blood.

The door opened slowly. Even in the near darkness, he saw the hesitant movement of his visitor. Not his brother. Some amount of relief lowered the choking tension to a more tolerable level. His eyes had days ago adjusted to the lack of light.

Juanita cautiously peeked around the partially opened door. *"Señor?"* Her voice was small and worried. She should be worried. She had played a part in this vile plan, had made herself an accomplice to his brother's selfish scheming.

In spite of the many reasons to doubt the possibility, hope stirred. Had he at last gained an ally? Or was this another trick?

"Have you had a change of heart, woman?" He asked this in English, refused to speak the native tongue of his betrayers. He had known this woman since he was a small boy. His mother had trusted her, had allowed her to look after her only children. Were his mother still alive, she would be gravely disappointed. There was no longer any loyalty in this family.

Juanita slipped into the room that had served as a prison for the past month, or had it been longer? On some level, he had reconciled to the likely fate that he would die here.

The light that followed Juanita into his prison accentuated the somber features of her thin face and her downcast gaze. He imagined that guilt kept her from looking him in the eye. He was being held prisoner in his own birth home. He had given up on the possibility of ever seeing the light of day again. His own people had turned on him, motivated by whatever threats made or gifts offered by his monster of a brother.

"I have, *señor*," Juanita confessed sadly. "You were right. He is evil. I have heard whispers that he plans to cut off your head—" she shuddered "—when he returns. No matter what you've done, I cannot allow him to harm you this way."

The threat of death was not unexpected. Why else would he be held prisoner like this? There was no turning back now. Whatever his brother was up to, he would leave no loose ends to fray. Yet even as the anger against his last living blood relative expanded inside him, he yearned for answers. His heart wouldn't simply let go of the need to know the answers as to why he had come to be in this position, at the mercy of his own kin. What had changed? Why the sudden determination to come against him…after all this time? There had to be some scheme in place.

He should have gone to the authorities years ago and put a stop to his brother's dealings. As a child, he had promised his mother that he would look out for his brother. Even then, she had known that something was not right with her eldest child. Maintaining his allegiance to that promise had been a mistake; looking the other way for so many years was a crime.

If he survived what was to come, he would settle this score once and for all.

"And what is it I have done that has brought about my imprisonment and impending death?" he asked the woman hovering with such uncertainty.

She eased back a step, positioning herself in the open doorway as if she feared she might need to quickly run away. Still, she refused to meet his gaze. "*Señor*, there is no need to speak of the past unless it is to pray for mercy on your soul."

Her hand trembled as it came to rest on the door in preparation for yanking it closed if necessary. Would she rather lock him back up in this room than answer a simple question?

"We must speak of it, Juanita," he insisted, "for I have no idea why this has happened." Other than the fact that his brother was as insane as his vile acts would suggest. But there would be much more than that. The need to uncover this plan sent much-needed adrenaline pumping through him. "Tell me what it is that you believe I have done."

For several moments, he was certain she did not intend to answer. Finally, her mouth worked mutely for a moment and then the words tumbled out. "You killed them, *señor*. All of them." Her voice trembled. She cleared her throat and began again. "Your brother put you here to protect you until he could ensure the authorities were satisfied. But I have learned that he plans to kill you himself, not protect you at all. I cannot permit such a thing. Your *madre* would not want me to allow this end, no matter your crimes."

This made no sense. He had not killed anyone. "Who have I killed, Juanita?"

"The missionaries," she whispered, then crossed herself. "You killed them all."

Shock radiated through him, rendering him momentarily unable to speak. "You are sure they are dead? All five?" His voice was quavering.

Juanita nodded jerkily. "The authorities are saying the rebels did the killing. Your brother saw to it that your name was kept from the trouble that has finally grown quiet. But now he plans to kill you so that you cannot do such a thing again. It was an act against God the Father." She crossed herself once more. "Your brother says that your death is necessary in order to obtain forgiveness for you as well as for himself." At last she lifted her gaze to his. "I have known you since you were a small boy. I cannot watch you die by the hand of your own brother. Forgiveness or no forgiveness, it is not right."

"What shall we do about this, Juanita?" He wanted to rise up from his position on the floor. To urge the woman who had known him for most of his life to act now. There was no time to waste. But he did not want to risk frightening her with any sudden moves. In addition, the price could prove to be very high if Juanita's participation in his escape were discovered before an end could be put to the enemy—his own brother.

"You must hurry back to your home in the north, *señor*," Juanita offered. "You must go now. There can be no delay. Eduardo has heard that your brother is already on his way here. He will not follow you to the north, as you well know. You must never return to Mexico. No one else can die in the Reyes' name. God will not forgive any of us, I fear."

He had not killed anyone, but Juanita was right about one thing—no one else should die in the Reyes' name, period. "How am I to go back to the States, Juanita? I have no papers. No money."

She exhaled a careworn breath. "Eduardo makes a way. Your brother's private plane waits. You must hurry. I have clothes for you."

"What will you and Eduardo do when my brother finds me gone from here?" Eduardo, Juanita's husband, had taken a great risk, as had Juanita.

She shook her head. "There is no time to talk of this. You must go."

He got up slowly. Even though she knew his intentions, Juanita gasped when he took a step toward the door.

His chest tightened at the idea that anyone would consider him threatening. That was the part of this ugly mess that he hated the most. His own brother had used him to create fear…to kill.

"Juanita," he said softly, "I have not killed anyone. If the missionaries—" his throated constricted "—are dead, then my brother or his men killed them. You surely know I would never do such a thing."

Those five men, volunteers from the Basilica de Guadalupe on the north side of Mexico City, had been working with him in a small southern village devastated by last year's floods. They had rebuilt many homes already, but there was much more to be done. Now those men were dead if what Juanita said was to be believed. What in God's name did his brother hope to prove?

"I have been thinking that you did not," Juanita admitted, her voice grave. "But I do not know the truth, *señor*. Flee this place. If your heart is pure you will flourish again."

If only it were that easy. "I understand." His brother could be charming and utterly persuasive when he chose. No one wanted to believe the depth of his depravity.

"You must hurry, *mi hijo*."

"Thank you, Juanita."

Their gazes met briefly in the near darkness. Years had passed since she had last used that endearment. If they survived, he would ensure that her attempt to do the right thing was well compensated. Of the handful who knew of this despicable arrangement, no one else had dared to offer a hand in support. Those who had looked the other way would not be forgotten, either.

He followed Juanita from the prison. His breath sawed in and out of his lungs despite his attempt to stay calm and steady. If they were caught, Juanita would die. His own fate might very well be no better, though most would not dare attempt to use lethal force to stop him for fear of his brother's reprisal. In any event, what did he have to lose? His fate had already been decided by his brother. A sharp pain pierced his chest at the thought of those men who had lost their lives already. Innocent men who had done nothing more than attempt to help those less fortunate.

His brother would pay this time.

Fury bolted through him. For the first time in his life, he felt certain he could do what needed to be done, putting aside that long-ago promise once and for all.

It was time for his brother's reign of terror to end.

Chapter Three

Key Largo
Time Unknown

Renee woke with a start. She frowned, feeling groggy. She swallowed, licked her lips. Her mouth was dry, tasted bitter. A strange odor lingered in her lungs, making her gasp for more air.

Where the hell was she?

She rolled onto her side, only then realizing that she lay on the cold tile floor. A shiver quaked through her. Damn, she was cold. Struggling up to a sitting position, she surveyed the room. It was nearly dark, the space lit by a single lamp in one corner.

A brown couch, two stripped chairs and a single oak table with a lamp. A den, maybe? But there was no television or game tables of any sort. No windows and just one door.

The image of a man subduing Paul Reyes flickered to the forefront of her hazy thoughts.

She scrambled to her feet and rushed to the door. She braced against it and twisted the knob.

Locked.

Renee looked around again as she slumped against the wall. Whatever inhalant they had used to put her out still had her equilibrium off-kilter. Her reasoning was fragmented. Her balance out of whack. *Wear it off.* She pushed away from the wall and walked around the room, slow and steady at first. Moving around would help her body metabolize the remnants of the drug. She wished for water. It was ironic that a whole ocean of water sat right outside while she was thirsty.

Evidently, one of the men had taken Paul Reyes and the other had locked her in here. Had they killed him? Were they Victor's men? Was Victor here?

She had to get out of this room.

The longer she walked, the clearer her mind became. She couldn't be sure how much time had passed. There was every reason to believe that she was in the basement since there were no windows. She went back to the door and gave it a couple of kicks and a few body slams. The door wasn't budging. She moved on to the wall next to the door that separated this room from the next. Smooth, painted. Not concrete or cinder block, which was good. It looked and felt like drywall. If that was the case, then it would be about half an inch thick, attached to either steel or wood two-by-fours installed at a set distance apart. She wasn't sure of the exact distance, but figured at least twelve inches.

Only one way to find out.

She needed more light. After unplugging the lamp, she moved to that same wall and plugged the lamp in the nearest socket. Then she discarded the shade so that the full force of the light would be available. Shining the light slowly over the wall, she searched for imperfections. Any indication of the nail or screw line to confirm her assumption. A smile nudged her lips as she found what she was looking for. She set the lamp aside and started knocking on the wall until she felt certain she had found a space between the two-by-fours.

Then she turned, facing away from the wall and kicked backwards, pounding her foot into the drywall as hard as she could, about eighteen inches above the floor. She kicked hard. If there was anyone close by, they would come running soon.

She repeated the process again and again. The slight give her action produced assured her that she had guessed right about this particular interior wall being composed of drywall.

Her leg started to give out so she shifted her position and used the other one, again putting all the force she possessed behind the effort. After a few more well-placed kicks, she got what she wanted: a hole. From there she pulled and tugged, breaking away the drywall and revealing steel studs. That left the layer of drywall on the other side of the studs the only barrier between her and escape. An electrical wire that likely linked the sockets in that room snaked through the studs about a foot off the floor. The wire's presence wouldn't be a problem. All she had to do was be sure she kicked above it as she'd done before.

Thankfully, no one showed up to stop her.

Maybe it was her imagination, but the process went a little more quickly this time. Before long, she had herself a hole about four feet high and around twelve or fourteen inches wide. Careful of the wire, she wiggled out between the studs.

For the first time, she had reason to appreciate the fact that her brother had put his fist through her living room wall once. Otherwise she might not have thought of this. At least he'd been good for something.

On the other side was what seemed like a corridor. It was too narrow to be a room, but there was no light at all for her to have visual confirmation. She dusted herself off and felt her way along the wall. She encountered another door, opened it and flipped the light switch. An overhead light came on, illuminating the space to reveal a bedroom. A telephone on the bedside table had her rushing over to it. Dead. She dropped the receiver and moved back into the corridor.

The direction in which she'd been headed was a

dead end, so she turned around and went the other way. She opened two more doors, one lead to what appeared to be a storeroom cluttered with leftover pieces of furniture and boxes of discarded clothing. The other door led to another bedroom. Again, the phone was dead.

At this end of the corridor was a staircase. She took a couple of deep steadying breaths before she started upward. The electricity was on, but so far the phones were dead. When she'd come into this house, the sky had been clear. She didn't remember hearing about any bad weather headed this way, so the dead phone lines were more likely related to the two intruders who had shown up and locked her down here.

Though no one had come running while she kicked through the wall, that didn't mean she was alone in the house. Her senses on high alert, she took the final steps up and moved into the kitchen, braced for most anything. The hurricane shutters were still locked in place, shielding the view through the windows. The metal shutters would be pretty much impenetrable, eliminating the windows as an exit. Since she didn't know the deactivation code for the security system, there was no way to disarm it.

As she moved through the ground floor, a lamp here and there provided enough illumination to discourage her from switching on additional lighting. The shadows provided by the dim lighting might prove beneficial.

Her heart pounded hard against her sternum as she progressed from room to room, checking phone lines and looking for anything useful. The computer had been disabled, the monitor smashed and wires cut at the back of the hard drive, rendering the system worthless. She found her purse on the floor near the front door where she'd dropped it. Her cell phone and gun were gone. They'd taken her ankle holster as well, she realized abruptly. So far she hadn't found any bodies, dead or alive, in any of the rooms she'd checked.

The front door was locked. She considered the keypad next to it. Red lights blared at her, warning that the system remained fully armed. If she unlocked and opened the door, the alarm would go off and the police would come. At least that was the way it worked under normal circumstances.

Might as well give it a try. There was nothing else she could do here. Maintaining her cover didn't appear necessary at this point. Paul Reyes was long gone…or dead.

She turned the lock button, then gripped the knob, gave it a twist and…nothing. She twisted the latch built into the knob again. This time, the knob turned, but the door didn't budge.

Frustration sent a prick of panic along her nerve endings. She wiped her sweaty palms on her slacks and reached to try again. Her gaze settled on the dead bolt. No wonder it wouldn't open. She'd forgotten to unlock the dead bolt.

Apparently her brain was still suffering the after-effects of the drug or she would have noticed that sooner. Exhaling a ragged breath, she started to reach up, then realized that this was the kind of dead bolt that required a key for locking and unlocking it. No turn piece on the dead bolt.

"Damn."

Don't panic, she reminded herself. Find another door. She turned around to retrace her steps. Why would those scumbags just leave her here? Why not kill her and dispose of her body? Where was Paul? If he was dead, where was his body?

Her heart started to thump hard again. Had Victor taken his brother from her reach? Had he somehow known why she was here? That seemed unlikely.

She hesitated at the bottom of the stairs. Before she did anything else, she had to be sure he wasn't up there. Her gaze followed the elegant staircase as it wound upward to the next floor. She couldn't imagine why he would have been taken upstairs and then murdered, but then murder didn't always make sense.

He wasn't in the basement or anywhere on the first floor. If the upper floor was clear, then she would know for certain he'd been taken from the house. Dead or alive. She placed her hand on the cool metal banister. Get this part over with.

Listening intently, she climbed the stairs. The upstairs corridor went left and right. The walls were richly paneled in a natural wood that glowed like warm honey. The floor was carpeted, muffling the sound of her footsteps. She went right first. Three bedrooms, each with its own bath. All with dead phones. No bodies. No usable weapons.

At the other end of the corridor was a single set of double doors. The master bedroom suite, she presumed. She opened the doors and turned on the overhead light. Two chandeliers twinkled, spilling a brilliant glow over the room. Same rich paneling as in the hall. The wall nearest the door offered floor-to-ceiling shelves lined with books and lovely objects the owner had collected. A big king-sized bed sat against the opposite wall. Several windows adorned with lavish curtains. Still, no blood, no body. The telephone was out of commission, just like all the others.

There was a massive walk-in closet and lots of fancy suits. A wall safe and dozens of pairs of shoes. Jewelry. A person could have set up an entire men's department with what was in that one closet.

Seemed like a hell of a large wardrobe and bling for a recluse.

The master bath epitomized the term *luxurious*. No working phone, no body. Nothing appeared out of place.

What the hell was going on?

It wasn't until she'd got halfway across the bedroom headed for the door that she noticed what looked like a painting on the wall was actually a framed plasma television. Using the remote, she turned it on, mainly to see if it worked and to check any possible alerts that might explain part of what had happened. A news channel bloomed to life on the wide screen. The sound was muted but the crawler revealed no weather alerts. She started to power it off when she noticed the Security button on the remote. She pressed it. The channel instantly went to a multi-view screen that displayed various exterior locations around the property. The front door, back door, garage entry as well as the dock, the driveway and an overall rear property panorama.

It was dark outside. The security screen showed the time as 1:15 a.m. She'd been out for hours. Her car and the Maserati were still parked exactly where they had been on the front parking patio.

This was nuts.

She tossed the remote back onto the bed and turned to go, but stopped dead in her tracks.

Her gaze collided with dark eyes…eyes she'd seen before.

Paul?

She searched the grim face…noted the day's growth of beard. She didn't remember that.

He wasn't wearing the same clothes he'd worn when she arrived.

Victor?

Her heart rammed against her sternum. She

couldn't be sure. The urge to flee exploded inside her, but before she could put thought into action he spoke.

"Who are you?"

She blinked, confusion defusing her fear.

"Why are you here?" he demanded in that same silky voice she'd found so pleasant only a few hours ago.

Could this be the same man?

"I'm—"

He held up a hand to silence her, his gaze suddenly riveted to the television screen. She turned her head just far enough to look there as well. The air evaporated in her lungs.

Men dressed in black fatigues and armed to the teeth were crawling all over the property. Police? Two men were at the front door preparing to knock it down with a battering ram.

A hand clamped around her right arm. Her attention snapped back to the man now standing next to her.

"If you want to live, you'll do exactly as I say," he said sharply, his fingers tightening with each word.

"That's the police," she bluffed. "I called them." She would have but the phones were dead. But her bluff might work.

One beat, two. "No," he countered. "You didn't call anyone."

It didn't matter, she realized, whether this was Paul or Victor. It appeared to be bad either way. She lifted her chin in defiance of the trembling that had started in her limbs. "They'll bust in here looking for me. But I suppose that's a risk you'll have to take." More bluffing, but it could work.

Mentally measuring his callused grip on her arm and the distance to the door, she considered how far she would get before he caught her.

"Those men are not here to rescue you," he said flatly. "You can come with me or we will both die."

Renee glanced at the monitor. She could hear the ramming against the front door as she watched the action playing out on the screen like a cop flick. The men would be inside in seconds. They looked official. Could she trust that assumption? She turned back to the man still clutching her arm. If he was Paul Reyes, she needed him to bait his brother. If he was Victor, then she had accomplished her mission. All she had to do was survive long enough to let Gates get his hands on him.

Right now, her best option was to go along with him. She needed him—at least for a little while longer.

"Where are we going?"

"This way."

He ushered her to the far side of the bedroom to the wall lined with bookshelves that likely separated this room from the next. He touched something on the underside of one of the lower shelves and a section of wall opened outward. As she stood there gaping, he grabbed her arm and ushered her inside the secret room. The breakaway wall closed and what she concluded were hidden locks clicked into place.

The lighting was dim, but she could see quite well. A cot sat against one wall. Shelves filled with supplies of all kinds, including food and water, were stacked in the back section of the room. Three small monitors blinked to life, each one displaying a different area in the house or the property outside.

"What is this place?" she whispered.

"You don't have to whisper," he said. "The room is soundproof."

A panic room, she realized after closer inspection. She'd heard of these. There was probably a telephone in here. One that had a separate line, just like the electricity. That was the whole point of one of these rooms. A person could hide in safety, and nothing done anywhere else in the house would affect the protected environment. She covertly glanced around. The phone was probably stowed behind supplies or built into the monitoring system. The movement on the screens distracted her. A dozen or more men were prowling through the house. In here she couldn't hear a sound as they shuffled from room to room in those heavy black boots.

Who were these guys? As if one of the men shown

on monitor two had heard her question, he turned away from the camera. Large, block style white letters were emblazoned across his back:

D...E...A.

Adrenaline surged. One of those men could be Gates. She held herself still, risked a look at the man standing a few feet away. If he was Victor Reyes, this could be the moment she'd come here to make happen.

As if she'd somehow telegraphed the thought, he turned his head and stared straight into her eyes.

"Who are you?"

His question startled her, but she suppressed any outward expression. "Don't you know?" Could this be Paul Reyes? She'd met Paul, had gone over the proposed gallery contract with him. He had been observant, infinitely charming and confident, with a calm but forceful manner. However, this man seemed agitated, uncertain, harsh even. His lean frame was all muscle...his hands were not smooth and soft as Paul's had been. Now that she studied him more closely, the stubble on his face was no mere day's growth...more like three or four.

"Who are *you?*" she demanded, turning the question back on him. Her breathing slowed just a little as her ability to reason overrode her initial trepidation. Surely if he had intended to kill her, he would have done that already. She was relatively certain at this point that he was not armed. The confusion he radiated was the one element that gave her pause.

"Answer the question," he ordered, his tone gruff.

"Renee Parsons," she lied, sticking with her cover for all the good it would do. "I represent a gallery in L.A." She amplified the indignation in her expression, as well as her tone, just to make sure that he knew she was not happy. "I came all this way to work out a deal to show the paintings of Paul Reyes in our gallery. What the hell is going on here? Who are you?"

For several seconds he didn't respond. If this was Victor Reyes, as she suspected, did he not know the truth about who she was? Could she be that lucky? When had he arrived? Then again, if he wasn't aware of her true business here, why had he shown up? Stepping onto American soil was a death sentence. Killing a cop was a capital offense. He was certainly aware of the risk he had taken making this personal appearance. Why not simply walk into his brother's home and do whatever he'd come here to do? Why the game? And if this was Victor, where was Paul?

Her breath caught when two of the agents entered the master bedroom and looked around. Every instinct urged her to scream at the top of her lungs, maybe pound on the wall that separated the panic room from where the men stood. But he had said this room was soundproof. If she took that risk and it didn't pan out, she would have accomplished nothing more than making this man angry with her. It was bad enough that she was trapped in here with him; she didn't need him ticked off.

"I do not understand."

His comment dragged her attention back to him. Bewildered, she said quite frankly, "Well, you're not in that boat alone." He had to be playing her. Whatever his hidden agenda, she wasn't going to let him trap her into saying or doing anything that would get her into more trouble than she was already in.

The men methodically tearing apart the house belonging to Paul Reyes captured her attention once more. What were they looking for? The two who had scanned the bedroom moved on to another room.

She turned to her host—or abductor. "What if they find us? Aren't you worried?"

He watched the monitors for half a minute. "They won't find us. This room is undetectable."

Her focus settled on the monitors once more. "I'd hate to be you if you're wrong."

Silence thickened for several minutes. She folded her arms over her chest and pretended to be unaffected by her present circumstances. She had no idea what this man had planned, but she would be damned if she would allow him to see just how terrified she was. She hated admitting that to herself, but she was pretty damned scared.

He turned around. She gasped, then cursed herself when he assessed her at length. Without commenting, he crossed to the shelves and removed two pouches of water. He offered one to her.

She started to decline, but that bad taste still

lingered in her mouth and her throat was cotton dry. She accepted the pouch and followed the instructions for opening it. Though the water was room temperature, it felt good against her throat.

For several minutes, he continued to watch this defacing of the home without comment or outward reaction. Her curiosity swiftly got the better of her.

"Where is Paul?" she asked, deciding that she might as well get him talking again. Once these guys found whatever they were looking for or decided to call it quits, she would be left alone with this guy. Maybe not a good scenario.

"My brother was in this house with you?" he countered.

Was he hedging? Avoiding her question? "Yes, your brother was here with me." As if she would have been in the house alone. "The two gorillas who showed up last night took him." She really couldn't say for sure they did, but that was the only conclusion she could reach. "They locked me in a room in the basement."

His brow lined as if he were working hard to make sense of what she had told him. "These men, what did they look like?"

This was getting stranger by the moment. If this guy wasn't the man she was with last night, and clearly he wasn't, then he had to be Victor. Why would Victor be standing here asking her these questions? Why the hell would he be here, period, unless he'd gotten wind of her true agenda? That was unlikely since she'd only gotten here an hour before trouble had shown up. Surely a man who hid out in Mexico couldn't have acted that quickly.

Since her response was necessary for the conversation to resume, she shrugged. "Big, muscled-up guys. Both wore black." She nodded to the monitors. "Not like these guys, not uniforms, just casual civilian clothes."

"My brother did not know these men?"

How did she get this across to him? "He told me to run. One of the guys stuck a gun to his head. I'm pretty sure if he knew them, he didn't like them very much."

More silence.

He moved closer to the monitors and studied the goings-on. "This is wrong."

Did he think that he could fool her into believing he was Paul by acting as if none of this made sense to him? Not going to happen.

He turned to her as if he'd sensed her conclusion. His timing was eerie.

"I am Paul Reyes. This is my home. The man you met last night was probably my brother Victor. These men—" he gestured to the monitors "—must be looking for him."

"I'll need proof," she challenged. As it stood, she had absolutely no reason to believe him. The whole situation was out of hand. Whatever his game, she wasn't playing along. "I saw Paul's work, spoke with the gallery owner. She spoke highly of how well Paul handled his last show. She—"

"Mallory Rogers?" he interrupted. "Ms. Rogers has a discriminating eye for art, that much is true, but we have never met."

Renee felt her gaze narrow, but she kept her immediate response of "yeah, right" to herself. "Ms. Rogers seemed to know Paul quite well." In fact, Renee got the distinct impression the two had a connection of sorts.

The man now claiming to be Paul Reyes shook his head. "Impossible. We have never met."

Strange. He sounded completely sincere and yet he had to be lying. He couldn't be telling the truth. Other than the fact that the two men could pass for twins, this guy was nothing like the man she'd met last night. The button-down shirt he wore was plain, a faded blue, the material distressed cotton. Well-worn jeans and sneakers. His black hair looked shaggy, as if he needed a trim. No. This was wrong, somehow. He couldn't be Paul Reyes, the refined artist who lived in this extravagant house.

"Why would your brother pretend to be you?" That was the real question. She could be open-minded as long as the facts backed up the conclusion. If the man who had represented himself to her as Paul was, in fact, Victor, what was his motivation? Why would a ruthless drug lord come to Key Largo and pretend to be someone he wasn't? Victor's M.O. usually included killing anyone in his way, not masquerading as that person. She was certain if the man with whom she'd chatted last night had been Victor Reyes and he had wanted her dead, she would be dead. Not to mention the risk he would have taken coming here. What would have been his ultimate goal? He'd have to be pretty damned motivated to come here, considering he was on DEA's wanted list.

Her mystery man didn't answer right away, then he said, "My brother and I have not spoken in years."

"Your brother doesn't appreciate the business you do?" she suggested, recognizing the risk that she might inflame his fury but willing to take it. Every good prosecutor knew how to lead a witness. Someone was lying to her, the man last night or this new guy. If not for the stubble that couldn't be faked, she would even go so far as to believe they were one in the same.

His gaze remained steady on the monitors. "My brother refuses to acknowledge the passion I feel for our people. Or—" he glanced at her then "—for my work."

She had to hand it to him, he had his story and he was sticking to it.

"I don't know why he would lure you here under false pretenses," he went on, the lines on his face deepening with something like regret. "Or why he would assume my life. But I am quite positive that it is not for good."

Ah, so he wanted her to believe that the man she'd met last night had stolen his identity. The idea wasn't impossible, she supposed, but where was his proof? "Can you prove that you're Paul Reyes?" Even as she asked the question she mentally acknowledged a cold hard fact. She couldn't say that he wasn't Paul based on the photos she'd seen. Neither Paul nor Victor had ever been arrested, which meant no fingerprints. Damn. There was something no one had given any real consideration. She'd come here assuming the man who lived in this house was Paul Reyes. Unless one or both had distinguishing physical marks not readily visible, making a conclusive identification might be next to impossible. There had been nothing in the file about any particular marks that might set one man apart from the other.

But why would his brother pretend to be him? The DEA wanted Victor fiercely. Surely he would not be so arrogant as to believe that no one would notice that he'd taken his brother's place. Again, she was back to the idea of motivation. What compelling reason did Victor Reyes have to do this?

"I cannot prove anything at the moment."

Therein lay the rub.

"Then how can you expect me to believe you?" And where did that leave her?

The man who might or might not be Victor Reyes

turned to look her in the eyes. "For the same reason I believe you are Renee Parsons."

Well, he had her there. And, unknowingly, he had just proven her point.

"You said this was your name," he continued. "I have no reason to believe otherwise."

Aha! "But I do have reason to believe otherwise about you," she argued. "I've already met Paul Reyes. Why would the other man have lied?"

That dark gaze probed deeper than was comfortable, but she held her ground. "I cannot answer that question. I can unconditionally say, however, that whatever Victor's plans, he must be stopped."

For the first time since he'd grabbed her by the arm and ushered her into this hidden room, she considered that this whole thing could be some sort of elaborate hoax. For what end? In her experience, men like Victor Reyes didn't go off half-cocked. He planned. He manipulated. He succeeded. There would be no glitches.

This was a definite glitch.

"If the man I met last night was Victor," she offered, "and if he has, for some as yet unknown reason, assumed your identity here in Florida, where have you been? Why were you not aware of his activities?" She gave herself a mental pat on the back for coming up with a perfectly logical question to which he would have difficulty professing he didn't know the answer.

"I was working in a village in Oaxaca." At her puzzled expression, he clarified. "Oaxaca is a state in southern Mexico where there is much poverty." He sighed, the sound grievous as if even the thought of the place disturbed him. "Many of the strong, young men who grew up there have escaped to the United States to work in the fields and vineyards since there is no real money to be made at home. Only the women and elderly are left behind. Last year's floods brought much hardship, and there was no one to look to for help."

Renee thought of his callused palms. "You were helping rebuild the village?" She could believe that, but his work there had nothing to do with here and now.

"I was one among many."

He looked tired. She stared at his hands when he shoved his fingers through his hair as if he needed to clear his head of the burden straining his thoughts. The image made her wonder how an artist could take such risks with the hands that created his beloved art. Wasn't he afraid of injuring himself?

Wait. That was assuming he was Paul Reyes and she wasn't ready to make that assumption just yet. She needed more concrete evidence.

"So you were away helping with the rebuilding and your brother stole your life?" Hadn't she seen a movie with that same story line? It wasn't that the idea was implausible; it just seemed awfully convenient at the moment. Everything she had on Paul Reyes indicated he rarely left his home. Working as a volunteer among strangers didn't fit with his usual M.O.

"Yes."

"You have witnesses who can confirm you were there and who will uphold your assertion that you are Paul Reyes the artist?"

He inclined his head, searched her eyes, his lacking some of the intensity she had noticed before, the change insinuating he had come to some sort of realization. "Perhaps. I cannot say for sure." His expression went blank as if he feared giving away too much. Then he said, "You do not speak like an art buyer, Ms. Parsons."

"How would you know?" she shot right back. "You've never met one…have you?" He'd insisted that he'd never met Mallory Rogers, the gallery owner in Key Largo. If that was true, there was every likelihood that he had not met anyone else in the business. At least not more than once, and then most likely only in the briefest of encounters.

He smiled. The unexpected act caught her totally off guard. That single action entirely changed the way he looked; even his posture relaxed visibly. Gone was the intimidating harshness, replaced by an undeniable gentleness that seemed far more natural.

"You are correct, Ms. Parsons, I have not."

"Renee."

His questioning look made her want to bite off her tongue. Maybe that was too fast. Don't second-guess, she reminded herself. But she didn't let him see the way she faltered. She had a mission. Lure Victor Reyes into a trap. If this man was Paul Reyes, she needed his cooperation. If he was Victor Reyes, she needed only to prove it…somehow.

"You can call me Renee."

"Renee," he parroted.

"You say someone in the village where you volunteered might be able to confirm your identity?" she ventured, since they were on such good terms now.

The last remnants of the smile she'd appreciated disappeared, replaced by what looked like sadness.

"Some have died."

She blinked, refused to be taken in by those dark, soulful eyes. He could be lying to her, probably was. "I still don't see the motivation for why your brother would want to pretend to be you." If she kept coming at him with that same question, eventually she'd get a real answer, or at least a different one.

His expression closed completely. "I told you. I have no idea." He turned his attention back to the monitors.

She supposed that helping to rebuild a village would give a man that weary, weathered look. He could be telling the truth about that part. But the rest of his story was just too circumstantial—not to mention that the timing was way coincidental. "What brought you back now? How did you hear about what your brother was up to?" If he'd been in southern Mexico, who had made him aware of his brother's activities?

He didn't shift his attention from the monitors. "One month ago, I unexpectedly returned to our childhood home in Merida to secure additional manpower. My brother's men imprisoned me there. I was held against my will until last night. I had no idea why."

The DEA guys appeared to be winding down their search. Her pulse quickened at the idea that they would leave soon and she would be here alone with whoever the hell this guy was. She settled her gaze on Reyes. "How did you get away?" Follow the logic, find the faults in his responses and she would find the lies and hopefully part of the truth.

"A member of the household staff finally recognized my helplessness in my brother's schemes and arranged for my escape. I did not ask why the sudden change of heart. I was anxious to get away."

"So there is a household staff who can confirm your identity?"

His gaze collided with hers. "If any of them are still alive, yes."

Her gaze narrowed. "Why would your brother kill them?"

"For the same reason he will kill me or anyone else who gets in his way."

Movement on one of the monitors jerked both their gazes back there. Four of the men had returned to the master bedroom. Each picked a different section of the room and started a new search. One zeroed in on the bookshelves.

Reyes tensed.

Renee looked from him to the monitor and back. "Are they going to find us?" She wasn't so sure that was entirely a bad thing…but she needed to be sure who this man was before anything else happened or anyone, even the DEA, interfered.

"If they do—" those dark eyes connected with hers once more "—then my brother will have won."

Chapter Four

Chicago
Thursday, May 3, 3:00 a.m.

Jim heaved a breath and scrubbed the sleep from his burning eyes. He'd fallen asleep at his desk waiting for a call from Vaughn. She still wasn't answering her cell phone. He hadn't heard from her since the morning before. Almost twenty-four hours had passed. Something was definitely wrong.

A light rap on the door to his office snapped his attention upward. Who the hell would be here at this time of the morning? He was confident he'd locked both the front and rear entrances.

"I decided if you weren't coming home, I'd have to come to the office."

He smiled. Tasha, the chain holding her key to his office twirling around her finger. "What about Jamie?"

"Our daughter spent the night with her grand-mother."

Tasha, his wife of just over two years, entered the room and sat down on the edge of his desk, tossed her keys aside. His gaze slid from the length of toned legs revealed by the short black skirt to the flash of cleavage allowed by the devil-red blouse. Tension rippled through his muscles, some more than others.

"The time got away from me," he offered as his gaze swept over the woman he loved more than life itself. How strange it felt to love someone that much. He hadn't realized just how much he loved her until he'd held their daughter in his arms. He'd never felt anything quite like that. "I fell asleep. Just woke up." She looked damn good for it to be so early in the morning.

"Victoria is worried about you," she said as she slipped off one high-heeled shoe and then the other before scooting more fully onto the desktop.

His mother, Victoria Colby-Camp, worried about him too much. But, as a new father, he'd learned that worry came with the territory. He could no longer say he didn't understand.

"She always worries." He licked his lips as his gaze raked his lovely wife once more. "You'd think she would be too busy to worry about me. The new Colby Agency building is under way. Between that and running the business out of a temporary location, she should have her hands full."

"You know your mother better than that." This time when Tasha moved, she slid around to his side of the desk, pushing files and papers aside as she went. She sat with one bare foot on either side of him, spreading her legs and causing the skirt she wore to slide to the very tops of her shapely thighs. "It'll take a hell of a lot more than someone blowing up her building to distract her from what she loves most."

He grunted, too focused on devouring his wife with his eyes to form any words.

"FYI, Mr. Colby, I worry, too." She started to unbutton her blouse. "I get really worried when you don't come home at night." The last button released from its closure and she shouldered out of the silky blouse, leaving only a lacy black bra behind. "But mostly," she added as she pulled his chair closer with her feet, the rollers sliding easily on the hardwood, "I just miss my husband."

He didn't bother explaining that he could remedy that problem. He kissed her instead, kissed her long and deep. Then he pushed out of his chair and leaned her back on his desk, clearing a path as he went. The rest of his staff wouldn't be arriving for hours. There was time.

He made love to her right there. She needed him. Everything else would have to wait.

Chapter Five

The four men had torn the bedroom apart in their search, evidently hadn't found what they were looking for, and left. Paul Reyes allowed himself to relax when the team designated as DEA had gone.

He had to wonder if this exercise had been for looks. To make it appear as if an investigation were under way. But what did this have to do with him?

The house had been quiet for almost one hour. His guest had stopped asking questions. Her silence proved to be as disconcerting as her tedious interrogation. She sat on the cot, her arms folded over her chest as if she felt the need to protect herself from him. He posed no harm to her, but telling her so might be premature. Assuming she preferred her distance, he leaned against the wall rather than joining her on the cot. As tired as he was, he could not let his guard down completely.

He was not sure how she fit into this perplexing scenario, but her presence could not be happenstance. Perhaps he should pursue his own line of questions. The immediate danger had passed for now. There might not be time later. If she was an enemy who represented a threat to him, he needed to know. The possibility that she was working with his brother could not be overlooked.

"How long have you lived in L.A.?" He started with the basics. Lies were most often discovered through the most elementary venues.

"Three years," she said automatically.

No delay in her response. Perhaps this answer was true. Or practiced.

"Yet you have not lost your southern accent." He was quite confident she had not lived her entire life in L.A. The west coast ability to sound "culturally anonymous" was missing. Hers was not such a thick drawl, more soft and slow…sweet, even when she was frightened or angry. An inflection pleasing to the ears.

"I made it a point not to. We're quite prideful in Georgia."

She was lying, at least in part. He had recognized those same indicators when she had told him her name. The telltale signs played out on her face, with a widening of the eyes as she glanced away and a compressing of the lips. He was not sure if her presence was relevant to what his brother was up to, but he would know in time. Patience, he had concluded, was the best route for reaching this woman. The task would not be a hardship. She was a beautiful woman. Dark hair and golden eyes. The pale creamy slacks and blouse she wore clung nicely to her womanly figure. And she was aggressive. Aggressive and intelligent. An exciting combination if their state of affairs were of a different nature.

She stood and settled that bold gaze on his. "Is there any reason why you can't just let me go now? Those men are long gone. I'd like to get out of here. This isn't exactly how I planned this trip to the Sunshine State."

Strange that she would ask this question now, seemingly out of the blue. Her sudden turnabout further roused his suspicions.

"There is only one reason," he said in answer to her question.

She waited for him to go on, her expression carefully restrained.

"You were with my brother yesterday. I must know the true reason for your visit." He steeled for her reaction. "Until I know what Victor is really up to, I cannot allow you out of my sight." She started to argue, but he stopped her with an upraised palm. "For whatever reason, you are a part of this. I must know that reason."

"He couldn't have known I was coming to see him," she protested. "I came unannounced. Used the local gallery as an opportunity to get past the gate."

This was the truth, or what she perceived to be the truth. He felt certain of that, but the response did not answer his question.

"But something happened during your visit," he maintained. "An event that coincided with my sudden release. Can you think what that might be?" He had been held prisoner for nearly one month. Juanita's explanation for his abrupt release no longer held any merit. Those DEA agents had shown up within a half hour of his arrival here. That was no coincidence. He might not have the experience of his brother in such matters, but he was no fool. He had walked into a setup gone wrong.

"No. Of course not." She looked away and stared at the floor, then at the static images on the monitors.

She was lying again. This disturbed him greatly, even as he understood that his reaction to her decision to lie was irrational. He had no reason to expect the truth from this woman. Unfortunately, there was a part of him that never ceased to expect the best from all. He should have learned better long ago.

"We should rest while we have the opportunity," he suggested, seeing no point in pursuing the issue just now. Fatigue pulled at him, clouded his ability to concentrate and form proper conclusions. Perhaps she would grow agitated and start to talk a bit more openly.

Her gaze snapped back to his as if his decision to put the matter aside for now had prompted her determination to do precisely the opposite. "Shouldn't we be trying to find your brother? How do we know he's even still alive? He might be injured and need help."

"My brother has never needed anyone in his life," he said with far more disdain than he'd intended. He modulated his emotions and, a great deal more calmly, said, "If we proceed without rest, then we are doomed to failure."

He knew this firsthand. He hadn't slept more than a few hours in days. The exhaustion clawed mercilessly at him. She was surely tired, as well. The longer he kept her to himself, the more likely he could wear down her defenses. He needed to know who she was and why she had appeared at his home. He had no worries about his brother's health. It was his, and perhaps hers, that was in danger. What he needed more than anything was her full cooperation. Isolation would work in his favor. He had never in his life taken a person hostage, but perhaps that was what this was. He needed her with him, no matter what she wanted or needed. Was that not the same thing as kidnapping?

"You need not worry about my brother," he said finally. "Unfortunately, he is far too hard to kill to have surrendered so easily. Things are not as they appear, I assure you."

She stared at him defiantly. "There are people who will be worried about me. I need a phone."

"There will be no phone calls now." At the fury that

lit in her eyes, he added, "If you do not cause me trouble, perhaps I will allow you to use the phone later." After I know your true agenda, he qualified silently.

Resigned to his decision, she plopped back down on the cot and curled her legs beneath her. She leaned against the wall and closed her eyes. If she went to sleep, perhaps he would be able to rest his eyes, as well. He was very tired. He needed to reason out what this latest turn of events meant.

He settled onto the floor and leaned his head against the wall. First his brother kills a handful of innocent missionaries, then he imprisons him in the family home. How could the dedicated people who had worked for their parents have believed anything that they were told by a man as cruel and demented as Victor?

Paul had assumed that fear had kept those who knew him from coming to his aid. Juanita and her husband, the housekeepers, and George, the gardener and groundskeeper, all three knew him...knew he was not capable of such violence. But perhaps it was not fear. Had his brother promised them money? Protection? The three were quite old now. Perhaps fear for their futures had driven them. He simply did not know.

What he did know was what he saw with his own eyes. His home here in Key Largo had been taken over by his brother. Signs of Victor were everywhere. The lavish car. New extravagant furnishings. All of it was in excess. Paul scarcely recognized his own home, so much had changed. How long had his evil sibling been pretending to be him? Months, at least.

Something had precipitated this move. Something with far-reaching implications. Had the new president of Mexico decided to consider the extradition petition the United States had made for Victor Reyes? Whatever the reason, his brother obviously wanted or needed his freedom from the ugly past that dogged his every step. The only way to achieve that was to slough off all aspects of his former self. The authorities would not be satisfied without indisputable proof that Victor Reyes was gone for good.

Paul was certain that was why those agents were searching his home. They had come expecting to find him. He would have been arrested as the venomous drug lord Victor Reyes, tried and possibly executed. Victor would have been free to assume Paul's life, a crime-free life. That had to be what this was about.

Such a good plan. Perhaps it might have even worked for a short time. But he knew Victor. He was a devil. He would never have been satisfied leading a normal, quiet life. He would have ended up ruining this life just as he had his own.

Paul had spent many years living in his brother's shadow. As children, his older brother had always been the one in charge. As an adult he was the one to make headlines while Paul lived quietly, happy with nothing more than his work. He'd kept himself so apart from the world, there was no one here who could vouch for his identity. Only Juanita, Eduardo, and George, back in Merida.

Victor would kill them, too. That was how he would retire them. Yet they foolishly trusted him.

Somehow Paul's leaving home so many months ago to devote himself to helping those less fortunate than him had provided the opportunity his brother needed. It had been years since Paul had even visited Mexico. But news of the horrendous problems in Oaxaca had propelled him to help his people. No matter that he had lived in the United States for more than a decade—Mexico was still his country, the residents there still his people.

He should have come home to check on things in Key Largo periodically. He should not have assumed that a mere caretaker would be able to protect his home or warn him in time in the event of trouble.

The thought speared through Paul's chest. Where was the caretaker? Had Victor fired him while pretending to be Paul, or had he killed him? Regret for his many mistakes tore at Paul. He should have been watching. He should have never believed that his brother would simply let him be. That had never been Victor's way.

Now, Paul had only one choice. Face Victor and end this once and for all.

That would not be such an easy feat, considering Victor had many ruthless men at his disposal.

Paul had no one. Not a single living being who

could help him. He looked at the woman who had
fallen asleep. Except perhaps her. She was here for
a reason that involved his brother. He was sure of it.
Many people had attempted to take down his brother
by using Paul for access. Was that her reason for
being here? If so, he might be able to use that to his
advantage. But it was unclear as yet whether she
was friend or foe.

It was entirely possible that Victor had left her
here to finish him off.

6:30 a.m.

THE NIGHTMARE woke Renee from her sleep.

She blinked, rubbed at her eyes and struggled to
get her bearings.

Panic room…with one of the Reyes brothers.

She settled her attention on the man who leaned
against the wall, his eyes closed. Whether or not he
was asleep, she couldn't say. He hadn't moved since
the last time she had awakened and taken notice of
him sitting on the floor.

Closing her eyes, she tried to banish the lingering
images from the nightmare.

He had been strapped to a shiny steel gurney, two
IV lines running into his arm. She'd been watching
through a viewing window along with half a dozen
other people, mostly family members of the two
victims he was convicted of murdering so heinously.

As she had watched he had turned his pale, thin face toward her and mouthed, *Why didn't you help me?*

Bastard. She hadn't helped him because he would not allow her to help. As soon as she had learned what really happened, she had attempted to have the verdict overturned—the verdict she had fought for and won.

Stop it. Enough. The whole thing was out of her hands. The execution had been stayed, which meant the governor of Texas would determine if the prisoner deserved a second chance to prove the innocence he initially denied. Whatever happened now was completely out of her hands.

She opened her eyes and refocused her attention on the man who claimed to be Paul Reyes. There was nothing about him that gave her reason to believe he was telling the truth. From his calloused palms to his manner of appearance, he did not fit the image her mind had shaped of an artist capable of creating such beauty on the canvas.

My line of work.

Then again, there were things about the man she had met last night that didn't quite fit, either. But she had chalked those up to differences in language, communication lapses. His few out-of-sync words were hardly reason to challenge his identity.

There was the way he had looked at her…as if she were the prey to be conquered and devoured. That had made her immensely uncomfortable. And that remark about fitness being important to his image.

That still nagged at her. Why would such an extreme recluse be concerned about his image? The idea shouldn't surprise her. Latin men were known for their machismo. But she'd discovered no indication that Paul Reyes operated with that attitude, but the files hadn't been all-inclusive.

Those few inconsistencies she had noticed last night did not mean that the man she'd met and with whom she'd talked shop had lied about who he was.

Since her captor still appeared to be sleeping, maybe she could try and use the telephone. There had to be one in here. What millionaire wanted to be stuck in his safe room with no way to call out?

"Have you made up your mind about me, Renee Parsons?"

His question made her jump. She hadn't realized he had opened his eyes and was staring at her. Perfect. There went her chances of looking for the telephone.

She dropped her feet to the floor and righted her twisted clothes. She cleared her throat and met that probing gaze. "I don't know how you think I could do that since you've given me no proof."

Another of those slow smiles she'd reluctantly admired tilted his lips. "Ah, yes, the proof."

He pushed to his feet and stretched. She followed his movements with far too much interest that could not be attributed to her assignment. Their commingled scents of warm flesh with a tang of fear thrown in had permeated the small space and had her feeling particularly out of sorts.

"I find this situation oddly amusing," he said with no hint of humor in his tone.

He reached for a pouch of water, offered one to her, but she shook her head. She was far more interested in what he had to say than she was in nourishing her body. She would probably regret it later.

He took a long drink, then explained, "Who would have considered that I might someday need to prove my own identity in such a way?" He gestured to the monitors. "This is my home and yet someone else has taken up residence here." He massaged his chin thoughtfully. "This is my face and yet another whose is so similar could claim what is mine as his own."

Renee sensed his desperation. His movements, his voice generated that sensation of near panic and yet he appeared calm to a degree that somehow lessened the hysteria quite clearly gnawing at him.

His gaze locked with hers. "You will believe what you choose. Your business with my brother, however, is another matter. I must know why you are here."

The tension filling the small room thickened, turned palpable. She could not deny how badly he wanted or needed to know what was going on, but from what perspective? Was Victor using her to bear witness to his theft of his brother's life? Is that why she was left here last night? If this man won her over, would she be confirming the wrong brother?

Was last night the same scenario from the other side of the coin? And yet, how could Victor or Paul Reyes have known who she was or when she would arrive? If she went with the theory that they could not have known, then all that had happened in conjunction with her arrival was coincidence.

She did not believe in coincidence.

Somehow, all or part of this chain of events had been meticulously planned. The only questions were by whom and how.

"My name is Renee Parsons," she stated for the record. "I represent a gallery in L.A. I came here to discuss art with Paul Reyes."

That dark gaze bored into hers and he moved, walked straight over to stand toe-to-toe with her. She trembled, but quickly grabbed back control.

"Then we have a problem, *Renee*," he said softly, the quiet words carrying a lethal message she couldn't miss. "Because I am certain my brother wants me dead. If, as you say, you are innocent in this grand scheme, I would surmise that as a witness to recent events, it is quite possible that he will want you dead, as well."

"Are you trying to frighten me, Mr. Reyes?" She inclined her head, searched those fathomless eyes. "It feels like that's exactly what you're doing."

"Yes," he confessed. "If that is what it takes to make you see the magnitude of this situation, then I will gladly terrify you."

Well, then, let the games begin. "I'm afraid we may have a problem," she said, not backing off even as he seemingly leaned nearer.

"And what is that, besides the obvious one, of course?"

His gaze flicked down to her lips. She shivered in spite of her determination not to.

"If you're Paul Reyes, as you say, then why should I be afraid? Paul Reyes is an artist who uses paint and a brush to pour out his emotions."

To her surprise, he reached behind him and produced a handgun, a .38 revolver. She hadn't seen that one coming. That put her right back at square one.

"Perhaps the artist has learned a hard lesson."

He stroked her cheek with the barrel of the weapon. Her lips compressed into a firm line, but she refused to allow the quake rumbling through her to surface.

"Why did you come here?" he demanded, the hand holding the weapon now hanging at his side. "Answer me truthfully and you will have nothing to fear."

If only it were that simple. She had no idea who this man was. He could be Victor attempting to determine her agenda. She could answer his question honestly and he could kill her here and now—if he was Victor.

"I came to do business with Paul Reyes."

Fury tightened his jaw. "Liar." He spat the word at her, those sculpted lips vibrating with the rage he felt.

"I tell you what," she countered, "why don't you paint me a picture and we'll settle this once and for all."

His nostrils flared with outrage. Oh, yes, that was what she needed. To see his real reactions. If this man was Victor Reyes, he would come unglued at her boldness. Victor had no use for women other than as sex objects. No way would he put up with her smart talk.

"You wish to inflame my fury. I understand your game, Ms. Parsons." He visibly calmed, or gave the impression of doing so. "But you have a valid point." He shoved the .38 into his waistband and grabbed her hand.

She didn't resist as he towed her toward the door. He surveyed the monitors for a moment, then entered a code and the door swung open.

Renee kept her victory cry to herself. She had accomplished her first goal: getting out of that tiny prison. If she were smart, the first chance she got she'd make a run for it. But then she still wouldn't know if he was Victor or Paul. She refused to fail in her first assignment. She had to stick with him for now. As soon as she found a way to contact Jim, she would give him an update on what she had learned so far. She needed to know why the DEA had shown up here. Had they been looking for Victor Reyes? What or who had tipped them off that he was here?

If he was here.

She arrowed a sideways glance at the man currently manacling her arm. Maybe they knew something she didn't.

Reyes led her through the bedroom and down the stairs. The entire house was a mess. Seeing the chaos firsthand made the reality all the more appalling.

Pausing at the front door, he glanced outside, then entered a sequence of digits into the security system keypad. The hurricane shutters on the windows slowly rolled upward, revealing the amazing views she had admired last evening.

The battered door and its damaged locks hung haphazardly from the hinges. He didn't bother trying to close it; it wouldn't have discouraged anyone who wanted to get inside. That was another thing. Why the hell hadn't the alarm gone off when the agents entered the house?

She stared back at the keypad even as Reyes lugged her along the entry hall.

"Why didn't the alarm go off when those men broke down the door?"

"The alarm for the exterior doors had been deactivated. That is why it did not go off when I entered the house."

That made sense, she supposed. But who deactivated it? She was pretty sure it was armed when she and Paul—the other Paul—attempted to escape.

By the time he stopped dragging her forward, they had moved through the great room and into what she would have called a sunroom overlooking the ocean, except that it was clearly a studio.

Paintings were propped against the wall all around the room. An easel with a fresh canvas sat in the middle of the space. Supplies lined shelves and probably filled the many drawers in the massive pieces of furniture positioned against one wall. As she passed the easel, she touched the blank canvas. Her fingertips came away dusty.

She swiped her palms together. "You planning a new painting?" Seemed as if he'd been in the planning stages quite a while, but then he'd said he'd been away.

"One day." He gestured to a small sofa. "Sit."

She wandered over to the sofa, curious to see what would happen next. The overstuffed yellow pillows welcomed her. Much better than the cot, she decided.

Reyes picked up a drawing pad and pencil and settled onto a stool a few feet away from her. He repositioned the .38 to the small of his back, the movement awkward somehow. He hung his feet on the rungs as if he'd sat this way a thousand times. The scruffy sneakers fit with the rest of his attire…but didn't work with the image of the man she'd formulated after studying his history. Could she have been that wrong about him? Or was her mind doing exactly what he wanted it to…buying into his story?

"Relax," he said, his gaze connecting with hers. "Most people like to play the part of subject."

She leaned back into the soft pillows and draped her arms along the back of the sofa in hopes of releasing the tension humming inside her. "I didn't know you worked with live subjects."

He lifted that dark gaze to hers. "Usually I don't." He let her think what she would and turned his attention back to his work.

His fingers were long and more slender than she'd noted before. She studied his movements for grace and dexterity. She saw both. Each time his gaze lifted to dissect some aspect of her face, her breath stilled. It was ridiculous, she knew, but somehow she couldn't help the reaction. Maybe it was being his subject. What girl hadn't fantasized once in her life about sitting for some great artist?

But this wasn't a fantasy. This was real. And the stakes were far too high for her to let him draw her into the engaging trap he was so carefully constructing.

"Do you always eat your lip that way?" Those eyes latched fully onto hers.

She stopped chewing her bottom lip as if she'd been caught hiding exculpatory evidence. "What?"

He licked his lips. "The way you bite your lip, do you always do that?" He stared at her mouth as he asked this.

"Is there a point to your question?" she demanded, flustered. What the hell did that have to do with anything? Why didn't he just draw the stupid picture so she could assess his talent?

He looked at her so long without speaking that she was sure he hadn't intended to. Then he said, "You don't realize your effect on men, do you?"

Okay, now he was really reaching. She got up. "This is crazy. Let me see what you've done."

"The drawing is not finished. Sit." He nodded to the sofa.

This wasn't going to prove anything if he kept toying with her. Was he buying time? What?

"I don't know what your goal is," she said, letting him hear the accusation in her tone, "but I know you're playing some kind of game and I don't like it. What's going on here?"

He slid off his stool, took the three steps necessary to stand directly in front of her. "Then we are at the same place, Renee Parsons, for I do not know what is going on here, either. Since this is my home—" he pounded his chest with his fist clutching the pencil "—my *life*, I would very much like to know the truth. Can you help me with that?"

For the first time since this insanity had started, she felt compelled to believe he might be telling her the truth.

She held out her hand. He stared at her palm and then, with only the briefest hesitation, he placed the drawing pad there. The image, as he'd said, was unfinished, but it was her. The likeness unmistakable, incredibly well done. If he wasn't Paul Reyes, he was damned good with a drawing pad and pencil.

"Do you believe me now?"

She held back the *yes*. "Maybe."

The muffled sound of doors slamming shattered the silence in the house.

"Someone is here," he whispered, echoing her thought.

He grabbed a remote from the table next to the sofa and turned on another of those plasma televisions camouflaged by a picture frame to look like wall art. The security screen came into focus. A black SUV was parked near her rental car and two men were getting out.

"Those look like the two guys from last night." She recognized the taller of the two without question…the second, she wasn't completely sure.

Reyes turned to her. "Go out this way." He gestured to the French doors that opened onto the rear patio. "Hide beneath the dock. You'll be safe there."

"What?" She dragged her attention from the screen. "What're you going to do?"

"Go," he urged as he withdrew the .38. "Go now!"

She didn't have time to formulate a reason not to do as he said, so she did exactly what he told her to do without looking back.

Chapter Six

Renee stopped at the bottom of the steps, flattened herself against the wall and slowed her breathing. She couldn't just run.

Had those men come back to kill her and Paul or Victor or whoever the hell he was?

She held her breath and listened.

The doors to the patio were open…maybe she could hear something. She'd give most anything for a weapon. They would take his .38…or maybe he would try to use it. Those guys would kill him. They were professionals. Burning fear seared through her.

"Put it down!"

Tension rippled through her. She remembered that voice from the night before. Definitely the same guy.

"Kick it across the floor."

Damn. There went the .38. At least he was cooperating. That would keep him alive for a while.

Would there be more weapons in the SUV belonging to these scumbags? A cell phone? OnStar?

Adrenaline firing through her veins, she moved to the corner of the house and surveyed the situation, then took off for the front of the house. The SUV was parked between her rental and the front steps. Maybe fifteen yards from her current position, with the tailgate facing her. There was nothing but open ground between her and the vehicle. It was a risk, but Reyes was probably dead if she didn't do something.

If he wasn't already. She hadn't heard any shots, but they could be using silencers.

She'd just summoned the courage to make the move to the SUV when a man exited the front of the house. Dressed in black just like last night, he rushed down the steps and to the vehicle.

She held her position, listened as much for his movements as anything coming from inside the house…like a scuffle or gunshot.

He opened the driver's side door and reached inside. When he drew back, he had retrieved a phone.

Well, there went her chance of borrowing his phone.

She tilted her head and strained to pay closer attention when he began to talk.

"Yes, we have him."

Pause.

"No. The woman is gone. He said she was gone when he arrived. Kicked her way out or something."

Her heart thumped. They hadn't just wanted her out of the way. There was more to it than that. How could that be? It felt as if they had been expecting her arrival. That wasn't possible…unless someone had double-crossed her. Double-crossed the Equalizers.

She needed to talk to Jim Colby.

"Yes. I'm certain."

Another pause, this one longer.

"Take him now?" Pause. "Yes, I understand."

He tossed the phone back into the vehicle and headed for the house.

Take him now?

Where would they be taking him? Back to Mexico?

She couldn't lose this guy. Whether he was Paul or Victor—and at the moment she was leaning toward the former—if she let him get away, she would fail and another innocent man would die.

She couldn't be responsible for that happening twice in one lifetime.

The idea that he'd lied to protect her by saying she was gone was another point on his side, but she didn't have time to worry about that right now.

Paul or Victor, she needed him. Preferably alive.

Without a second thought, she lunged for the rear of the SUV. She glanced toward the house. Still clear. Her hands shaking, she reached for the rear door. The SUV was an extended version with the side-by-side doors that opened into a large cargo space. The absence of a third-row seat made for more cargo room. There was a large bag, like a black plastic bag for yard trash, in one corner and a couple of shovels tossed in next to it.

She didn't have time to check out the contents or the bag or to dwell on the idea of why these creeps would be hauling around shovels. Careful of the shovels, she climbed inside and eased the door shut.

Did she have time to grab the phone? Check for a weapon?

Both?

Might as well take the time.

She started over the seat and voices coming from the front of the house had her ducking back down.

She curled up into the smallest ball possible, snuggled against the seat and then attempted to slide the bag in front of her. What the hell did they have in this bag? It weighed a ton.

The approach of footsteps had her pushing harder on the bag. It moved just enough to block most of her. It was at that exact instant that she considered that the two killers might just open the cargo doors and put Reyes back here. No way was she hidden well enough not to be seen if they opened those doors.

Why hadn't she thought of that?

She tugged at the bag, trying to pull herself more fully behind it. The plastic tore and she jerked her hand back, but it was too late; she'd made a gaping hole. She clamped her mouth shut and told herself not to even breathe.

From inside the bag, part of a face stared at her. An older man. Gray hair. Pale blue eyes. That was when she smelled it—death.

A scream burgeoned in her throat.

The rear passenger door opened. "Get in."

The growling voice was different from the guy's who'd made the phone call. The second man from last night.

She swallowed back the scream. Looked away from the bag as best she could without moving enough to make a sound.

The vehicle shifted as someone got into the backseat and the front seat simultaneously. Doors slammed. Seconds later, the front passenger door opened and someone else got in. The engine started as the final door closed.

Relief allowed the constriction around her chest to ease marginally. They weren't going to open the rear doors yet. Thank God.

"I can't exactly fasten my safety belt with my hands tied like this."

Renee's pulse hitched at the sound of Reyes's voice. If she reached up she could touch him, she realized. She dared to turn her face just enough to see the back of his head above the headrest.

"Maybe you'll get lucky," the killer who'd forced him into the backseat taunted, "and we'll crash before we get there. Save us the trouble of killing you."

Renee bit her lips together to stifle the gasp that caught in her throat.

They were going to kill him.

She had known that was a strong possibility, but to hear the words…

"Where are you taking me?"

"No questions." This from the driver, the man who'd made the phone call.

"Damn, do you smell that?" the man driving asked.

"We gotta bury that old bastard," the other one agreed.

No one said anything after that. Renee could hear the sounds of the city outside the vehicle each time he stopped for what she presumed was a traffic signal.

She wished she had the weapon they'd taken from her last night or the one Reyes had given up this morning. She wished there was a tire wrench in the cargo area instead of shovels and a dead body, but there wasn't.

No problem. She would just have to figure out another way to keep their plans from fruition.

If both killers got out at their destination, she could go for the phone in the front seat. But it would be too late for help to arrive and stop them from killing Reyes, not to mention her.

The self-defense classes she had taken after the kidnapping outside the courthouse, in her former career as a prosecutor, had helped her so far, but this was vastly different. There were two of these guys, and they both had guns. That one time she'd been held at gunpoint by the husband of a woman accused of overdosing her terminally ill father, she'd known that he wasn't really a killer. The man had simply been desperate to save his wife from a murder charge. All she'd had to do was stay calm and wait for an opportunity to disarm him.

This wasn't going to be nearly so simple.

Minutes crawled by. She watched out the rear window in hopes of getting some idea of where they were headed, but that didn't help. What she could see rarely changed, the sky interrupted only by power lines and the occasional building. The roar of the wheels on the pavement underscored the silence inside the vehicle.

She didn't know how much time passed, but the sky eventually gave way to trees. Lots of trees.

A forest.

Where would they go to find a forest this dense in south Florida?

Of course.

Everglades.

The realization dawned at the same time that Reyes finally spoke again.

"Why are we going into the park?"

Renee knew only two things about the Everglades: saw grass and alligators. Neither of which she wanted to know beyond pictures in a book.

When their abductors refused to answer, Reyes asked another question.

"What does my brother want?"

Why couldn't he say his brother's name? It would make her life so much simpler.

Yeah, right.

She was in the back of an SUV that was headed into the Everglades where a man would die and, evidently, where two would be buried. And the minute she was discovered, she would die, too.

Nothing about this was simple. Hadn't she been yearning for complex?

Be careful what you wish for....

"He wants you dead," the front passenger said with a chuckle. "Then, when they find what's left of your body, there won't be enough to cause any trouble."

Oh, hell.

Renee swallowed the bitter taste of bile.

Her first assignment, and she was going to get herself killed. Jim Colby had been right; maybe she hadn't been up for this one.

No. She refused to give up.

Stay calm. Pay attention. There's always hope.

All she had to do was look for the opportunity.

"He doesn't possess the courage to take care of this personally?"

Renee winced. Was Reyes trying to get these guys ticked off? Not that anything he said or did at this point was going to stop the inevitable, but there was no need to hurry it along.

"He doesn't like wasting his time."

"Or getting his hands dirty," Reyes suggested in a bitter, scathing tone that said more about how he felt about his brother than any words could.

He really was bucking for a battle. The man was unarmed and tied up. These two jerks were going to kill him because his brother had ordered the hit. Now was not the time to be mouthing off.

"Shut up," the driver ordered.

Reyes said nothing more.

Renee allowed some of the tension to seep out of her muscles. She would need all her energy to figure a way out of this.

The vehicle slowed and took a turn. The road felt rougher now. A side road deeper into the park? She didn't know. She'd never been here before. Didn't want to be here now.

The trees were so thick at this point that it was like dusk outside, and it wasn't even ten o'clock in the morning yet. She worked at keeping her breathing slow and soundless. With the conversation at a standstill inside the vehicle she couldn't afford to have anyone hear her breathing erratically. Besides, she had no desire to inhale any more of the poor dead man's stench than necessary for survival.

She thought of how she had been betrayed and how devastated she had been. She'd worked that case alongside her mentor, Austin's esteemed district attorney who had visions of becoming a Texas senator. She'd admired and respected him. Her primary goal had been to achieve the kind of legendary status he had in his distinguished career. But she'd made a mistake. He hadn't been the great man she'd thought he was. In the end, no one had believed her. He had lied and an innocent man had been ushered into Texas's infamous fast lane to execution.

But her revered mentor wasn't the only one who had betrayed her. *He* had as well. He had allowed her to hate him...to believe the worst about him. To protect her.

And now her brother was on death row, alive this day only by virtue of the last-minute decision of the governor of Texas.

She blinked back the sting of tears. Sometimes she hated him for what he'd done. Other times, she wanted to break into that damned prison and rescue him the way she'd rescued him a million times as a scrawny kid.

I've never done one damned thing right in my entire life. Just let me do this one thing right, Sis. That's all I ask.

The idiot! How could he have believed that confessing to murders he hadn't committed was doing the right thing? For God's sake! And not just any murder. Two of the most heinous killings in Austin history. The whole state had wanted someone to blame.

Stupid, stupid.

How could her own brother have been that stupid?

They hadn't spoken for months after he'd been arrested. She had hated his drug use and inability to pull his life together for so long that she didn't remember the last time she'd thought of him in a favorable light.

Though she hadn't been primary on the case, she'd supported her boss. The press had eaten up the idea that the suspected murderer's own sister had helped present the case against him.

Damn him for letting her do that. Damn her for not letting it go…she just had to keep digging until she found the truth. And then he silenced her. She'd had no choice but to walk away.

The SUV came to a stop and Renee's attention snapped back to the present. Judging by the even thicker canopy of trees, they were deep in the middle of nowhere.

The front doors opened and the vehicle shifted as the two scumbags in charge of this outing got out. She held her breath, hoped they wouldn't open the rear door just yet. She needed an opportunity first. Just in case, her fingers curled around the handle of the closest shovel. She might die in the next few minutes but, by God, she would go down fighting like a wildcat.

The rear passenger door opened. "Get out."

Reyes followed the order without comment.

The door slammed shut.

Renee lay very still for a moment. Then another.

They were going to kill him. Then they'd come for the dead guy and the shovels.

She had to do something.

Fear pounding in her chest, she raised herself up into a partial sitting position and peered over the seat. Outside, a few yards from the front of the vehicle, the two men stood, their backs to her. Reyes waited beyond their position, facing the two bastards with the guns, his hands tied behind him.

There was only one thing she could do.

Now or never.

She climbed over the rear seat, her gaze not leaving the men. Slowly, afraid she'd make a sound, she levered herself over the console and into the driver's seat. She scooted down low so that her head wouldn't be a target. Her fingers were icy as they closed around the key in the ignition.

Do it, she ordered, or he dies.

She twisted the key. The engine started.

One of the killers shouted something like, "What the hell?"

She rammed the gearshift into Drive and stomped the accelerator.

The SUV lunged forward.

More shouting.

She hoped like hell Reyes had the good sense to get out of the way.

She peeked above the dash just in time to see that she'd run out of road and was about to barrel into the woods.

She cut the wheel right and braked hard.

The vehicle careened sideways, cutting through underbrush.

A teeth-jarring stop later, she scrambled out the door, hesitated long enough to grab the cell phone that had flown into the floorboard and ran like hell. The dense forest swallowed her up.

The shouting behind her was too close for comfort.

She had to run faster.

Underbrush slapped at her legs. She ignored it. Faster. Harder. She couldn't stop.

Gunshots exploded in the air.

She weaved right and then left.

She couldn't tell if they were shooting at her or at Reyes.

No time to look back.

Run.

Her heart slammed mercilessly against her ribcage.

Don't look back.

Don't stop.

Or you'll die.

Chapter Seven

Chicago
7:30 p.m.

Jim Colby checked the time again. More than thirty hours since he'd heard from Vaughn. He was worried. She should have connected with Paul Reyes by now. And she should have checked in again.

He'd contacted DEA Agent Joseph Gates at 5:00 a.m. this morning. Gates was supposed to check out the situation and get back to him, but that was hours ago. If he didn't hear from Vaughn or Gates by midnight, he was going down there.

Maybe the thing going on with her brother had her too distracted. He'd hoped putting her on a case would help. That might have been a mistake. She hadn't told him about the situation with her brother; he'd found that out on his own. He'd known something was going on with her. He'd made a few calls, reached out to some of his contacts at the FBI and with the U.S. Marshals. It might not help, but it couldn't hurt. He knew people in high places through his mother, and her agency was a useful tool. According to his sources, Vaughn's brother, Matthew, had confessed to the murders but Vaughn had insisted he was innocent—even after initially helping present the case against him. But something or someone had shut her up, ultimately causing her to leave Texas. If there was a way to help Vaughn's brother, the people he knew could make it happen.

The telephone rang and Jim grabbed the receiver. Connie and the others had gone home a couple of hours ago.

"Colby."

"The situation down here doesn't look good."

Joseph Gates.

Jim tensed. "What do you have?"

"We've had an internal snafu."

Jim scrubbed at his forehead. This was not the news he'd wanted to hear. "What the hell kind of snafu?"

"According to the briefing I just sat through," Gates began, "a fellow agent's contact in Marathon called in the impending arrival of a private aircraft from a small airfield on Mexico's Yucatán Peninsula shortly after midnight this a.m. The aircraft refueled and returned immediately to Mexico, but this gung-ho agent got there in time to snap some covert photos. The single passenger was listed as a George

Gonzales. But imagery analysis confirmed that it was Victor Reyes."

Tension roiled in Jim's gut. "And?" There was more. All of it bad, if the vibes he was picking up from Gates were any indication.

"Rather than going through the regular channels, my knuckleheaded colleague assembled an assault team and moved in on the residence of Paul Reyes in Key Largo. Victor Reyes was suspected of having gone straight there from the airfield."

Jim swore repeatedly under his breath.

"My sentiments exactly," Gates muttered.

"Where's Vaughn?" Jim braced for the worst. He should never have assigned her to this case. But the idea of bringing down a major drug lord was high on her priority list of things to do in her new career. Whether she admitted it or not, it was likely due to her brother's troubles with drugs. Initially Jim hadn't seen any problem with giving her the case. She was female, a necessary requirement to get the job done. She was prepared. All she had to do was get close to Paul Reyes. When the time was right, he and Johnson, along with Agent Gates, would have assisted in the takedown of Victor Reyes. It wasn't supposed to happen like this.

"Don't know. The house was empty. No sign of foul play other than a hole in the wall in a room in the basement. Vaughn's purse was found in the residence, and her rental car is still parked outside. No blood. No bodies. No nothing."

Fury knotted inside Jim. "How the hell did this happen, Gates? I thought you said this case was off the books. That you were doing this dark."

"We're grilling the agent involved just to make sure he wasn't somehow connected to Victor. Hell, Jim, I don't know the answer. I'll do everything I can on this end to find Vaughn."

That just wasn't good enough. Jim clenched his teeth to hold back the words.

"The good news is," Gates offered, "Victor Reyes is here somewhere. All we have to do is find the SOB."

"Yeah." A determined fury ignited deep in Jim's gut. "Keep me posted." Gates agreed to keep him informed and Jim hung up the phone. For several seconds, he stared at it.

Whatever had gone down with the DEA, it wasn't on the up-and-up. If Jim discovered that Gates was playing him, there wouldn't be any place on this damned planet the bastard could hide. But that would have to wait. For now, he needed to do what he could for Vaughn. He needed eyes and ears where this was going down. He needed someone on her side. Gates was supposed to have been his immediate backup on this in case anything went wrong. He'd failed. He was no longer dependable.

Jim picked up the phone once more and entered the contact number for his newest associate, Sam Johnson. Johnson picked up after the third ring.

"This is Jim Colby." He paused a moment to give Johnson a chance to turn down the volume of the music playing in the background. "We have a situation," Jim explained. "I'd like you to do what you do best."

A few minutes later, after laying out the situation, Jim placed the receiver back into its cradle. Sam Johnson was a former forensics expert. If there was anything to be found where Vaughn had been since her arrival in Florida, he would find it. Having him on site would also allow for immediate action in the event Vaughn needed him.

Damn it. This wasn't supposed to happen. Vaughn was only supposed to get to know Paul Reyes. Once she got close enough, he would have been used to lure Victor to this country. After all, Paul was Victor's only living family. According to Gates, Victor was protective of his brother despite present circumstances. The plan had been well thought out; nothing was supposed to have gone wrong.

How the hell had this gone to hell so fast and furiously?

A buzz signaled that someone was at the front entrance of the brownstone that served as the offices for the Equalizers. Surprised at having anyone show up this late, Jim stood. Wouldn't be Tasha, she had a key. Could be a customer, he supposed, even at this hour. He didn't bother turning off the light as he left his office. If it was a customer he'd be right back.

At the bottom of the stairs, he flipped the switch that lit the wall sconces in the lobby. He crossed to the door, unlocked and opened it.

"Did I catch you on your way out?" Victoria Colby-Camp asked with a skeptical look on her face.

Forcing his tension to recede, he mustered an amiable tone. "I was just about to call it a night." He stepped back, opened the door wider. His mother had not come all the way across town at a time when she was usually relaxing with an after-dinner glass of wine with her husband unless she wanted to talk. "Come on in. We can talk while I square away my office."

Victoria stepped into the lobby and he closed up behind her. Since she knew the way to his office as well as he did, she preceded him up the stairs. The distinguished navy suit with matching pumps was classic Victoria. As usual, not a hair out of place. His mother, whether commanding the troops at her private investigations agency or seeing after his six-month-old daughter, was always poised and in charge. Just one of the things he loved about her.

In his office, she made herself comfortable while he cleared his desk. She would get around to whatever she had on her mind in her own time. He'd learned patience since crashing back into his mother's life.

"Tasha tells me you haven't been home for dinner a single night this week."

So that was what this impromptu visit was about. "I have a couple of sensitive cases going right now." He met her scrutinizing gaze. "I'm sure you understand." Jim didn't remember much about his early childhood; most of his memories before age eight had been so thoroughly wiped or corrupted that, were it not for a couple of good psychiatrists, he might not have any. Months of intensive therapy, and a few special treatment sessions he'd just as soon not repeat, had extracted enough recall for him to know that his parents had loved him dearly. He had lost that knowledge for a lot of years. Hatred and bitterness had consumed him during that time.

But that was behind him now.

"Jim," his mother said, her eyes worried, her tone weary, "I know this new venture is extremely important to you. No one wants the Equalizers to succeed more than me." She sighed. "But I see you making the same mistake your father and I made twenty-odd years ago."

This surprised him. "Mistake?" He understood that his mother still blamed herself for his kidnapping, but that was unfair to her. She'd had no idea what the man who had stolen him away from his home was capable of. How could she? What had happened was not her fault, nor was it his father's. It had taken two decades for him to understand that, but he knew it now.

She held his gaze with desperation in her own

when he would have shifted his attention back to the papers on his desk. "Your father and I were so fixated on getting the Colby Agency off the ground back then that we didn't pay attention as closely as we should have to what mattered most. We likely missed warning signs that evil was about to strike. It was a mistake."

"Mom." Jim rested his hands on his desk, leaned in her direction and poured all the assurance he possessed into what he was about to say. "You didn't do anything wrong. Leberman–" he hated saying the name out loud, he despised even thinking it "—wasn't going to stop until he'd hurt you and Dad." He didn't use the more familiar terms very often, but she needed to hear them just now.

Her deep shuddering breath told him exactly how much the past still weighed upon her. Then she stood, straightened her suit jacket and smiled as if she'd put it behind her and moved on all in one breath.

"You're right, son, I know that." She glanced pointedly at the clock before meeting his gaze again. "Just don't take your family for granted. You might turn around at the least expected moment and find someone you love gone. You'll ask yourself what was the last thing you said or did, and it won't be right or enough. And you won't ever be able to make it right or enough."

"I hear what you're saying." She'd given him this speech a couple of dozen times recently. "How's the construction going?" Might as well shift the subject to her and her "baby."

She smiled. "The Colby Agency is rising from the ashes right on schedule. We should be moving in by September."

That was one of the things he loved most about his mother—she was unstoppable. No matter how hard life got, she just kept on charging ahead.

"Outstanding."

She skirted his desk and kissed him on the cheek. "Now, go home. Your wife and daughter need to spend time with you."

His mother was right. "Give me a minute. I'll walk out with you."

He was going home. Johnson would find Vaughn…if she wasn't dead already.

If she was, some-damned-one would pay.

Chapter Eight

Florida Everglades
after dark

It was so damned dark.

Renee was positive that she was in the clear at this point.

Problem was, she didn't have a clue where she was.

She'd been running for hours.

Peering down at the cell phone's screen, she resisted the impulse to shout *yes*. Finally she had service. Only two bars, but it could work.

After entering the number for the office, she held her breath as she waited for the call to go through.

"Colby."

Relief made her knees weak.

"Jim, it's Renee."

"Vaughn?"

His voice was broken.

Damn it. Not a good connection.

She looked at the screen, moved first one way and then the other until the second bar appeared once more. Then she froze.

"Can you hear me okay now?"

"There's some static, but go ahead. Are you safe?"

Renee resisted the urge to look around the dark woods. "I'm in the Everglades. Two of Victor's men tried to kill us and we're on foot. Otherwise, I'm good to go." She was fairly certain that the man who'd been with her was Paul. As sure as she could be, anyway.

"Is Paul Reyes with you?"

"He's out here somewhere, just not with me."

"Are Victor's men still on your trail?"

"Possibly."

"Is this your cell phone?"

"No, I lifted it from one of the guys who brought us here."

"Okay, listen to me carefully, Vaughn."

She took a deep breath, let it out slowly.

"The men who are after you may use this phone to track you. So as soon as we're finished here I want you to turn the phone off and don't turn it on again unless it's an emergency."

"Got it."

"Now, give me as many details as you can about your location."

"Paul mentioned a park. He said something like,

'why are we going into the park?' We weren't on the road that long after leaving Key Largo. Maybe thirty or forty minutes."

"Anything else?"

She racked her brain. "No. Nothing I can recall."

"All right. I assume you don't have supplies."

"Just the phone."

Saying it out loud made the idea sound even worse.

"There are park rangers throughout the area. Find a ranger's station if you can and you'll find supplies. I don't want to send a search party in there for you unless it's absolutely necessary. Johnson's on the ground down there. I'll see what he can do. Maybe he and a guide can find you and bring you out."

He didn't have to explain his reasons for not wanting to send a search party. That would require bringing Gates up to speed.

"It's someone in the DEA, isn't it? That's where this thing went wrong," she asked. Her mission should have been simple. She should be wining and dining Paul Reyes right now, not running for her life in a swamp.

A moment of silence lapsed. "Why do you say that?" her boss inquired noncommittally.

"Those guys were all over the Key Largo residence just minutes after Paul arrived from Mexico. They had to have been given advance notice. Something was wrong with the whole situation."

"You've lost me, Vaughn. What do you mean after Paul arrived from Mexico?"

She filled him in on the events of the past twenty-four hours and wrapped up with, "I think Victor is trying to pin his whole sick existence on his brother so he can walk away with a clean slate and a new life."

"Find Paul Reyes if he's still alive," Jim ordered, "and lie low as long as you can. Keep him in the dark, if possible. He might not cooperate if he learns why you're down there."

She'd decided to go that route already.

"Look," she began, hoping like hell she had the guts to see this through, "if we make it out of here alive, I don't want to get ambushed by the DEA. This may sound crazy, but maybe you should keep Johnson on top of Gates. He's the only one who knew I was coming. This all happened almost immediately after I arrived at Paul's residence. The whole setup seemed to have been arranged for me to believe that Paul had been kidnapped by his brother's henchman. But there was a glitch. Somehow Paul showed up and screwed up the plan."

"All right. But if you get into trouble, use this phone. I don't want you dead, Vaughn. Do you hear me?"

"Yeah, I hear you." She looked around again, trying her best to peer through the blanket of night. "If I can find Paul, and he's still alive, we'll get out of here somehow."

She ended the call and shut down the phone

before sliding it into her bra strap. The slacks she wore had no pockets, so her choices were limited.

Drawing in a deep breath, she scanned the darkness around her. Despite her brave talk to Jim, if she got out of this alive it would be a miracle.

It would be nice if the moonlight could cut more effectively through the canopy of trees, but that was wishful thinking in this jungle. The mosquitoes hummed around her as if she were the dinner buffet on tonight's menu. She slapped at her neck. What she would give for some insect repellent.

She had been moving in a sweeping pattern in hopes of encountering Paul. So far she hadn't encountered anything that wasn't indigenous to the area. Resting for a bit, while she was still on dry land, would most likely be the smart thing to do. He could be close by. Maybe he would catch up if she took a breather.

Not knowing where the forest merged with the ocean of muck and saw grass was her biggest concern. She had no desire to find that territory. Her sense of direction had worked fairly well so far. If her luck held out, she might just make it until daylight without running upon anything that hadn't had dinner tonight.

Dread settled heavily in the pit of her stomach when she considered that Reyes might very well be dead. Those scumbags had fired off several rounds. That could mean they hadn't hit their target. Or maybe it meant they hadn't got her in addition to their primary target. She'd have to operate under the assumption that Paul was out here somewhere, maybe even looking for her.

Giving up was something she had no intention of doing…again.

As her breathing slowed since she was no longer moving in a dead run, she grew more aware of the night sounds around her. Frogs calling in loud, deep voices, and the high-pitched cry of insects. Once in a while the hoot of an owl or the splashing of water would jerk her attention one way or the other.

She tried to shake the shivers, but that wasn't happening this side of sunrise. As long as she was out here in the dark, her imagination was going to work overtime. Though she had never visited the Everglades, she had some idea of the range of animal species that called this habitat home. The only friendly ones, as far as she was concerned, were the white-tailed deer and the various types of birds.

Snakes, spiders, alligators, to name a few, were not exactly her choices in roommates.

But there was no avoiding the residents here. She'd done her share of camping as a kid, so she wasn't entirely out of her element in this setting. Just out of her comfort zone.

Rest a few minutes and start out again fresh. Find Reyes and select a place to lie low until the dust settled. Victor Reyes was somewhere in Florida, and someone in the DEA appeared to be on his side. Maybe she was jumping the gun, but she'd learned her lesson about trusting the so-called good guys. She was sticking with the facts. Namely, Gates was the only person in Florida who had known her mission details, when and where, et cetera. All hell had broken loose, and here she was trekking her way through the wilderness with killers on her tail.

Since there were no other facts to refute those two, she had to go with that scenario. Someone in the DEA, either Gates or someone he'd entrusted with this information, was dirty.

She used her foot to tamp the ground around her chosen tree that would serve as a temporary lounge. Then, her heart thundering foolishly, she crouched down and felt around with her hand. Damp and cool earth interrupted only by the exposed, tangled roots of a tree she couldn't identify in the dark, but no critters that she could readily recognize by touch.

Carefully, she eased down into a sitting position and leaned against the gnarled tree. A scurry through the underbrush to her right snapped her attention in that direction. Snake? Too noisy. Gator? Too light. Bird? Maybe. Which ones were nocturnal? She couldn't recall. Well, except for the owls.

She sat perfectly still and listened, allowing her muscles to relax after hours of brutal punishment running through the wilds with nothing but dainty sandals for protecting her feet.

The whisper of something solid slipping through vegetation was unmistakable. What sounded like a muffled footstep, then another.

Goose bumps rose on her skin.

This could be company.

Human company.

Something upright for sure.

Were there bears in the Everglades?

Maybe.

She eased into a crouch and braced for defending herself. Part of her wanted to run like hell. Stay very, very still, her more rational brain cells ordered.

Keeping still won out.

She didn't even breathe.

Closer. The interloper moved slowly but steadily. Just one, she decided.

Almost upon her now.

She prepared to launch an attack.

Her heart practically stopped when whatever it was rushed through the underbrush behind her and just kept going.

A deer. She hadn't been able to see it, of course. It was dark, and the animal had been behind her. But she was sure it was a deer.

Or a panther.

A chill went through her.

There weren't that many panthers around anymore, but there were still a few.

Whatever kind of creature, it was gone now.

She relaxed.

Five more minutes and then she would restart her search for Paul.

Her eyes started to grow heavy. She jerked them open and got to her feet. If she kept sitting there, she would fall asleep. Might as well start moving again.

A hand abruptly clamped over her mouth.

Renee screamed, but the sound was trapped in her throat.

She scrambled to get away, but a strong arm hauled her up against a solid body.

"Do not be afraid, Renee."

She stilled.

Reyes. Paul.

As she pushed his hands away, she turned to face him, for all the good it would do in the dark. "What the hell do you mean sneaking up on me like that?"

"Keep your voice down," he whispered.

She shut up. Listened. Even the frogs and insects had gone silent in expectation of trouble.

"I thought you were dead," she snapped, suddenly and irrationally frustrated that he wasn't, or maybe because he'd caught her off guard.

"I thought I was, too."

Okay, calm down.

"Are they still out there looking for us?" she whispered. The idea that they might give up for the night was probably just a pipe dream.

"I don't think so." His body was very close to hers.

Close enough for her to feel the heat from his skin. "But we should proceed as if they are out there."

He was right. She wouldn't have made any noise at all if he hadn't scared the hell out of her.

"How did you find me?" she demanded. It was dark. They were in a swamp. His vision and hearing couldn't be *that* good.

"I have followed you for hours. I did not want to get too close until I was sure it was safe to do so."

She supposed that made sense. He'd had the advantage, after all, since he'd been behind her.

"Were those Victor's men in the SUV?" They were the same guys who'd manhandled her the night before. The same ones who'd taken the first man who'd claimed to be Paul Reyes. The more she thought about that whole strange event, the more she was certain she had been set up. It all had happened far too conveniently.

"My brother's men. Felipe and Rafael. His personal bodyguards."

She supposed it shouldn't surprise her that he knew them by name. "They were going to kill you."

"Yes. They killed my caretaker, as well. I had feared as much when I returned to find my home in…such condition."

The man in the garbage bag. She shivered. Poor guy.

"So, he really is trying to assume your identity?" she asked as if she still couldn't believe it. That was her conclusion, based on the few available facts, but for now he didn't need to know what she knew.

"Yes, it would seem so."

The resignation in his voice made her feel sad for him. She knew exactly how it felt to have your brother use you. His scumbag brother provided the drugs, and her stupid brother used them. Both uncaring about the lives they ruined. The whole idea stank.

The silence went on a little too long. If she were going to keep her cover in place, there were questions he would probably expect her to ask.

"We should probably hole up here for the night unless we have company." If they kept moving, they could run into real trouble that had nothing to do with Victor's men.

"I agree. Continuing to move around in the dark will only get us more lost."

With that decision out of the way, it was time for those expected questions.

"Why does your brother want to kill you and assume your identity?"

"To escape his past." He tugged her downward as he settled onto the ground.

She didn't mind sharing a tree with him, but it did make for close quarters. "You've been estranged for years?" she asked, pushing on with her questioning.

"Yes. He resided in Mexico. I lived here." He

exhaled a heavy breath. "Until I could no longer ignore the needs of my people."

She remembered he had said that.

"About one year ago, I began spending more and more time in Mexico."

That, she had to admit, made sense. A few of the more recent paintings she'd seen were of historic churches and quaint villages, when most of his other work centered on the water and the sky. One particular scene of the sunset on the water was her favorite. The color and detail were so vivid. Breathtaking. She thought of his calloused hands, and she felt an ache deep inside for the man who would risk those talented hands to help others. Startled, she dismissed the sensation.

"You hired this caretaker to see after your home in Key Largo while you were away?"

"Mr. Harbin. I called him frequently enough to ensure all was as it should be. The past six months in particular, I was unable to get home, but all appeared to be well. Until one month ago. I was unable to reach Harbin."

When his brother had imprisoned him in their childhood home in Merida.

"In all your trips to Mexico, you never ran into Victor?"

"No. My brother maintains a home somewhere in Mexico City. Even I do not know where. He prefers his anonymity."

That answer certainly went along with what she knew about Victor Reyes.

Silence elapsed between them, but the world beyond their tree trunk was anything but silent. The insects seemed to cry out for something only they understood; the nearly constant high tempo was punctuated by the rhythmic bass of the frogs.

"Tell me about your childhood." She didn't really need to know about his early life, but it seemed to be a reasonable question, one she would ask a new acquaintance under other circumstances. "Was your family wealthy?" That they owned property and a staff was maintained spoke of money.

"My family was wealthy enough. We had what we required and more."

"Your parents are still alive?"

She knew the answer to that one, but she would be asking it as well as a number of others. He couldn't know that she knew. Their roles had reversed. He had held her hostage on some level at his home for a few short hours, but now he was her hostage, in a manner of speaking. She would be in charge of their movements, as much to protect him as to use him. If Victor Reyes opted to stay hidden, whether on American soil or not, they would need Paul to lure him out of hiding.

Her mission was back to where it should be. Keeping Paul Reyes close at hand. Encouraging him to trust her. Until they had his brother in custody.

"No, they died. There is only Victor and me. We were happy as children. There were the usual sibling rivalries. Nothing…dramatic."

His hesitation made her wonder what he'd just remembered. "Why does he want to steal your life?"

A beat of silence. "Because he is afraid."

"What causes his fear?" she pushed.

More of that deep silence.

"Sorry," she offered. "I shouldn't have asked."

"He barters in illegal goods."

That was putting it kindly, in her opinion.

"What does that mean, exactly?" Too much prying would definitely give her away, but this seemed like a logical question. So far, she appeared to have gained some ground in the area of trust.

"Drugs."

"As in cocaine or something like that?" she ventured.

"Yes."

"I'm sure your parents were devastated with his decision to become a part of that world."

"They died many years before that," he corrected. "They were killed in a boating accident. We were on vacation. My brother and I were the only survivors."

That had to have been horrifying. "How old were you?"

"Twelve. My brother was fourteen."

Renee couldn't imagine being left all alone at

that age. "Who took care of you? Did you have other family?"

"No other family. We were raised by the caretakers of our family home."

She wondered if the reason Paul painted all those waterscapes was because his parents had died in the water. Asking would be too personal.

"Why were you in the SUV?" He opened up his own line of questioning. "I told you to hide."

Tension vibrated along her nerve endings. What she heard in his voice sounded a little like suspicion. She couldn't fault him there. In his shoes, she would be pretty damned suspicious.

"What do you mean?"

"Why would you take such a risk to save a man who had held you at gunpoint just a few hours ago? That seems out of character for an art buyer."

She winced. She would need a damned good answer for that one.

"I couldn't do it," she admitted. "I got around the house and intended to make a run for the gate," she fabricated, "when I heard one of the men make a call. He said something about taking you somewhere. I was afraid they were going to hurt you, so I did the only thing I could think of. I hid in the vehicle."

She took a breath, hoped her explanation would allay his suspicions.

The sounds of nature filled the lull that dragged on for a couple of minutes.

He was thinking, she decided. Trying to determine if her responses were reasonable. She could see how her actions looked a little suspicious. She'd gone after defendants for less.

"So you set out to rescue me, did you?"

The amusement had trumped the suspicion. Good. "Yes. I suppose I did, though I had no idea how I would manage it or exactly why I would need to." She relaxed a fraction. She'd barely skated out of that one.

"The expression on the faces of those men was quite priceless when the SUV's engine suddenly started."

She bit her lower lip a second. "I didn't consider that I might run over you in the process. I just knew I had to do something fast."

"Understandable. I headed for the trees the moment their attention shifted to the vehicle. Your timing was remarkable."

"Luck," she admitted. "I was desperate. At that point, I knew they were going to kill you." He didn't need to know that she'd utilized the only weapon at her disposal. Luck had nothing to do with it. It was about thinking on her feet.

"I take it you believe I am who I say I am at this point."

He was looking at her, or at least his face was turned toward her. She looked at him, in his direction, anyway. She could vaguely make out his form, but she couldn't really see him. Nor could he see her, she would wager. That he wanted to sense her total reaction should have concerned her, but it didn't. She was confident of her standing with him now.

"I'm convinced you're telling me the truth."

"Was it the drawing?"

"That was part of it."

"Ah, but I could still be lying," he countered. "Perhaps Victor has a gift for drawing. Drawing and painting are very different."

The hair on the back of her neck lifted, not from fear but from anticipation. He was enjoying this sparring with her. "You could be, yes."

"But you do not believe I am."

"No, I don't believe you are."

"As you said before, you have no real proof."

"True," she confessed. "But I can't imagine why an artist who creates such beauty would want to kill his own brother or anyone else. And you're definitely the artist in the family."

More of that silence that was filled with a thousand sounds.

"It's more than the drawing," she went on when it likely wasn't necessary. "It was the way you held the pencil…the way your fingers moved with each stroke of the lead against the paper."

Maybe she'd said a little more than was necessary. She shifted her attention forward, drew her knees up to her chest and wrapped her arms around them. "Anyway, I believe you're Paul Reyes."

"You saved my life, I am in your debt."

He was closer somehow…leaning toward her. If she turned toward him now…no, she couldn't do that. Too close—way too close. But the desire to do so was strong. She shivered.

"Are you cold?"

"No."

"When this is done, perhaps I may be able to properly show my gratitude."

That was an invitation for more than simply dinner. Didn't take a crystal ball to pick up on that. She would have had to be deaf not to have noted the nuances of hope and desire and plain old lust in his deep voice.

"You do understand that I'm asking you to my home for a social occasion," he clarified. "That is not something I do often."

"Yes…I understand. I'm just…considering what to say."

He laughed softly. "I am afraid that if you feel compelled to consider what to say, then the answer is perhaps not one I wish to hear."

She laughed, couldn't help the response. Maybe because she was tired…maybe because he was so close, she couldn't get a grip on her emotions. "The answer is yes, okay?"

"Yes. Okay. That is a good answer."

Nature's music crowded in around them again. For the first time since he'd grabbed her in the dark, she felt totally exhausted. She needed sleep, but the threat that could still be out there made her second-guess the idea. Victor's men could show up any second.

"Are you worried that Victor's men will find us?"

He picked up on her feelings far too easily. "The thought crossed my mind."

"We could take turns sleeping."

"That could work."

"You sleep first, I'll keep watch."

Tempting, but letting down her guard wouldn't be a good move. "I'm not sure—"

"Wait. You will sleep better if you are comfortable." He wrapped those long fingers around the arm closest to him and before she could fathom his intent he'd ushered her into his lap. "You saved my life. This is the least I can do for you."

Incredibly, she got the distinct impression that he meant exactly what he said. Had any other guy made this move, she would have been certain he was only trying to get her in his lap.

"Really, I'm okay."

She started to scoot away, but he closed his arms around her and drew her to his solid chest. "This is good. Sleep. Morning will be here before you know it. We will have quite a walk ahead of us."

Or run, she added silently, if Victor's men found their trail again.

Her cheek rested against his shoulder, her face

turned into his neck. She would be lying if she said this wasn't much better. This was…great.

"I fear they will look for us again when it is daylight," he added softly. He sounded resigned to the possibility.

"I think you're right. We have to be prepared for that possibility."

He'd lived here for years. Had recognized that those men were bringing him to the park. Maybe he knew the area.

"Can you find your way out of here?" she asked, hopeful.

"Perhaps."

She bit her lip and sighed wearily. If he thought he knew the way out of here, he would want to lead. She'd have to find a way to deal with that in the morning.

He laughed softly, the sound rumbled deep in his chest. "We will find our way out, or the park rangers will find us. I suspect that is why my brother's men gave up so quickly. The sound of gunfire carries. The fear of being caught by park authorities may have hastened their concession to defeat, at least for the moment."

He'd taken her sigh as worry. Good. "You're right, they're probably long gone for the night."

"You may sleep then, no?"

Sleep. In his lap with his arms around her? Definitely no. She lied, "Yes, thank you." Her body was beginning to heat up in places that weren't conducive to sleep. He appeared to have the same problem, judging by some of the contours nudging her backside. But he was right—if she didn't rest she would be no good tomorrow. Just as he wouldn't be.

Sleep, she ordered. Don't think about his body and the way it felt to be this close to him.

If only those frogs and crickets or whatever they were would lull her to sleep. Things would be much clearer in the morning.

As long as she didn't wake up dead.

Chapter Nine

Friday, May 4th, time unknown

He woke with a start.

Dawn had crept its way through the trees and offered enough light for him to barely make out his surroundings. He had not intended to fall asleep, but exhaustion had eventually claimed him. If Victor's men had not found them by then, he doubted they were still looking in the dark. However, with dawn's arrival, the search would begin anew. Nothing would be left to chance.

He could not be certain, but he sensed that he and Renee were still amid the thirty-eight acres considered traversable park land. This could be helpful. Park rangers frequently roved the area. The chances for rescue were quite significant, whether he could find the way out or not.

This was good.

The woman in his arms still slept soundly. She

would need her strength and her courage to make the journey back to a more civilized trail. There were many trails and narrow roads; it was only a matter of finding one before his brother's men found them.

Perhaps he underestimated her. She had, after all, climbed into that SUV with the intention of doing what she could to help him.

She snuggled against him, the movement of her soft body arousing his to the point of pain. He held his breath until the near overwhelming sensations eased.

On one level, he did not fully trust her, but on all others he wanted to learn all there was to know about her. Her heroic efforts to go out of her way to help him were troubling, as was the timing of her arrival. He could not disprove that she was an art buyer from Los Angeles as she claimed, but her arrival at his home at the same time his brother decided to put his scheme into action seemed too large a coincidence. That she had not run while she had the chance on not one but two occasions did not bode well for her complete innocence in this puzzling scenario. Surely a mere art buyer would have fled for her life at the first opportunity.

Then again, had she done so he would be dead right now.

He wanted to believe her. She had, in fact, saved his life. For that, he owed her his allegiance, at least temporarily.

It had been a very long time since he had allowed anyone close enough to make him wish for things he did not have. He wanted for little and the idea of wanting more seemed far too selfish. Yet he could not push aside this need she had awakened.

If she turned out to be his enemy, he could not say that he would not be disappointed. For now, he would give her the benefit of the doubt. Perhaps she was an adventurer. He spent so little time with others that he was not at all sure his judgment was adequately balanced. Once thing was certain—American women were very different from those of his homeland. Maybe if he had bothered with a social life, he would not be so quick to jump to conclusions regarding a strong, determined woman.

A sound in the distance, a snap or crack, jerked his attention from his foolish thoughts. With the sunrise came a satisfied silence from nature. The insects no longer trilled and the frogs had stopped their deep croaking. There was only the sound of the leaves stirring when the breeze roused them and the occasional splashing of water as the natives to the park went about their morning rituals of survival.

But this sound had not been a noise created by nature.

"Renee," he whispered against her soft hair.

She sat up instantly and looked around.

He touched a finger to his lips.

Another noise grazed his senses, this one slightly closer.

Her eyes widened with recognition. She heard the intrusion as well.

Getting up without making noise was not an easy feat, but necessary all the same. He checked the area where they had spent the night, plumping and straightening the flora to ensure it did not draw attention. After surveying the area around them for the most effective possible route of escape, he took her hand and started the painstaking movement away from the approaching trouble. Waiting to see if a park ranger was simply making his rounds this morning would be too much of a risk. He hastened his step as soon as it appeared safe to do so.

The deeper they moved into the park, the thicker the vegetation. The path grew more narrow as the swamp closed in on dry land. He couldn't be certain that continuing in this direction was safe or logical.

He stopped. She stayed close behind him and did not ask questions. The slightest sound could give away their location. He listened long enough for his heart rate to return to normal and to conclude that trouble had not picked up their trail.

Pushing onward could prove detrimental if help was close by. The thicket of mangrove trees to his right might provide a temporary hiding place until he could determine whether the approaching party was help or trouble. A ranger would be able to radio for help and could direct them to safety much more quickly than he could hope to do with the aid of a compass or map.

He weaved his way through the dense foliage until he reached the thicket he had spotted. The vegetation and soft soil that abutted the trees provided the perfect haven for snakes and alligators. He had no choice but to proceed cautiously and wish for the best.

She stalled.

He looked back, couldn't risk speaking to her. He could only urge her with his eyes and hope she would understand that they had no other choice.

Movement twenty or so meters back the way they had come propelled her into action. She gingerly took the same path he had.

Once stationed behind the mangroves, he permitted a deep breath. They were close now. The fact that those approaching had started to move so quickly, as if they had suddenly picked up a trail, negated the possibility of a park ranger. A ranger would have no need to rush. He was certain this was trouble.

Renee felt the air flee her lungs when one of Victor's men, whom she'd had the misfortune of bumping into twice already since coming to Florida, came into view. She peered between the twisting throng of branches as he came closer. Behind him were two other men. All were heavily armed. As she watched, the men broke ranks, taking off in different directions.

She was certain that the only reason one of them hadn't already approached their position was that they stood in water about twelve inches deep in the snakiest-looking spot she'd seen so far. No one in his right mind would hide here. She shuddered inwardly as she considered those facts.

Even a brief visual examination of the weapons the three carried made her damned glad that Paul had chosen this spot.

Two of the men had disappeared into the woods on either side of the one progressing in their general direction. This one seemed to be in charge, she'd noticed from their previous encounters.

Her heart bounced against the wall of her chest when he continued to move closer and closer to their hiding place. Paul's arm went around her as if he'd sensed her mounting trepidation.

If they were murdered out here, would their bodies be found before the animals ate their fill? She bit down on her lower lip to stop its annoying trembling. Her life had been threatened before. Bomb threats at the courthouse. Warnings that if she proceeded with a case she would be harmed in some way.

But this was a little different. There were no armed sheriff's deputies standing between her and the possibility of danger. And she didn't have a weapon.

There was only this man. She glanced at him from

the corner of her eye. A man who rarely left his home, an artist who likely had little, if any, defensive or offensive training. And sheer determination.

Victor's hired killer stopped as if he smelled or sensed his prey. Renee froze, her heart staggered. The scumbag was no more than ten or twelve feet from their position. Slowly, he scanned the area.

It was at that precise second that Renee faced one of the toughest challenges of her life. If she survived this first mission that had taken a definite turn for the treacherous, this would be, in her estimation, one of the defining moments of her true courage.

Something slithered through the murky water, curved around her left calf, its cold skin sliding against hers, forcing goose bumps to rise on her body like tiny knots of absolute terror. She clenched her jaw. Didn't dare breathe.

Seeming satisfied, the man moved on. So did the snake or whatever the hell had slinked around her leg.

Renee took a jagged breath, let it go. Still, she didn't dare move. The tiniest sound could bring one or all of Victor's men charging back toward their hiding place.

The urge to look behind her was suddenly overwhelming. What if one of the others had made his way around to come up behind them?

Another glance at Paul and she knew he'd considered that very possibility. With his body positioned at a slight angle, he watched behind them for a time before turning his attention back to the more apparent danger. If she looked past his profile, she could see beyond him, as well.

Endless minutes dragged by. If they moved too soon, one of the thugs might hear them. So they held still.

Her legs, above and beneath the water, had started to itch. The way the slinky fabric of her slacks stuck to her skin only make matters worse. The urge to move back onto dry land was almost unbearable. Mosquitoes were feasting on her, but she didn't dare fan them away or swat at the pesky predators.

Jim Colby would be worried if she didn't call in again soon. Obviously Victor hadn't been caught, since his men were still out looking for Paul.

The possibility that Agent Joseph Gates was working against them made her furious. What had he hoped to gain by being a part of this? Their client, Darla Stewart, believed she could trust him. Her dead brother, the cop, had trusted him. That made Gates the lowest of the low. An accessory to a cop killer…to the man responsible for drugs pouring into their country, tainting their youth…such as her own brother.

God, she needed to check on that situation, as well. For all she knew, a new date of execution could have been set. But he didn't want her involved; she had to let that go. Not your problem, she reminded herself, clenching her jaw to hold back the emotion that rose in her throat.

This was her job. Getting this guy safely out of this damned jungle. Helping to bring down a mass murderer and his accomplices.

Focus. Wait until it was clear and then start moving. Get as far away from these bastards as possible.

Locating a park ranger would be good. He would have supplies at his station and the means to get out of here without further incident. She could definitely use a long, cool drink of water about now. But if Victor's men were anywhere around when that happened, the ranger would end up dead, as would the two of them.

Putting as much distance as possible between them and those lowlifes was imperative.

Paul leaned closer, put his lips to her ear. "Let's go."

Nothing would make her happier than getting out of this swamp, but what if they hadn't waited long enough?

"Shouldn't we wait a little longer?" Her lips were so dry the whisper came out roughly. She moistened her lips and willed her heart to slow its sudden hammering.

"I believe it's safe." He eased out of their hiding place first. He barely made a sloshing sound. She hoped she would be as fortunate.

Holding her breath, she climbed out after him. Hardly a sound. Relief washed over her.

Her leather sandals were sodden. Honestly, she didn't know how they had held together this long.

Looking back at the mucky area where they'd hidden, she shuddered.

Paul took her hand and headed back the way they had come.

He moved faster with every step, still taking care to remain as noiseless as possible. She let him lead for now. As long as they were moving away from the danger, she couldn't say she would have done anything differently.

Not much she passed looked familiar. Since she'd been running for her life when she'd come this way and taking time to notice the landscape had been the last thing on her mind, that wasn't surprising. Then it had become dark and she'd had enough trouble avoiding head-on collisions with trees.

Paul hesitated. To get his bearings, she presumed. She scanned the waist-deep underbrush and dense tree population for anything even remotely familiar.

She would have been okay if she hadn't looked up.

Major mistake.

Never in her life, not even in her grandfather's barn, had she seen such massive spiderwebs. They sprawled from tree to tree.

And then she saw the occupants. Big spiders. Some bigger than others, but all huge in comparison to the ones she'd seen in her lifetime. Yellow-and-black-striped legs. Big bodies with red spots.

Fear curled its way around her chest, squeezing out the last of her breath.

She could deal with snakes if necessary. In fact, there wasn't a lot that scared her.

But she hated spiders.

Paul tugged her forward. She stumbled, blinked, then jerked back to the here and now.

"Don't look at them," he murmured.

Wouldn't help. Not now. She knew they were there.

"We must hurry," he urged softly.

He was right.

She forced her feet back into action, refused to look upward again. She didn't want to know if there were more of them.

A shout somewhere behind them sent a new kind of fear gliding through her veins like ice.

"This way."

Paul dragged her back into the densest part of the wilderness around them. The soil was mucky. She knew what that meant—they were headed into water again.

Snakes. Alligators. Lots of friendly critters. She glanced up and shuddered. And spiders.

The heat had already grown stifling. Unlike her, the tropical vegetation appeared to thrive in the desert-like temperatures. All the muck and water, she reasoned. The combination made for an environment literally swarming with life.

Up ahead, she saw an egret. It appeared to consider their approach at length before deciding that taking flight wasn't necessary. The beauty of the wild orchids momentarily took her mind off the idea of spiders and guys with guns.

Paul headed for dryer land, urging her toward a cluster of trees, pine and another species she didn't readily recognize.

The new hiding place was somewhat more bearable, considering they weren't standing in a foot of water. But she could see a narrow, murky strait not far from where they hid. A turtle lay sunning itself in a spot where the sun somehow managed to cut a path through the reigning trees.

Not far from the turtle was a shape that almost blended in with the vegetation. She strained to see if maybe it was just a decomposing tree trunk. Movement warned her it was no rotting log. Big eyes blinked slowly before the greenish black form slid into the water and moved away. Thankfully, the prehistoric-looking creature glided off in the opposite direction from where she and Paul were hiding.

Alligator.

She wondered where the egret had got off to. Her memory was a little sketchy on the eating habits of gators, but she was fairly sure egrets were on their diet.

She had a feeling that Paul's choice in hiding places had more to do with the enemy's movements than comfort.

He leaned close. "They are expanding their search grid. We are going to have to keep moving."

She'd reasoned as much. She met his gaze, saw

the worry there. The cell phone tucked into her bra reminded her that she had that one option, but turning it on might lead the enemy right to them. Jim had told her not to use it unless it was an emergency. "Which way do you want to go?"

Paul inclined his head in the same direction the gator had taken.

Perfect. That would have been her first choice, gator or no gator.

The mucky ground sucked at her feet, made walking hard, made keeping quiet even harder.

As if the Man Upstairs wanted to make things even more interesting, the wind started to kick up. Distant thunder rumbled.

Minutes later, rain was coming down in sheets. She couldn't see the lightning streak the sky, but she could feel the charge in the air and the accompanying thunder kept her ears ringing.

They walked as long as they could in spite of, and mostly against, the weather. When it became impossible to see, Paul ushered her toward a mass of tall tropical vegetation that bordered another copse of gnarled mangrove trees.

She was soaked to the bone. She leaned against a tree and wiped the rain from her face. The downpour was starting to let up and the shield of the thick canopy where they stood helped considerably.

Paul stood near the edge of the cover, watching to ensure they hadn't been followed.

Somehow they had to get out of here. Finding their way out of this jungle was going to be impossible if they had to keep evading their would-be killers and backtracking. Hanging around here was not going to work for lying low. All Victor's men would have to do to win this chase was bring on the dogs for tracking. She couldn't take the risk that the idea would occur to them.

She had to get Paul out of here.

But she couldn't do that if they had to stay hidden.

Her stomach rumbled and she ignored it. Food was way down the priority list just now. Water, however, was essential. All the more reason to try and spot a ranger's station.

The rain let up enough for them to start moving again. The sooner they were out of here, the better.

She joined him at the outer perimeter of their hiding place. "Do you think we should keep going? Try to find our way out or to a ranger station?"

He nodded. "There has been no indication that my brother's men followed us this way. The rain may have sent them seeking cover."

But their paths could always intersect, she didn't bother mentioning. There was no guarantee, no matter how careful they were, that they wouldn't get caught.

She was well rested, thanks to Paul. If she stayed alert and kept moving, they would make it. All she had to do was stay focused.

"This way." He took her hand as he did each time and tugged her after him.

She didn't resist. She had gotten used to the feel of his roughened palm meshed with hers.

IT WAS NOON.

He wiped his forehead with his arm and stared up at the portion of sky he could see through the trees. The heat had created a sauna effect. His clothes had partially dried, but the sweat slowed the process. They had been walking for hours. He was certain Renee was tired and thirsty, as was he.

He could not determine if they were headed in a useful direction. There had been no other indication that the men sent to find them were close by. That, at least, was good. The more distance between them, the better.

Renee pulled on his hand. "Wait."

Turning to face her, he instinctively performed a quick scan of the area. There appeared to be no trouble. His gaze settled on her.

"What's that?"

He looked in the direction she pointed, then strained to better see what appeared to be a dwelling of some sort. Not very large.

"A ranger's station," she suggested hopefully.

"Perhaps."

He considered the corner of the small building, or what looked like a building, a moment longer.

Judging by the level of the light, whatever it was it seemed to be in or near a clearing.

"You stay here," he said to Renee, "until I have checked the situation."

She shook her head. "No way. I'm going with you."

Arguing would be a waste of time. The determined set of her shoulders and the grim line of her mouth warned him that she was not going to be dissuaded.

As they neared the edge of the clearing, the designation of the small building as a ranger station became visible.

He felt very grateful that they had finally reached assistance.

Beyond the ranger station, the tropical forest gave way to a seemingly endless river of saw grass.

He hesitated, listened. It was very quiet. Too quiet. This concerned him for reasons not readily apparent.

Next to him, she noticed, as well. "Is anyone here?"

"The rangers have certain areas to oversee," he offered, as much to convince himself as to convince her, keeping his voice low. "Perhaps this one is out making those rounds."

He told himself that was the case, but there was something about how deserted everything was that did not feel right. His instincts were vibrating with warning.

"Maybe there's water."

She pushed ahead of him, and he hurried to slow her.

"We should proceed with caution."

She stared at him for a moment, and something like trust flashed in her eyes. "You're right."

This understanding or trust softened him, made him feel an even stronger need to protect her. He took her hand and she let him, as before, but this time the accompanying feelings were stronger, deeper. Foolishly he wondered if she felt this connection, as well.

Most likely not.

Together they eased closer to the building. He rounded the corner first and moved to the only door. She was close behind.

The door was not locked. Inside, he found what he had expected—a desk, shelves and cabinets.

But no park ranger.

And no radio.

Renee checked the desk, the shelves and cabinets. "Shouldn't there be a radio?"

He looked around again himself, double-checked the places they had both already considered. "Perhaps the radios are portable and the rangers carry them." This was very disappointing.

"At least there's water." She gathered pouches of water and packets of food from the supply cabinet. She studied the available offerings. "Looks similar to the field rations the military use."

Since they had no choice but to wait for the ranger to return, satisfying their hunger and thirst would be beneficial in the event walking out of here was still necessary. He tore open one corner of a water pouch as per the instructions and passed the pouch to Renee, then opened one for himself. Seated on the desk, they ate the food from the foil packets without conversation. He was certain she was as tired and hungry as he was, which prevented the usual pleasantries.

"How long do you think it'll be before the ranger returns?" she asked. "We could stay here until then. Maybe avoid running into trouble again."

He could not speculate with any accuracy on when the ranger would return. Since the building had been unlocked and food supplies were available, he felt sure someone had been there that day. Why would he leave the door unlocked? The policy didn't seem like a very good one to him, but he wasn't certain of the usual protocol.

"I would not be able to guess under the circumstances." He considered her second question. "We can stay here as long as it feels safe."

She stood, gathered and discarded the empty food and water containers before settling her gaze back on him. "Under what circumstances?"

Sharing his concerns would only make her more uncomfortable, but she had a right to know. "The door was left unlocked. We have been here nearly an hour and no one has returned."

She walked to the window and stared out. "That's what I thought." She turned back to look at him then. "Either the ranger who mans this station is missing in action, or he didn't show up today. In which case, I have to wonder who unlocked the door."

He understood what she was thinking. His brother's men may have been here already, or possibly they had run into the ranger while tracking their prey.

The lock and chain on the desk suggested that the small building was usually locked and that a key had been used to unlock it. Since the place had not been left torn apart, he would assume Victor's men had not been here, or if they had, they had not been inside for more than a quick check to determine if anyone was hidden here.

Renee stood by the window, staring out into the treacherous natural beauty. He set his concerns aside momentarily so that he could admire her. It was a selfish indulgence, but he was weary and in need of inspiration. The ivory-colored slacks were soiled and wrinkled, but they did not detract from her appeal. Her hair was a wild mass but that only made him long to thread his fingers there and feel its silky softness.

"How did the ranger get here?" She swiveled toward him. "You suppose he walked?"

He tugged his thoughts back to less precarious emotional territory and considered the acres of saw grass. "Airboat, perhaps."

She shrugged. "But where is the boat?"

He saw her point. "He could be out on a rescue mission. He may have left in a hurry and forgotten to lock up."

"So we continue to wait?"

He flared his hands. "Unless you would prefer to take our chances out there." He nodded to the wilderness beyond this small shelter. "The ranger will return eventually." If he is able, he added silently.

She regarded his suggestion a moment. "There's food and water here. It's dry." She glanced around the room. "No spiders."

He smiled. "Agreed."

"I vote we stay here. Someone's bound to show up sooner or later," she said resolutely.

"Then we stay."

She walked over to the supply cabinet. "There's toilet paper in here. I think I'll take a walk."

He got to his feet. "We should stay together."

Her hands went up Stop-sign fashion. "Sorry. Not for this."

Before he could argue the point, she walked out the door. If she needed privacy, he could understand that, but he didn't like the idea of allowing her out of his sight.

Two minutes.

If she did not return in two minutes, he mentally ticked off the seconds, he was going after her.

Chapter Ten

Renee surveyed the area she'd chosen once more.

Locating a spot that provided adequate privacy wasn't a problem. She took care of necessary business as quickly as possible, her senses alert to every sound, every movement.

The rain had helped considerably in losing those guys. But how long would their good fortune last? Lying low in the ranger's station could work for a while, but staying in one spot was dicey business.

She glanced around before stepping from the shielding bushes. Clear. The sooner she was back inside with Paul, the safer she would feel.

But first she had to try and get through to Jim again. He'd told her to lie low as long as possible. This seemed like as good a place as any, but she couldn't put off checking in any longer.

She turned on the phone. No service. Damn it. Shutting it off, she shoved it back into her bra and glanced around to make sure it was still clear. When she started forward again something on the ground at the edge of a thicket of dense undergrowth snagged her attention.

She crouched down, stared intently at what appeared to be part of a flashlight. Easing closer, she reached out to touch it.

Hard, plastic. She grasped the yellow surface with her finger tips and dragged it toward her. Definitely a flashlight, but it was stuck…or something.

She pulled a little harder. The flashlight cleared the bushes along with the hand still gripping it.

Renee toppled backward. Clamped her hands over her mouth a split second before a scream escaped.

Her heart pounding mercilessly, she stared at the flashlight and hand. The hand was attached to an arm that disappeared into the bushes.

Don't scream, she commanded herself as she lowered her hands from her mouth. *Don't scream.*

Her arms and legs shaking so badly she could hardly organize her movements, she crept closer to the clump of bushes. She parted the branches and took a look.

Male.

Lying face down.

Uniform.

Definitely dead.

Struggling to control her breathing, she touched the man's hand, the one closest to her and still clasped around the flashlight.

Cold. Stiff. Rigor mortis was already present in the extremities. He'd been dead several hours.

As a woman, she wanted to run back to the ranger station as fast as she could. The logical, trained former prosecutor wanted to determine his identity without further contamination to the crime scene.

She should go get Paul.

Chewing her lower lip, she looked toward the station. That would only waste time.

Just do it. She reached into the back pocket of the dead man's trousers and withdrew his wallet.

Breathing slow and deep through her nose to control the roiling in her stomach, she searched until she found what she needed. Driver's license. Dennis Frisk of Marathon, Florida.

She replaced the wallet and wiped her hands on the legs of her pants. Okay.

She jerked her head up at the sound of foliage rustling.

Someone or something was coming.

She scooted behind the bushes concealing the dead man and willed her lungs to hold the air inside.

Paul's profile came into view.

She let go a breath of relief, then stood.

"You okay?" he asked, not coming any closer.

"I…I think I found the park ranger."

Paul was at her side before her brain acknowledged that he'd moved.

She crouched next to him as he squatted down to

take a look. He touched the man's neck to check his carotid artery. She noticed the strange angle of his head then. Whoever had killed him had done so up close and personally by snapping his neck.

A shudder quaked through her.

Paul started to turn the man over.

"What're you doing?" She grabbed his arm to stop him. "This is a crime scene." She was certain he realized that, but apparently he didn't comprehend the rules that went along with that designation. And why would he? she realized too late to take back the words.

His gaze collided with hers. "Looking for a radio or cell phone."

Oh. She should have thought of that. She also should have thought of how he might view her resolve not to violate a crime scene. Not exactly something a regular civilian would think of in a situation like this. Maybe he would assume she'd been watching too many crime scene dramas on television. The fact that she had checked the victim's wallet had been instinct.

And he was right about one thing. They needed help. A radio or phone that actually got service out here would make life a lot easier. Even as an officer of the court, she recognized that end would certainly be a legitimate reason to take the risk of breaching a crime scene. The idea that he might find her ability to be this close to a dead guy without falling apart unusual had her taking steps to undo that image.

She looked away as if the sight were far too gruesome to endure.

Paul exhaled a heavy breath. "Let's go back inside."

She met his gaze and nodded. He pulled the flashlight loose, in case they needed it, she supposed, then offered his free hand to her.

She placed her hand in his and allowed him to assist her to her feet.

This ranger's death couldn't have been coincidence. The men looking for them had done this. She was certain. This was the way she and Paul would end up if they didn't get out of here first.

Inside the small station, she hugged her arms around herself and paced. How the hell could they get out of here? Clearly, lying low here was not a good idea. They had no idea which way to go. There were at least three men out there searching for them.

They were screwed if she didn't get her act together and come up with a new plan.

She should have a better handle on the situation. Think. Her frustration gave way to determination. She had to look at this like a trial. When the case started to crumble, you backed up and regrouped. Revised and rerouted.

Standing around here wondering if they would be rescued or murdered was not the right course of action. She turned her attention to her companion, who seemed to be studying a map.

"We should find our way out of here before it gets dark," she announced.

Paul glanced up. "I agree. I think I've located our position on this map."

"Excellent."

She went back to the supply cabinet and grabbed a couple of packets of water and joined him at the desk. She handed the water pouches to him. "Put one in each pocket. I don't have any pockets or I'd do it."

He did as she suggested, then pointed to the map. "We are here," he said in that vaguely accented voice that made her shiver with something that definitely wasn't fear. "We need to reach this location." He pointed to another spot on the map. "There is a lodge and a café. Perhaps we can find transportation there."

Sounded like a plan.

"Can you get us there?" As long as he thought his help was crucial to their survival, chances were he'd stay close to her. She needed him to believe they were in this together. They were, to a degree. He just didn't need to know why she was involved. His co-operation was essential. The other side of that was the idea that she wanted him close…maybe more than she wanted to admit.

He looked at the map again, then at her. "I believe so." He tucked the flashlight into the back pocket of his jeans. "It's quite a distance. We might not make it before dark."

She nodded her understanding. "We'll give it our best shot."

Outside, she hesitated. Any cop worth his salt would likely argue her reasoning, but she just couldn't walk away like this. It might be hours before Frisk was found. He'd most likely been murdered early in his shift, but who knew what time his relief would come. "We should move his body inside." It was a miracle the carnivores hadn't been after him already.

"You keep watch. I will move the body."

He'd get no argument from her. She was happy to allow her companion to play the "guy" on that score.

Once Frisk's body was in the station, they headed back into the heart of the forest with Paul leading. He'd studied the map. The sun was still high in the sky; the time was maybe two or two-thirty. That left about four or four and a half hours until dark.

They had to move fast. She did not want to spend another night out here with Victor's men tromping around after them.

THEY FOUND THE LODGE shortly after dusk.

If she hadn't been so exhausted, she would have thrown her arms around Paul and kissed him. She told herself that it was nothing more than gratitude, but that was a lie. He'd done a great job of leading them out of the wilderness. It might have taken her twice as long. Working together as a team had proven much more useful than allowing him to know that, for now, he was ultimately her hostage. She didn't need a weapon or threats to keep him close, cultivating his trust had worked far better.

Until they had Victor Reyes in custody, Paul was their ace in the hole. But he didn't need to know that. The instant he realized what she was up to, he would likely bolt. She didn't believe for an instant that he would want to help his brother in any way. But she doubted that he would choose this route to stop him. The image of the two of them battling to the death made her shudder inwardly.

They remained in the edge of the woods and watched before moving forward.

"Three of the rooms are occupied."

Looked that way to her, too. The other rooms were dark, with no vehicles parked in the designated slots. "I count ten vehicles total. The others must be patrons of the café."

"Or employees."

She agreed. No black SUV, but that didn't mean Victor's men weren't around. There could be a whole lot more than the three she'd met so far. She couldn't be sure what other makes of vehicles they might have at their disposal.

Only one way to find out.

One of them had to go in. Putting him at that kind of risk was out of the question.

It had to be her.

Using her fingers as a comb, she attempted to tame her hair. She smoothed her blouse as best she could. Her clothes were dry, if not clean. "I'm going in."

He put a hand on her arm. "No. I'll go in."

She shook her head. "If any of his men are hanging around in there they might not recognize me, but they'll damned sure know you." Paul and Victor were practically twins; neither could deny the family tie.

"No." Paul's grip tightened.

His protectiveness made her feel warm inside even as it annoyed her. She could get used to the whole I'll-take-care-of-you mentality…to a degree, she amended. But now wasn't the time. "I'll be okay." She gently tugged her arm free of his hand. "Just stay out of sight until I check out the situation."

"Three minutes," he warned. "If you are not back in three minutes, I will come for you."

"Give me five, okay?" Since he didn't have a watch, she wasn't sure how he intended to accurately measure the time. Better a little more than not enough.

He didn't agree, but he didn't argue, either.

He needn't have worried. She wasn't about to allow him out of her sight any longer than absolutely necessary.

At the entrance to the restaurant, she smoothed her hand over her hair once more and took a deep, bolstering breath. She looked like hell, but there wasn't a lot she could do about it.

Now or never.

She opened the door and stepped inside. The scents of grilled and fried foods had her stomach grumbling. Thankfully there was no hostess to way-lay her. A dozen tables with Formica tops and chairs sporting yellowed white vinyl seats filled the black-and-white-tiled dining area. A buffet-style bar took up a good portion of one side of the room. A couple of patrons perused the selections, plates in hand. Double doors led into the kitchen.

The cashier was busy ringing up a customer. Renee walked over to the counter and picked up a menu. She peered over the menu instead of at it so that she could survey the occupants of each table. No one that looked familiar to her. Most were families. Husband, wife and children. She doubted any of Victor's henchmen would be traveling with their families. If the world were lucky, those guys wouldn't be procreating.

"Did you want to place a take-out order?"

Renee laid the menu aside and produced a smile. Just when she'd decided she didn't have a plan, in-spiration struck.

"No. I'm here to see my cousin." She gestured to the busboy who was clearing a table across the room. "Thanks anyway."

The cashier shrugged and turned her attention to wiping the counter.

Renee wet her chapped lips and considered a moment what she intended to say to the young guy she'd claimed was her cousin. Tall, skinny, blond hair, good tan and old enough to drive. He didn't look up until she'd walked all the way over to the table where he worked. "Hi." She hung on to her smile. "Looks slow around here tonight."

He surveyed the room. "You shoulda been here earlier. It was a madhouse."

This was a whole hell of a lot harder without a gun. She had no choice but to rely on her powers of persuasion. At least in the courtroom she had a captive audience. It wasn't like the jury was going to tell her to get lost or run out on her.

"Look," she said, finally latching onto an idea that didn't include the phrase *help me out or I might just end up dead,* "I hate to bother you while you're working, but my car won't start. I think the battery's dead. I was wondering if you'd give me a jump."

A frown tugged at his expression as he looked around at the four or five tables that needed to be cleared. Evidently he'd been right. She'd gotten here right after the rush.

"Please," she urged. "I really could use your help."

He sighed. "Okay. Where's your car? I'm out back."

"I'm right out front."

"Come on." He grabbed the shallow tub of dirty dishes. "I have to get my keys."

"Thanks. I really appreciate it."

Renee followed him through the kitchen. Two

cooks and a dishwasher glanced up, but didn't bother looking for more than a second or two.

Her busboy settled his load onto the stainless steel counter next to the guy washing dishes by hand. "I'll be right back."

"You shouldn't be taking a smoke break until all those tables are bused," the dishwasher groused. "You get behind, I get behind."

The busboy flipped him off as he grabbed his keys from the table by the rear exit. The dishwasher rolled his eyes and dived back into his work. Renee kept that stupid smile tacked in place as she followed the young man out the back door. She hoped the dishwasher didn't get suspicious and come out to see what they were up to.

"He's a jerk," the busboy said, then motioned to the blue pickup truck that easily fit into the category of antique. "That's mine. Hop in. We'll drive around to where your car is parked." He shot her a smile. "My name's Kenny, by the way."

"Renee," she returned as she climbed into the passenger seat as he slid behind the wheel. "You live around here?"

"Florida City," he said as he lit up a smoke and then, as if out of consideration for her, he rolled down his window. "How 'bout you?"

She shook her head. "Just visiting. I took a trip in the park that ended badly."

He started the engine and pulled the gearshift into

Reverse as he looked her up and down. "You get lost out there?"

She started to lie, but decided that since she undoubtedly looked like that was exactly what had happened she might as well 'fess up. "Yeah. Spending the night in a swamp wasn't exactly how I pictured this vacation going," she fibbed. "I don't think I'll be coming back anytime soon."

He grinned. "Folks get lost all the time. They still come back."

Not me, she didn't bother saying. She'd seen all the nature she cared to for a long time to come. Give her the streets of Chicago anytime. She didn't have a problem with danger, but she'd take the threat of thugs in city alleys over alligators in the wilderness any day.

He drove around the end of the building and braked. "Which one's yours?" He surveyed the vehicles in the main parking area.

Now came the tricky part. "I was wondering—" Surely they wouldn't fire him if he drove her and Paul into town. She was just desperate enough to ask anyway. It was either that or ask to borrow his truck. She doubted the latter would go over very well.

A big black SUV rolled up to the front of the café and parked.

For three full seconds, her mind refused to register what her eyes saw. Then the two men whose faces were permanently burned on several of her brain cells got out of the vehicle and she was forced to acknowledge that it was really them.

Which put a totally different spin on things.

"Hey, Renee, which car is yours?" the driver griped. "I have to get back in there or my uncle'll be big-time mad."

So much for the power of persuasion. Her attention turned back to the driver. "What did you say your name was?"

His frown deepened. "Kenny."

"Look, Kenny." She watched the two men enter the café. Evidently the third man was dead, lost or in another vehicle. "Those guys who just went inside are after me." Her gaze locked with his. "They're really bad dudes. I need to get out of here." Now for the possible deal breaker. "I need to borrow your truck."

At his confused look, she added, "I'll leave it parked in town. You can pick it up tomorrow."

He laughed, the sound lacked any humor. "You're joking, right?"

"Sorry. No."

His jaw slackened in surprise, but then he said, "Look, this isn't really my truck. I could get in big trouble if my dad finds out."

She stared straight into his eyes and told him the truth. "I could get dead."

"Get out of the truck," a deep, Latin-influenced voice rumbled.

Renee's gaze shot past the busboy to the man who jerked the driver's side door open.

"Get out," Paul reiterated in case the kid didn't get it the first time.

"What the hell's going on here?" Kenny turned to her. At her shrug, he demanded, "Are you two for real?"

"Just let us borrow your truck, Kenny," she urged, "and everything will be fine."

Kenny shoved the gearshift into Park, and got out. Paul climbed in behind the wheel and jammed the transmission into Drive once more. He jammed his foot against the accelerator and the vehicle rocketed forward.

"That was totally unnecessary," she grumbled as she watched Kenny stalk back off toward the rear of the building. If he went in there and announced what had just happened, which he most likely would, those guys would be out here on their tail so fast. Damn. They should have just brought the kid with them. But then he might have got hurt.

"You weren't having such good luck convincing the young man to cooperate."

She didn't argue with him. She kept her attention on the front of the café. No sign of Victor's men yet. She didn't know if the head start they were gaining would be enough, but it was something.

The café was almost out of sight when the door flew open and two men burst out.

"Damn it!"

"They're coming?"

"They're coming." There was no way in hell they were going to outrun these guys in this old truck.

"Turn off somewhere!"

"What?" Paul demanded.

"Turn. Left. Right. It doesn't matter. Just turn!"

Paul made a sharp left turn. Tires squealed and Renee barely stayed in her seat.

The truck bumped over the rougher gravel side road.

"Turn off the headlights," she urged. "Hurry!"

Paul shut off the lights. He drove a short distance, parked and cut the engine.

They turned simultaneously to watch the main road they'd abandoned in such a hurry.

One minute turned into two, then three.

If they were lucky the bastards would drive right on by. But if they slowed...if they used a spotlight or something to look...they were done for.

The black SUV roared past.

Renee breathed a major sigh of relief.

"Good call," Paul said softly.

"We should just sit tight for a while." She relaxed into the seat.

He leaned his head back and exhaled loudly. "Another good call."

The night sounds of the Everglades invaded the interior of the truck. The air was thick with humidity.

She turned toward the man behind the wheel. She couldn't really see him, just the outline of his profile. But she didn't need to see. She had memorized the way he looked, the way his lips moved when he spoke. Such a kind, restrained man. How could he be the brother to such a violent, evil being?

"You have something to say?"

The sound of his voice made her shiver. She shifted in her seat, faced forward. This was not the time to feel this damned attraction. As if she had any control over how her body reacted to the sound of the man's voice.

"No…I'm just trying to figure out where we go from here." At least that was what she should be doing.

"He will not stop."

She turned toward him once more. Part of her wanted to tell him that she knew how this kind of betrayal felt. Having one's brother play the part of deceiver made the devastation all the worse. She could not think about that right now. It was a miracle she and Paul were both still alive. Getting bogged down in her past would not promote staying that way.

She had to stay focused on the present.

"I know," she agreed, her own voice as somber as his had been. Victor would not give up until one of them, he or Paul, was dead.

"Who are you, Renee Parsons?"

She could lie some more. Maintain her cover until she could contact Jim Colby and bring Paul to safety. But that wouldn't change a thing. Without Victor, all of this would be for nothing. And there was no guarantee that if Paul knew the truth, particularly the part about how she'd kept the truth from him, that he would cooperate.

She needed him to finish this.

There was no point in adding more lies to the growing mass already mounting between them. They were way past that.

Her best bet—until she could come up with a better plan—was to distract him.

Once the notion was born, there was no stopping putting thought into action. She leaned toward him, kissed his jaw, just the lightest brushing of her lips against that warm skin. The quivering sensations that bombarded her stole her breath. The fingers of his right hand fisted in her hair before she could draw away. He pulled her closer so that he could claim her mouth with his. She opened at his touch, parted her lips for his complete possession.

His touch was tender yet thorough. This was a slow, utter indulgence of the senses. His lips felt firm and somehow soft and smooth. Slowly, his left hand moved up over her torso to settle on her breast. She whimpered at this touch, wanted to do something with her hands, as well. Her fingers splayed on his chiseled jaw, delved into his silky hair. She wanted to be closer. Needed to mesh more fully with him. An urgency swam through her blood, making her ache for more than just this kiss. She wanted him to hold her in his arms as he'd done last night.

His tongue delved into her mouth, slid over places she had never known to be so sensitive before. She trembled, felt the tension begin to build. Impossible. They were still fully dressed. He couldn't bring her to this place with just a kiss.

And yet here she was. Close to the edge.

She moaned, panted with the rising need. She wanted more than this. She wanted…

Victor's killers could come back at any second.

Renee pulled free of his possessive kiss.

She reminded herself to think about what the hell she was doing.

"We're not safe out in the open like this."

His hesitation had her heart lunging into her throat. What if he insisted on questioning her further? What if…

"Where shall we go?"

The strain in his voice could be about his own desires…or it could be a thinning of his patience. No time to dwell on that.

"We could go back to my hotel. They won't expect us to risk going back there."

"And then?"

He was looking at her. There wasn't enough light for her to see his eyes, only the shadow of his face.

But he was looking straight at her. He wanted answers. He deserved answers.

Just not right now.

"Then we'll figure this out."

Chapter Eleven

Key Largo
7:45 p.m.

"It doesn't look good, Mr. Johnson."

Sam Johnson regarded DEA Agent Joseph Gates for a moment before he responded. "There's no blood. No sign of a struggle. Nothing." Sam stared out the wall of windows at the fantastic view of the ocean that served as a permanent backdrop to the property of Paul Reyes. "It's as if no one was ever here." His gaze met that of Agent Gates again. "Except for the fact that her rental car is out front. I find that disturbing, Agent."

Gates nodded. "As do I, but you have to understand, Johnson, this is Victor's M.O."

Sam had gone to Renee Vaughn's hotel first thing that morning and found nothing. The woman was just as neat with her toiletries as she was with her paperwork at the office. Then he'd checked out this place. The home of Paul Reyes was clean.

Almost as if someone had wiped every damned surface to ensure nothing would be found. Vaughn had told Colby that the DEA had torn the place apart. There was absolutely no indication the house had been searched. In Sam's experience, when a place was this clean, it probably had been wiped. The motive in this case eluded him. If Victor was in-country, why? Why take the risk? What was he after? Better yet, what or who was after him?

And if Vaughn was certain that the man traipsing through the Florida Everglades with her was Paul Reyes, then who the hell was this guy?

Sam leveled his attention on the other man in the room—the one claiming to be Paul Reyes. "How many men usually accompany Victor?" he asked. According to what Vaughn had told Colby, two had escorted them from this location.

"A minimum of two."

"Mr. Reyes, are you sure there was nothing taken from your home? No money, passport, nothing?" Sam didn't like this guy. Maybe because he had reason to believe he was lying; Vaughn's word counted, in his opinion. Whatever the case, he just didn't care for the jerk.

The man claiming to be Paul Reyes had agreed to cooperate after reporting a run-in with his brother's men, who had abducted Renee Vaughn. He had barely gotten away.

Reyes moved his head slowly from side to side.

"I'm afraid, Mr. Johnson, that my brother is quite self-sufficient. I would have nothing of consequence to him. We have not spoken in many years."

"Why do you suppose he came here looking for you?" This was the part that stuck in Sam's craw. Victor Reyes stayed clear of American territory for fear of being arrested. Why would he show up at his brother's Key Largo residence out of the blue, so to speak? Why kidnap Vaughn? How could he have known who she was or that she was here to lay a trap for him?

According to Vaughn, Victor was attempting to assume Paul's identity, thus allowing Paul to take the fall for his crimes. Made sense, if it were doable. The two could pass for twins, and neither had a lot of paper on who he was. Lack of dental records, finger-prints, et cetera, left the possibilities wide open.

"I can only assume that he was warned that some-one had been sent here to use me against him. Per-haps he intended to not only stop your friend, but also to ensure I could no longer be a trifle to him. Or perhaps he believed Ms. Vaughn was someone im-portant to me, and he wants to use her to lure me into some sort of trap. I can only guess."

To Sam's way of thinking, the identity theft was the most likely scenario, but even it had major holes in the timing and success possibilities. Men like Victor Reyes simply didn't act without covering all the bases. Playing it safe was how he'd avoided prosecution all these years. Seemed a little strange for him to deviate from that strategy now. "How do you suppose he learned that Vaughn wasn't Renee Parsons?" Sam proposed. "There was only one person who knew about this operation besides my people." He turned to Gates, his expression openly accusing. "Isn't that right, Agent Gates?"

The agent's gaze narrowed. "Are you accusing me of something, Mr. Johnson?"

Sam shrugged. "I haven't decided yet."

"I am sorry, Mr. Johnson," Reyes said, shattering the tension suddenly pushing the air out of the room. "I have no idea how my brother knew anything. Personally, I was completely fooled by Renee." He looked to Gates and then back to Sam. "I was under the impression that she was an art buyer from Los Angeles, just as she said."

Maybe so. "You have no hired help?" Sam wanted to know. "No one who can confirm your activities during the past forty-eight hours? Or who could report those activities to your brother?"

Reyes lifted his expensively clad shoulders and allowed them to fall once more. "You may ask Mallory Rogers, the art gallery owner with whom I do business, or any of my neighbors. I have no staff and I seldom leave my home, other than for occasional gallery showings."

"No shopping?" Sam pried. "No dates?" The idea that he insisted he rarely left the home didn't quite sit right with Sam. This guy had that whole macho attitude going on, from the clothes to the way he held himself—shoulders back, feet wide apart, chin lifted arrogantly. Someone who was spending some major bucks. Sam had worked around the celebrities in the Los Angeles area long enough to recognize designer rags. Not to mention the car and the furnishings. Didn't act like any recluse Sam had ever encountered.

"All my needs are brought here to me," Reyes insisted. "I have no need for a staff. A service comes in once per week to take care of the housekeeping. I'm never here when they come. As I said, anything I need is delivered right to my door."

Sam cocked his head and eyed him with mounting suspicion. Suspicion he didn't mind sharing with his new pals. "Are your female friends delivered here to you as well?"

"Mr. Johnson," Gates said, his tone reprimanding, "We are very fortunate that Mr. Reyes has agreed to cooperate fully with us. Let's not go out of our way to insult him for no reason."

"Sorry." Sam wasn't. The only thing he felt was more suspicious of the man claiming to be Paul Reyes. Something was off here; he just hadn't put his finger on what it was yet. But he would. Vaughn would have her reasons for believing the man with her was Paul Reyes. Sam's only hesitation was the idea that the real Victor Reyes would have the nerve to stand in the room with the DEA all around him and not even flinch.

But then, the guy was one sick SOB from what he'd read in Reyes's file.

"I hope," Reyes offered with a sincerity Sam couldn't deny visually, "that your friend is safe, Mr. Johnson. My brother is a vicious killer. If I can help you stop him, I would very much like to do so."

Sam needed to touch base with Jim Colby and give him an update, but he had just one more question. "Why the sudden change of heart?" he asked Reyes. "For years, the DEA has attempted to nail your brother. You've never offered to help before. What'd you do, wake up with a conscience this morning?"

Gates shifted with his escalating discomfort at Sam's attitude, but he kept his mouth shut on this one. Sam didn't really care if Gates liked him or not. He wasn't here to make friends.

For three tension-filled beats, he wasn't sure the man would respond to his blatantly skeptical question about his moral standards.

"I do not agree with Victor's way of life," Reyes said with equal bluntness, "but he is my brother. However, when his men came into my home and tried to kill me, he crossed the line. He is no longer my brother."

Sam nodded. He understood perfectly. If Gates hadn't liked his line of questioning thus far, he sure as hell wasn't going to like this. "So, you didn't care how many kids he was killing with his drugs, but the minute he endangered you, you're happy to come forward. Do I have that straight?"

"Johnson," Gates warned.

Reyes held up a hand. "It is all right, Agent. I understand Mr. Johnson's meaning perfectly. Yes, I suppose I loved my brother more than I should have. That is my mistake. I shall carry that burden with me for the rest of my life. But now I am prepared to do the right thing. I will help you in whatever way possible. Let me do this, Mr. Johnson, and perhaps the Father in Heaven will have mercy on my soul."

Sam searched his face, his eyes. Maybe this guy was on the up-and-up. Maybe not. Sam would reserve judgment until he had the lowdown from Vaughn. Whatever the case turned out to be, he'd made his point. "I was out of line," he admitted to get back in the good graces of the agent glaring at him. Sam pulled his cell phone from his pocket. "I have to check in with my office." He started to turn away, but hesitated. "There is one other thing, Mr. Reyes, that might be helpful to my investigation."

"Whatever I can do," Reyes repeated.

"Since you and your brother look so much alike and neither of you have ever been printed for any reason, it would be great if we could dig up some identifying physical trait that would confirm who's who. Or better yet, medical or dental records. Can you help with that?"

Gates exhaled his frustration. "Now you're accusing Mr. Reyes of lying about who he is," he suggested.

Sam smiled. "You have to admit, that's about the only way any of us are ever going to know for sure."

"He is right," Reyes agreed. "This must be settled once and for all. Perhaps I can assist you with this matter. You are correct, my brother and I are very similar from the outside. But there are differences."

"I'll need more than just your word," Sam challenged.

Gates interrupted, "You know we don't have any medical or dental records on the Reyes brothers."

"Actually," Reyes interjected, "I may have something useful."

Tension rippled through Sam. How convenient.

"What're you talking about, Paul?" Gates wanted to know, evidently as surprised to hear this as Sam.

"I may have indisputable proof," Reyes assured, then he smiled. "You will see. I am Paul Reyes. If your friend is still alive, and I pray that she is, it is most definitely my brother Victor who is with her."

Chapter Twelve

Time Unknown

What was she hiding from him?

Paul looked both ways before pulling out onto the long deserted stretch of highway.

He was still grappling with this powerful emotion that had taken him by the throat the instant their lips met. He struggled to focus on driving. Victor's men could decide to turn around and come back at any moment. He had to be prepared.

But he couldn't stop thinking about her.

She sat within arm's reach, the taste of her still on his lips.

Never had he felt such a fierce need to claim a woman. The urge was primal and certainly unreasonable. He knew very little about Renee Parsons, and he suspected that she was not being fully honest with him.

No, he did not suspect, he *knew*.

Logic did not stop him from wanting her so very badly.

Perhaps the insanity that had descended upon his life just over one month ago, combined with running for their lives for the past thirty or more hours, had driven him to this place of ill reason. He could not say for sure.

He released a breath of frustration and tightened his grip on the steering wheel.

For now, survival was of primary importance. His first objective must be to get Renee to a safe place, and then he would do what he already knew he must.

Face Victor.

Otherwise this would never end.

One of them had to die. There was no pretending anymore.

"What is the name of your hotel?" he asked, shattering the suffocating silence.

"The—"

She twisted around in the seat. "Oh, God. It's them."

"What?" He stared at the rearview mirror. Headlights bobbed as a vehicle pulled onto the road from a side road just as they had done not more than five minutes prior.

Even as he watched the vehicle roared closer, the headlights bearing down on them.

"Faster! You have to go faster," she shouted.

He floored the accelerator. The old truck lurched forward.

"Dammit! No signal."

He glanced at her. She held a cell phone in her hand. Where had that come from? The boy? Kenny? Had she found it in this truck?

She reached across his lap. "They're going to ram us. You need to get your seat belt on." She snapped the old-fashioned lap belt into place.

The SUV bumped them before she could get her own snapped around her hips.

Renee slammed into the dash.

He grabbed for her, then swerved to keep from hitting the ditch.

"I'm okay!" She rubbed the side of her head. "Just drive!"

He heard her lap belt snap, and he relaxed a fraction. At least until he glanced at the rearview mirror. "They're coming again!"

He braced against the steering wheel. Renee moved her feet into position on the dash to brace for the crash.

The impact sent the old truck spinning off the road.

Paul tried to control the vehicle, but there was no use.

The truck roared into the underbrush, coming to a rocking halt in the muck.

"Get out!" she shouted as she struggled with her seat belt. "Run!"

He released the latch of his seat belt and shoved the door open.

Doors slamming jerked his attention to the side of the road some twenty meters away.

They were coming.

"Get out, Paul!" she urged. "My door is jammed."

He stumbled out, his feet sinking into water up to his knees. She scrambled out behind him.

"Run!"

Too late.

"Don't move or you're dead."

Renee put her hands up. No need to pretend. They were caught. Better alive and captured, than fleeing and dead.

"Good girl," one of the jerks said as he reached for her.

"Don't touch her," Paul growled.

The sound of a fist connecting with his jaw made Renee's stomach clench.

"Give me your hands," the other scumbag demanded of Paul.

He thrust out his hands, but didn't take his eyes off her. She tried to tell him with her eyes to stay calm, to let them do this, but she wasn't sure he could see the urgency she needed him to. The moonlight was brighter than last night, especially considering they were clear of the trees, but it was still damned dark.

"Let's go."

Her personal scumbag shoved her toward the SUV. She didn't give him any grief. She climbed the slight embankment and headed for the vehicle. Thankfully, Paul did the same.

Renee was loaded into the front passenger seat while Paul was pushed into the back.

"Make one mistake and I'll blow his brains out," the lowlife climbing into the backseat said to her, as if she didn't get the point of the gun jammed into Paul's temple.

They drove back to Key Largo, but didn't go to Paul's house. Instead they went to a house on the low-rent side of the village. Once inside, she and Paul were forced into what might have been a master bedroom. The carpet had seen better days, and there wasn't a stick of furniture. To her supreme relief there was an en suite bath. The windows in both rooms had been boarded up on the inside, and there was nothing in the bathroom except the fixtures.

One of the men patted her down, didn't find anything, and then moved on to Paul.

She'd lost the cell phone in the truck when they crashed, so she didn't have anything for them to find. Neither did Paul.

"What are we doing here?" she demanded when the man was about to leave them in the room.

He hesitated at the door just long enough to look back at her. *"We,"* he said smugly, "are waiting for our next orders. You two are waiting to die."

The door slammed behind him, and a lock was snapped into place.

She took a moment to picture that guy with a bullet between his eyes, then she exhaled as if ridding her body of the foul thought.

"Let's see if we can get each other untied," she said to Paul. He stood very still watching her. She wasn't sure whether he was in shock or had decided that he couldn't trust her. She didn't want him to start asking questions again. At this point, the last thing they needed was doubts between them.

His hands were bound tightly. Too tightly; blood seeped past the ropes around his wrists. Bastards.

She struggled with the first knot until she got it loose. The second one was a bit easier to free. Pretty soon, the nylon rope fell away.

Taking his turn, he worked with the rope binding her until he'd freed her hands.

"Thank you." She rubbed her wrists where the rope had chaffed the skin.

"You're bleeding."

He touched her forehead just above her right eye. She winced.

"Come."

He took her hand as he had several times during their journey through the Everglades and led her into the cramped bathroom. There was no soap or towels, but there was water. As she watched, he ripped off a piece of his shirt and rinsed it over and over, until he was satisfied that it was as clean as it was going to get. Gently, he dabbed at the injury on her forehead.

His face was intent on her, his hand shaking ever so slightly as he worked.

She'd caught a glimpse of herself in the mirror and it was a pretty scary sight. A shower would be great. And clean clothes. But she feared that neither of those things were going to do her any good.

If they didn't get out of here, they were both dead.

"We need bandages." He frowned as he studied the small gash.

She was pretty sure stitches wouldn't be necessary, but a couple of butterfly tapes would be useful. "I'll be fine."

He dropped his hands to his sides. He looked tired and defeated. She wished there was something she could say to lighten the situation, but there wasn't. This was bad. Really bad.

She took the piece of fabric he'd used as a cleaning cloth from him and rinsed it repeatedly. Then she washed his wrists where the rope had torn the skin. She tossed the cloth into the sink and smiled at him. "Now we're both good." It was a lie, but it sounded upbeat.

He settled that dark gaze on hers. "We have a problem, Miss Parsons."

That was the understatement of the decade. "Yes, we definitely have a problem." She glanced around the tiny bathroom. "But for every problem, there's an answer. We just have to find it."

Was that trepidation she saw in his eyes?

"This is a different problem."

A frown furrowed across her brow, making the gash sting. "I don't understand."

"I want very much to make love to you right now, but we have a dilemma." He glanced toward the door leading back into the bedroom. "The timing is not so good."

The heat his admission inspired was nothing short of an inferno. She restrained the need to grab him by the shirt front and show him he wasn't the only one feeling that way. That kiss had set her on the edge and, despite being nabbed by Victor's men, that need still hummed inside her. "You're right, the timing stinks."

For what must have been a full minute or maybe two, the silence expanded between them. She couldn't remember the last time she'd felt this awkward.

He wanted her. Her gaze settled on his face. She wanted him. There was a very good chance that they were going to die in the next few hours.

What the hell.

"Perhaps, I have misread—"

Her next move stalled whatever he'd intended to say. She grabbed him by the shirtfront just as she'd imagined doing and kissed him hard on the lips.

She drew back just far enough to draw in a breath. "The next move is yours," she said when he did nothing but continue to stare at her mouth.

Her challenge prompted him into action. He

peeled her blouse up her body and over her head, then dropped it to the floor. For long seconds he admired her breasts, his breathing growing rapid and uneven.

She gasped when his fingertips grazed the tender flesh at the small of her back as he reached around to lower the zipper of her slacks. She shivered…urged him to hurry.

Paul tried to hurry, but his hands were shaking. She was beautiful. He wanted to see all of her… every shadow and curve. Her skin was so soft and warm. He wanted to taste it. Unable to resist, he pressed his mouth to her shoulder. She quivered, and his body jolted with an answering ripple of pleasure.

He ushered her slacks down her legs, following the fabric downward so that he could lift first one foot and then the other to free her of that encumbrance altogether. He slipped her sandals off, set them aside. While he knelt in front of her, his fingers curled in the lacy fabric of her panties and glided the sensuous material down and off as he had the slacks.

When he stood, before he could unbutton his shirt, she had taken control. She released each button, then pushed the shirt off his shoulders, allowing it to fall to the floor. And then she removed his sneakers and trousers as he had done hers.

When her soft fingers eased his briefs downward, he caught his breath. She pressed a soft kiss against his hip, allowing his erection to nuzzle her shoulder. He shuddered at the incredible vision of her kneeling before him.

He pulled her to her feet and braced her against the wall. He groaned when his body meshed fully with hers. The contrast of her smooth, soft flesh against his hard body was almost unbearable. She reached up to touch his face, her hand trembled. He kissed those trembling fingers and slid his palms around her waist and up her torso to her jutting breasts.

She cried out as he squeezed. His own body jerked with mounting need. He continued to massage and knead those full, lush breasts, her urgent pleas driving him mad. He nuzzled his face in her hair, loved the silkiness of it.

He lifted her, settled her against his waist. The tip of his erection pressed against the damp heat waiting for him. Never before had he wanted anything this much.

"Hurry," she urged.

He shook his head and smiled. "No hurry."

He started at the tip of her nose. He kissed her slowly, thoroughly, learning each new part. Her closed lids. The line of her jaw. The hollow of her throat. That place between her breasts where her heart beat so frantically. And then he suckled each breast until she writhed against him. Her hands moved over his back, her legs wrapped around his waist. She wiggled, tried to usher her bottom down onto him, but he would not allow the full contact…not yet.

Renee couldn't take any more of this. If they were interrupted…she might just die. They had to hurry.

"Stop," she cried.

His head came up, those dark sexy eyes glassy with desire. "You wish me to stop?"

Just looking at him nearly made her come. "No," she said, her voice thick with lust. "I want you inside me. Now."

Those brown, almost black eyes searched hers. She couldn't bear it. She kissed him. Let her lips meld with those firm, full male ones that could work such utter magic.

With one arm around her and using the other for leverage, he lowered her onto that generous erection that had her so hot and bothered.

He flexed his hips, pushed inside her…not all the way but enough to have her moaning with the incredible sensation. He kissed her harder. She shifted her hips, needing more. His body trembled. Finally, he was at the same place as she was, and instinct took over. He thrust deeper.

His lips pulled away from hers just a fraction. "Is that where you want me?"

"Yes." She nipped at his bottom lip.

He moved slowly at first, making her crazy, making her sweat. She pleaded with him to hurry. He ignored those pleas, choosing instead to go painfully slow and ever deeper.

She couldn't hold back any longer. The pleasure cascaded around her, dozens of tiny little explosions. He lunged after her, thrusting faster, harder, until he came apart just as she had.

He pressed his forehead to hers, panting for air. "I am sorry," he said between harsh breaths.

She choked out a laugh. "I'm not. That was amazing!"

He shook his head. "No, I'm sorry I have put you in danger. I swear on my mother's grave that I will do all within my power to protect you."

She caressed his jaw, wished they could make love again. "We'll protect each other, but right now we need to figure a way out of here before our hosts decide it's time to take us to that command performance with death they mentioned."

He kissed her lips one last time before lowering her feet to the floor. The glow shimmering inside her was like nothing she'd ever felt before. Amazing. Amazing and perfect.

After taking care of essentials, Renee wiggled back into her panties and grabbed for her slacks.

Paul reached for his trousers and she touched his back, tracing a six- or seven-inch scar on his lower spine. The scar appeared to be the result of surgery. Not recent, she decided, since the scar looked smooth and any discoloration had long ago diminished. Judging by its location, she guessed it was a spinal injury, but she couldn't be sure. "What's this?"

He thrust one leg into his trousers, then the other. "This is a very old story." He grabbed his shirt. "Are you sure you want to hear it?"

"Yes." She slipped on her blouse. That was the kind of distinguishing physical mark that could confirm who was who. Maybe he hadn't thought of that.

"I was only ten. My brother and I were playing in the barn. I fell from the loft. The damage was more severe than anyone realized, but I was young. The true trouble did not come for a few months. Surgery was necessary, but I was very fortunate that the damage was to a disk very low on my spine."

She stepped into her sandals. "What do you mean you were lucky?" Any spinal damage sounded bad to her. She tugged the straps onto her shoes.

He shrugged those broad shoulders. "If the damage had been here—" he reached around and touched her back just below her shoulder blades "—or higher, the use of my arms or hands might have been affected." He flared his hands. "My work is who I am…why I breathe. I would not be whole without it."

If any doubt had lingered about this man's true identity, that statement obliterated it. He would rather be able to paint than to walk.

"We should hurry," she said, blinking back her

foolish emotion. Man, she'd fallen hard for this guy. She'd definitely be leaving that part out of her report.

There was no way to guess how much time they had. The best way to look at it was that they probably wouldn't have enough, so moving in a hurry was necessary.

Renee studied the way the windows were boarded up. That route would take too long and would make a hell of a lot of racket. She couldn't exactly kick her way through a wall this time. Those scumbags were in this house somewhere.

They needed a distraction.

But first they had to have a strategy.

She had it.

Only he wasn't going to like it.

"It's you they need." She looked him square in the eyes. "I'm expendable."

"Renee—"

"Think about it," she argued. "Victor needs you to complete this scheme of his. I'm not relevant to the outcome. Chances are they'll kill me before we ever leave this house." This was the sticky part. "Unless they have reason not to."

"Fine." He crossed his arms over her chest. "We'll give them reason." His face darkened with worry. "How do we do that?"

She chewed her lower lip, tried to come up with the best way to say this. "The thing is," she started off, "they need me to keep you cooperating, right?"

He nodded, suspicion slipping into his expression.

"If you escape, then they'll need to keep me alive until they have you back where they want you."

He was already moving from side to side before she even finished the statement. "This is not a good plan."

"It's a great plan. They can't kill me if they need me. We have to make them need me."

"And what am I supposed to do when I escape? Assuming we can make this happen."

More dicey territory. "You have to call a friend of mine, Jim Colby. Have him get word to Sam Johnson that you need him."

A frown tugged at his features. "Who are these people?"

She should tell him, but there might not be time.

"I'll have to explain everything later. We can't risk that Victor's time line will preempt ours."

"What shall we do?"

"How long can you hold your breath?"

"A minute? Two?" He looked skeptical, but didn't appear put off by the question.

She quickly ran through the plan she'd hatched. He argued over several points but, in the end, he agreed to do things her way. That he didn't ask any unnecessary questions was a surprise, but he was as aware as she was of the time crunch here.

As Paul got comfortable on the floor, Renee took a couple of deep breaths. Then she screamed.

Screamed a bloodcurdling, at-the-top-of-her-lungs kind of scream. Then she pounded on the locked door for effect.

When the door flew open and one of the men stormed in, his weapon readied for taking down whatever got in his way, she started ranting, "You have to help him! Something's wrong!"

Paul lay on the floor, his body shuddering violently as if he were having seizures.

"What the hell happened?" the scumbag snapped as he shoved his weapon back into his waistband at the small of his back.

"I don't know," Renee wailed as she looked from him to the other man loitering in the door. "He just fell down and then he started shaking. You have to help him!"

Paul suddenly went limp. Renee didn't have to be close to know he'd stopped breathing on cue.

The man kneeling next to Paul leaned closer to see if he was breathing. The man at the door wandered closer to the ongoing drama.

"Is he going to die?" Renee cried.

"He ain't breathing," the guy hovering over Paul said to his cohort.

The other man swore.

As the man leaned close again to try to feel any sign of breath on his jaw, Paul raised his head and snagged the man's ear between his teeth. The man screamed.

The other man moved toward the trouble. Renee

rushed him. Her unexpected move sent him stumbling sideways.

"Don't move!"

The jerk's grip on Renee tightened, but he didn't have time to go for his gun. Paul had the other man's weapon aimed directly at his chest.

"Let her go," Paul snarled.

Dammit. That wasn't the plan. "Just go!" she shouted at him. He wasn't supposed to try and take her with him.

"Back off," he warned the man who still had an iron grip on her arm. "Back off," he repeated. To Renee, he said, "Take his weapon."

She pulled free of the man's loose hold and took his weapon.

"Nothing you do will matter," the man whose ear was bleeding profusely snarled. "He's going to kill you. You know that whatever Victor wants, Victor gets."

Together, Renee and Paul backed out of the room. She quickly snapped the padlock into place.

"We need the keys to the SUV," she said.

He nodded.

The blow came from behind. She didn't see it coming. But she felt it.

Right before the floor flew up to meet her.

Chapter Thirteen

Saturday, May 5, 12:05 a.m.

Victor had Renee.

The third man they had encountered in the Everglades, as well as two faces Paul did not recognize, had ambushed them at the house when they had attempted to escape.

Paul had been given his instructions. He had been left at the house where they had been held. Victor's men had provided a wristwatch and a car. Nothing more. One of the men remained to watch him from his vehicle parked on the street. If he attempted to leave early or to stop for anything along the way, Renee would be executed.

Whatever Victor's plan, nothing had been left to chance. Not a single detail had been overlooked. This was the grand finale. There would be an audience, Paul was sure of that. Too much careful preparation had gone into the meeting to assume otherwise.

He drove through the gate to his home…or the place that used to be his home. It did not feel like home now. It felt empty, hollow. He had spent years holed up in this place, pretending he needed no one else. But he had been wrong. He did need some-one…he needed Renee.

There were doubts about her. She was certainly no art buyer from L.A. But he knew for certain that she was not involved with his brother's scheming. Whatever her hidden agenda it was not in support of Victor.

If he survived this night, he would know all there was to know about her. That would be his new pas-sion. All else would be secondary.

Paul ascended the steps to the front entrance. The house was utterly quiet.

But the danger was here. He could feel it in the air. Could smell the vile scent of his brother's presence.

Strangely, the front door had been replaced. He reached for the handle, expecting it to be locked, but it was not. He stepped inside the cool, silent interior. It was dark. Somewhere deeper in the house, there was light. He followed the hall until he reached the great room. He hesitated at the door. The only light in the entire house, as far as he could see, was a lamp on the table next to his favored chair inside this room.

In the chair sat his brother.

He made no move to get up. He simply sat there watching, waiting.

"I've been waiting for you."

"Yes, I am aware of that."

It amazed him that the two of them could be so similar on the outside, almost twins, and be polar opposites inside, where it mattered most.

Victor Reyes had no heart.

"You've made quite a mess of all this." Victor shook his head. "Very unlike you, *brother*."

Hearing the term uttered from his vile mouth made Paul shudder.

"I only did what I was forced to do in order to thwart your plan," he countered, enjoying the fury dancing in the other man's eyes. "This is my life and my home. You are not welcome here."

"Ah, but you're wrong." Victor stood. "This is my life…my home."

"Perhaps you have become too intimate with the products you distribute, Victor. I am quite sure you are aware that the authorities will be only too happy to discover you on American soil. You can not hope to pull this off. There are witnesses who know us, dear brother. They will not lie for you."

His brother laughed long and loud. "Foolish, foolish, *brother*. Do you not know me better than that? There are no loose ends. There is no one left."

Anger tightened Paul's jaw. He'd killed them all. Juanita, Eduardo and George. "Do not call me your brother. We are no longer brothers. I should have killed you long ago."

Victor sighed dramatically. "Yes, it would have been so much simpler to have ended this long ago. I tried to kill you when we were mere children, but you refused to die. Our mother watched you closely after that, as did that bitch Juanita, and another chance did not come."

Paul's gut clenched with hatred. On some level he had known that his fall from that barn loft had not been an accident. "You are nothing to me," he sneered, his contempt a palpable force throbbing inside him.

Another of those loud, obnoxious bouts of laughter. "Oh, yes, we are brothers. But in a few minutes there will be only one, and that one will be me." He thumped his chest. "Paul Reyes, the passionate painter who lives such a reclusive life that anyone could take it from him and no one would be the wiser."

"You will not succeed," Paul argued vehemently. "Your only creations are pain and death."

Victor flared his hands and nodded. "That is true. But, alas, the devastating moment to come will force me into an early retirement. How could I possibly continue to create after my only brother attempted to kill me in my own home? The price of *my* paintings will skyrocket."

A new blast of fury detonated inside Paul. "I have

no intention of attempting to kill you," he challenged. "I will never make it so easy for you. You will have to kill me if you want me dead." He held out his hands. "I am unarmed and I refuse to fight you."

Victor's expression turned venomous. "But it is exactly that simple. It is already done. All that is left is the part where you die."

"Then kill me." Paul pounded his chest. "I am here. Why not do it now? If that is your intent. Why bother with this charade."

His brother was right, in part. Without family or friends who knew him well enough to confirm his identity, there really was no other way. Other than dental X rays, and his brother would have ensured that those had been destroyed. He was all too sure of himself not to have taken care of that matter already.

Paul had no idea if there were any old medical records of his back surgery. He had been only a boy. His brother would have covered that, as well. Victor left nothing to chance.

Victor walked slowly, cautiously in Paul's direction, as if he feared for his own safety.

Perplexed, Paul braced for an attack.

His brother threw his arms around him and hugged him as if he were happy to see him, as if none of what had just occurred was real. "Reach into the back of my waistband, *brother*," he said, "and take the weapon."

"What are you doing?" Paul tried to push him away but Victor held on.

"Take it," he commanded.

Paul didn't fight him, but neither did he obey his command. "No," he challenged. "You will not triumph. You are forgetting that I have the scar from the last time you tried to kill me." Remembered pain burned through Paul. As a child, he had believed his brother when Victor claimed the push that had caused him to fall had been an accident, but a part of him had always known the truth. The idea had haunted him. Now he knew why.

"Give me credit, dear brother," Victor said, "I would never forget such an important detail." His hold turned brutal. "Take the gun. Now. Or she dies."

Pain arced through Paul. "You will kill her anyway," he said, the words like daggers twisting in his back. If he went along with Victor, she would die. His only hope was to fight him.

"I'm sure you don't want her to be hurt." His brother smiled at him, the expression sickening. "Do as I say and I will let her live. No one will believe anything she says. She has no proof of what she believes."

"I want to see that she is safe."

As if Victor had been prepared for this very moment, one of his men appeared in the doorway leading into the entry hall. He held Renee in such a way that snapping her neck would require nothing more than a quick jerk. The terror blasted through Paul's veins.

"Take the weapon," Victor murmured for his ears only, "or she dies now."

Paul snatched the weapon from Victor's waist-band and stepped back far enough to aim it at the bastard's chest. "Let her go, or I will kill you."

Victor staggered back as if he actually feared for his life. He did not smile but the expression on his face was one of victory. "Goodbye, brother."

RENEE COULDN'T let this happen.

She screamed, "Nooooo!" She jerked free of the hands restraining her and rushed toward Paul.

A shot exploded in the room, shattering glass at the same instant that her body collided with his.

Time seemed to lapse into slow motion as they crashed to the floor together.

The air rushed out of her lungs with the impact.

Instantly, time snapped back and the room was suddenly overrun with armed DEA agents.

Half a dozen voices were shouting, but she didn't hear the words. She was too busy checking to ensure Paul wasn't hit.

"You're okay?" she demanded.

He blinked. Nodded. "Yes."

Strong hands suddenly lifted her to her feet.

Paul was on his feet in a flash, jerking her away from the man who'd pulled her up. He ushered her slightly behind him, protecting her.

"Step away from him, Vaughn," Johnson ordered.

It wasn't until that moment that Renee realized that all those armed agents had their weapons aimed at Paul.

"Get the hell out of my way, Johnson," DEA Agent Joseph Gates ordered. "This man is my prisoner."

"Stand down, Gates," Johnson ordered. His aim steady on Paul, he glanced briefly at Gates. "You tell your men to back off until I have some answers."

The weapon Paul had been holding lay on the floor. There was glass on the floor near one of the French doors. That was when Renee understood that the weapon that had been discharged had been fired from outside…by one of those men. Seven men, all outfitted in full ambush gear like the ones who'd ransacked the house, were bearing down on Paul and Sam Johnson. And her.

"This would have been settled with that one shot if you hadn't interfered," Gates snapped at Johnson. "You interfered with a federal operation. You're going down for that, Johnson."

Gates had shot at Paul? Why?

"What's going on, Johnson?" Renee demanded.

"Step away from him," Johnson repeated. "And we'll talk about this."

"He tried to kill me," Victor Reyes shouted. "You saw him," he said to Renee.

The gun in Paul's hand had been aimed at his brother, but she couldn't say with any certainty what had been going on or why he'd ended up with a weapon. He certainly hadn't had one the last time she saw him.

"Move," Johnson commanded her. To Gates he said, "Keep him out of this until we have a definitive answer."

"What the hell are you talking about?" Renee started to move around Paul, but he stopped her.

"Stay behind me," Paul urged.

"Turn around," Johnson said to Paul, "and lift your shirt. I need to see your back."

This was about the scar.

"What the hell is this, Johnson?" she demanded.

He glanced at Renee. "We have hospital records that prove Victor Reyes had surgery at age eleven. I need to see his back."

Renee shook her head. "He tampered with the records." She shot a look at Victor. "He's using this to fool all of you." This time, she glared at Gates. He had intended to kill Paul—would have, apparently, if Johnson hadn't interfered.

What was to stop him from doing it now?

Moving out of Paul's reach, she darted around in front of him.

"Renee—"

She held up a hand to stop his argument. "Lower your weapon, Johnson." How could they fall for this?

The same way you did.

She had. She'd believed Victor's lies at first. Before she'd met the real man.

"I saw the medical records, Vaughn," her colleague argued. "This has to be sorted out. There is still some question as to which of these guys is Victor Reyes." He shot a nasty look at Gates. "Some of us got a little trigger-happy before the answers could be ferreted out. But we've got it under control now."

"There is no question," Victor roared. "Agent Gates, are you going to allow this? He tried to kill me!"

Renee thought of the scar on the back of the man with whom she had made love. She had promised herself that she would never be fooled by anyone again. That she would never trust anyone again. Not completely.

But she did. She trusted this man. She thought of the story he'd told her about that scar, and she was certain. Absolutely certain.

"He's lying," she said to Johnson as she jerked her head toward the man she knew to be Victor Reyes. "He changed the records. Something. But he is not Paul Reyes. This man—" she gestured to the man at her side "—is Paul Reyes."

Johnson's gaze held hers for two beats. "You're certain about that?"

At that second, she did the one thing she had sworn she would never again do. "Positive."

Johnson lowered his weapon and turned to

Gates. "You heard the woman. You almost killed the wrong man."

"You are dead!"

All eyes shifted to Victor Reyes at the same instant that he snatched a weapon from under his shirt.

Weapons discharged, the explosions deafening.

Renee was suddenly on the floor, with Paul on top of her like a shield.

Victor Reyes lay a few feet away, his open eyes unmoving, a small round hole in the center of his forehead leaking blood.

Renee couldn't move.

Voices.

Frantic movement all around her.

Paul.

"Are you all right?" She searched his face as he attempted to lever his body off hers.

"Yes. Are you hurt?"

"I'm okay." She scrambled out from under him and helped him to his feet. He seemed somehow disoriented. Well, he had just witnessed the execution of his brother. Shock, maybe.

He blinked. "I…"

He collapsed onto the floor.

"Paul!" She dropped to her knees beside him. "Paul!"

Johnson appeared next to her, shouting orders over his shoulder. "Get those paramedics in here now!"

Renee whirled around to see that someone was doing as Johnson had demanded. She hoped like hell that meant the paramedics were on standby somewhere close.

She turned back to Paul. "Was he hit?" she asked Johnson, who was examining him.

He ignored her question and rolled Paul toward her, onto his side to check his back, she presumed, since he leaned over him and took a look. He swore and Renee's heart tumbled toward her stomach.

"What?" she demanded.

Again he ignored her. He gently lowered Paul onto the floor. "Reyes, can you hear me? If you can hear me, talk to me, man."

"I hear you."

His voice sounded weak and thready, but he was still with them. Relief flooded Renee. She leaned close. "Help is on the way, Paul." She struggled to keep the tears out of her voice. "You'll be fine, just hang in there, okay?"

His gaze shifted to hers. She was pretty sure he smiled...his lips tilted ever so slightly, but it was so hard to tell with the tears blurring her vision.

"You still haven't told me who you are," he said thinly, the words crushing her. When she started to explain, he whispered, "Renee...Vaughn?" His face went lax and his eyes closed.

Johnson pushed her out of the way and assumed a position she recognized all too well.

He leaned his cheek close to Paul's face. Paused. Then tilted his head back and commenced CPR.

"Oh, God." She started to shake.

Two paramedics burst into the room and took over.

Johnson dragged her out of the way.

"I don't understand." She watched the paramedics intubate and bag Paul so that air could more easily be forced into his lungs to keep his heart beating. How could this be? There wasn't even that much blood.

"Look at me, Vaughn."

She couldn't take her eyes off Paul as the paramedics prepared to move him.

"Vaughn." Johnson pulled her around to face him. "The .22 entered his back…close to his spine. You need to brace for the worst."

"I have to be with him."

Johnson let her go, even though she knew he had questions.

All the questions and reports would just have to wait.

As she followed the paramedics out of the house, she heard Johnson shout, "Where the hell is Gates?"

Chapter Fourteen

Miami Trauma Center
6:30 p.m.

The hours had all run together.

Renee wasn't even sure what day it was.

Paul had been airlifted to Miami's Trauma Center. Some cop whose name she couldn't recall had driven her here despite the DEA's insistence that she stay behind and give her statement. Johnson had basically told the man in charge where to go and what to do when he got there. In his opinion, the DEA had enough to do figuring out what had happened to their man Gates, who had conveniently disappeared. At least now Renee understood how Victor had known when to precisely plan his moves.

She could truthfully say that she was glad that bastard was dead.

Over and over, her mind had played Paul's last words to her. The idea that her deception was the last thought he had about her made the agony almost unbearable.

A neurosurgical team had started the process of removing the bullet three hours ago.

Paul was stable, but the prognosis was unknown.

The bullet from the .22 had entered at an angle, lodging close to the spine. Apparently when Paul had stood up, the bullet had moved closer, pressing against nerves, paralyzing his upper body and making breathing difficult.

Grief so overwhelming rushed over her each time she thought of it that her stomach clenched mercilessly. He couldn't die. He just couldn't.

She remembered what he'd said about his previous back injury, about how he was glad it had been low on his spine so that there was no risk to his arms and hands. Surely God wouldn't take that from him now.

She closed her eyes and fought back the tears.

"Vaughn."

She opened her eyes to find that Jim Colby had sat down beside her. He'd arrived a few hours ago.

She dabbed at her eyes with a tissue and took a deep breath. "Hey."

"Any news yet?"

She shook her head.

"I wanted to let you know that I tracked down the admin clerk who changed the hospital records in Mexico City. The hospital's attorney has already faxed a statement to the DEA that Paul Reyes was the one who had the surgery, not Victor."

"Does that clear up any questions?"

"Yes. The case against Victor Reyes is officially closed. Apparently he had been planning to take over his brother's life for several months. The newly elected Mexican president was considering allowing Victor's extradition. Gates gave in to Victor's persuasion when the price was right. The bastard actually talked Darla Stewart into coming to us for help to set this whole thing in motion. Paul was to be the scapegoat."

Renee's jaw hardened with hatred. She hoped Victor Reyes burned in hell. She hoped Gates got what he deserved, as well.

Before she could say as much to Jim, the door opened and one of the doctors who had spoken to her before the surgery entered the small waiting room.

She pushed to her feet. Jim stood next to her.

"How did it go?" Please, she prayed, let him be okay.

"He came through the surgery very well," Dr. Kilpatrick explained, his tone cautious.

"Any permanent damage?" Jim asked the question she couldn't bear to utter.

Dr. Kilpatrick considered his words carefully. "It's difficult to tell at this point. The swelling obscures the issue. There was no structural damage to the spine, which is very good. However, we have to assume since sensory control, including the involuntary act of breathing, was hampered, that there may have been enough pressure to cause bruising. Frankly, this can go either way. He may recover without any permanent damage, or he may not. Only time will tell. Could be hours, could be days, before we know for certain."

Jim asked a few more questions and thanked the doctor. Renee couldn't stop thinking about how devastated Paul would be if he couldn't paint anymore.

Would he even want to live if that turned out to be the case?

"When can I see him?" she asked before the doctor could get away.

"Not for a while yet," Kilpatrick said gently. "Someone will come for you when he's awake and able to take visitors."

When the doctor had gone, she dropped back into her chair, her legs unable to hold up her weight any longer.

Jim resumed his seat beside her. "Would you like me to make a fresh pot of coffee?"

The current pot had scorched on the warming plate.

She shook her head. "No thanks."

"You did a good job, Vaughn."

Somehow it felt as if she'd failed. Sure they'd got Victor, but Paul was…seriously injured.

"If you hadn't warned me about Victor's plan,

Gates would have taken Paul down. We wouldn't be here. We'd be at the morgue."

She shuddered. "Was that the plan?" She turned to Jim. "To execute Victor Reyes without a trial?" Not that she actually gave a damn, but the wrong man had been targeted.

"According to the agent who assumed control of the case after Gates disappeared, they were only going to take Victor out if he didn't surrender voluntarily. We had no way of knowing Victor had a little setup of his own."

None of those final moments she'd witnessed made sense. "I'm still unclear about how Paul ended up with a gun?"

"Felipe Santos, one of Victor's personal bodyguards, spilled his guts for a deal. He says Victor set the whole thing up. He had two weapons on him as the sting went down. A .38, which he forced Paul to take when they hugged. Apparently he knew Paul wouldn't try to shoot him unless he forced the issue."

"That's why he dragged me into Paul's line of sight at that moment," she realized out loud.

"Right," Jim confirmed. "Victor had taped the second weapon, the .22, to his side beneath his shirt in case things went wrong. He had no intention of letting his brother survive."

All the hatred she felt for the man came rushing back. She rubbed her forehead, didn't want to hear any more of this. She just wanted good news about Paul.

"They haven't located Gates yet?"

Jim shook his head. "They will. Don't worry."

She prayed he was right.

"Why don't I go get you something to eat?" Jim offered.

She was relatively certain that she couldn't eat, but she appreciated the offer. "I'm okay for now."

"All right, then." He leaned back in his seat. "We'll just wait it out."

And that was what they did. Jim Colby sat right there beside her for hours…too many to count. Conversation was sporadic, but just having him there helped.

Exhaustion had gotten the better of Renee and she'd dozed off when the door to the private waiting room finally opened once more.

A nurse offered a smile when Renee looked up.

"Can I see him now?" Renee was on her feet and at the door before she had cleared the haze of sleep from her head. Her pulse tripped into triple time.

"Ms. Vaughn, Dr. Kilpatrick wanted me to let you know that Mr. Reyes is awake and breathing completely on his own now."

Renee's knees went weak with relief. "That's great. Can I see him?" she repeated, wondering why the nurse just didn't take her to him.

"You can, but it's imperative that he not move and that he not be overexcited."

Renee nodded. "I understand."

Jim gave her a nod. "I'll wait here for you."

She followed the nurse to the ICU. Paul's cubicle was directly across from the nurse's station. The glass walls allowed a full visual on all patients in the unit.

"We can only give you five minutes, Ms. Vaughn."

Renee would take whatever she got.

She moved up next to Paul's bed. "Hey," she said softly as she took his hand in hers.

He opened his eyes. "Hey." His voice was rusty. He licked his lips.

"The doctors say you're doing great." She smiled, fighting hard to keep the tears at bay.

"That's what they tell me."

He looked so unnaturally pale. Her heart squeezed. "I can only stay five minutes. But I'll be back as often as they'll allow." That his fingers remained limp in hers filled her stomach with dread.

"Tell me quickly," he murmured, his voice so low she could barely hear it.

"Tell you what?" She caressed his jaw. Wished she could crawl into the bed with him and just hold him close. He looked so vulnerable.

"Who are you? I must know."

That ache welled inside her. "My name is Renee Vaughn. I work for the Equalizers." She shrugged. "It's sort of a private investigations firm."

His brow wrinkled in confusion. "You were investigating me?"

She bit her lip for a second, then told him the truth. "Your brother. We were investigating Victor."

"You needed me to get to him." As dull as his dark eyes were from the injury and the surgery, she could see the regret and disappointment glimmering there.

"Yes."

He took a deep breath. The harsh movement worried her. Was he okay? Had she upset him?

"I am very tired now." He closed his eyes.

She pressed a kiss to his forehead and placed his hand back on the sheet.

There was nothing else she could say. If he never wanted to see her again, she would have no choice but to understand. He'd been dealing with betrayal and deception his whole life. She doubted if he wanted any more of it intruding in his life.

"I'm sorry, Ms. Vaughn," the nurse said from the door, "that's all the time for now."

Renee thanked her and left the cubicle. As promised, Jim Colby waited for her outside the ICU.

"There's a U.S. Marshal waiting." He gestured in the direction of the private waiting room for family members of surgical patients. "He's says that it's urgent that he speak with you."

Bewildered, she met his gaze. "I don't understand."

"It's about your brother, Vaughn. You need to do this. I'll be right here. If anything changes I'll let you know."

Embassy Suites Hotel, Miami
9:00 p.m.

RENEE HESITATED outside Room 618. She wasn't sure she wanted to know anything else about her brother. For two years she'd been told she couldn't go near him—orders that came straight from him. He didn't want her anywhere near him. No matter what new evidence she uncovered, she was not to speak of it. There was nothing she could do but stay away. So she'd done just that. She'd left Texas and tried to start over in Atlanta.

She couldn't imagine why anyone on her brother's case would come all the way to Miami or would want to talk to her. Or why the hell she would bother letting them bring her here.

"He's waiting, Ms. Vaughn."

Renee looked up at the marshal standing next to her. He'd been kind and patient as she ranted about her reasons for not wanting to ever hear her brother's name again. He'd known she was reacting on emotion.

She squared her shoulders and took a deep breath. "All right." Jim had arranged for her to have a shower at the hospital, and he'd rounded up new clothes for her hours ago. So she looked halfway respectable, not that it mattered. She wasn't here to impress anyone, frankly she didn't know why the hell she was here.

Marshal Farnsworth rapped on the door twice and it opened. A stern-looking man in a dark suit, with the same demeanor as Farnsworth, stared at her, then glanced at the man next to her. "We're ready."

Ready? Ready for what? Just what the hell was going on here?

Marshal Farnsworth nodded.

"Come in, Ms. Vaughn," the other man said as he moved away from the door.

Her heart had started to pound by the time the door was closed behind her. Had her brother been executed while she was out of reach? She'd scarcely had time to think about the situation as she'd run for her life. Now that he was dead, did they want to hear about her theories regarding her brother's innocence? That didn't make sense. Unless they suspected wrongdoing. A little late for that.

"This is highly unusual," the unidentified man started off, "but your brother was insistent."

"Ma'am, this is Marshal Owens," Farnsworth said. "We're transitioning Matthew."

She was totally lost now. "What are you talking about?"

"Please, sit down." Owens motioned to a chair in the room's sitting area.

The room was a suite. From the doors on either side of the room, she'd say a two-bedroom suite.

She sat. The quicker this was over, the sooner she could get back to Paul.

"I'm going to let your brother fill you in, then we

have to go. The longer we stay here, the greater the risk."

The idea that he'd said her brother had stunned her, she barely heard the rest of what he had to say. Her brother was sitting on death row in a Texas prison…wasn't he?

The two marshals stepped out into the hall, leaving her alone. The door to one of the bedrooms opened and her brother appeared.

"Hey, sis."

The fury that rose so rapidly was irrational, but something over which she had no control. She sprang to her feet. "What's going on here, Matthew?"

He was out?

Alive?

More incredible, he was speaking to her?

He walked over and hugged her. At first she stood there, her arms limp, her thoughts churning wildly, and then instinct took over. She hugged her brother fiercely, battled back the tears she refused to shed for him yet again.

He drew back. "I don't have much time, so I'll be brief."

They sat down and she listened as her brother told her an incredible tale of fear and desperation. He'd confessed to the murders of two of Austin's socially elite only because he'd had no choice. When Renee had learned the truth and attempted to help him, the threat shifted to her. That was the reason he'd pushed her out of his life—to protect her. Unbeknownst to the real killer, a man key to a Mafia-like organization in Texas, Matthew had started cooperating with the FBI. Since Renee had been out of his life and out of Texas for two years, all deemed that it would be safe for her. As of midnight the night before, Matthew Vaughn was dead, executed in a Texas prison. The Mafia in Texas was under investigation and already a dozen had been indicted, including the man who'd terrorized Renee and her brother—the real murderer.

It was over.

There was just one problem.

Matthew had to go into the Witness Protection Program. This would be the last time Renee ever saw her brother.

10:38 p.m.

RENEE WAS EXHAUSTED by the time Marshal Farnsworth dropped her off at the hospital's lobby entrance. She wasn't sure how she would ever talk the nurses into allowing her to see Paul at this hour, but she had to try. Jim Colby had promised to stay. He'd given her his cell phone and would have called if Paul's condition had changed.

She and her brother had cleared the air between them. They'd laughed and cried and, most importantly, made peace. She had assured him that she would be safe with Jim Colby. She'd never met a man quite like him before. His firm was aptly named—the Equalizers. Jim Colby evened the odds for those who had nowhere else to turn. It wouldn't matter how the DEA handled their investigation; she'd lay odds that Jim Colby would see to it that Joseph Gates was found. Just as he had seen to it that the marshals treated her brother with the utmost care and respect. Though the investigation into her brother's case had already been ongoing, the Colby name had ensured that Matthew got what he deserved—a second chance.

For the first time in a long time, Renee smiled a real smile. She was proud to be a part of Jim's group. She was proud of her brother.

She headed across the lobby for the bank of elevators. If she hadn't been lost in thought, maybe she could have avoided the collision with another visitor.

"Excuse me." She looked up at the man with whom she'd collided.

Gates.

"This way, Vaughn."

She didn't have to see the weapon in his jacket pocket; she felt it nudging into her ribs.

"I didn't think you were this stupid, Gates."

"Shut up and move," he muttered as he ushered her in the direction of the hospital's parking garage.

"If I were in your shoes I'd be deep in Mexico or some other place where the law couldn't reach."

He didn't respond, just kept ushering her forward. The corridor was deserted, which meant the parking garage would be, as well. There were probably security cameras, but those wouldn't help her a whole lot. Someone would view the tape later and determine that yes, indeed, she had been kidnapped and/or murdered by Gates. But she'd be dead.

The one thing she knew for certain was that she could not allow him to get her into a vehicle.

The double doors that separated the hospital from the garage slid open, and he pushed her forward. The smell of gasoline and oil filled her nostrils. She had to think fast.

"You believe having a hostage is going to assure your safe passage?" she suggested. "You've seen too many movies, Gates. You should know better than that."

He slammed her against the passenger side of a car. He laughed. "No, Vaughn, this isn't about safe passage." He leaned his face close to hers. "This is about payback. I want Paul Reyes to know what his failure to cooperate cost him."

She was the one laughing now. "Come on. You think he cares about me? I was working under cover, using him. He knows that now. He won't care if you kill me."

Gates jerked the car door open. "Oh, yes, he'll care. I saw the way he protected you. He's lying in that hospital bed right now because he took a bullet for you."

Now or never.

She was dead for sure if she didn't try.

Throwing all her weight behind the move, she slammed her elbow into his gut.

He grunted, bent forward.

She twisted out of his hold.

She ran.

He grabbed her by the hair, jerked her backward. The pistol's barrel rammed into her temple. "Don't make me kill you here."

He shoved her into the front seat. "Scoot over. You're driving."

As she took her time sliding across the bench seat, she scanned the interior of the car for a weapon. She needed something…anything.

The keys.

She yanked the key out of the switch before she'd slid behind the wheel. She turned on the man settling into the passenger seat. With her left hand, she shoved at the weapon. She stabbed the key into the side of his neck, going for an artery.

The pistol discharged.

The windshield shattered.

She was straddling him, struggling to keep the pistol away from her head. Blood squirted from his neck…splattered across her face. Another explosion from the pistol. The bullet whizzed past her ear. Too close.

If she could hold him down…

Twist the key in his neck…

He screamed.

They fell out of the car onto the concrete floor.

"Don't move!"

She didn't have time to look up, had to hold Gates off her.

A foot came down on top of the hand still clutching the gun.

Renee looked up, still struggling to hold Gates away from her.

Sam Johnson.

Gates collapsed on top of her.

His eyes were open, unblinking.

Damn. She rolled him off her and scrambled up.

Johnson toed the gun free from Gates's limp fingers. "Guess you'd better go in there and tell 'em you've got one for the morgue."

Renee nodded.

She'd killed a man.

Johnson steadied her when she swayed. "It was you or him, Vaughn. Don't sweat it."

She was still nodding, somehow unable to stop the bobbing of her head.

Security flooded the garage. E.R. personnel rushed in to attempt to resuscitate Gates, but it was too late. Just as well. The bastard didn't deserve to live. He belonged in hell with his friend Victor.

Johnson gave his statement to a cop while she was

questioned by another. She didn't remember the cops arriving. Time seemed to be on fast-forward and she couldn't catch up.

The DEA arrived.

Renee learned that Jim Colby had ordered Johnson to keep an eye on her, just in case Gates did exactly what he'd done. She'd have to thank Jim later.

Right now, she just wanted to see Paul.

6:00 a.m.

ONCE THE POLICE and the DEA were through questioning her, Jim had forced her to get some sleep. Her statement was confirmed by the hospital's security cameras, so she was in the clear. Johnson had brought her yet another change of clothes and she showered, washing away the traitor's blood. Then she admitted defeat and slept in the nurses' lounge.

She hadn't wanted to, but Jim had insisted. ICU rules wouldn't allow her to see Paul until six this morning.

The idea that she'd had to kill Gates still seemed on the fringes of reality. Jim told her that the shock would wear off, and reality would set in later. She would need counseling. He knew someone who could help her work through it. Right now, she was just glad it was over.

Her heart was running away in her chest as she neared Paul's cubicle in the ICU. She wanted to see him desperately. Wanted to tell him that she hadn't intended to hurt him in any way. But she was scared to death he would tell her to go away and never come back.

For once in her life, everything was fixed. She had a new career that made her feel that what she did mattered. She and her brother had made amends. They both deserved to live happily ever after. But her happily ever after hinged completely on this man.

He was awake.

"I understand there was excitement last night," he said, his voice not quite so rusty this morning.

She nodded. "Gates is dead."

"Good."

Renee stood at his bedside, but this time she didn't reach for his hand.

"You look much better this morning," she offered in a cheery tone that sounded fake even to her.

He was watching her, assessing what he saw. She resisted the impulse to look away. She had to face whatever his decision turned out to be. No more running away. She'd done enough of that. She'd run away from Texas to escape the reality of what had happened between her and her brother. She'd run away from Atlanta because she couldn't deal with the trust necessary to prosecute a case again. She'd tried to fit in again—to belong to the world of politics and prosecution in Atlanta's high-profile DA's office, but she just couldn't. The past kept coming back to haunt her…making her doubt her esteemed colleagues… making her doubt herself.

No more running away.

He reached up, caressed her cheek with his fingertips. She leaned into his touch. Then he smiled. "I'm glad you're safe." He lowered his hand back to the bed, the movement seeming to have cost him a great deal of strength.

It hit her then. He'd moved his arm. Touched her face. Hope bloomed in her chest.

His answering smile melted the ice of fear that had chilled her. "They say I'll make a full recovery."

Tears slid down her cheeks before she could stop them. "That's great. Really great."

He placed his hand on hers where she clutched the bed's side rail. "It's time you properly introduced yourself to me."

Relief gushed through her. "Renee Vaughn, from Texas, originally."

"Well, Renee Vaughn from Texas, we have much to talk about." He squeezed her hand. "Many plans to make."

She leaned down and placed a soft kiss on his lips. "Many plans."

Their gazes locked, and he looked at her with all the passion that she'd seen when he was making love to her. "First thing, I want to paint you."

She bit her lower lip to stop its trembling. "I think that can be arranged."

She kissed him again, this time with a definite promise of things to come.

Chapter Fifteen

Chicago
Saturday, May 12, 11:15 p.m.

Jim Colby parked in front of his house and exhaled a heavy breath.

He had missed dinner with his girls again.

Today had been a busy one for a Saturday. Several new cases had come in. Pretty soon, he would need to hire an additional associate if Tasha opted not to join him at work.

Not that he could blame her. The idea of leaving their daughter in the hands of anyone besides close family was something neither of them was prepared to consider.

He went inside and locked the door.

The house was quiet.

He was sure Tasha had left dinner for him, but he was too tired to eat.

As quietly as he could, he trudged up the stairs.

He peeked in his daughter's room and, as tired as he was, he smiled down at her. So sweet, so beautiful. Just like her mother.

He eased out of her room and went to the bedroom where his wife would likely be asleep, as well. He peeled off his clothes and slid beneath the sheet and snuggled up to her backside. It felt good to lie down; having her sweet body close was just icing on the cake. He was still amazed that she loved him. That their child was so perfect…that his life was real.

Tasha turned over and sighed contentedly. "You're home."

"Mmm-hmm." God, she smelled good. He nuzzled her neck.

"Your daughter said da-da tonight."

Jim's heart constricted. "Seriously?"

"Seriously."

And he'd missed it.

"Don't worry," she stroked his jaw, "I got it on video."

"Thank you." He kissed her forehead. What else was he going to miss?

"Victoria was here."

He stilled.

"She's worried about you, Jim. She thinks you're working too hard. Some of the cases you're taking are pretty dangerous."

"Starting right now," he said, ushering her beneath him, "I promise I will not come home later than seven. And I will be more selective about the cases I take." If he didn't, his mother was going to move into the office with him. Already, she stopped in two or three times each week, checking on him and assessing the cases he accepted. As much as he loved her, her concern was moving into the interference zone. They were going to have to have a serious talk. He was a grown man; he didn't need his mother looking over his shoulder.

"Good. I like having you home for dinner." Tasha looped her arms around his neck. "Just remember, Victoria loves you. She wants to protect you, just like we want to protect Jamie."

"Except," he murmured against her neck, "I don't need protecting. I'm a big boy."

Tasha moved against him. "I can see that."

He pushed the regrets and worries aside and made love to his wife. Right now was all that mattered.

Tomorrow would take care of itself.

He would see to it.

And Victoria would just have to get used to the idea that her son could take care of himself.

End of story.

* * * * *

COLBY VS COLBY

BY
DEBRA WEBB

This book is dedicated to the City of Los Angeles,
one of the coolest places on earth. A place where
nothing is as it seems and all is as it should be.

Chapter One

"And there she goes," Jim Colby murmured as he watched the young woman dart across the dark, deserted street. "Victim number three is in position."

Sam Johnson moved his head from side to side. "How can these kids be so gullible?" He just didn't get it. With the news reporting way too often on the dirty business of runaways being sold into slavery, he just didn't see how anyone could be so oblivious to the dangers. And yet it was happening right in front of his eyes, as he sat watching from a beat-up Chevy Impala.

"Time to shut these scumbags down."

Following Jim's cue, Sam exited the passenger side. The vehicle's interior light had been disabled to ensure they weren't spotted by anyone watching the street.

Using the vehicles parked along the block as cover, Sam stole halfway up the block before pausing to survey the situation once more. Jim had taken the direct route to the office building abandoned by day and used for criminal rendezvous by night. Jim would put in a call to Chicago PD for backup as soon as he verified that all known players were in position. The Equalizers could tag and move in on this group, but the final arrests had to be made by official law enforcement personnel.

Sam hustled across the street and crouched at the rear of an SUV. If these scumbags had any spotters keeping watch, they were either asleep or blind. He steeled himself for possible confrontation and ran the last twenty yards to the northeast corner of the building inside which the despicable transaction would go down.

According to Jim, the location had once been an adoption agency. Sam found that ironic since the business taking place here most recently involved another sort of adoption: the selling of young women to the highest bidders.

Three females, ranging in age from seventeen to twenty-six, were inside. Two of those three didn't realize just yet that this was going to be one of the luckiest days of their lives. The third victim was a plant. Connie Gardner, the receptionist from the Equalizers, had agreed to step into that role. At twenty-six, Connie didn't look a day over twenty-one. Having a great body and the right look ensured she fit the profile.

Top priority was neutralizing the bad guys while maintaining the safety and well-being of the three women about to be auctioned via a private chat room on the Internet. If those scumbags inside knew what was good for them they would keep their hands off Connie. She knew how to make life miserable in a New York minute.

From his position at the main entrance, Colby tapped the mike to indicate all players were now present and visually accounted for.

Sam eased around the corner of the building, surveyed the back parking area and then hustled over to the ground-floor rear entrance. He tapped his collar mike, giving Colby the signal that he was in position. Colby would call his contact at Chicago PD and four minutes from now the world as these jerks knew it would change forever. Unfortunately, another group would take their place far too quickly.

As if to warn that the night was about to take a turn for the worst, another kind of change came earlier than Sam had anticipated. One of the hoodlums barreled out the rear entrance and ran square into him.

Sam and his startled attacker tumbled to the

ground and rolled as each attempted to gain control of the other. Sam resisted the urge to use his weapon. His enemy had dropped his weapon when they hit the ground. No need to use excessive force. His assailant went for Sam's throat. Weapon or no, the guy was determined to win this battle. At least until Sam applied just enough pressure to the carotid artery. The man slumped, unconscious. Sam shoved him off and clambered to his feet.

After tucking the lout's weapon into his waistband, Sam moved back into position at the rear exit and listened. If the unconscious chump had been sent to retrieve something, then his pals would get restless when he didn't return in a timely manner.

Sending a *complication* signal to Colby, Sam prepared to very carefully risk opening the door.

A weapon discharged inside the building, the sound shattering the silence and derailing Sam's plan. The cacophony of screaming and yelling had him rushing through the door, weapon drawn.

Two men were facedown on the floor, one was on his knees with Jim Colby's weapon boring into his sweating forehead. The two female teenagers were huddled together. Connie Gardner held a weapon she'd obviously taken from one of the men and was instructing the dudes on the floor to stay put.

Since everything appeared to be under control inside, Sam went back outside and dragged the guy who'd tackled him back inside with the others. The scumbag had started to rouse, but didn't attempt to break free.

"What happened in here?" Sam asked Connie.

She looked furious and not the least bit frightened. "They wanted to make sure we weren't wearing wires or tracking devices so they demanded we take off our clothes. Big mistake."

Sam resisted the urge to grin. Considering no one was dead he figured this team of lowlifes had gotten off easy. Connie was not one to be pushed around and she definitely knew how to use a weapon.

The wail of sirens indicated the arrival of the police. Tonight chalked up one more for the Equalizers. Chicago's finest had been trying to nail this operation for months. The man currently begging for his life in a position of humiliation in front of Jim Colby was the suspected ringleader. A few months from now, when he was in prison with guys ten times worse than him, he would be wishing Colby had put him out of his misery.

A sense of accomplishment filled Sam as he kept a bead on the others while Connie reassured the two young ladies who had thought they were coming here tonight to be extras in a movie. Their dreams had turned into nightmares, but at least they had lived to see their mistakes.

One hour later, Sam piled into the Impala with

Connie and Colby to head back to the office. It was almost midnight and he was relatively sure the silence was indication that both his colleagues were as exhausted as he was. The euphoria lingered in spite of the quiet and the fatigue. Sam genuinely liked playing the hero, no matter the risks involved. He loved his job. It beat the hell out of obsessing about the past.

As Jim Colby slowed for a changing traffic signal, he reached into his pocket and dug out his cell phone which was evidently still set to vibrate.

"Colby."

Sam didn't really pay attention to the conversation, but he did pick up on the change in tension in his boss's tone. Jim Colby was clearly not happy with the caller and/or the subject of the call.

Colby closed his phone and shoved it back into his pocket. "We have a command performance tomorrow morning," he said with a quick glance into the rearview mirror at Sam.

That couldn't be good. "The detective in charge has a problem with our statements?" Seemed a little fast to have gotten feedback, negative or otherwise, only minutes after they'd driven away from the scene of a sting operation. Usually the questions came later. Not that Sam was worried. Jim Colby might bend the hell out of the rules, but he never crossed the line, at least not more than a step or two.

"This has nothing to do with tonight's operation." Colby sent another look in Sam's direction. "We have an appointment at eight sharp at the Colby Agency. Victoria needs to see us."

Now Sam understood the irritation.

Jim Colby's *mom* had called.

Checking up on her son had gotten to be a regular routine for the lady. And judging by the muscle flexing in Colby's jaw, it was not appreciated.

The real question was, why would she want to see Sam?

Colby Agency
Wednesday, June 5, 8:00 a.m.

JIM COLBY WAS twenty-eight years old. He was married with a daughter. He had opened the doors to his own cutting-edge firm just this year. The Equalizers were swiftly making a name for themselves as the place to go when all else failed.

He had faced death on more occasions than he could recall, and he'd doled it out far more times than any man would want to admit. The possibility of having his wife or child hurt was the one thing in this world that scared him; otherwise he was fearless. And yet here he sat, with dread tying his gut in knots as he waited for his own mother to call him into her private office.

Not that he was afraid of his mother; he wasn't.

But her need to protect him, to ensure his every move was cautiously executed was, frankly, making him nuts. Since the birth of his daughter, his mother's hovering had only gotten worse.

"Jim."

He looked up to see Mildred, his mother's personal assistant and longtime friend, approaching the sitting area outside Victoria's office. Pushing to his feet, he propped a smile into place. "Mildred."

"Victoria is ready to see you now." She directed an acknowledging nod at Sam Johnson as he stood. "If you don't mind waiting, Mr. Johnson, it will only be a few more minutes before you can go in, as well."

Jim felt his gaze narrow with suspicion. What was Victoria up to? He sent Johnson a "beats me" look as the man resumed his seat.

Mildred led the way to the door on the other side of the small waiting area and opened it. "Let me know if you change your mind about coffee."

Jim didn't respond, his entire attention already focused on the room beyond the door Mildred had just opened. The setting was a little generic, not at all his mother's usual elegant style, but this building was only temporary office space. The agency's new home was still under construction.

He walked in, instantly feeling his tension escalate to the next level. The Colby Agency had that effect on him; always had. He imagined most anyone who entered the inner sanctum of the head of the Colby Agency—temporary or not—experienced the same. For more than a quarter of a century, the Colby Agency had stood head and shoulders above the rest as the most prestigious private investigation agency in Chicago, perhaps in the whole country. Jim admired his mother and all she had done.

"Jim, thank you for coming."

"Victoria," he acknowledged.

His mother indicated the wingchair to his left. "Please have a seat." She settled into the leather executive chair behind her desk.

It wasn't until Jim moved around the chair she'd designated that he saw the other person already seated in the room. Female. Blond hair, brown eyes. Thirtyish. Posture rigid. Gaze assessing. A cop.

The woman extended her hand. "Hello, Mr. Colby."

Yep. Definitely a cop. She had that formal bearing, that watchful eye.

Jim pumped the lady's hand once then looked to his mother for an explanation.

"Please make yourself comfortable, Jim. This is Detective Lisa Smith. She and I will explain everything."

He lowered himself into the chair, analyzing the three words uttered by the woman seated next to him when she'd shaken his hand. "West Coast?" he asked, turning his attention to Detective Smith.

"L.A.," she confirmed.

Now he got the picture.

"Jim, Detective Smith flew in to Chicago yesterday. She came directly to my office with some concerns of which I believe you need to be aware."

Major patience was required to keep his temper in check. He'd already gotten the picture. "What kind of concerns?"

"You may or may not know, Mr. Colby," Detective Smith began in that careful tone cops used when they intended to tell you something that would actually tell you nothing at all, "but the three men who murdered Sam Johnson's fiancée allegedly belonged to a notorious L.A. gang known as the Crew."

He met her gaze with one that cut her no slack. He understood exactly why she was here, and he didn't like it at all. "I am very much aware of the kind of thugs who raped and murdered Anna Denali. The bastards deserved what they got, and if you're here looking for conclusions as to whether or not Sam Johnson had anything to do with their executions then you've come to the wrong man."

The detective didn't back down. "I'm not here for your conclusions, Mr. Colby. I'm here for the truth," she said frankly. "Sam's name has come up in recent gangland rumblings. There's still a contract out on him, and someone has recently decided to provide the necessary motivation to see that it's fulfilled."

"And," Jim countered, "you wouldn't mind clearing up that unsolved case sitting on the corner of your desk in the process. Isn't that right, Detective?"

Detective Smith's gaze held his, but he saw the faintest flicker of indecision.

"Jim," Victoria cut through the mounting tension, "Detective Smith's first obligation is to protect. That's why she has come to us rather than launch an official investigation of her own."

Jim's attention never deviated from the detective. "Really? Or maybe your lieutenant didn't think there was enough evidence to launch an official investigation so you're on your own."

Another glimmer of doubt told him he'd hit the nail on the head.

"I considered coming to you first," Detective Smith said. "Now I'm glad I listened to my instincts. You obviously can't see beyond your own uninformed deductions regarding a case about which you've heard only one totally unobjective side."

Jim laughed softly, but there wasn't a damned thing pleasant about it, any more than there was about the irritation churning inside him. "You would be correct, Detective." He stood, leveled a firm stare on Victoria. "I'm quite certain you can decide what cases your agency should take without any assistance from me. This meeting is over."

He turned his back and headed for the door. Right now was not a good time to speculate what the hell Victoria had meant calling him here, much less taking this pointless case. He'd form his conclusions when he'd cooled off and could think more rationally.

"Jim."

Hesitating wasn't something he would have done in the past. But there he stood at the door, making that hopeful pause…giving Victoria the benefit of the doubt. He needed her to trust him. This meeting, the detective's presence, screamed of distrust and doubt.

"I'm taking this case," Victoria said, "for *you.*"

Fury kindled, diminishing the hope and amping up his already soaring tension. He turned to face his mother. "I don't need protecting, Victoria. I can handle anything that comes my way. You of all people should be aware of just how well I can do that."

Victoria didn't falter. He hadn't expected she would. "I would like to offer a compromise."

"What kind of compromise?" He shouldn't stand for this…but she was his mother. Changing her mind would take nothing short of a presidential veto.

That Detective Smith kept quiet told Jim hat she and Victoria had already discussed the likelihood of this reaction and that the two had agreed on this so-called compromise. That only annoyed him all the more. Unreasonably so.

"The police aren't going to investigate the threat to Sam," Victoria suggested, "until someone has actually committed a crime against him, and that might be too late. I'm certain you don't want Sam hurt any more than he already has been."

That much was true. Jim dropped his hand away from the door. "So, you're going to look into the case." He didn't need her to spell it out. The Colby Agency took cases like this all the time. But this was Jim's associate. The case should be his. It should be handled by the Equalizers.

"Actually, one of my investigators is going to work with Detective Smith," Victoria explained. "Detective Smith knows the territory and the facts surrounding what happened to Sam's fiancée better than anyone. Her knowledge and contacts are crucial."

"Why send one of your investigators?" Jim countered, determination and some amount of arrogance nudging him to push the issue. "As invaluable as Detective Smith's knowledge of the case and her contacts might be, Sam Johnson's would be even better. This case should be his. He's the one with the most to lose."

Even from across the room he noted the slight shift in his mother's posture as she said, "He's too close. The case is too personal for him."

Jim resisted the impulse to laugh. "We both know

that rule is only applicable in theory. It has no place in real life, otherwise Detective Smith wouldn't be involved in this case."

Victoria held his gaze for several seconds. Whatever she said next, she could not deny his assertion.

"Perhaps you're right. Why don't we call in Sam and see what kind of compromise we can reach?"

Jim didn't miss the way the detective tensed at the suggestion. Interesting. If she was on the up-and-up she had nothing to hide.

"You have a problem with that, Detective Smith?" He shifted the conversation back to the lady from L.A.

She turned fully to meet his gaze. "Absolutely not."

"Good." Jim looked back to Victoria then. "This is the only right way to do this. I don't think we want to go down that other road."

Victoria nodded once in acknowledgment of the line he'd drawn. Jim opened the door and gestured for Johnson to join him.

As he entered the room, Jim said, "Johnson, I'm sure you know Detective Smith from L.A."

Johnson stopped in the middle of the room. His gaze collided with the detective's.

Smith rose from her chair. "Hello, Mr. Johnson."

The tension that rippled through Jim's associate was more than just surprise. There was something between him and the detective. Something more than the ugly history of the homicide investigation.

"Detective Smith," Johnson said before glancing over at Jim.

"Detective Smith has come all the way from L.A.," Jim noted, working hard to keep the sarcasm out of his tone as he brought his associate up to speed, "because she believes there is some threat to your life."

"There's talk," Smith explained, "that the Crew is planning a hit on you."

Sam digested that information for three or four beats. "And you felt compelled to deliver that message in person?"

Definitely something between these two. Jim saw it in his associate's posture and heard it in his voice.

Smith blinked once, twice. "I think it's past time we got to the bottom of what really happened. That way maybe we can stop this before someone else has to die."

"The truth is," Johnson said with a bluntness that held everyone in the room silent, "your department couldn't care less if I die. This isn't about helping me, and you know it. It's about solving a case that baffled L.A.'s finest, and I don't mean my fiancée's murder."

Jim had to give Detective Smith credit, she held her ground. Her navy slacks and pale blue blouse were pristine, not a wrinkle, and her poise was nothing less than professional. When she spoke, her voice was strong and steady.

"My partner would like nothing better than to nail you, that's true," she admitted, "but I don't share his theories on what really happened. What I do believe in is the truth. I think it's time we knew what that was." And then she made a major strategical error. "I also think you're way overdue to stop running from the past."

Sam Johnson executed an about-face and stalked out of the room.

Jim didn't follow, but he did offer the detective a bit of sage advice. "If you want his cooperation, it's best not to insult him until he's committed."

Smith squared her shoulders. "I'll talk to him."

To Jim's surprise, she took off after Johnson. He had to give her credit; the lady was definitely determined.

"I hope you understand why I'm doing this, Jim."

Jim studied Victoria for a bit before saying exactly what was on his mind. "You're the one who needs to understand. I'm not that little boy who vanished twenty years ago. You have to stop punishing yourself for that, Victoria. It wasn't your fault. You need to come to terms with the reality that I'm a grown man. I survived twenty years in hell without you. I don't need you looking over my shoulder now."

He didn't want to hurt her, but he had to get that through to her…somehow.

Chapter Two

Sam cleared the stairs leading down to the second floor of the Colby Agency's temporary home. One more floor and he'd hit the lobby and be out of there.

"Johnson, wait!"

He hesitated on the landing halfway between the first and second floors and closed his eyes for five seconds in an attempt to calm the rage simmering inside him before he said something he would regret. Detective Lisa Smith had no business showing up here. Damn it!

"What do you want?" he demanded when she hesitated one step above him. What did she hope to accomplish by coming here? He was just beginning to enjoy his new life. He didn't need the past barging in.

"I want the truth, Johnson. You can't keep running away from it." She rested her hand on the railing and took the last step down to stand toe to toe with him. "As long as I have a breath left in me I'm going to keep haunting you. You should know that by now."

Oh, yeah, he knew. He'd gone through months and months of hell because of her and her partner. The last four months of long-awaited peace weren't nearly enough to banish those dark days.

He looked directly into her eyes, let her see the resolve in his. "You're wasting your time, Detective Smith. You won't ever know what happened. You can dog my every step for the rest of my life. It's not going to work." A ragged, involuntary exhale reminded him that he'd been holding his breath.

"Then we have a problem, Sam," she said with a fortitude that matched his own. "Because it's going to take both of us to stop what's going down back home even as we speak." She lifted her chin and ratcheted up the warning in her eyes. "And I'm not going back to L.A. without you."

He leaned closer, heard her breath hitch at the unexpected move. "No, Detective, *we* don't have a problem. *You* have a problem." He knew his civil rights forward and back. No way could she make him go back without a court order. If she'd had one, they wouldn't be having this discussion right now. She would have arrived with her partner and all would have been handled swiftly and by the book.

As if he hadn't said a word, she took another shot

at convincing him. "Lil Watts has issued a new contract on you. You'll be lucky to survive the week. No one close to you will be safe. Maybe you've forgotten how these guys work."

Sam looked away, remembered terror slithered beneath his skin in spite of his best efforts to suppress any and all emotion. He still had a sister in L.A. Parents. None of whom understood his decision to leave…could never know his reason. The words he refused to utter aloud stuck in his throat. His family was supposed to be safe as long as he stayed away. That was the deal.

"When did things change?" His voice was bitter, brittle, as he leveled his attention on the detective once more.

"About two weeks ago." Her eyes told him she wanted to back up a step, but she stayed put. "I guess you didn't hear about it. The Man is dead. Murdered. Lil Watts took over. He's shaking things up. Every damned gang in L.A. is restless. I think he wants to set his own precedents. Make himself look superior by having his long-awaited vengeance on you—the one that got away."

Sam knew the gang members weren't the only ones nervous. The riots of 1992 hadn't been forgotten by anyone who'd lived through them. She was right. He hadn't heard. He'd stopped watching the news a long time ago. But her revelation certainly explained why she was here. The Man had made the deal with Sam, and he was dead.

That meant one thing: open season on Sam Johnson and anyone he cared about.

"What's the standing order?" There would be specifics. It wouldn't be enough just to make him dead. Lil Watts liked pumping up the drama and the gore. Like Napoleon, his small stature dictated that he constantly attempt to make up for what he lacked in size. He wouldn't rest until he'd made a circus act out of the situation and proved just how big and powerful he was to the world he now represented.

"Your head," she said bluntly, "delivered to him on the proverbial platter. He chose six of his most devoted followers—whichever one brings him what he wants gets to be his right-hand man."

Now there was some heavy incentive. A scuzz-ball's wet dream.

"So, basically, I'm a dead man."

Those brown eyes searched his before she nodded, her expression grim.

If Sam was nowhere to be found, the more ambitious and intelligent of the chosen hunters would go for his unsuspecting family. He didn't need the good detective to tell him that.

"What about Sanford?" Detective Charles Sanford had hated allowing Sam to walk away. He'd taken it badly when he hadn't been able to prove

Sam's involvement in the murders of those who had killed Anna. Sanford hadn't given Sam a minute's peace as long as he had remained in Los Angeles.

"In a nutshell," she replied, "he's hoping to be the one to ID your remains." A weary sigh escaped her. "He doesn't know I'm here. The whole division thinks I'm on vacation in Mexico."

Sanford would love nothing better than to dance on Sam's grave. No surprise there. The truly startling idea was that *she* was here. That she'd warned him what was going down. "If your partner finds out you lied to him he's not going to be happy." Sanford wasn't the type to forgive this kind of perceived betrayal, no matter if justice was Smith's primary motive, and Sam wasn't entirely sure about that. Sounded a little too simple to him.

"I don't intend for him to find out," she countered, the frankness in her expression credible.

He got the picture now. "You think we can do this under the radar?"

Another of those barely discernible nods. "We'll go in dark. Keep a low profile while we try and neutralize this situation before anyone gets hurt. If we prove you weren't involved in the murders, assuming you weren't, then Watts should back off."

"Impossible." She was out of her mind. If this was her way of getting him to come clean about what really happened, she could forget it.

"It's the only way I can help you." For the first time since she'd arrived, he saw a flicker of trepidation in her eyes. "You have to trust me, *Sam.*"

He ignored the new kind of tension that filtered through him when she used his first name like that… like she cared. He couldn't afford any soft feelings where this woman was concerned. "What you're suggesting, Detective—" his gaze bored into hers "—will not set me free. It will only get us killed."

"You're dead, anyway."

He couldn't argue with that. "There are far better ways to achieve a promotion, Smith." If she wanted to make the next pay grade she should focus on kissing up to the brass, not digging around in cold cases that would get her six feet under.

Her one hand resting on the railing, she plowed the fingers of the other through her hair as if her patience had thinned. "I told you—"

"I know what you told me," he cut in. "Don't play games with me, Detective. Give it to me straight. If I'm going back to L.A. with you, I at least need to know you're not a head case. I have no desire to go dark with a cop who's suicidal."

Well, hell, he'd really messed up now. He'd given her that inch she wanted so desperately. He'd admitted that he was going back to L.A. It wasn't as if he had a choice. When had his brain staged a mutiny and decided he was going with her?

This time when she met his eyes there was no trepidation. That unyielding determination was back, full force. Maybe even had a little anger in the mix. "I want to help you get your life back…for real."

That tug he hadn't felt in months—not since the last time they'd stood this close—had him fighting the need to lean closer…to taste the grim line of those lush lips. Oh, yeah. Ten minutes around her and he'd already lost his grip on reality. He had to be out of his mind to even consider what she was proposing.

He was a fool, that was for sure.

Sam drew back a step, mentally shook off the too-intense moment. There wasn't any going back now. "We should go back to Victoria's office and work out the particulars."

"Does this mean you're going back to L.A. with me?"

If she was surprised at his decision, she kept the reaction carefully concealed behind that inflexible cop demeanor she'd yanked back into place.

"It means I'm going back. Whether I go with you or not is yet to be seen."

He walked around her and headed up the stairwell.

It wasn't like he had a choice. He couldn't let Watts carry out his vengeance on his family.

Going back to L.A. was the last thing he'd ever expected to do.

Ironically it probably would be the last thing he ever did.

LISA SMITH couldn't take the first step upward. Not yet. His answer had shocked her. She hadn't expected him to agree to go back to L.A. quite so easily. Not in a million years, actually.

A dozen steps up he abruptly stopped and turned to her. "You coming?"

Heat rushed up her neck and across her cheeks. If he noted her hesitation, thought for one second she couldn't handle this, he would refuse to cooperate. She knew the kind of man she was dealing with here. "Yeah. I'm right behind you." She took the steps two at a time until she'd reached the one just below him.

Instead of giving her his back and resuming his climb upward, he studied her...too close. She banished all emotion. Stared right back at him. Whatever he was thinking, she wouldn't have him reading her. She remembered all too well just how good he was at that particular skill.

When he decided the intimidation wasn't going to work, he turned forward and headed back up to Victoria Colby-Camp's office. Lisa didn't draw a deep breath until they were inside that neutral territory. Victoria had agreed to help her. That put her on Lisa's side. Strange, that decision also seemed to pit her directly against her own son. Lisa wasn't sure of the story there.

Jim Colby still stood in front of his mother's

desk, looking annoyed at the whole situation. Victoria remained calm and as regal-looking as when Lisa had first met her yesterday afternoon.

"I have to go back to L.A. and handle this," Sam said to Jim Colby. "There really isn't any other way."

"I can send Anders with you," Jim suggested. "You'll need backup."

Sam shook his head. Lisa had known he would do that.

"I have to do this alone."

Lisa held up both hands stop-sign fashion. "We do this my way, Johnson. I'm the one with the badge." No way was she going to have him going vigilante. Again. He had to understand who was in charge, here and now. Now that she knew he was going back, she could afford to push the boundaries a little. The glare he pointed in her direction told her what he thought of that idea.

"I would much prefer," Victoria interrupted, maneuvering easily through the thick tension radiating between Lisa and Johnson, "sending one of my investigators at least in a support capacity."

"Support would be helpful, as long as there's no question who's in charge." Lisa looked from Victoria to her son, Jim Colby. Both were determined to help, but she needed him to be onboard with her. Jim Colby kept whatever he was thinking to himself.

Johnson, however, did not. He moved his head firmly from side to side. "No one else gets involved. The only way to do this is by slipping into that world, the less fanfare the better. It's too risky to drag anyone else into the situation."

Lisa couldn't argue the validity of that particular point, but backup could make the difference between success and failure. She couldn't call on anyone in Homicide for support of any nature. If they figured out what she was up to, the chief would have her shield. Not to mention that Chuck would probably request a new partner.

"We'll need logistical support," Lisa argued, infusing as much logic into her tone as possible. "We can't go under deep cover and handle any necessary logistics at the same time."

Johnson appeared to consider her assertion. Good. She'd made him think. The operation they were talking about was extremely dicey at best. Any and all help behind the scenes that didn't come from LAPD would be beneficial.

"All right. Logistical support and that's it. No one goes in except me."

There he went again. "And me," she reminded, setting him straight.

He looked away, gave his attention to his boss. "I need to make arrangements for my family." His sister was ten years his junior. She still lived with his parents while she completed her doctorate at UCLA.

"I'll send two of my investigators to serve as security," Victoria offered. "I have several who are the absolute best to be found."

"Anders will provide logistical support," Jim Colby said to Sam, choosing not to comment on his mother's offer. "Anything you need, you let him know. He's been in far worse places than L.A.'s gang world."

Johnson said to Lisa, "Spencer Anders is former Special Forces. He spent most of his time in the Middle East. He could handle this with his eyes closed."

"Good." She didn't mention that she already knew Anders was former military. She'd run a complete background check on the Equalizers the day Johnson went to work there. "There's a flight that leaves at three this afternoon. We could be on it," Lisa suggested. The sooner they were on their way the better, in fact. She didn't want him having any extra time to reconsider.

"That'll work," he agreed, though it didn't sound as if his heart was in the decision.

"Let's use the agency jet," Victoria offered as she pushed out of her chair. "That way the two of you can brief the others en route, and equipment transport won't be a problem. Airport security makes getting across country with the necessities for an assignment like this nearly impossible."

Victoria was right. A private aircraft would make travel considerably less complicated for all involved. Excellent idea or not, Lisa couldn't help noticing the increasing tension in Jim Colby. His posture grew even more rigid and his jaw tightened to the point that a muscle repeatedly contracted there. Apparently, he was not pleased with what he presumed to be Victoria's interference. When running that background check, Lisa had learned that Jim Colby was Victoria's son. Evidently, Victoria had remarried since her surname was now Colby-Camp. Maybe that was part of the problem. Whatever. Lisa was no shrink, but her gut instinct told her that there was an explosion coming between these two.

Or maybe Victoria was unhappy that her son had started his own firm rather going into the family business. Lisa had wondered at that. Evidently Jim had drawn a line in the sand, professionally speaking, and Victoria just kept crossing it. A standoff, Colby versus Colby. Lisa would just as soon not be around when those two reached their breaking points. And it was coming, fast, that much was as plain as day.

Jim turned to Johnson. "We should get the communications equipment together. I don't want you out of touch with Anders."

"And fire power," Johnson added.

"I'll instruct the pilot to prepare," Victoria said to no one in particular, though Lisa suspected what she wanted was for her son to acknowledge her act of support.

"Can we be ready to go by three?" Lisa looked from one man to the other. She recognized that Victoria needed certain information, starting with takeoff time.

Johnson shifted his attention to her, though reluctantly so. "Three will give us plenty of time."

Jim Colby nodded. "We'll rendezvous at the airfield at two-thirty," he said to Victoria.

His comment felt like a dismissal to both her and Victoria, but Lisa wasn't going anywhere without Sam Johnson. No way was she going to risk him taking off on her and doing this on his own.

"I don't see any reason to hang around here," she said with a glance in Victoria's direction. "I can drop my rental off and join the two of you for preparations," she said to Jim Colby. "If—" this was the tricky part "—Johnson doesn't mind giving me a ride from the rental car agency."

Johnson stared straight at her. For three beats she was certain he was going to say no.

"I can do that."

He didn't want to, his body language shouted that message loud and clear, but for some reason he didn't turn her down.

Lisa offered her hand across Victoria's desk. "Thank you for your help, Mrs. Colby-Camp."

Victoria shook her hand. "I'll see you this afternoon, Detective Smith. I'm certain that we can find the truth you're looking for and neutralize this volatile situation for Mr. Johnson."

Hoping like hell she was right, Lisa turned to Sam Johnson. "Are you ready?"

To Jim Colby, Johnson said, "I'll see you back at the office."

Colby confirmed with a nod. "I'll just finish up here."

With Johnson right behind her, Lisa left Victoria's office without a backward glance. She could feel the tension mounting once more, pushing the air out of the room. Mother and son weren't finished by any means.

The trip down the two flights of stairs was made without conversation this time and with every bit as much tension as before. They'd reached the parking lot before Johnson said a word to her.

"Which rental agency?" he asked without so much as a glance at her.

"Budget."

"I'll meet you there."

She wanted to say no. To tell him that she'd rather stay close behind him or have him follow her.

"Okay." At least she knew what kind of car he drove and his license plate number. She'd just have to keep him in her line of sight.

Lisa headed for her rental, keeping an eye on Sam Johnson as he strode toward his own sedan. She got into her car and started the engine. The opportunity to hit the street at the same time he did wasn't possible, but she did fall in three cars behind him.

She gripped the steering wheel in a death lock as she waited for an opportunity to maneuver closer to his black sedan. A stop light caught her after he'd passed through it.

"Damn!"

Her heart thudding in her chest, she waited for the green. Her foot instinctively shifted from the brake to the accelerator the instant the light changed. She'd never catch him now.

The cell phone in her pocket vibrated. Not taking her eyes off the back of Johnson's car, she dug out her phone and took a breath.

"Smith."

"Hey, Smith, where the hell are you?"

Lisa's pulse skittered. Her partner, Charles Sanford.

"I'm…headed to a spa appointment," she lied. "Where the hell are you?"

She cut right, edging between two cars, which left only one between her and Johnson.

"I figured you'd still be in bed. You're supposed to be partying, hanging out in the bars all night. Isn't that what singles do when they go to Cozumel?"

She glanced at the digital clock on the dash— 9:20 a.m. Two hours earlier in L.A.

"I had to take the first appointment of the morning to get this particular masseur. He's supposed to be the best." She bit her lip and hoped he'd go for the lie.

"Oh-ho, I see how it is. Well, enjoy. I just wanted to check in and make sure you were be-having yourself."

"Thanks, Chuck. I'll see you next week."

Lisa closed the phone and slid it back into her pocket. Was her partner suspicious? She couldn't be sure. She'd given him no reason to be…but he was no fool. He'd been at this a whole lot longer than she had. He knew she was obsessing over the news about Johnson. In fact, she'd used that as her excuse for the abrupt vacation. The timing had worked out perfectly. Her parents were away on vacation with friends, as well, so she didn't have to worry about them calling to check up on her.

Still, her story might not be enough for her partner.

Pushing her partner's call aside, she changed lanes, tried to get behind Sam's car. She'd almost caught up with him. As she moved closer, a look at the license plate told her she'd made a mistake at some point since leaving the Colby Agency parking lot.

This wasn't Johnson's car.

Where was he?

There was no other vehicle matching his for as far as she could see.

With no other choice, she drove to the rental agency and parked. No sign of Sam Johnson in the lot.

Just her luck. Less than an hour after coming face-to-face with him again and he'd lied to her already.

So much for finding the truth.

Chapter Three

Sam watched Lisa Smith climb out of her rental car and survey the lot. She was looking for him. He shouldn't keep her guessing like this, but he needed to be sure of her motives. He'd played a little switch-and-bait with her, falling in between a couple of other black sedans and then abruptly making an exit while she followed the others. Even with that one traffic signal to his advantage, he could only assume she'd been distracted, otherwise he wasn't sure he would have fooled her so easily.

He'd taken a shortcut to the rental agency and parked where he could watch her arrive.

When she walked out of the rental office, an overnight bag in her hand, and took another long look around the lot, he decided to put her out of her misery. He backed out of the parking slot where he'd waited, then pulled up right in front of her.

She tried to act as if she weren't surprised as she

stowed her bag in the back, then slid into the passenger seat, but he knew better.

"Did you get an unexpected call?" he ventured as he merged into the traffic on the street.

Her startled glance in his direction gave him his answer. He'd been guessing, of course. But a cell phone call was the most likely culprit whenever a driver got distracted. Since she didn't have any passengers, hadn't been eating while driving and there hadn't been any traffic incidents to vie for her attention, then the cell phone was the probable candidate. He'd gotten away from her too easily to believe that one traffic signal had done the trick. This lady was trained in surveillance.

"Or maybe you made one," he went on when she couldn't decide how to answer. "Maybe to let your partner know how and when we were arriving."

The line of her jaw tightened. She didn't have to be looking at him for him to sense her anger. He'd ticked her off by suggesting she was keeping something from him. That she didn't deny his charges didn't bode well. The detective was hiding something, it seemed.

"Detective Sanford called," she said crisply, maintaining that steady watch on the traffic in front of their car.

"Did you give him an update on me?" He should

have known that she wouldn't be working alone. The cop mentality was pair oriented.

"I told him I was on my way to a spa appointment." She looked at him then. "He thinks I'm in Cozumel on vacation."

Sam fixed his attention on the street as he maneuvered through midmorning traffic. "If I find out you're lying to me—"

"You won't."

Instead of driving directly to the office, he turned in the direction of his place. He might as well pack a bag and check the aquarium. Once preparation was underway back at the office, he didn't want to have to break away for anything as menial as grabbing his toothbrush. He'd driven a dozen or so blocks before she spoke up. He hadn't expected to get that far.

"Where are we going?"

"My place." He took the next left. "I'm sure you already know the address."

She didn't bother denying his charge. He imagined that she knew all there was to know about him except the details of why and how the three scumbags who murdered Anna were executed.

He couldn't really hold that against her. He'd done his research on her, as well as her partner, not long after his fiancée was murdered. At the time, he'd considered it his job to know if the cops on the case were up to snuff.

"I know a few things myself. Lisa Marie Smith," he said out loud, mostly to unnerve her. "Thirty-one, born in San Diego, graduated Berkley with a degree in criminology. Made detective just over five years ago, much to the annoyance of your male peers. Assigned to homicide one month later. No family in L.A. Never been married. One dog."

She continued her steady gaze out the windshield. "The dog died. Old age. I'd had him since I was in high school."

"That's a shame." He slowed the car and took a right turn. "I'm sure you miss him." He'd had a dog once. But the animal had gotten so attached to Anna that he'd literally grieved himself to death after her murder. Sam had decided after that he'd stick with fish.

Anna. He didn't say or think her name very often. He banished the images that immediately attempted to intrude on his thoughts. Anytime he did he was sorry for it. She was gone. There was nothing he could do to bring her back. Her parents hated him, held him responsible. He couldn't blame them. He was responsible. It was his fault Anna had died.

"Nice place," Smith said as he made the final turn.

His thoughts drifted back to the present with her comment. He parked in the driveway of his Oak Park home. The price he'd gotten for his Hollywood Hills home would have bought something much larger and in the ritziest market available in Chicago, but he hadn't been looking for glamour or square footage.

This place gave him the peace and quiet he needed.

By the time he'd gotten out and rounded the hood, she had already emerged from the passenger side. He led the way up the walk and to the door.

"Seems quiet," she remarked.

"It is." Since school was out for the summer, there would be a little more excitement around the neighborhood throughout the day. Otherwise the neatly manicured lawns were clear of clutter and people during the morning hours.

First thing, he checked the aquarium and filled up the automatic feeder. He could be gone for two weeks and not have to worry. Fish didn't need to be walked or boarded at the kennel. Didn't need baths or any particular attention. Just a clean tank and food.

Uncomplicated. That was his new motto.

Smith stood in the middle of his living room looking around. He hadn't bothered with any decorating and, admittedly, the furniture left something to be desired. But he didn't spend much time here so he didn't actually care. He'd sold his house in California fully furnished. Too many memories to bring any of the stuff with him.

"Have a seat. I'll only be a few minutes."

His new home had two bedrooms, one he'd

turned into an office. That was the one part of his past he'd kept, his research books. As a forensics scientist, he'd used reference materials daily. So far he hadn't really needed them in his new job, but it didn't hurt to have them around.

He grabbed a duffel from his closet and stuffed it with two changes of dark-colored clothes, gloves and the necessary toiletries. He threw in a mini flashlight and a small first-aid kit.

"You kept your reference books."

Sam turned at the sound of her voice. She stood in the open doorway, but made no move to enter his bedroom. That she'd peeked into his home office didn't surprise him. A cop didn't stop being a cop just because she or he wasn't on official duty.

"I did." He zipped the duffel and lifted it off the unmade bed. "I'm ready."

"You didn't keep any pictures of her?"

She stayed in that doorway almost as if she intended to have her answers before she let him pass. Evidently she'd already had herself a better look around than he'd realized.

"No." He'd sold or put away everything, except the books, related to the past.

"You shouldn't pretend she didn't exist."

If those brown eyes hadn't looked so sincere, he might have considered that she was baiting him, but he could see that she was serious.

"She's dead. She doesn't care what I pretend." He moved toward the door, expecting the nosy detective to step out of the way. She didn't.

"That's how you're dealing with it?"

What the hell did she want from him? The last time he'd spoken with Detective Lisa Smith she'd been convinced he'd killed three men in cold blood. Did she believe she could get close to him like this and find that truth she wanted so badly to know?

"Let's get one thing straight."

She still didn't back off, just looked directly into his eyes.

"My personal life is off-limits. It's none of your business. End of story."

"Strange," she said with a puzzled expression. "I thought this whole thing was personal. Three members of a notorious gang killed your fiancée, then ended up dead a short time after. Lil Watts wants you dead. Sanford wants you on death row. What part of that do you feel *isn't* personal?"

He stepped directly into her personal space and cranked up the irritation in his tone when he spoke. "This is never going to work, Smith."

"Probably not," she agreed without a glimmer of trepidation as she stared up at him. "But I don't see any point in pretending I don't want answers or that how you're dealing with the past doesn't matter."

"Stick to the facts related to the case," he ordered.

"We're not friends. We've never been friends. How I'm dealing with life in general isn't your concern."

She pivoted on her heel and walked back into the living room. He watched her go, tamped his emotions back down to a more manageable place.

If he got even an inkling that she was working a scam on him, this liaison was over.

For now he had no choice but to go along with her. He'd been out of touch with life in L.A. for more than four months. He needed the detective to get him back up to speed. Then he might just have to break out on his own. That option would be in her best interest, anyway. If she hung around him too long she would likely end up dead.

The Offices of the Equalizers
1:45 p.m.

"THAT SHOULD COVER IT." Jim Colby shuffled the stack of reports they had just gone over. The reports included everything from seven-day weather forecasts to topographical maps of Los Angeles County.

The communication links were wireless and the tracking devices were state-of-the-art. Spencer Anders would serve as backup. Sam wasn't exactly sure how that would work in real time, but he had to say he was glad for the support as long as Anders stayed out of the line of fire.

"You have a question, Detective Smith?"

Sam looked from Jim Colby to Smith. She'd picked up one of the reports from his stack and appeared to be studying it.

"I'm wondering how a private citizen in another state was able to get hold of an arrest record." She dropped the report back onto the stack. "I don't think I could have gotten it any faster."

Renee Vaughn, another of Sam's colleagues here at the Equalizers, stood. "I'm a former assistant prosecutor," she said with a quick smile. "I know the ropes, Detective. However, if you take issue with our under-the-table contacts, I would suggest you take it up with the boss." She aimed a wider smile at Jim Colby.

Smith held up both hands. "I have no issues with your tactics. I'm impressed, that's all."

The tension in the room reduced significantly.

Spencer Anders grabbed a gear bag. "We should head for the airfield. Wheels up in one hour."

Sam picked up the remaining bag. "Let's do it."

LISA CLIMBED into the backseat of the SUV belonging to Jim Colby.

"The pilot's sitting on ready," Jim announced as he closed his phone and started the vehicle. "Victoria has Brett Call and Jeff Battles rendezvousing with us there."

Lisa wondered why Jim called his mother by her

first name. Perhaps it was an effort to keep the conversation on a strictly professional level. But it felt like more than that. The tension she'd noted between the two went deeper than a need to maintain professionalism.

The drive to the private airfield utilized by the Colby Agency took just over half an hour. Spencer Anders and Sam Johnson kept a running dialogue regarding the gear they carried and the possible technical problems they might encounter. Lisa didn't mind that they left her out of the discussion loop. More than once she noticed Jim Colby watching her in the rearview mirror. She'd been with Sam Johnson since he'd learned of her presence in Chicago, so she was relatively sure the two men hadn't talked privately. Maybe she was being paranoid, but she had the feeling that Jim Colby was suspicious of her.

Then again, his conclusions about her could have more to do with Victoria taking her case than with anything else. Time would tell, she supposed.

Once at the airfield, Jim followed the signs to Hangar 3. Another SUV, black like the one belonging to Jim, waited. The Lear jet sat on the tarmac, fueled and ready for takeoff.

Lisa unloaded as soon as the SUV was parked. She joined the others at the rear and handled her own bag. Both Anders and Sam carried their personal bags, as well as a gear bag. There was more they'd have to come back for, the additional weapons and more sensitive communications equipment.

As they strode toward the aircraft, the occupants of the other SUV emerged. Victoria Colby-Camp and three men, members of her staff, Lisa presumed.

"Detective Smith," Victoria said as she approached, "this is Ian Michaels, my second in command, and investigators Brett Call and Jeff Battles."

Lisa shook hands with each of the men. Ian Michaels had the dark, mysterious look of a true spymaster. Jeff Battles would blend right in on any West Coast beach with his surfer-guy tan and blond hair. Brett Call had the broad shoulders of a football linebacker, but the red hair and freckles gave him the appearance of the boy next door. Judging by what she'd learned about the Colby Agency in her research, there was probably a great deal more than met the eye with these gentlemen.

"Don't hesitate to call on Jeff and Brett," Victoria reminded Lisa. "The Colby Agency's every asset is at your disposal."

"Anything you need," Jim Colby interjected with a look first at Lisa then at Sam, "I'm one phone call away."

Something like fear flashed in Victoria's eyes, puzzling Lisa for a moment, then she recognized it for what it was. Concern for her son's well-being.

Lisa considered the tall, well-muscled man in question. It didn't make sense for Victoria to worry on that level. The guy certainly looked as if he could take care of himself in most any situation. But there was something more, beyond the obvious. Lisa had noticed it before.

"Sam," Victoria said, drawing his attention to her. "Brett and Jeff are prepared to follow whatever instructions you feel appropriate for the protection of your family. I would suggest that Jeff tag around the university with your sister. He fits the proper profile."

"Those decisions will be made en route," Jim pointed out. Though his tone was cool and calm there was no mistaking his insistence on maintaining the lead.

Glad when the time came, Lisa was the first to go aboard the aircraft.

"Good afternoon, Detective Smith. I'm Race Payne, I'm your pilot." The tall, slender man gestured to the seating area that had all the markings of an elegant conference room. "Looks like you get first pick."

"Thank you." This was definitely traveling in style.

"You may keep your bag with you or stow it in the luggage closet at the rear of the passenger cabin."

She thanked him again and moved on to the seating area. Once she'd selected a seat close to a window, she dropped her handbag there and carried her overnight bag to the storage area. There was a minibar and a short corridor that led to the toilet and another door that was unmarked. She wondered if that was a private room or a store room.

"Private conference room."

Startled, she turned to face Brett Call. "Oh, thanks. I wondered about that."

Brett stashed his bags. "This is my second flight on the Colby bird." He hitched a thumb toward the bar. "Would you care for refreshments?"

Lisa shook her head. "I'm good, thanks."

Anders and Johnson had already taken their seats. Jeff Battles put his bag away and joined Brett at the bar for refreshments.

Lisa hoped it wasn't going to be this "us against them" the entire flight. In some ways, they were on opposing teams, but the operation was a joint effort. Behaving that way would be in the best interest of getting the job done.

After settling into her seat, she watched the men who represented the Equalizers. They spoke quietly as they moved through a stack of papers similar to the ones they'd viewed in Jim Colby's office. Hopefully, the two would be sharing that information with the Colby Agency representatives.

Deciding not to wait and see, Lisa spoke up as soon as Battles and Call had taken their seats. "Shall we start the briefing?"

Spencer Anders took charge. "Mr. Battles, you will be assigned to Mallory Johnson." Anders provided a photo and background info sheet on Sam's sister. "As Mrs. Colby-Camp pointed out, Mallory is a student at UCLA and you'll fit in well there."

Jeff took the photo and info sheet. "Will Miss Johnson be aware of my assignment?"

Sam shook his head. "I think it would be better if they didn't know."

Lisa was surprised at that. Was he purposely leaving his folks in the dark just so he didn't have to see them? Would he even notify them that he was in L.A.?

"Your parents are retired?" Brett inquired.

"Yes." Johnson handed photos and the needed info to Brett. "You might have a hard time keeping up with them on the golf course. Other than that, you'll find their routine fairly mundane."

"I'll maintain a command post of sorts," Anders added. "As soon as I have the location, I'll notify the team."

The *team.* That was a step in the right direction. Lisa saw an opportunity to take it one step farther. "We can use my place as the command post."

All eyes turned to her.

"The location is central, quiet and out of the high-traffic areas."

Anders nodded. "Good."

She felt Sam's gaze on her, but she avoided eye contact. "There are two phone lines, one's for a fax. My neighbors are older so they don't get out much. As long as you keep your vehicle parked in the garage there shouldn't be any questions."

"What about your partner?" This from Johnson.

Lisa's gaze met his. "He has no reason to drive by my place."

The sound system vibrated, signaling the pilot was about to make an announcement. "Ladies and gentlemen, please prepare for takeoff."

Safety belts were fastened into place across laps. Johnson was still studying her as if he suspected she'd volunteered her home for some reason that would be detrimental to him. Lisa focused her attention out the window on the people still standing near the SUVs.

Victoria Colby-Camp and her son Jim Colby waited, not quite side-by-side, since several feet separated them, for the plane to roll toward takeoff. Both watched the aircraft as if their full attention was required for proper function.

What was it between those two?

Lisa stole a glance at Sam Johnson. He'd redirected his attention to the reports spread across his lap. This uneasiness between the two of them was multifaceted for sure. There was the rage still simmering inside him at the loss of his fiancée. She sensed that emotion even as he outwardly denied it. Lisa had watched him lying in agony in that hospital room as he'd slowly recovered from the near lethal beating he'd taken that night. Before being allowed to lose consciousness, he'd been forced to watch the brutal rape and murder of the woman he loved.

Closing her eyes, Lisa shoved those images away. She'd gotten far too attached to him during those long months she and Sanford had been assigned to the case. Then the three suspects had gotten themselves murdered. Heinously so. Everyone in the division, all the way up to the chief, suspected that Sam Johnson had gotten his revenge. But there hadn't been a trace of evidence tying him to any of the scenes. Sanford had grilled him repeatedly. Followed him, harassed him, actually. Lisa had tried to pull him back, but Sanford was senior and he refused. Until the chief had ordered them off the case.

Then, three days ago, all hell broke loose. Lisa had known when The Man died that Sam Johnson's name would come up again. Somehow, Johnson had entered into an unholy alliance with the deceased leader of the Crew. His death had unleashed months of pent-up rage against Johnson. Now he was a wanted man. On more than one front. Charles Sanford would like nothing better than to nail him for multiple homicides.

When Lisa looked Sam Johnson in the eye, she

couldn't say that she was 100 percent sure that he *hadn't* killed those men, but she couldn't say he had, either. He'd had motive, that was certain. Means? She supposed so. Opportunity? Probably. But did he possess the ability to disengage emotionally so completely that he could kill not just in cold blood, but in a truly evil manner?

Lisa didn't think so.

Unfortunately, she couldn't be totally objective about that. Mainly because she'd fallen for the guy during those long months of watching him grieve. But she couldn't tell a soul, least of all him.

She felt his eyes on her once more. The woman in her pondered whether he'd ever felt that connection—that thin thread of electricity that somehow tethered them. She turned from the window, met his assessing gaze.

No matter what happened, she could never let him know how she felt. Not only would it be a mistake ethically, she was also certain it would be a huge personal error in judgment. He could never know.

If she'd been smart she would have closed the file on this case months ago. Tucked the whole package into a box and filed it away with all the other cold cases belonging to L.A. County's Priority Homicide Division.

As she held that analyzing stare, she had to admit that perhaps she wasn't nearly so smart as her detective's examination would indicate. But this had nothing to do with her intelligence level. This had to do with keeping Sam Johnson alive. If they didn't extinguish the volatile situation surrounding the murders of those three scumbags once and for all, Sam Johnson was going to pay the price:

His head delivered to the new man in charge.

Chapter Four

The Colby Agency jet touched down in the Sunshine State's Santa Monica Airfield at 5:00 p.m. Sam was the last to leave the plane. Tension rippled along his nerve endings. Irrational anxiety had clamped around his chest in a breath-halting grip. He'd sworn he would never come back here, not for anything. His family visited him in Chicago now and again, but coming back here alive was going back on the bargain he'd made.

Yet, here he was. He took the final step down onto the tarmac. Detective Lisa Smith was right, he wouldn't last long once word got out. He'd be lucky to survive this night much less the next one.

Truth was he was dead, anyway. There was no way he could hope to defuse this thing—to pretend otherwise would be a major joke on himself. If he managed to protect his family, that would have to be enough. Watts would never permit him to leave California alive. It would be a matter of pride.

Spencer Anders closed his cell phone as he approached Sam. "The rental agency dropped off the requested vehicles." He gestured to four black sedans parked near the hangar. "Keys are in the ignitions."

Anders turned to Detective Smith then. "I'd like to get set up at your place as quickly as possible."

She fished the keys from her purse and handed them to Anders. "I assume you know the location. I'll be sticking with Johnson and—" she swiveled her attention to Sam "—I doubt that's where he wants to go first."

Anders accepted the keys to her house with a nod and no argument.

Sam didn't argue her decision, either—it would be pointless. She wasn't going to let him out of her sight. As much as he hated to admit it, he was relatively certain her assistance would come in handy. He just hoped it didn't get her killed. But she was determined. He doubted anything he could say would change her mind about going with him. Why waste the effort?

"I'd like to get Call and Battles into position," Sam said to Anders. The two Colby Agency investigators were already loading their bags into two of the rentals. They understood as well as Sam did that there was no time to waste. Once word of his arrival was on the street, things could go downhill in one hell of a hurry.

"Check in with me when that's done," Anders said before heading to the third vehicle. "I don't want you out of touch for more than a couple of hours."

"Got it." Sam followed Smith to the fourth sedan.

"Would you like me to drive?" she offered.

He started to say no, but he surprised himself by saying, "Yeah."

After instructing Battles and Call to follow, Sam climbed into the passenger seat.

"I thought you might want to take in the sights," Smith commented as she drove away from the hangar.

Sam didn't respond. He'd only been gone a few months. He doubted that much had changed. Frankly, he didn't care one way or the other. He checked the side mirror to ensure Call and Battles were behind them as they merged into traffic. Anders had opted to stay on the boulevard while they took the expressway. Detective Lisa Smith lived off Santa Monica Boulevard in Century City which was pretty much a straight shot in the direction Anders chose.

Sam's folks lived a world away, in the affluent Bel-Air community. He wasn't too worried about Call being noticed hanging around in the exclusive neighborhood. Paparazzi hung around celebrity homes all the time. Not that his folks were celebrities, but there were plenty in their neighborhood.

Once in a while the local cops would advise the paparazzi to move on, but no one was ever surprised when they came right back.

"Your parents miss you."

Sam turned and stared at the detective's profile. "How would you know that?" If she had been talking to his folks…

"I call now and again to see how they're doing." She said this without looking at him.

The anger he'd kept at bay since putting life in L.A. behind him started to boil in his gut. "You have no right keeping tabs on my folks or me."

"You're wrong." She glanced at him this time. "Until this case is solved, I have every right. It's *my* case."

Sam held back the first response that rushed to the tip of his tongue. He knew this wasn't simply about clearing her record of the failure. As much as he wanted to say just that, it would be a lie. Lisa Smith was dedicated to the job. He'd known that about her long before he'd found himself a victim.

He'd worked with the L.A. County Forensics Division. For years he'd been one of the leading evidentiary experts. The techs brought in the evidence, and Sam put it all together. He'd been pivotal in solving many, many homicides. That dedication to duty had cost his fiancée her life. He'd ensured a murderer got his due, and she had paid the price.

Sam pushed the memories away. He couldn't change what had happened one night on La Cienega Boulevard nearly two years ago. It was too late to protect Anna. Way too late to make that right. But he had to protect his family. No one else needed to die because of his decisions.

"You should talk to them," Smith suggested quietly. "Let them know you're here. It's not right to keep them in the dark."

His jaw hardened against the idea that a hell of a lot wasn't right about this, but that didn't help. "The less they know the better off they are."

"Lil Watts doesn't have the same principles his uncle had. Your family's innocence in all this won't keep him from doing whatever he decides to do."

He didn't need her to tell him that. The Man, James Watts, had been a man of honor despite the fact that he'd been one of the instrumental forces in forming the Crew. Though he'd levied vengeance swiftly and fatally, he'd never once killed a man who hadn't deserved to die. The generation that came after him, including his beloved—however whacked—nephew, operated more often on impulse than honor.

Sam didn't say any more on the subject. No need to. He'd made up his mind. Nothing the detective said was going to change it. Instead, he watched as the sun dropped low in the sky, spilling its fading orange glow over the L.A. skyline in the distance. No matter what the detective said, he couldn't let sentimentality or foolish dreams get in his way.

Protecting his family was the best he could hope for. Staying alive was too much to ask.

LISA PULLED TO THE SIDE of the street directly across from the home belonging to the parents of Sam Johnson. She'd been here numerous times before. More often than Johnson needed to know, that was for sure. The house was obscured by the trees, the driveway one that wound deep into the unusually large lot before reaching the residence. The area was quiet and the surrounding homes hidden by the well-wooded landscape. This part of Bel-Air in particular was thick with trees, one of the few lushly forested neighborhoods in the L.A. area.

Call and Battles had joined Lisa and Johnson in their rental.

"Mallory should be in her evening class at this time," Battles advised. "I'll head there now unless you have additional directions."

His attention focused fully on the home where he'd grown up, Sam said, "You might want to put a tracking device on her car. Mallory can be tough to keep up with. She's had so many speeding tickets it's a miracle she hasn't lost her license already."

"I'd planned to do that," Battles acknowledged. "And perhaps one in her handbag or book bag."

"I'll relocate every few hours," Call put in, "keeping the house in my line of sight. If the neighbors on either side are on vacation I'll attempt to get closer to the property via that route."

"I'd like an update every four to six hours." Johnson shifted to face the men in the backseat. "If anything at all looks or feels wrong, I want to know it."

Call nodded. "I understand."

The two Colby Agency investigators exited the car and moved to their separate vehicles. Battles headed for the university while Call settled in on the shaded street for the evening.

"Are we ready to catch up with Anders at my place?"

Johnson pulled his attention from his parents' home and rested it on her. "First I'd like to go by the cemetery."

"It's still daylight," Lisa countered, "that's not a good idea." He'd be a sitting duck in that situation. She couldn't be sure that Watts or his people knew Johnson was back in L.A. already, but there was no need to take such an unnecessary risk.

"I can go with or without you."

She could squabble with him, maybe make him angry, but needed his cooperation. To that end, she had to go along with his request even when she didn't feel it was in his best interest.

"All right. Hillside Memorial it is then."

That he looked surprised that she had caved so easily told her that he'd expected to be able to use her resistance as an excuse to part company.

She'd made the right decision.

Hillside Memorial was in L.A; not that far, but evening traffic had gotten heavy, slowing them considerably. Convertible tops were down, music thumping, commuters were celebrating the passage of hump day. It would be all about Friday for the next twenty-four hours. That was the thing about Southern California: the weather was always perfect. One could admire the array of beautiful plants, one or the other always in bloom, and the well-kept lawns along Sunset Boulevard before the residential area gave way to the edgy clubs and restaurants. Amid such beauty it was difficult to believe that anything bad ever happened here. But that was only one side of this vibrant city.

Night would fall and other streets, those beyond the reach of all the glamour and glitz, would fill with the restless souls of those living in the depths of desperation and poverty. A vivid contrast where being a part of a gang, notorious or not, was the closest thing to belonging some people ever got.

Sam Johnson had crossed the line that separated

that life from his own. He'd found the single piece of evidence that sent Lil Watts's older brother to prison for murdering two cops. Lil had avenged his brother's incarceration by ordering the execution of Sam's fiancée. For Lisa, the story ended there. But she needed to know what happened after that. Who executed the three men who had carried out Lil Watts's orders? If it was Sam, why had Lil refrained from avenging their deaths until now? Why would James, The Man, have kept him in check until his death? What did James owe Sam…if anything? Why had Sam left L.A.? The memories? Or was that part of the deal?

Plenty of questions, not enough answers.

Hillside Memorial Park was deserted when they arrived. The air had grown cool and crisp as the sun slid lower into the mountains and canyons circling the city. Lisa stayed two steps behind Johnson as he walked through the rows of the buried along Sunset Slope. Lisa's nerves jangled as she repeatedly surveyed the cemetery, ensuring no one was watching.

Anna Denali's headstone was black granite and lay flush with the ground. The clean lines of her name and dates of birth and death were all that marred the sleek surface. No testaments to her short life, no cameo photos. An only child, her death had devastated her parents. They held Sam Johnson wholly responsible for what happened. Lisa didn't have to hear the words to know he held himself responsible, as well.

She stayed back, giving him plenty of room, as he knelt down and touched the marker that designated the woman he'd loved.

At thirty-one, Lisa was beginning to wonder if she would ever have a man feel for her what Johnson had felt for Anna Denali. Lisa had been too wedded to her job to have a decent social life. Her partner teased her nonstop that if she didn't find a man soon it would be too late to bother.

Maybe it was watching Sam Johnson agonize over losing the woman he loved that had driven the point home so completely. Lisa hadn't been completely happy with her life since. But then she hadn't been able to do anything about it since she'd been hung up on a man who was not only victim but suspect.

Such a waste of energy.

Not to mention really dumb.

Cutting herself some slack, how often did a woman spend eleven months focused so damned intently on one man? It would have been pretty hard to walk away unattached to the guy.

Her partner liked pointing out that her male counterparts didn't have that trouble. Not that she'd admitted her slip to him, but he joked about other female detectives who got involved with suspects.

In reality Lisa wasn't involved. And Sam Johnson wasn't a suspect anymore, not technically. If she could get to the truth, maybe her partner would finally let the idea that he was guilty go. Maybe Sam Johnson's life could go back to normal.

Maybe even hers would.

Watching the emotion tearing him apart as he kneeled next to his fiancée's grave wasn't exactly the fastest route to accomplishing that feat. She needed so badly to put this case behind her once and for all. As hard as she'd tried, she just couldn't get past it with all these unanswered questions haunting her.

As if he'd picked up on her thoughts, Johnson stood. "Let's go." He didn't wait for her to respond but strode back to the car.

The drive from the cemetery to her bungalow was filled with the same silence as when they'd left his parents' home. If that was the way it was going to be she would have a heck of a time learning anything at all from him. So much for cooperation. So far she'd been the only one putting forth any effort.

She parked down the block from her house. Dusk had invaded, providing some amount of cover as they hurried along the sidewalk, bags in hand. The lack of through traffic and pedestrians provided some sense of security as she scrutinized the area. There was no reason for anyone to suspect they would come here. Still, caution had to be her watchword. Sam Johnson might have a death wish, but she didn't.

"We'll enter through the back," she suggested as she cut through the narrow length of side yard that separated her house from the row of high hedges along the boundary of her neighbor's yard.

On second thought, she pulled out her cell and put in a call to Anders so he would know they were coming in. She had no desire to get shot by someone on their own team—assuming this was in fact a team effort. Their group possessed all the markings of a team, but the essential element of full collaboration was yet to be seen.

"We're at the back door now," she told Anders.

The door opened as if he'd been waiting there for her call. They hustled inside and closed out any prying eyes. The less they were seen in the open the better.

"You have several messages on your landline from your partner," Anders informed her. "I'm beginning to wonder if he really believes you're on vacation."

Lisa suppressed the initial reaction of irritation that he'd listened to her messages. "You're certain they're recent?" She was bad about erasing old messages.

"All in the last thirty-six hours. The most recent one was the only one listed as a new call. Have you been remote-accessing your machine?"

"No. I never check my messages remotely."

There was no reason for her to. Anyone she needed or wanted to hear from had her cell number. Why would Chuck do this? She dropped her bag and walked over to the answering machine to listen for herself. Four messages, all in the past thirty-six hours as Anders said, all repeating the same question: "You home yet, Smith?"

Her partner knew damned well she wasn't supposed to be home yet.

"Is it possible he has the code for accessing your machine?"

Lisa glanced at Sam, annoyed. "No. Why would he?"

Sam shrugged. "Maybe to see if you're checking your messages from here."

"He knows I hate answering machines," she argued. "The only reason I have one is because my mother complained that she could never reach me. She hates cell phones. Even then it sat in the box for months before Chuck forced me to hook it up...." He'd insisted she do it to keep her family happy.

"Did he help you do it?"

"No." Her gaze connected with Johnson's. "He set it up for me."

This was nuts. Why would he leave her messages and then check to see if she'd accessed them?

Because that would mean she was home, since she didn't know the remote access code. Why would

Chuck resort to such extreme measures to keep track of where she was on her own time?

"We'll have to leave a new message," Anders said quickly.

"Or he'll know someone has been here," Johnson added. "First we need a recording."

Anders searched the array of items he'd spread across her coffee table. "Got it." He used the palm-size machine to record as the last message Chuck Sanford had left was replayed.

This was crazy. Before she could argue, Sam was placing a call via his cell. When her machine picked up he played the recording of Sanford's voice into his cell phone. He did this only once, since there had only been one new message. The machine recorded it as if Chuck himself had just made the call.

"No answering your home phone," Johnson told her as he put his cell away. "No checking your messages."

She put up her hands. "Wait. This doesn't add up. Why would my own partner do this?"

"Because," Johnson said, as he placed his gear bag on the sofa, "he obviously doesn't believe you're on vacation. He thinks you're up to no good."

Unfortunately, her partner would be right. Lisa would be the first to admit that Chuck didn't like that she obsessed about Sam Johnson's possible inno-cence in the slaying of those three men who'd murdered his fiancée, but would he go this far to check up on her? Maybe, if he was worried about her. But that didn't make the tactic one motivated by some sinister agenda as these two obviously believed.

Still, why the hell had he learned the manufacturer-installed access code to her answering machine? Had he been banking on the idea that she wouldn't change it because she wouldn't ever use it?

What would be his motive?

Johnson planted his hands on his hips and fixed her with a look that said listen up. "Whatever you might be thinking, if we're going to be on the same team, we have to get one thing straight."

She matched his stance. "What's that?"

"Everyone is a suspect, even your beloved partner. If you really want to defuse this ticking bomb as much as you say, you're going to have to look at all involved in what happened with an eye toward assessing the possibility of their involvement. No one is exempt."

"Not even me?" If he considered her a suspect, then he needed his head examined.

"You're not the only one who can do a thorough background check, Detective," he said pointedly.

And then she knew he had learned her little secret. Even her partner didn't know about that.

"My brother's death doesn't make me a suspect," she argued, heading him off.

"Your brother died as a result of a gang shootout

in a retail store parking lot. You were twelve, your brother was fifteen. Don't pretend it didn't have an impact on your life. That's motive, Detective Smith. No matter how you look at it."

Why not put all her cards on the table? "You're right. It is motive. It's motive to become a cop. To try and stop gang killings before they happen, one at a time."

She hated the way he looked at her with his expression all full of sympathy. "This is L.A., Detective, gangs are a fact of life. So is murder. You aren't going to change that. The only thing you can hope to do is survive peaceably next to each other."

"I guess we'll just have to agree to disagree," she said resolutely. "Anna Denali was murdered by three gang members. If your version of the story is to be believed," she pointed out, "then one or more other gang members killed those three and left you looking like the perpetrator. It has to stop somewhere. Someone has to try and make a difference. Might as well be me."

The sympathy morphed instantly into fury. "I tried to make a difference, Detective," he said bitterly, "and look what it cost me."

"Are we ready to prep?" Anders asked, breaking the ensuing tense silence.

"Yeah," Johnson said, "we're ready."

His gaze never deviated from hers. It was like

he wanted her to argue with him, to prove they couldn't get through this night as a team, much less the next. But she held her tongue. If this effort didn't work, it wouldn't be on account of her stubbornness. He also stayed clear of her theory about who killed those bastards who murdered his fiancée. Maybe if she kept at him he'd admit what he knew at some point...hopefully before one or both of them were dead. Lisa pushed her frustration aside and listened up as Anders went over the gear.

Wireless communication links would keep her and Sam in touch at all times. Since Anders would be out of range, they would check in every few hours via cell phone. Tracking devices would keep him aware of their positions. The devices were small microfiber ones, which prevented detection by the naked eye. Anders would serve as the go-between for the team watching the Johnson family. That way everyone was apprised regularly and similarly.

Since Johnson insisted on a little night surveillance, Lisa changed into dark slacks and a dark pullover. L.A. nights could turn cool rapidly so she selected a lightweight blazer. She carried a black cap for tucking her hair into, but she wouldn't wear it until she needed to. She fastened her ankle holster in place and slid her .22 automatic into it. Her service revolver would be too bulky.

Sam dressed in jeans and T-shirt with an open, button-down shirt over it to hide the weapon tucked into his waistband. She didn't bother asking if he possessed a permit to carry a weapon. He'd be a fool not to carry, considering where they might end up before this night was over.

With a gear bag packed with additional rounds, flashlights, a detailed map of L.A. and surrounding communities, and Johnson's small first-aid kit, there really wasn't anything else to do. They had the cover of dark now. The only question was how he intended to make his first move.

"What's our plan?" She looked from Johnson to Anders and back. This was as far into the plan as they'd gotten on the plane.

Sam grabbed the gear bag. "Now we go put the word out."

Fear swelled in her throat. "Exactly what word is that?"

His gaze collided with hers. "That I'm back and ready to see who thinks they're big enough to fulfill that contract."

He had to be kidding. "Are you out of your mind? We won't last five minutes out there tossing your name around. We need to assess the situation. Measure the trouble waiting on the street without making our presence known."

Anders stayed out of the discussion, which told Lisa that he wasn't so hip on Johnson's plan, either.

"You can go with me and do exactly as I say or else you can stay here." Sam shrugged. "It's your call, Detective."

As she stood there too stunned to speak or act, he walked right past her headed for the back door.

"You can't possibly agree with this," she said to Anders.

"The only way to start the domino effect," Anders explained, "is to push the first one down."

"What domino effect?" Evidently these two were on some kind of wavelength she'd missed entirely.

"When you want the truth, Detective Smith, you start a chain reaction, and whoever has something to hide will always try to stop the momentum. All you and Sam have to do is start that reaction and wait and see who goes against the inertia."

She laughed, the sound was dry and wholly lacking in humor. "And stay alive in the process."

Anders acknowledged her point with a dip of his head. "That would be the most desirable scenario."

Lisa stalked off in the direction Sam had taken. Maybe if she hurried he wouldn't leave her behind. If he intended to get himself killed someone had to be there to call it in.

Assuming he didn't get her killed in the process.

Chapter Five

9:15 p.m.

The Box.

Skid Row.

A human calamity. A drug supermarket where gang members from all over this city and surrounding areas came to peddle their wares—usually crack and heroin. A place where addicts and people with psychiatric disorders were found every morning sleeping on the sidewalks. The open use of drugs and five-buck tricks in the portable toilets were as common as breathing.

Sam had thought this ugly side of his hometown was something he wouldn't be facing again in this lifetime. So much for future planning.

"I hope you know what you're doing."

Sam glanced at the woman in the passenger seat. Cop or no, armed or not, anyone with half a brain would be a little nervous in this neighborhood. But this was the closest thing to a safe zone he could hope to find within the territories of violence located in and around L.A.

Rival gang members stood on the same street corners taking care of business. Everybody was just doing what they had to do to survive, and all involved respected that—the faintest glimmer of that "honor among criminals" that The Man, James Watts, had lived and died by.

Sam wondered how long any honor would last with the up-and-coming generation of gangbangers. With what he knew about Lil Watts, not long for sure.

He parked in an alley between a rundown hotel where presidents and silent-film stars once stayed— before the area was swallowed up by the evil forces of drugs and desperation and a restaurant that had closed at nine.

"Leave it parked here and it'll be gone when we come back," Smith said with a long assessing look around. Dumpsters lined the far end of the alley, the smell of grease and food refuse permeating the air. "Assuming we make it back."

"It's cool," Sam assured her. He climbed out, grabbed the bag from the backseat and locked the doors.

Sam surveyed the dark alley, lit only by one meager streetlight, taking note of the tents and the cardboard condominiums already erected and occupied for the night. By 8:00 a.m. every last one would disappear, just in time for the gates on shops to go up as they opened for business. Tourists and shoppers who visited only by the light of day would never get even the slightest hint of the nocturnal residents who camped out here every night.

Sam retrieved the bar of bath soap he'd taken from Smith's shower and marked the windows on the car to protect it from exactly what she had predicted.

"That may or may not work," she countered, obviously not inclined to put much faith in those who lived by the laws of the street.

He put the bar of soap away in the duffel and considered his handiwork. The emblem he'd used, representing a fierce South Central gang, would likely ward off any trouble. Men had been killed for grievances far more trivial than stripping a vehicle belonging to a rival gang member. He was counting on that history to make the difference.

"It's a chance we'll have to take," he said in answer to her warning. She didn't argue, but she didn't agree, either. That surprised him, but then he remembered that she was the one who needed his cooperation. She wasn't going to make any unnecessary waves.

Panhandlers with their cups outstretched lined the sidewalk beyond the alley. Sam kept his attention straight ahead. He had no desire to see the dull, listless eyes of those who had somehow managed to avoid drug addiction any more than he did the glittering ones of those verging on violent impulses by the chemicals flowing through their weakening veins.

As they entered the hotel, the once-opulent marble lobby smelled stale and musty and was in need of a cleaning. The silence and poor lighting instantly took one's senses to a higher level of alert. The clerk behind the counter looked as if he'd rather be anywhere but here. He pushed a registration card toward Sam without saying a word in welcome or instruction.

"I'd like a view of the street," Sam told him.

The clerk grunted, which Sam took as an affirmative response.

"We're getting a room?"

Sam glanced at Smith. "Yeah."

Like before, she didn't bother with any more questions. He filled out the short form, handed the clerk a bill sufficient to cover two night's room rate and accepted the keycard.

Smith didn't inquire as to his plans again until they were in the elevator headed upward.

"You're going to have to let me in on your strategy. I don't like operating in the dark."

She was annoyed at his highhandedness. Too bad. He kept his attention on the floor numbers as the slow-moving elevator idled past each. She wasn't going to walk away if he didn't play nice. He wasn't that lucky. "I don't have a plan."

Besides, he didn't have a plan, not really. Not one she would like, anyway.

She was really irritated now. But the elevator stopped and the doors slid open before she could launch what would likely be a debate or tirade. Maybe her patience couldn't keep up with her desire for his cooperation.

Sam led the way to the room, unlocked the door and waited while she went in ahead of him. He'd hesitated in a gesture of ladies first, but he doubted she cared about manners. The cop in her would want to check out the room first, would consider it her God-given right.

He'd no more than gotten the light turned on and the door closed when she lowered the boom.

"You take a room in a hotel that's a regular stop on the coroner's route and you expect me to just go along? Get real, Johnson. I need a heads-up on your strategy before this goes any further. I've been patient for about as long as I'm going to be."

Just as he'd thought. He dropped the duffel on the bed and walked over to the window. "I'm waiting for the right time. When that time comes we'll play our moves by ear." He pushed the worn drapes aside and considered the maze of seemingly innocuous streets below.

Despite her impulse to question him further, Lisa made a decision to continue cooperating. Hopefully he would do likewise when the time came. Maybe if she gained his trust, he would tell her the whole truth. As much as she hated to admit it, part of her wanted to do exactly as he'd suggested, put that old case to bed once and for all. But mainly she wanted to prove to her partner that Sam Johnson hadn't killed anyone. It was the only way he would ever really have his life back. Running away to Chicago hadn't changed anything. He had to know that.

She'd told herself a hundred times that he wasn't her problem. That she should just let the whole thing go. But the need to get this case right, to settle all the questions, wouldn't let go. This one had gotten to her. She refused to believe it was the man alone that kept haunting her.

He stayed by the window, staring out at the less-than-scenic view. The city lights far beyond the streets below offered a kinder background to the danger lurking just outside these walls. This whole situation could be handled so much easier if he would only tell her what had happened last year. His refusal to discuss any of it only made him look guilty. Add to that the fact that he didn't care what anyone thought about him one way or the other, and the result was one major roadblock.

The cell phone in her pocket vibrated, startling

her. Evidently hearing her breath catch, Johnson glanced back at her. Embarrassed at being caught on edge, she averted her gaze and focused on the call.

"Smith."

"Detective, this is Spencer Anders."

Anticipation zinged inside Lisa. "Yes, Mr. Anders." Her gaze met Johnson's as he turned to face her.

"An unmarked vehicle posted across the street from your house about forty-five minutes ago. It's not your partner, Sanford, but it's definitely a cop."

Why would the department have someone on surveillance at her place? "You're certain?"

Anders's hesitation told her he wasn't accustomed to being second-guessed. "I ran the license plate. The vehicle belongs to Los Angeles County's police department. It's listed to a Detective Hernandez."

Hernandez? What the hell? He was in Homicide. Why would he be watching her house? She doubted it would do her any good to ask Anders how he'd managed to run a plate, especially at this time of night. She didn't even want to know how he managed access to the system, period.

Pushing the irrelevant detail aside, she asked, "Your presence hasn't been detected?" If word got back to Chuck that she was working with Johnson there would be a lot of awkward tension to deal with. Technically, since she was on vacation and she wasn't breaking any laws—at least not yet—what she did was no one else's business. But this would become the whole division's business if word got out before she'd solved this case.

"I spotted him when he arrived. He has no idea I'm here."

If she were damned lucky, it would stay that way.

Then came the question she'd expected Anders to ask. "Do you know of any reason why someone from your division would be watching you?"

There was only one.

"I can only assume that Chuck suspects I'm up to something besides vacationing in Cozumel." The admission was bitter on her tongue.

"I'll keep you posted on Hernandez's movements."

Lisa thanked him and closed her phone and slid it back into her pocket. The idea that her partner didn't trust her stuck in her throat along with a host of emotions from anger to a feeling of betrayal.

"Chuck Sanford has a man hanging out in front of my house," she told Johnson.

"Are you surprised?"

That irritation he seemed to be able to rouse so easily reared its frustrating head. "What's that supposed to mean?"

"Your partner wants to pin those murders on me." Johnson shifted his attention back to the view out the window. "He knows you well enough to understand that you didn't just up and decide to take a vacation at the same time that Lil Watts is plotting to get his hands on my head. You surely realized that before you came to Chicago."

On some level maybe she had. Mostly she'd been disgusted with Chuck's attitude, but she wasn't giving Johnson the satisfaction of knowing the full extent of the tension already simmering between her and her partner of five years. Her sense of loyalty wouldn't let her charge onward without giving him the benefit of the doubt for a little while longer.

"Are you saying you didn't commit the murders?" Johnson's statement about her partner wanting to pin the murders on him seemed to indicate that mind set. But the admission would be a first. Sam Johnson had spent the last year keeping his mouth shut, sitting back and letting Homicide try its damnedest to prove him guilty…knowing, based on the glaring lack of evidence, that it wouldn't happen. If she was smart she'd walk away from this right now.

But she couldn't.

And, damn it, she hated that weakness.

"I'm not saying anything about the murders, Detective," he returned pointedly. "We're talking about you and your partner and his vendetta against me." He turned to stare out the window once more, his profile set in stone. "Have you ever considered why he wants to nail me so badly?"

Only one of the wall sconces in the rundown room

worked, but even with the poor lighting it was easy to see the grim line of his lips. There had always been something, some source of friction between Johnson and Chuck. Not that her partner had ever admitted it, but she'd picked up on it more than once.

"Charles Sanford is a twenty-five-year veteran of LAPD's Priority Homicide Division," she argued. "He likes solving his cases. Failing to get the bad guy makes us all look bad. He and I just have a different opinion of who the bad guy is in this case."

"Keep telling yourself that, Detective," Johnson said, with a sidelong glance at her, "if it makes you sleep better at night."

He wasn't getting off that easily. She walked to the window and stood bedside him but kept her eyes front and center on the view beyond the window. This close, looking him square in the eyes wouldn't be a good idea. "How can you complain about the way the investigation was handled when you declined to cooperate? We had no choice but to work around your refusal to give us the full details we needed. Our hands were tied."

"If you'd had evidence against me, you would have arrested me, but you didn't."

He turned his face fully toward her, those gray eyes penetrating. The tension abruptly shifted to something more personal with her standing so close and looking so deeply into his eyes. The realization that they were shoulder to shoulder with only the thin fabric of their clothes separating their skin made her heart jolt against her sternum. This close, every line and angle of his face reminded her of the nights she'd spent sitting at his bedside…waiting for him to surface from the coma those bastards had put him in.

"I keep telling myself," she said as she searched his eyes, "that your refusal to talk couldn't possibly have been about protecting anyone else. I mean, why would a guy protect the people responsible for the murder of the woman he loved and planned to marry?"

His guard went up so fast the harshness of the change took her aback, forced her to take a moment to regroup before she went on. "But it felt exactly like that was what you were doing."

He leaned toward her, as if he wanted to intimidate her, but the only thing he succeeded in doing was making her pulse skip erratically. "Things aren't always what they seem, Detective. If you looked closely enough you'd find that out."

This was the way it had been with him from the beginning. Every response was a question. Every explanation was a riddle.

"You've said that before," she countered, "and I've yet to see whatever it is you keep alluding to. Maybe this truth you believe exists only in some reality you created to camouflage what really happened."

He turned that piercing gaze back to the street below. "Then maybe you aren't really looking."

Square one. That was where they always ended up.

A muscle flexed in his jaw, belying his relaxed posture. He could be right. She studied that stony profile a moment longer. Perhaps she hadn't been looking closely enough, but she was looking now.

"What is it you're afraid of, Johnson? I know you want to protect your family, but this seems like something more. I was there during your recovery. I'm certain you're not afraid for yourself. You spent nearly a decade ferreting out the evidence to put dozens of bad guys away. What is it that scares you so badly that you'd keep the identity of a murderer a secret?"

He glared at her. "Other than for the safety of my family, I'm not afraid of anything, Detective. Don't mistake my determination to settle this in my own way for fear. This isn't about fear."

She moved her head from side to side, disgusted. "You do it every time. You say a lot, but you don't tell me anything at all."

"It's time to go." He stepped away from the window, let the shabby drapes fall back into place.

"Have you decided where we're going yet?" That he refused to keep her briefed made her want to draw her weapon and demand that he cooperate.

"It's not far." He checked his weapon. "You sure you want to do this?"

"I'm not letting you out of my sight."

Sam hated dragging her along. As much because she distracted him on some level as because of the idea that she could get herself killed following him around. The problem was neither one of those excuses was going to keep her from tagging along. He might as well make the best of her participation.

"You'd better leave your jacket behind," he warned.

She wanted to question him as to why, but she didn't. Instead she ditched the jacket that hid all those lush curves outlined so well by the black attire.

He looked away, kicked himself for noticing.

Once the door to their room closed behind them, he opted for the stairs rather than the elevator. Acquainting himself with all routes of escape could come in handy. Once he made his presence known, staying out of sight would elevate to a matter of prime importance. Every step had to be carefully calculated. It was the only way to do what had to be done without getting killed before he'd attained his goal.

Outside he took a right on the sidewalk. It was past ten now. Those who had a penchant for partying would be out en mass. The beggars and dealers were thick on the sidewalk. The smell of drugs and body odor heavy in the night air. Every imaginable means to escape reality was here for the taking if a guy had the cash. Two blocks farther there was a club, the Sahara. That was his destination.

As they neared the club, the deejay's music thumped above the boom boxes stationed on the street corners and the stereos of the cars cruising by. Cronies of Lil Watts frequently hung out at the Sahara. It was one of the few clubs where members from various gangs gathered without clashing. Sam wanted to send the scuzzball Watts a message. A few minutes in the Sahara and someone would recognize him. Word would get to Lil faster than the speed of light. As big as L.A. was, each segment of the population had its own methods and grapevines. Word of mouth was a powerful tool especially with cell phones keeping the world in touch.

The door of the club opened and the loud hip-hop spilled out behind a couple of shady-looking characters who swaggered out. Probably stringers. The runners used for going back and forth from the dealer to the mass of customers gyrating on the dance floor. Nothing like service with a personal touch.

As Sam neared the club entrance Smith stalled. "You have to be kidding."

He reached for patience, didn't find it. "Listen, if you can't handle this situation, then maybe you should go back to the room. This is the way it has to happen. *This* is my plan."

"You really do have a death wish, Johnson."

He considered her a moment, but decided not to debate her assertion. There had been a time in all this when he had been teetering on that edge, just wishing someone would give him the right push. But no more. He had a new life in Chicago and he wanted this done so he could get back to it. If Smith was nervous about his plan, she should say so now. Once they got inside, any second thoughts would be too late.

"The question is—" he draped his arm around her shoulders, felt her tense "—do you really want the truth badly enough to do whatever is necessary to get it?"

Well, he had her there. Lisa didn't answer, he knew what she wanted. She let him guide her into the club as if they were a couple out on the town. He paid the cover charge and merged into the crowd. The crush of bodies and the deafening throb of music fragmented her thoughts. The suspicious looks cast in their direction didn't slow Johnson's plunge through the throng. The weapon in her ankle holster felt a world away. She'd been in spots like this before, but always with her badge visible and her weapon more accessible in her shoulder holster. Going in like this she felt naked and vulnerable.

Johnson located a vacant spot at the bar and claimed it. He kept his arm around her shoulders and her body drawn close to his. That part was for show. Her foolish heart didn't appear to know the difference since it pounded unreasonably. Now wasn't a good time to silently rail at herself for being hung up on the guy, but later, when she wasn't compacted amid a couple hundred dope heads she would give herself hell for allowing the reaction.

The bartender, whose physical description fit the bill of big, bad and one-smart-remark-away-from-going-ballistic, paused to get their drink order, though didn't bother asking what they would have. Instead he waited, pulling off the whole silent and brooding act to the max.

Johnson looked at her. "Beer?"

She nodded. Why not? She wasn't technically on duty.

"Two beers," he said, holding up two fingers and then pointing at the bottled brew in the hand of the nearest patron so he wouldn't have to shout against the blare of music.

Lisa resisted the impulse to take stock of the club. It was instinct to evaluate her position in any given situation, but that would only reveal the fact that she didn't belong here. Not an optimal scenario by any stretch of the imagination.

Johnson leaned his head close to hers. "You see those two guys at the other end of the bar?"

She glanced that way without turning her head. "Yeah." Two skinny guys who looked as if they had recently escaped rehab.

"One of them used to work for Lil Watts. I don't know about now, but you can rest assured that any opportunity to gain brownie points would be pounced upon."

This was precisely what she had feared he had in mind.

She lifted her lips to his ear so she could keep her voice down as low as possible. "I don't think this is a good idea, Sam." She used his first name to really get his attention and because her heart was thundering in her chest and messing with her ability to think straight. She could see this ending badly far too rapidly. Just being here was dangerous enough without calling unnecessary attention their way.

He turned his face to hers, so close she could feel his breath on her lips. He dodged her mouth barely and rested his lips fully against her hair to whisper directly in her ear. "I know what I'm doing. You're going to have to trust me, Smith. Can you do that?"

For several tension-filled beats she couldn't decide how to respond. Maybe it was the distraction of his jaw pressed against her cheek, or his lips lingering close to her sensitive lobe...but she couldn't think nearly quickly enough to react appropriately.

She'd made up her mind that she was going to see this through when she went to the Colby Agency. Backing out now would be a mistake. She needed to know the truth. And whether he would ever admit it or not, he needed it, too, for more reasons than just protecting his family. Instinct nudged at her, warning that he was as much in the dark on some level as she was. But she needed to be able to prove that…to prove what really happened. There had already been way too much speculation.

The only way they were going to get this done was to do it together.

She lifted her chin, accidentally brushed her lips against the lobe of his ear when she'd meant to stop just short of doing that. She felt him tense. So, she wasn't the only one feeling the vibes of this nonsensical attraction.

"I can do that…for a little while."

The plop of bottles against the counter drew her attention to the bartender who waited for payment. This wasn't the sort of establishment where a patron could run a tab.

Sam tossed a couple of bills on the counter before handing one of the sweating bottles to her. He picked up the other and downed a swallow. She got a little lost in watching the movement of his lips, his throat and his fingers on the bottle. Taking a drink of the cold brew, she reminded herself of something very, very important. She couldn't be 100 percent certain that the man standing so close wasn't a brutal killer.

But she would take her chances and trust him.

She told herself it had nothing to do with all those long nights she'd watched him lying there so close to death, but the truth was she couldn't be sure about that, either.

Whatever the case, it was way too late to change her mind now.

Johnson was suddenly wrenched away from her. She pivoted in time to see a big guy go nose to nose with him.

"I know you," the huge man growled.

"Well, then," Johnson said far more calmly than he had a right to, "you have me at a disadvantage, because I don't know you."

Before Lisa could go for her weapon considering she was hemmed against the bar by the two men, Johnson had whipped out his 9 mm with his free hand and shoved it into the underside of the big guy's fleshy chin. The atmosphere around them changed instantly…anyone standing close by went on alert, fully prepared to kill or be killed if necessary.

"But I'm willing to get to know you a whole lot better if you're interested," Johnson offered.

Four more men crowded in around them. Lisa's fingers itched to go for her weapon or her phone, but she knew better than to make any sudden moves. Not with these guys looking all too ready for a shoot-out.

"Nah," the big guy with the barrel of Johnson's weapon jabbed in his throat said, "I don't see no point in wasting my time getting to know a dead man."

He let go of Johnson's arm and Johnson lowered his weapon.

The big guy glanced at his buddies. "Let's go. This place's too crowded."

When the men had moved away, Lisa put a hand on Johnson's sleeve. "We should get out of here."

Sam picked up his beer. "Finish your drink. There's plenty of time."

She tried to be as calm as he was, but that wasn't happening. Had Johnson forgotten how quickly even a cop, especially one without backup, could get dead in a joint like this? The best training taught a cop when to use her common sense. *This* was bad. The beer tasted bitter on her tongue…and every eye in the club felt as if it was cutting through her back like a bullet.

They would be damned lucky to get out of here alive.

Chapter Six

Jim Colby's cell phone vibrated on the bedside table. He reached for it and Tasha snuggled closer to him. Ignoring the call crossed his mind. This was the first night he'd gotten home at a decent hour in days. He'd like it to carry through the whole night. But a call coming at this time of night was generally not good news. He peered at the display to identify the caller before answering. He hated to risk waking up his wife, but depending upon the caller...

Victoria.

No way could he ignore a call from his mother. He pressed the talk button. "Yeah."

"Jim, there's been a development."

"Just a minute."

As much as he hated to, Jim slipped out of the bed

and pulled the covers up around his still sleeping wife. He eased out of the bedroom and closed the door.

"What kind of development?" As he waited for his mother's response he walked quietly down the hall and peeked into his baby girl's room. She slept like an angel. He moved on to the staircase and started downward as he refocused his attention on the call.

"The Johnson family had to be briefed on the situation."

Jim stilled on the bottom step. "What do you mean 'briefed'?" He tamped down the suspicion and irritation that instantly twisted in his gut.

"Mallory confronted Jeff. I'm afraid there was no choice."

Jim's fingers tightened on the banister. "So you're telling me that your man Battles couldn't find a way to prevent blowing his cover?" It wasn't like a Colby Agency investigator to fall down on the job like that.

"I'm afraid it wasn't as simple as that. I made the final decision. Jeff felt the distance he was forced to maintain while keeping up with her schedule put Mallory in unnecessary jeopardy. In addition, there was a fiancé who complicated matters."

"Did you speak with Sam first?" Jim braced for the answer he already knew even before he asked.

"There was no time. Spencer indicated that Sam and Lisa were unreachable."

Jim forked his fingers through his hair. "You should have called me first." This situation between him and his mother had gotten entirely out of hand. Victoria couldn't seem to come to terms with his ability to take care of business. At first he hadn't minded, but things were different now. He was fully capable of making decisions. He didn't need her making them for him.

"Our people are working together as a team. I don't see the problem, Jim. Tasha told me this was the first night you'd been home in time for dinner all week. I didn't want to disturb your family time. I almost didn't call tonight at all, but evidently Mr. Johnson is refusing to cooperate and insists that Sam call him."

Great. Just great. Jim held his temper in check, as hard as that proved. "You're aware that Sam didn't want his family to be burdened with his presence in L.A."

"Yes, but I believe that was a shortsighted decision."

Enough. "Victoria, I appreciate that you're accustomed to running the Colby Agency as you see fit. But this is not solely a Colby Agency operation. Any deviations in strategy on this case should be run by me before being implemented. I thought we had an understanding."

"Jim, this shouldn't be about egos or who's in

charge. Lives are at stake here. There is no time for conference calls. I've been doing this for a very long time. My investigators are highly trained in providing personal security. I'm not so sure Sam understood the ramifications of his request to keep his family in the dark."

She simply didn't get it. It was all black-and-white and by the rules for her. Jim had learned first-hand that life didn't always follow the rules and there was far more gray than there was black-and-white.

"I can't change a decision that's already been enacted," he allowed as he strode into the kitchen for a drink. He was going to be up for a while. Damage control would be necessary. Sam was not going to like having his decisions reversed. Jim opened the fridge and reached for a bottle of water. "But this can't happen again, Victoria." He twisted off the top and downed a swallow while he waited for her reaction.

"I take it you don't agree with my decision."

Maybe he'd been too subtle. "This is primarily my operation. Sam and I make the rules. From this moment forward unless there is clear and present danger no changes are implemented without running them by one of us first."

Silence.

"That mindset is unreasonable, Jim. I appreciate your prospective, as well as Sam's, but I can't go along with a flawed strategy."

Jim set his bottle on the counter. This was the moment that had been coming for a long while now. If he just let it go, Victoria would never understand that she was stifling him.

"I'm not sure we should have this conversation over the phone."

More of that thick silence.

"This isn't a contest about who needs to be in charge, Jim. This is about making the right decisions. Are you questioning my ability to do so?"

"Evidently, you're questioning mine." He shook his head slowly, reached for the sweating bottle.

"I'm not questioning you, Jim, I'm simply looking out for all involved with this operation from a vantage point of nearly three decades of investigative and security work. I don't understand why you can't see that. You should trust my instincts."

"The way you trust mine," he suggested.

The hesitation before she responded was answer enough. She still saw him as that screwed-up guy who'd operated with only one focus: kill anything that got in his way. He'd changed. She, of all people, should have recognized that by now.

"I'm sorry, Jim, I can't make bad calls because I'm afraid of hurting your feelings. This is a business that requires swift, decisive action. There isn't always time to operate under strict protocols."

That was clear enough.

"You're right. From now on, I'll give the orders. If your people have a problem with that, I'll replace them with my people. Is that understood?"

"I don't think we need to go down that road, Jim."

He hated to do this, but she had to understand that this overprotective mentality had to cease. There appeared to be no other way to make her see that she was seriously stepping on his toes.

"I'm afraid we're already on that road, Victoria. Now, if there are no other questions, I need to do some damage control."

He didn't wait for her argument or even a response. He pushed the End Call button. For several minutes he stared at the phone. He'd just hung up on his mother. How the hell had they reached this point? It was as if she had slowly but surely come to distrust his every decision and deed. She'd been so supportive when he'd decided to go out on his own. Was this her way of letting him know how much that decision had hurt her?

The last thing in this world he wanted to do was hurt his mother…and yet there appeared to be no other way to get the point across.

Victoria Colby-Camp was not a woman easily swayed from her beliefs. If they didn't find neutral ground soon, he wasn't sure where their relationship was going to end up.

Chapter Seven

Sahara Club
Los Angeles

Sam placed his empty bottle on the counter. The bartender glanced in his direction, but Sam didn't give him any indication of needing a second round.

He pulled Smith closer. "Time to go."

Pushing his way through the crowd, he kept that arm tight around her. Though he knew she was armed and perfectly capable of taking care of herself, he suddenly felt solely responsible for her safety. If she got hurt in this place he'd have no one to blame but himself. No matter that the decision to come along had been hers, this was his problem.

He didn't breathe easily until they had cleared the door. Traffic had picked up on the street. The crowd had drifted into cliques on the sidewalks. The blocks between them and where he'd left the rental felt like a mile with every face they passed scrutinizing him. Or maybe he was only being paranoid. If word hadn't reached Lil Watts already it wouldn't be long. Getting off the street before that happened was imperative. Every move had to be timed perfectly for his plan to work.

Lisa pulled away from him as they turned into the alley. She moved around to the passenger side of the rental as he headed for the driver's door.

"Where to now?" she asked, clearly frustrated.

"I been protecting your interests, bro."

Sam's gaze shot across the top of the car. A young man stepped out of the shadows and toward Smith. He flashed the knife in his hand at her when she would have made a defensive maneuver. The man moved up behind her, wrapped his left arm around her waist to hold her and positioned the knife in a way that clarified his intent. His clothes were street rags, his face and arms grungy.

"I appreciate that. What do I owe you, *bro?*" Sam asked as he sent a reassuring glance at Smith. She didn't look scared, mostly she looked ticked off.

"I figure my expert skill's worth at least one dead president," he puffed out, feeling cocky now. "Old Ben Franklin might do the trick."

"I've got you covered." Sam ordered his heart to slow as he reached one millimeter at a time for some cash.

"Make sure that's your wallet you're going for, my friend." The jerk pressed the knife to Smith's cheek. "I'd sure hate to mess up her pretty face."

Sam pulled a one-hundred-dollar bill from his pocket.

The guy's eyes lit up. "That's what I'm talking about."

In that split second when he relaxed his guard, his full attention on the money, Smith pulled a move on him. An elbow into his gut with just the right amount of twist from her upper body sent him stumbling over her left leg which she shot out behind her as she made that turn. The momentum put the man on the ground.

By the time Sam rounded the hood Smith had drawn her handgun and had it pressed against the center of his forehead. "Why don't we call it your good deed for this lifetime?" she suggested.

"Whatever you say, lady," he urged, his eyes as round as Frisbees.

The knife lay on the ground just out of reach. Sam picked it up and looked it over before flashing it at Smith. "Too bad. Only six inches."

She backed off. "Next time," she warned, "you'd better have more than that when you come after me."

The guy scrambled up and ran like hell.

"I could've paid the guy," Sam said with a smile he couldn't seem to rein in.

"Get in the car, Johnson, before he comes back with his friends."

Before sliding behind the wheel, he retrieved a small towel from the duffel and cleaned the soaped symbols off the windows. He tossed the towel into the back and settled into the driver's seat.

"That towel's part of a matching set," she said as he started the engine.

"Don't worry." He backed out of the alley, careful of the pedestrians on the sidewalk. When he'd hit the street and shifted into Drive, he added, "I'll have it dry-cleaned."

"Where are we going now?" Lisa had presumed they would go back to the hotel. Since he hadn't opted to tell her any more details of his plan, she had no idea what came next. She'd tried to keep an open mind, but his determination to close her out was becoming tedious.

"I don't know about you," he braked for a light, "but I'm starved. I thought I'd find a drive-through. Burgers sound okay to you?"

"As long as they have fries." She could definitely eat. Lunch had been a long time ago.

The buzz of a cell phone interrupted the silence that ensued. Johnson removed the phone from his pocket. She told herself not to watch his every move with an avid interest that had nothing to do with solving the case, but the order went ignored.

"Johnson."

The way his lips compressed told her this wasn't news he'd wanted to hear.

"Yeah. I'm on my way now."

When he'd put the phone away she waited another full minute or so before she asked, "Trouble?" It would have made life so much simpler if he just chose to keep her informed.

"We have to make a midnight house call."

Another minute passed, and he still didn't say to where or to whom. "How many guesses do I get?" This was bordering on ridiculous. She could not operate in the dark!

"I have a command performance. My parents found out I'm here."

She hadn't agreed with him keeping his presence a secret from his family, but having them suddenly discover the truth didn't feel right. "How did they find out?"

His gaze steady on the street. "That part's not clear. However it happened, Jim Colby is not a happy man."

Considering Victoria's people were on security detail with Johnson's family, it only made sense that the leak had something to do with Battles or Call. If that were the case, Jim Colby's unhappiness would be with his mother. Lisa sensed the explosion coming ever nearer. She wasn't sure those two understood that they were about to cross a line of no return.

Lisa hoped for their sakes that mother and son got this thing worked out before it went that far.

Without the commuter traffic jams of the day-light hours, the drive to Bel-Air was accomplished in record time. Lisa had lived here her entire life and the transition from gaudy neon on the Strip to elegant architecture on the Bel-Air end of Sunset Boulevard still amazed her.

Both rentals belonging to the Colby Agency inves-tigators were in the driveway of the Johnson home.

"Do you want me to go in?" she asked when he'd parked.

Sam stared at the house for a few moments where he'd grown up before he responded. "Everyone else is in there, you might as well join the crowd."

Lisa emerged from the car and followed him to the front door. He reached for the bell, but the door opened before he could press it. An older version of Sam stood in the open doorway.

"You have some explaining to do."

No hello, no hug. His father was angry. Lisa felt uncomfortable being caught in the middle of this family business.

Inside, beyond the entry hall, Call and Battles waited in the luxurious living room. Lisa stayed there while Sam followed his father deeper into the house. She surveyed the room, admired the opulence during the awkward moment that followed.

"Nice place," Brett Call noted when their gazes bumped.

"Yeah." Lisa sat down on the sofa next to him. "What happened?" she asked Battles who still stood. Too restless to sit, she surmised.

"Sam apparently didn't know his sister has a fiancé." Battles rubbed the back of his neck. "Suffice it to say the guy had a problem with how I was watching his girlfriend."

It would have helped if they had been more fully informed as to the status of the various family members. "Don't feel bad," she said, mostly to make Battles feel better, "I'm pretty much operating in the dark. Following after Johnson like a lost puppy." It definitely felt exactly like that. She had no choice but to react rather than act, never a good scenario.

"So, Victoria gave you two the go-ahead to brief the family?" Without her son's permission. That part was easy to guess.

Call nodded. "It was the only solution." He glanced in the direction Johnson had disappeared with his father. "I'm certain Mr. Colby wasn't any more thrilled to hear about her decision than Mr. Johnson."

"I checked in with Spencer Anders," Call said, "to get word to you and Mr. Johnson, but he indicated that the two of you were unreachable and didn't seem inclined to interrupt."

To some degree she and Johnson *had* been unreachable. Still, sending a text message to either her phone or to Johnson's might have alleviated this tense reunion. At the very least the attempt might have satisfied Jim Colby.

"I'll ask Johnson to speak to Anders about the lapse in communications." She looked from Battles to Call. "We need this team working together."

Call nodded. "The results could be disastrous if we keep working around each other like this."

That was the problem. Sam Johnson had kept the whole world in the dark for the past year. She wasn't sure there was anything she could do or say that would change that.

And Call was right, the end result could be disastrous.

SAM'S ENTIRE FAMILY had been waiting for him in the den. His explanation of what he was doing here and just how much danger they were in didn't have the effect he'd hoped for. All three merely stared at him after his informative monologue.

"You expect us to live in fear?" This from his father.

"I have a life," Mallory said pointedly. "I have classes and a job. And," she emphasized, "a fiancé. It would have been nice to know about this, rather than learn what was going on by happenstance."

His mother waited until last to speak. "Are you

telling us that the leader of this gang wants you dead?" she asked.

Straight to the heart of the matter. "Yes." No use lying now. "I knew he would use one or all of you to get to me if I didn't come and face the music… so to speak."

"Why didn't Lisa tell us about this?" Samuel Johnson, Sr., demanded.

Lisa, not Detective Smith. Well, well, the detective had been busy since Sam's departure. She'd managed to get on a first-name basis with his father. That was a major coup.

"Because the only way I would allow her to be involved was if she did so on my terms."

"Son," his mother wrung her hands together, "why aren't you letting the police handle this? This is far too dangerous for you to try and do alone. These people won't hesitate to kill you to protect their secrets. The police have an obligation to protect you. Why don't you let them do their job?"

Mallory jumped up from her seat and started to pace. "Good grief, Mother, surely you know he can't go to the police. They think he's the one who murdered those three gangbangers. They'd like nothing better than to have him rotting away in jail. I think Lisa is the only one who believes he's innocent."

Well said. He'd always been able to count on his younger sister to stand up for him. There wasn't a single instance of her support in the past that he appreciated more than now. He was counting on her to help him persuade their parents to cooperate with their security detail.

"Well, perhaps," Samuel offered, "if he would cooperate with the detectives, they would be a bit more open-minded."

He and his father disagreed on that one, but he wasn't going there tonight.

"Detective Smith and I are going to get this straightened out." Sam was definitely appreciative of her participation just now. "But I need your full cooperation with your security detail. I can't protect you from this if you refuse to work with me."

He held his breath, prayed like hell they would go along. He didn't know what he would do if they refused to. Endangering their lives was the last thing he wanted to do.

"And if we don't?" his mother countered. She would much prefer he just turn all this over to the police and hope they would get the job done. But she was living in a fantasy world where scumbags like Lil Watts didn't exist. "Will you go to the police, then?"

So naive. But she was his mother and he loved her.

"If you refuse to cooperate, then I'll have no choice but to do what I have to do to protect you."

"Meaning?" Mallory prodded, her arms crossed protectively over her chest.

"I'll turn myself over to the gang leader who wants my head."

His mother's face paled, and Mallory's turned a brilliant crimson with fury.

"Was that really necessary?" his father groused. "Sam, you must know that we're worried sick about you as it is. You ran off to Chicago with hardly a goodbye or go-to-hell to us. What're we supposed to think?"

Sam took a breath. Hated himself for doing this to his family. But keeping them safe was far more important than sparing their feelings. "I'm trying my best to get on with my life. But this is beyond my control. You can either help me get through it or you can force my hand." He looked from one to the other, ending with Mallory. "What's it going to be?"

He could see in her eyes that Mallory wanted to demand more answers, but thankfully she appeared to see the desperation in his. "I'll do whatever you need me to do, Sammy."

He relaxed marginally. "Thanks, sis." He couldn't remember the last time she'd called him that or vice versa. It felt good.

Samuel Johnson cleared his throat. "Well, if it'll help you get through this, then we'll do what we have to do, as well." He stepped forward, putting himself within arm's reach. "Don't we always?" Then he pulled his son into a bear hug. "Just don't get yourself killed."

Sam held on for longer than he meant to, but he just couldn't help himself. Then he hugged his mother, who cried, and then Mallory, who cursed him softly, but he knew she didn't mean a word of it.

"When this is done," his sister whispered in his ear before pulling away, "I'm going to kick your ass for putting us through this."

He hugged her tighter. "And I'll gladly let you."

When the Johnsons had composed themselves, Sam called the others in and they ran through a quick briefing to make sure everyone was on the same page. As much as he loved his family, he was glad to get out of there.

He couldn't bear being in their presence with the knowledge hounding him that his being there could get them killed.

"Where to now?" Lisa asked as Johnson turned the car around. He'd given an impressive pep talk in there about cooperation and team work. Funny, all that enthusiasm appeared to vanish into thin air as soon as they walked out the door.

"Back to the hotel."

She should have guessed. "You know there are people who likely saw us come out of there earlier tonight. That's one of the first places Watts will look when he gets the word."

Johnson pulled out onto the street. "That's what I'm counting on."

She'd been right all along. He did have a death wish.

"SLEEP IF YOU NEED TO."

He stared at the window as he made this statement. That was where he'd stationed himself as soon as they'd arrived back at the hotel.

"Fine." One of them had to get some sleep.

She took off her sneakers and socks, put her ankle holster in the drawer of the bedside table and her .22 under her pillow. After folding down the worn-out comforter, she lay back on the cool sheets. They looked clean enough. She was fairly certain the less-than-pleasant odor in the room was the carpet. She closed her eyes. Johnson had already turned out the dim sconce, leaving the room dark but for the light coming in through the window.

Sleep really would be a good thing. Even though she'd gotten into a reclining position and closed her eyes, her brain wouldn't shut down. She kept seeing images of shoot-outs and the shiny steel blades of knives.

"You know they're going to kill you, don't you?" she heard herself ask.

Had he really considered the reality that they were trapped in this fleabag hotel? A flimsy locked door wasn't going to protect them from anyone who really wanted in.

"They're going to try."

The deep, gravelly sound of his voice made her restless. She refused to open her eyes. Looking at him would only make it worse, make her feel those things she wasn't supposed to feel. Dumb, Lisa. Really dumb.

"It would be so easy to get you the kind of backup you need if you'd only tell me the whole story, Sam." She did open her eyes then. Why did he refuse to tell her the truth? He was an expert in finding evidence when all others would give up, he surely understood how important the truth was in any scenario. Everything looked different when the real story was told. No matter how guilty he appeared, coming clean could make all the difference. She'd been telling herself for a year now that what he was hiding couldn't possibly be anything that would incriminate him. She just couldn't believe he would have killed those men that way.

Gutted like fish. What kind of person ripped a man's intestines out of his body with him still breathing?

Not this one.

She was certain.

He turned away from the window. The drapes fell back into place behind him. "Do you really want to know the truth? You talk about it like it's some sort of drug that will give you the rush you've waited for your whole life." He took a step toward the bed. "But are you sure you *really* want to know?"

Lisa scooted up to a sitting position as he took a second step. "I asked, didn't I?"

"The incision was as clean as if a surgeon had set a scalpel to the flesh," he said as he sat down on the edge of the mattress, forcing her to move over to accommodate him.

"I read the autopsy report," she reminded him.

Johnson looked directly at her, his gray eyes distant as if he were remembering the images rather than recalling the autopsy report. "The first man suffered a heart attack before he'd even bled out. But the last two, they were younger, stronger, they felt every second of the pain until there was no longer enough blood in their vessels to keep their heart pumping. And they couldn't do a thing to help themselves because their hands and feet were tied. They were helpless. Just like she was." The distance disappeared and rage blazed, turning those gray eyes to liquid steel. "They tied her up just like that and then took turns having her. When they'd finished they gutted her. I remember every second of every minute she lived until her heart finally stopped."

For the first time since she and her partner had found the first of those three victims, she had to ask herself if she'd been wrong. Could Sam Johnson have killed those three lowlifes?

One corner of his mouth twitched with the beginnings of a smile. "Makes you wonder, doesn't it?"

She shoved at his chest. "You bastard. That's what you want me to do."

The door flew open and banged against the wall. A dozen men poured into the room.

Lisa was on her feet with her weapon leveled before the first one reached the bed.

"Don't move," she ordered the one nearest her position.

The sound of rounds being racked in half a dozen weapons jerked her attention to the business ends of the guns, all aimed directly at her head.

"Lower your weapon, Smith," Johnson said. "This is one of those no-win situations they talked about at the police academy."

Knowing he was right, but hating like hell to admit it, she lowered her weapon. Before she'd slid her finger away from the trigger, the .22 was snatched out of her hand. Johnson's 9 mm was taken, too.

"You have an appointment." The man who appeared to be in charge informed Johnson with nothing more than a condescending look in Lisa's direction.

Johnson flared his palms. "I'm all yours."

Lisa hoped like hell he was so calm because he knew something she didn't.

Something that meant they weren't going to die.

Chapter Eight

The streets looked empty as they drove through the Southside community. Not surprising. People didn't come out at night for fear of ending up as some form of collateral damage. At night these streets were owned by the guardians who protected their turf at all costs.

Sam glanced back at Smith. The guy in the red bandanna on her left held an AK-47 while the one on her right, directly behind Sam, preferred a .40 caliber handgun. The twenty-year-old Chevy was pimped-out to the max, complete with bulletproof glass, as was the SUV leading the four-vehicle convoy.

As they neared their destination, sentries stood on the corners, putting through calls on their cell phones to signal that the convoy was arriving. The small single-family bungalows on either side of the street gave way to high-rise apartment buildings with their graffiti-covered, bullet-pocked walls.

Farther down the street, the lights of a church stood out like a hopeful beacon in the night…just a little too far away to be of any use.

Sam wasn't worried about dying tonight, not from these guys, anyway. Their red bandannas and the tattoos they bore marked them as Nation, not Crew. Lil Watts was the latter. Whoever had requested his company tonight had nothing to do with the threat to his life.

Unless, of course, there was a price on his head that could settle some score that needed to be resolved between the two infamous gangs. No way to know for sure. Sam's only choice was to wait and see. He hadn't expected this reaction to come first, but as long as the reactions were occurring he had to consider his endeavor so far to be successful. He doubted that Smith saw it that way, but she was looking from a cop's perspective. During the past year, Sam had learned to put all he thought he knew aside. This world had its own rules. Recognizing and respecting those rules was a huge step in the direction of survival.

The scattering of duplexes beyond the high-rises were rigged for battle. Bars on the windows and guards stationed at every door. Headquarters, Sam presumed. This block would be their destination.

Once the SUV had pulled into the short driveway of one bungalow, the Chevy halted at the curb.

Doors opened and drivers and passengers unloaded. The guy with the .40 cal prodded Sam toward the house while the AK-47-toting thug hustled Smith in that direction.

Inside they were taken to an empty room and abandoned.

"Maybe you've forgotten your geography," Smith commented as she took in the twelve-by-twelve prison, "but this is not good. There are no homicides in this neighborhood. No drug dealing, no turf fighting. Nothing. This is where the trials are carried out—the decisions on who will live and who will die."

Sam tried to make light of the situation. "Well, at least we don't have to worry about dying here."

She walked over to the boarded-up window. "That's for sure. They'll take us someplace else to do that. This is the neighborhood Buster Houston calls home." She turned to Sam and waited expectantly as if she anticipated some particular reaction to the name.

He knew who Buster Houston was. Who didn't? A legend. One of the founding members of the Nation. Well into seventy, he preached peace and tolerance like a TV evangelist, despite the fact those around him were armed to the teeth.

"I'm curious to see what Mr. Houston has to say," Sam said, which clearly wasn't what she'd wanted to hear.

"Think about it, Sam," she said, using his first name again. He didn't know why that bothered him, but it did. "There's an agenda. This man doesn't waste his time. He wants something from us. That can't be good."

"Maybe."

She was right in that Houston wouldn't waste his time. But whatever he wanted wasn't necessarily bad for Sam's agenda. This could actually work to his advantage, so long as Smith's presence didn't create any unnecessary friction. The only cops found in this territory were dead ones.

The door opened and four men entered and took up positions around the room, each armed with serious fire power. Then Buster Houston walked in. Dressed completely in black, fedora included, his presence overwhelmed the room. Anyone even remotely versed in gangland history knew what a pivotal role this man had played. Despite his age he still radiated an air of danger.

"Sam Johnson," he said as he clasped his hands behind him, "your return surprises me."

Sam braced for retaliation. "Then you're obviously not in tune with the news on the street."

Houston shook his head, signaling his henchmen not to respond physically to the verbal disrespect. "What news would that be?" he asked Sam as if he had no idea what he meant.

"Watts wants my head. Surely you've heard about the edict he issued. Apparently my deal with his uncle is no good after his death."

Houston glanced at the guard standing closest to Smith. "What I have to say to that is between the two of us. I don't speak freely in front of anyone who carries a badge."

Lisa tensed. The impact of Houston's words hit her at the same time the man standing right behind her grabbed her arm and pushed her toward the door.

"Johnson," she urged, glancing back at him. Why didn't he tell this guy to allow her to stay?

When he didn't look at her or speak up, she knew that he didn't want her privy to the conversation.

So much for teamwork.

She was ushered into the hall and toward what had once been a kitchen but which now served as a waylay station for Houston's thugs.

Five men waited there. All looked dangerous, but she'd seen worse. Since the guard assigned to her didn't offer to restrain her, she relaxed against the counter and waited. Whatever Johnson and Houston had to talk about, she doubted it would take long. Most of these guys were men of few words. The idea that she and Johnson had gotten this far, unmasked and with their hearts still beating, was a major coup. Like Watts, Houston's home base moved so often that even the Gang Division of LAPD couldn't keep up with his location. This place would be abandoned by daylight.

That's why Houston wasn't worried about what she saw. Still, this was definitely an unusual encounter.

"I know you."

Her attention flew to the larger of the two men loitering near the refrigerator. He stepped forward, his eyes slitted with accusation. Déjà vu. Hadn't she and Johnson just gone through this in the club?

"You and your partner framed my cousin Sean Hastings," the gangbanger pronounced as if passing sentence.

His cohorts went on the alert, dark eyes glaring at her with that same accusation, while the man who'd spoken stepped into her personal space.

"He didn't kill nobody and he got fifteen." He sneered down at her. "You needed a suspect and you nailed an innocent man."

Lisa vaguely remembered the Hastings case. Last year. Shot his dealer for roughing him up. The kid had the murder weapon in his possession and he had no alibi. Her partner got a confession out of him. Lisa hadn't approved of his methods, but there were times when nothing else would get the job done, according to most veterans she knew on the force.

She should have kept her mouth shut. But the six

feet of angry hoodlum glaring down at her made the feat impossible.

"Sean confessed. He had the murder weapon in his possession. The case was cut-and-dried."

He laughed, as did everyone in the room. "Things are always cut-and-dried when a cop wants to close a case. Nobody cared, just another dealer shot dead and off the streets. Didn't make no difference who you nailed for doing the deed. An investment in the future, two for the price of one."

She couldn't deny his final charge. Any cop would be all the more pleased if a suspect with a long rap sheet got his due in a big way. One case, one trial, two criminals off the street. Made everyone, including the D.A., happy.

"That confession was bull," the guy said bitterly. "Maybe you don't know your partner as well as you think you do. Or maybe—" he leaned his face closer to hers "—you're just as bad as he is."

Lisa felt a spike of fear. If this guy got his buddies riled up, there could be trouble, whether the boss in the other room wanted it or not. She had two choices, she could stay cool and see how this played out or she could call this hothead's bluff.

"Maybe your cousin didn't tell you the whole story," she said, meeting that menacing glare head-on.

A muscle jumped in his tense jaw. "And maybe your partner is keeping you in the dark about the way things really work when a 187 goes down in certain neighborhoods. You should ask him sometime."

Lisa held his glower, schooling any reaction to his mention of the penal code for murder. "Maybe I will."

"Let's go," a voice called from the hall.

The guy glaring down at her backed off, and Lisa took her first deep breath since he'd spoken.

She pushed off from the counter, one of her five guards coming up behind her to ensure she moved forward. Johnson and Buster Houston waited in what had once been a living room. Since Johnson appeared to be in one piece, she assumed the conversation had been civil. As long as Johnson gave her a blow-by-blow accounting of what went on in that room she would overlook the fact that he hadn't insisted she be allowed to stay.

Houston said to one of his men. "Leave them the way you found them."

Lisa felt the tension in her muscles release fractionally. She doubted any of these men, who were closest to the leader, would dare cross him. Which meant she and Johnson might just live to argue about the way he'd handled this little consultation.

Johnson still hadn't said a word as they were loaded into the Chevy and headed back across town. Since he sat in the front seat with the driver, she couldn't exactly interrogate him. She couldn't even make eye contact unless he chose to do so. The guy who'd questioned her regarding his cousin sat in the backseat with her along with one of his pals. She kept her attention straight ahead.

That this guy believed LAPD had coerced a confession out of his cousin wasn't unusual. People believed what they would. It was easy to blame the police when a family member got into trouble or simply got caught. That was a big part of the trouble these days, no one wanted to take responsibility.

Lisa thought of her brother. He was an honor student and had never gotten into trouble. Bad timing had gotten him killed. Bad timing and people like the ones chauffeuring her and Johnson back to the Box. Her lips compressed together to hold back the anger she felt every time she thought of that tragedy. She'd told herself for more than a decade that she'd gotten past that painful event in her life. Her chosen career field allowed her to try to stop these kinds of lowlifes. Whatever had gone down with Johnson last year was somehow all tangled up in this world of communities within communities, each with its own laws of survival. She was now convinced more than ever that Johnson was innocent.

The question was, to what degree? He hadn't killed those three men, she was certain. But did he know who had? Was he involved on some level she hadn't considered before? Any man whose presence prompted a visit with Buster Houston represented a value of some sort on the street. Respect came at a high price in this seedy world.

What exactly had Sam Johnson purchased with his silence? A man like him, with no record and a stellar career within the law enforcement realm, didn't turn without motivation. Was protecting his family the reason for his continued silence? That would be the simplest deduction. But Lisa had a feeling that this strange alliance was anything but simple.

BY THE TIME they reached downtown L.A., Sam had mentally prepared for Smith's interrogation. She would have plenty of questions. More than he could answer, he felt certain. Considering what he'd just learned, maintaining her cooperation was essential. As soon as they were back at the hotel, he would touch base with Anders. Checking in with Battles and Call wouldn't be necessary for a few more hours. Both knew to call if anything came up.

When the driver pulled to the curb more than a dozen blocks from the hotel, Sam dragged his attention back to the here and now.

"It's almost 3:00 a.m.," Sam said to him, "I have no desire to take a multiblock stroll."

The driver swiveled his head, his hands still fastened on the steering wheel. "You're lucky to be walking at all. Now, get out."

Sam held out his hand. "Our weapons."

The driver met the gaze of one of his accomplices in the rearview mirror, then turned back to Sam, "Get out."

Sam got out of the car. When the two men in the backseat emerged, Smith scooted out right behind the guy on the passenger side. The trunk was opened, and their weapons and cell phones were returned.

"I think your boss intended for you to drop us at the hotel," Smith snapped at the taller of the two who'd kept her company in the backseat. "I'm sure he won't be happy to hear that you failed to follow his orders."

"He said to leave you the *way* we found you. He didn't say nothing about *where*." He opened the car door and got in.

The car spun away from the curb. Sam assessed the block in both directions. Empty. Dark. But that didn't mean squat in this district. The first sniff of motivation would bring trouble streaming out of the woodwork.

He shoved the weapon into his waistband at the small of his back. Smith did the same with hers. Money, weapons, two major motivating assets.

The good news was that this sidewalk was a straight shot to the hotel. The bad, that it was twelve blocks with hardly any working streetlights and the usual tents and cardboard condos. Somewhere in the distance, sirens wailed. Sweat seeped from

Sam's pores as he considered the numerous hiding places for those who liked to lie in wait for just the right moment to ambush open targets. Tourists and the lost, without gang-member status to protect them in this so-called safe zone, were no better than sitting ducks in a shooting gallery.

Sam grabbed Smith's hand. She didn't resist and started forward. Eyes straight ahead, senses on red alert, he moved quickly and deliberately toward their destination. He avoided trouble for six of those twelve blocks. But his luck failed to hold out beyond that.

"I got whatcha need, *man*," the scraggly looking hoodlum who scooted from a stoop into their path said in what was likely a fake Jamaican accent. "Rock, weed, powder…whatever makes your fantasies come true." His clothes were ragged. His mop of hair was pulled back in a haphazard braid.

"Not interested," Sam said as he pushed past him.

But the dealer wasn't going to let it go so easily. He grabbed Sam's arm. "Just trying to do business, *man*. Ain't we all?"

When Sam would have gone for his weapon, Smith pushed between them and got in the guy's face. "That's right, man," she mocked, "we all gotta make a living. Now get out of our way."

The standoff lasted another thirty seconds before the dealer sidled back onto his stoop that fronted a dry-cleaning shop.

Smith took the lead this time, grabbed Sam's hand and pulled him along as she strode quickly toward the hotel. He glanced over his shoulder several times to make sure the guy hadn't decided to follow. For the next few minutes he allowed his thoughts to wander to the feel of her smaller hand clutching his. She was strong but soft. A nice combination. Her long, blond hair bounced with each determined stride she took. Nice hair, too.

He couldn't remember the last time he'd really paid attention to the way a woman looked. A year… longer? Now definitely wasn't the time.

In the hotel lobby, they walked straight to the bank of elevators. As soon as the doors slid closed and the car started its upward glide, she launched the interrogation he'd been anticipating since leaving the headquarters of Buster Houston.

"What did Houston say to you?" She cut him a look. "I want the truth, Sam. No more games. We could have been killed tonight. I don't know what you've got on those guys, but for some reason we got a firsthand tour of a Nation hideout and we're still breathing. I'm through waiting for you to do whatever it is you've got planned. I want the whole story *now*."

"That's going to take some time," he offered, knowing damned well she wouldn't go for it, "and we both need some sleep right now."

"Not going to happen."

The car stopped and the doors slid open. She stormed to the room and waited for him to fish the keycard from his back pocket.

"We won't be sleeping until I know what the hell is going on."

Sam pushed the door open and waited for her to enter first. "Then it's going to be a long night."

He locked the door, slid the chain into place and went into the bathroom before she could say anything else.

After splashing some water on his face, he stared at his reflection. There was absolutely no way out of this that didn't include getting dead.

It wasn't that he couldn't bear the idea of dying. Truth was that for a long while after Anna's death he'd wished for the same. He'd gone out of his way to put himself in the line of fire, driving through neighborhoods with the highest rate of fatalities from drive-by shootings. He'd hung out in the clubs that catered to criminals. He'd practically worn a big sign that said, "Shoot me!"

But it hadn't worked. Then he'd realized how unfair that thinking was to his family. Before he'd made his decision to try living again, the three men who'd raped and murdered the woman he'd loved had gotten what they deserved.

Everything had changed then. There seemed no

escape. The cops were crawling all over him. His family was worried sick. But worst of all, L.A.'s gang world was suddenly focused on him. Talk about a hairy situation. Some had respected him for taking vengeance into his own hands. Others had despised him for daring to act like one of them.

Mainly he'd been scared to death that the wrong people would learn the truth and more people he cared about would be hurt.

He hadn't been able to concentrate on his work. He'd pretty much stopped caring about his future when Anna died.

Time was supposed to heal all wounds. But time couldn't fix this.

The only way to make this right was for someone to die.

Chapter Nine

8:20 a.m.

A sound penetrated the layer of sleep holding Lisa captive. She knew she needed to wake up, but she was tired. So comfortable. She snuggled closer to the warmth in her bed. Her next breath brought with it the earthy scent of warm male flesh. A smile tugged at the corners of her mouth.

Sam…

A jarring vibration shattered the sweet, dreamy state where she lingered on the edge of sleep.

Her phone.

Trembling on the bedside table.

Her eyes opened.

A slice of brilliant light cut through the darkness of the room. She blinked to focus her vision. The sunlight peeked in through the parting in the drapes.

Hotel.

The Box.

She tried to sit up, couldn't, then fumbled for her phone.

A groan rumbled against her ear. She turned her head to the left and came face-to-face with Sam Johnson. His arm across her chest had her trapped against the bed. The front of his muscular body was pressed along her side, every hard, lean contour registering instantly in her brain along with the heavy male thigh draped across hers.

She licked her lips and forced her attention back to the phone, which had started to vibrate in her hand.

"Sm—" she cleared her throat "—Smith."

"Smith, are you hung over?"

Chuck Sanford. Her partner.

The man wrapped around her roused, grunted as his hand closed around her breast. Lisa's breath caught.

"Oh, hell." Chuck laughed. "Did I catch you at a bad time? I figured you'd be up by now. I'll call you later."

"No." Lisa scrambled away from Johnson, who suddenly sat bolt upright. "It's okay." She stumbled into the bathroom and closed the door. "I'm up. What's going on?" Lisa looked in the mirror, grimaced. She looked like hell. Johnson had given her just a taste of that truth she'd demanded and then he'd insisted she get some sleep. He had promised to tell her the rest this morning. The last time she roused and looked at the clock it had been around five. Evidently, he'd opted to get some shut-eye sometime after that. She shivered at the memory of his body against hers, his hand on her—

"We had a major battle over on the corner of South Western and Vernon around four this morning. We don't know all the details yet but it was bloody. The one witness who would talk says a half-dozen perps wearing red bandannas mowed down these four junkies and their dealer. The dead are all Crew."

Lisa absently rubbed at her forehead in hopes of warding off the beginnings of a headache. It was a miracle there was a witness at all. People didn't usually want to risk becoming a fatality themselves by speaking up in situations like this. Too often the gang members were people they knew, people who knew them…who knew where they lived.

"Happens all the time, Chuck," she returned, shifting her attention back to the conversation. Time to make this real. "You felt the need to call me on my vacation to tell me about this?" The suspicion in her voice made her want to bite her tongue. That guy last night—this morning actually—had her second-guessing what she knew. Her partner was a good guy. One of the best.

"You're right," he said with a heavy exhale, "I

shouldn't have bothered you on your vacation."
Pause. "It's just that…"

Trepidation trickled through her. "What? Come
on, Chuck, you got me up. Spill it." This indecisive-
ness wasn't like her partner at all.

"Their faces were marked with an X drawn in
their own blood just like the three vics Johnson
swore killed his fiancée."

Lisa sagged against the sink. "Gunshot victims?"
He'd said they were mowed down. That generally
meant gunfire. She held her breath, praying that
this might be a break that pointed away from
Johnson in the year old case.

"Yeah. AK-47. Not a pretty sight."

"I, ah, appreciate you letting me know. So, you
think this might have a tie in to that old case?"
There had to be more to this call than that.

"Maybe. Maybe not. With Watts clamoring for
Johnson's head, it's hard to say what's going on.
Johnson hired some fancy P.I. agency out of
Chicago to serve as security for his family. The firm
where he works says he's on a job in New York. I
thought you'd like to know, since that case still
bothers you." Another of those overdone sighs. "I
guess what I'm saying is, you could be right. There
could be something to the idea that Johnson didn't
kill those guys."

She restrained the urge to shout *yes*. For months

she'd been telling him that there was something wrong about the case. He'd played her off every single time. That it took four more dead gangbangers to sway him wasn't good, but at least he was looking at the situation a little differently now.

The part about Johnson's current whereabouts abruptly filtered past all the rest. Chuck had been looking into where Johnson was. If word got out that he'd met with Buster Houston—with her in tow—her partner would hit the roof. She'd be suspended, and Sam Johnson would be under investigation…again.

"I won't say I told you so," she tossed back since that was what he would expect.

"Yeah, yeah, I know. Anyway, I'll let you get back to your *vacation*. I just thought you'd want to know."

"Thanks, Chuck. I appreciate it."

Lisa severed the connection and stared at her phone for a long minute. She considered the calls her partner had made to the landline at her house and his surveillance of her calls. Something was going on. Something more than he was telling her.

When she'd freshened up, she exited the bathroom to find Sam Johnson hovering outside the door. She started to rail at him for eavesdropping, but he brushed past her and closed himself up in the bathroom so fast she didn't get the chance. So maybe eavesdropping hadn't been his motive for loitering outside the bathroom door.

The need to find a deli or coffee shop gnawed at her stomach, but she ignored it. She went to the window and drew back the drape just far enough to survey the street below. The Box looked totally different by day. Gone were the tents and cardboard condos and the street people who utilized them. The cars of businessmen and women, along with delivery trucks, lined the curbs. There wasn't a single dealer slinging dope or prostitute showing off her wares. The scaffolding and Dumpsters provided a ray of hope for the future by the light of day. Long-neglected buildings were being reclaimed and rejuvenated as high-end housing.

Nothing was what it seemed. Two different worlds.

Her gaze drifted to the closed bathroom door; just as Sam Johnson was two different men. There was the focused man of science who'd once used his skills to help catch criminals, and then there was the man she'd met twenty-four hours ago…the wary, determined guy with no care for his own safety.

AK-47. Her partner had said that the victims in this morning's predawn gun battle were killed by AK47s. One of the men who'd escorted them on their midnight journey had been carrying an AK-47. Not that he would be the only thug carrying that kind of weapon on the streets of L.A. on any given night, but the fact did seem a little coincidental. Especially considering the way the victims had been marked after death.

Johnson emerged from the bathroom and she decided that now was as good a time as any for him to make good on that promise he'd made a few hours ago. She'd wanted the lowdown on his conversation with Houston at three-thirty this morning, but he'd put her off, insisting they needed to get some sleep. He'd claimed he needed to consider what he'd learned before discussing it.

He'd had four hours to consider, it was time for him to give it to her straight.

As if he'd read her mind, those gray eyes zoomed in on hers. "Let's get some coffee and talk."

It was about time.

THERE WERE PLACES in downtown L.A. that Lisa couldn't afford to be seen during daylight hours, but Coffee Joe's was not one of them. Though some areas of the Box were only a short walk from City Hall, this corner was several blocks clear of that cop sector.

With a decent breakfast behind them and a third cup of coffee steaming from their cups, Lisa had waited long enough. She'd already filled him in on the call from her partner.

"Okay, let's have it."

"Fifteen months ago I found the one spec of DNA amid a multitude of evidentiary items that placed Kenan Watts at the scene of a multiple homicide."

She knew that part. Two Los Angeles police officers had been the victims. "He got life, since we couldn't prove he was the shooter, just that he was there." The D.A. had even offered him a deal. All Watts had to do was finger the shooter and he'd get probation—as long as he had nothing to do with the shootings. He refused, which meant unless he was the shooter, one or more cop killers had gotten away scot-free.

"Two months after his indictment, Anna was murdered."

She and Chuck had gotten the case. Johnson ID'd all three perps from photographs in one of Homicide's many suspect books, and the perps were hauled in for questioning. When it came time for him to make the final identification, he insisted he couldn't be sure. Any physical evidence had been destroyed when her body was partially burned. Johnson's testimony was all they'd had. Without it they had no choice but to release the three perps.

Days later they were all three dead and marked with an X. Chuck insisted Johnson had backed out on IDing the guys so he could have his vengeance. Lisa hadn't been able to believe that…but she'd doubted herself from time to time. Like last night when he'd managed to be hosted by the leader of the Nation and walk away without so much as a wrinkle in his shirt to show for it.

"The Man paid me a visit."

The late James Watts, Kenan and Lil's uncle and only blood relative. She'd known it, damn it. Deep in her gut, she'd suspected this was the case. Lisa instinctively leaned forward. She'd waited for this for more than a year.

"He apologized for his nephew's mistake and assured me that if I kept my mouth shut that he would see that those three were properly punished." Johnson searched her eyes, his hesitation palpable. "So I did. It was the least I could do for Anna."

The woman in her wanted to cheer his decision, but the cop in her understood the ramifications of that judgment. He'd interfered with an official investigation and he'd had advance knowledge of the impending murder of three men, deserving or not. But she didn't say a word for fear he would refuse to tell her the rest.

"As promised, Watts delivered."

"And you let us bang our heads against the wall," she interjected, unable to keep the edge of bitterness out of her voice. As deeply as she understood the pain he'd been through and the probability that his decisions at the time were likely not made with a stable mental outlook, still he'd been wrong. He'd committed a crime.

"Lil Watts was furious. He was the one to order the hit on Anna, but James refused to execute his own nephew. He argued that I was responsible for Lil's brother going to prison, in a matter of speaking, and so we'd call that part even. I wasn't satisfied. I wanted Lil Watts to pay the price, as well. I couldn't think of anything else."

She recalled those days with far too much clarity. He'd worked night and day, walked around like a ghost of the man he'd once been. She'd worried that he would end up committing suicide.

"Finally James settled the issue for me. I could either leave town and stop looking for ways to get Lil, or my family would be executed. He'd given me every opportunity to put the past behind me and I refused. I wanted Lil to pay and he knew I would keep on until I nailed him for something even if I couldn't bring myself to kill him."

The revelation brought everything into perspective. "So you left L.A. to protect your family?"

He nodded, sipped his coffee. "That was our deal. I stayed clear of Lil Watts and my family would be protected."

"But the man who made that deal with you is dead now." The big picture came into vivid focus.

Johnson nodded.

That left him in a hell of a position. Without James Watts to run interference, Lil could force Johnson's hand. Could push the issue until Johnson had no choice but to surrender to him.

Or go to the police and risk being charged as an accomplice to multiple counts of homicide.

Wait.

"What about Buster Houston. Why did he get involved?" Houston surely wouldn't give one damn what happened to Lil Watts or to Sam Johnson. Houston was Watts's sworn enemy. Had he offered his protection to Johnson just to be pitted against Watts? That didn't make sense. Particularly not from a man who spouted peace and tolerance the way Houston did.

Johnson's guard went up then, setting her on edge. What the hell else could he possibly have to hide?

"Houston is prepared to help me deal with the situation on one condition."

"'Deal with the situation'?" she echoed. She didn't need a psychic connection to understand what that meant. "What's the condition?" Not that she was condoning his actions with anything Buster Houston suggested, but she needed to know what the man wanted. It seemed strange that a man that powerful in the gang world would need anything from Sam Johnson.

"He wants me to help him lure the person he believes is responsible for James Watts's death into a trap."

"Why would he do that?" Houston and Watts were enemies. Why would Houston care who killed

Watts? LAPD had assumed Watts's murder was gang related, there hadn't been any evidence to indicate otherwise.

Johnson studied his cup for a bit as if trying to decide whether he dared drink the rest.

Finally he said, "Apparently the two men had become friends in recent years. Secretly, of course."

She pushed her cup aside, done. "Why doesn't he just carry out his vengeance? If he knows the perpetrator, why does he need you? This doesn't add up, Johnson. You surely see that."

He looked directly into her eyes. "It adds up, Smith. Houston insists that the man responsible for Watts's death is a cop. This cop is part of a band of dirty cops. The two cops Kenan Watts murdered were about to ID these guys. Kenan was ordered to execute them. The only glitch was my interference, which caused Kenan to go to prison when he would have otherwise gotten off scot-free. James Watts's subsequent pronouncement that there would be no retaliation for the part I played evidently didn't go over so well, either, since someone decided to get him out of the way. This ultimately worked for all involved. Gave Lil a clear path to get at me and Lil would definitely be a lot easier to manipulate."

Stunned, Lisa couldn't speak for nearly a minute. Johnson couldn't be serious. James Watts had been an old man, one who promoted peace. To have killed him would have been a cold-blooded act of premeditation. Something she might expect from an angry rival gang member, but she damned sure wasn't ready to blame that on one of her colleagues. Nor was she about to take some gang lord's word about a group of dirty cops.

"Are you sure he isn't setting you up, Johnson?" she argued. That was the most probable explanation. Houston had an agenda and he was playing Sam Johnson. No doubt about it.

"I'm positive. The cop he wants to bring down is not only dirty, but the ringleader of a group of several others. He's playing God and on the take big-time. Houston says he can prove it."

"Well, then," she said, fury building in her belly, "he should prove it and let the authorities deal with it." She'd heard enough of this foolishness.

Johnson's gaze never deviated from hers. "You know that's a hell of a lot easier said than done," he countered. "And this cop is no rookie. He's a seasoned veteran with serious clout."

His last statement made her nervous. "What does this have to do with you or Anna?"

"This cop is the one who set the revenge against me in motion. Kenan Watts wasn't supposed to have gone to prison. He wasn't supposed to have been nailed period. But I wouldn't stop sifting through the evidence until I found something to use against him."

She held up her hands stop-sign fashion. "All right, so there's a dirty cop. I might go along with that, but a whole band of them? That's just more than I can swallow. So who is this supposed ringleader? Houston must have told you who he suspected."

"Yeah, he told me."

Lisa waited, none too patiently. This was a new twist in the whole mess, and she wasn't sure she wanted to waste her time listening. But if *he* was listening, she had no choice.

"Sanford, your partner."

Sam had put off telling her for several hours. Ultimately he'd had no choice but to hit her with this. The look of disbelief and astonishment on her face warned that the shock was fading and the reality would set in any second.

"There is no way my partner is dirty," she charged, her lips quivering with anger, her pupils flaring with the same, "much less leading a group of other renegade cops."

"If he's not, then he has nothing to worry about."

She shook her head. "Let's just pretend for a moment that he is responsible for what happened. How do you plan to prove it, and then what do you anticipate doing about it if and when you do?"

"I just want him to admit what he's done, provide

the names of the others involved, and then you can arrest the whole lot."

She wasn't listening to any more of this. "You've lost it, Sam. That's all there is to it. I won't be a party to this insanity." She owed her partner her trust. He'd saved her life more than once.

"What about the messages he keeps leaving on your machine? Anders said he left another one this morning before he called you on your cell phone."

"That makes him a cop with good instincts, not a dirty one. I'm the one acting outside the law."

He didn't want her down on herself. "If your partner has nothing to hide, then he can stand up to a little scrutiny. And don't forget that he stationed another detective to monitor your house. Why doesn't he trust you, Smith? Is he afraid you'll talk to me and figure out the truth?"

"He's protecting me," she said quickly. "He knows I'm hung up on this case, and he wants to see that I'm okay."

"You keep telling yourself that. But I have to be realistic. My family's lives are at stake here. Sanford is up to no good, and I'm going to prove it."

"So Houston can have him killed?" Those lush lips were set in a stern line.

Sam shook his head. "So Sanford can go to prison and get what's coming to him from some of those scumbags he sent there."

Smith scooted across the seat and stood. "I have to think about this. I can't make a decision like this on the spur of the moment. I need time."

He pushed out of his seat. "Don't take too long," he suggested. "My family has been hurt enough. I don't want them to suffer anymore."

"And what about you?" she returned crisply. "Do you care what happens to you in this equation?"

"I have to check in with Anders."

He couldn't answer her question. At one time he'd thought he no longer cared, but he didn't know anymore. No matter, that was as good a place as any to end the discussion.

He knew what he had to do.

All she needed to do was see that Sanford got what was coming to him when the dust settled.

The explosion of gunshots rent the air a split second before the plate-glass window shattered. Sam took Smith to the floor with him, using his body to shield hers. Glass fragments sprayed like hail from a sudden summer storm across the floor.

Then came the eerie silence.

Chapter Ten

Screams and cries reverberated in the coffee shop as if everyone present had erupted from their paralyzing fear at the same instant. Sam came up on all fours first to assess the situation. Whoever had done the shooting was long gone. The pedestrians on the sidewalk had started to move to the window to look inside the coffee shop, hoping to get a look at the carnage.

Sirens wailed in the distance.

They couldn't be caught in here. Word would go straight to Sanford that his partner had been dining with Sam Johnson.

Sam jumped to his feet, pulling Smith up with him. "We have to get out of here."

She'd drawn her weapon and was surveying the damage. "Was anyone hurt?" she demanded as she moved away from him.

Damn it. Didn't she get it? They had to disappear before the first officers were on the scene.

Smith walked the length of the shop, checking on those just finding the nerve to crawl from under tables and from behind the counter.

The man he used to be would have done that same thing...first. When had that changed? Had the events of the last year hardened him to the point that he would walk away before checking on the innocent bystanders?

Smith shoved her weapon back into her waistband and strode quickly back to where he still stood. "No injuries." She looked around. "There has to be a back door out of here."

He nodded, then followed as she hurried around the counter and into the kitchen. The hired help had either moved to the front of the shop or were still hidden, since the kitchen was deserted. The smell of burnt muffins filled the air.

Smith eased the back door open and ensured no cops had shown up in the alley just yet.

"Clear," she muttered.

He followed her out the door, rushed along the alley until they reached the far end of the block. They dropped into a more relaxed stride as they fell into step with the pedestrians on the sidewalk running parallel to the cross street.

Sam surveyed the street and the shop fronts on either side of the road, watching for anything out of sync...any sudden moves out of other pedestrians.

A dozen cruisers had closed in on the coffee shop. Smith took a left before reaching the hotel that stood between them and the coffee shop. She weaved between three other buildings until she reached the parking lot where they'd last left the rental car.

"Do you have a destination in mind?" he asked as he unlocked the vehicle. Apparently, she'd decided to give him tit for tat. He took one last long look around to ensure they hadn't been followed.

"My place."

He hesitated but decided it was better to get into the car before pursuing any debate. "Why your place?" He started the engine and backed out of the slot as she snapped her safety belt across her lap.

She turned those brown eyes to him. "I need my computer."

"If there's still surveillance on your place, going there might not be a good idea." He paid the parking fee and pulled out onto the street.

"We'll just have to work around that obstacle. I need to access my computer."

He didn't ask why. He knew. She wanted to do some research on his accusations. Wouldn't do her any good. Sanford and his cronies were too smart to leave tracks that easy to follow. But he would indulge her for the moment.

For now, getting and staying out of sight was an excellent idea.

JOHNSON PARKED THE CAR on the street adjacent to Lisa's own. She'd lived in this neighborhood for four years. She knew the residents who worked and those who were retired. Taking care to stay close to the hedge line she moved along the driveways and back-yards belonging to those already gone for the day.

Johnson had put a call in to Anders to let him know they were approaching from the rear. Anders would keep an eye on whoever had stakeout duty today just to make sure he stayed put.

"Your partner called again," Anders said as soon as she'd cleared the back door.

"This time," he went on as she went straight to the refrigerator for a cold drink, "he remotely erased all the previous messages."

Lisa refused to allow that bit of news to influence her at the moment. There could be a plausible ex-planation for Chuck's behavior. If she had to guess, she'd say he was suspicious about what she was up to, and she couldn't blame him for that.

"Colby wants a conference call," Anders said to Johnson. "He wants an update on where we are."

Johnson glanced at her, then said to Anders, "We don't know where we are yet."

Lisa ignored his pointed remark. At least he hadn't shared his groundless theories about her colleagues yet. She headed for the second bed-room she'd turned into an office, not bothering to respond. Her living-room sofa was a hideaway bed, providing space for overnight guests. Not that she ever had any. She was too busy with work. But it was always better to be prepared. In all honesty, she didn't really have time for much of a social life. This was the first time off she'd taken in years.

Lately, the loneliness had gotten to her a little more than usual. But like everything else that wasn't stamped priority, she didn't have time for that right now.

She sat down at her computer and scrolled through her files until she found the one she needed. Two murdered cops. As hard as she and Chuck had worked, they'd come up with insufficient evidence to nail the perp they'd caught near the scene until Sam Johnson had found that DNA. The idiot perp had spit in the faces of his victims. But then he'd realized that might be a mistake and he'd attempted to wash their faces clean of any saliva. He'd missed a spot.

Sam's stellar forensics work had nailed a major player in the gang world. The nephew of The Man: Kenan Watts.

She studied the reports she'd prepared. All seemed in order. Then she searched her files for the next cop-killer case. Three years ago. A rookie who'd been partnered up with a veteran. He'd been off-duty. Had gone to return a couple of DVDs and gotten gunned down in the video-store parking lot. Months after the shooting, his wife had come forward and insisted that her husband had suspected some kind of trouble in his division. Priority Homicide. He'd decided to go to Internal Affairs with his suspicions, but that never happened. When asked why she'd waited so long to bring this up, she'd insisted that grief had prevented her from delving into the matter at first.

That was another case Lisa and Chuck had gotten. The perp was never found. There hadn't been a single trace of evidence. Just another unsolved homicide in the City of Angels.

The fact was, none of this meant anything. There were hundreds of murders in the L.A. area every year. Sometimes, unfortunately, the victims were cops. But that didn't mean there was a conspiracy of bad cops against good cops.

If her partner was into something like that, she would know. She wasn't that naive or that blind. The detective sitting outside her house and the constant calls to check her answering machine were only because Chuck worried about her. Charles Sanford was her mentor. Her friend.

Next she read through the news articles that had been published on the murders. The investigation had been by the book, from beginning to end. What Buster Houston was suggesting was incomprehensible.

But the detective in her wouldn't let her blindly

insist that there was no thread of believability in his accusations. The best way to disprove a lie was to find the truth.

Easy enough. Jason Rivera, the cop who'd been murdered three years ago and whose wife had insisted he had been suspicious of some of his fellow officers, was the place to start. His partner was retired now, but he was still alive. And so was Jason's widow.

Asking all the same old questions might be a waste of time, but she intended to do this right. It was too important to do otherwise. If Buster Houston intended to use her partner for some agenda, only he knew about it. She had to disprove his accusations and put a stop to his plan. The shortest route to accomplishing that was to convince Johnson that Houston was wrong…was using him.

Sam briefed Spencer Anders and Jim Colby on the events of the past fourteen hours, including the drive-by shooting which had already been reported on every single local news channel. If the police had his and Smith's descriptions, the information hadn't been released to the media.

"Just one more thing," Colby said via the speaker phone on Smith's answering machine.

Sam and Anders shared a look. Sam doubted that

Colby had learned anything he didn't already know, but his tone was grim.

"If either of you receive any orders or instructions via Battles, Call or Victoria, I want you to confirm those directly with me."

Another look passed between Sam and Anders. "Is there a problem?" Anders asked, when Sam chose not to.

Sam understood exactly what was going on here. He'd spent a lot of years reading people, mostly dead ones, but a lot of the principles were the same. Victoria Colby-Camp didn't want her son delving into hardcore cases. Sam had watched her interference increase over the past few months. Jim Colby had reached his limit on patience. Sam hated to watch this wall go up between mother and son, but one of them had to be prepared to compromise and so far he'd seen no indication of either one leaning in that direction.

"No problem," Sam assured Colby. He didn't expect to be on the receiving end of many directives. Most of his decisions were real-time in the field. There was no opportunity to run his thoughts by anyone else. Like when they'd escaped that shootout this morning. He'd done what he had to do.

Smith entered the room. She'd showered and changed. Her long blond hair was still damp. As he watched, she twisted it around into a bun then clamped it with a clip to hold it into place.

"I have to follow up on a couple of loose ends." She reached for her handbag and her weapon.

Sam pushed out of his chair. "I'm ready."

Her gaze connected with his. "I need to do this alone."

"Not going to happen." He tucked his own weapon into his waistband. "You didn't let me take a single step without you right on my heels. I'm claiming the same right."

"Give me an update in three to four hours," Anders reminded as they headed for the back door.

They took the same route as before from her house to the car. This time she drove. Sam waited until they'd put a few blocks between them and her house before he questioned her plan.

"Where are we headed?"

"To see Jason Rivera's partner."

So she wasn't so sure about Sanford.

"Before you form any conclusions," she said testily, "this is for you, not me. I know Charles Sanford. I'm not worried. But I need you to see that I'm right before this goes any further. And while we're both still alive."

Sounded like a waste of time to him, but he would keep an open mind. If she could make a valid case, he would weigh it against the proof Houston had. First he'd have to get the man to show it to him.

FORTY-FIVE MINUTES LATER they arrived at the Glendale residence of one Detective Roger Cornelius, retired. The man lived alone since his wife had died the year before. He was confined to a wheelchair, but looked fit for a fellow without the use of his legs.

"You're sure I can't get you two some coffee?" he asked for the third time since their arrival.

"No, thanks," Smith assured him. "We don't want to put you to any trouble."

Sam didn't remember this particular detective. He knew most in Priority Homicide, but this wasn't one he'd ever worked with on a case.

"You said you needed my help on an old case," he said to Smith, his expression bright. Every cop, no matter how old or how ill, missed the investigative work.

Smith looked completely relaxed, but Sam knew that wasn't the case. She didn't want to do this, even though she hadn't said as much. Doubting her colleagues was not something she enjoyed. The woman had a great deal of pride in her badge and all it stood for. Sam admired that about her. The years on the job hadn't jaded her, and in this city that was a hell of an accomplishment.

"Your partner Jason Rivera's murder. How did you feel about his wife's assertions that he'd been on to some illegal activities within the division?

Didn't she even insist that his suspicions were the reason he was murdered?"

Cornelius's expression fell instantly. "Why would you bring up that nonsense?"

She held out her hands as if she didn't understand it, either. "Some perp brought it up during an interview. He claims he has proof that Rivera was on to something."

Sam tensed. She was pushing it a little too close for his comfort. He hadn't given her carte blanche to come in here and give away what they knew or their source.

"Hell, Lisa, you know that's crazy." Cornelius's agitation escalated. "That woman went off the deep end when her husband was murdered. She had to blame someone and it just happened to be us. If there'd been any truth to her allegations, why didn't she bring up that crap right after he was murdered? Besides," he went on, "you know every detective in Priority Homicide. There shouldn't be any question."

"There isn't," Smith assured him, her face packed with sincerity. "But I have to follow through on something like this so it doesn't come back to haunt us. The last thing we want is some jerk mouthing off to the press and word getting around that we refused to investigate the allegations."

Cornelius considered that for a moment. "I guess

you're right. The damn media exploits everything these days. What's Sanford saying about this?"

The slightest hesitation almost gave her away, but she recovered quickly. "Do you even have to ask?"

Cornelius snorted. "Hell, no. He's probably as ticked off as I am."

Sam watched as Smith led him right to where she wanted him from there. She was a damned good interrogator.

"Rivera was your partner," she said. "You didn't get any sense that he felt there was illegal activity going on in the division?"

The retired detective shook his head adamantly. "Not a clue. If he'd ever said anything like that, I would have set him straight. I don't know what he was thinking or if he was even thinking it. You know, maybe his wife made it up. She was wrecked about his death. They had two little kids, and I think maybe she just had a nervous breakdown or something."

"Did she seek counseling? I don't recall that she pursued her allegations."

"Nope. She let it go." He shrugged. "Who knows why? Probably because it was a fabrication. But she didn't pursue it, and that was the best for everyone. There was no need to tarnish her husband's reputation or the division's."

"You spent twenty years in Homicide, Roger,"

Smith noted. "I don't think we've ever had a dirty cop. We're the cleanest division in the department and it's because of good cops like you."

"Damn straight. We keep our noses clean and do our job. End of story. Anybody who says different is a liar, plain and simple."

"Did Rivera have financial problems?"

She slid that one in while the man wasn't looking. Again Sam was impressed.

"You know..." He squinted in concentration. "Now that you bring that up, there was talk after his death that he'd gotten into a bit of a bind. But I still don't believe he was going after the division for personal gain." He waved off the whole idea. "He was my partner. I think I would've known if he was up to something like that."

"I think you're right. Thanks, Roger." Smith stood and shook his hand. "I'll make sure this rumor gets crushed. Don't you worry about that for a minute. Rivera was a fine detective."

Sam followed her out of the neat ranch-style home and to the car where she slid behind the wheel. He glanced back at the house and did a double take. For a second he'd thought he saw Cornelius watching them go. Only, he wasn't doing so from the level of a man seated in a wheelchair, he was standing up. The blind snapped closed so quickly Sam couldn't be sure.

"How was it Cornelius ended up in a wheel-chair?" he asked as Smith backed out onto the street.

"A shooting. He still has a little feeling in his legs, but not enough to permit standing or walking. The injury forced him into early retirement. Happened right after his partner was murdered."

Sam stared back at the house a moment as they drove away. Interesting: a detective who hadn't had a clue that his partner was investigating the goings-on in his own division; who had been disabled by a gunshot; and who, Sam was certain, had been standing at that window.

Noon had come and gone and Sam's stomach rumbled in protest of his negligence. The lack of sleep was catching up to him, as well. With that thought came the memory of waking up entangled with Detective Smith. Her soft body had been pressed intimately along his. He'd been having the best dream when he'd awakened. She'd been under him instead of next to him, and he'd been driving deep into her. His body tightened even now at the memory. Not exactly smart of him to dwell on a fantasy involving one of the detectives who would like nothing better than to prove he'd somehow been involved with no less than three murders.

That was one thing a guy could count on. When it came to sex, intelligence had nothing at all to do with it.

He took his time visually perusing her profile. Nice high cheekbones and full lips. Soft skin. He'd liked waking up to the smell of her.

Funny, he hadn't had the first zing of attraction other than these feelings for Smith since Anna was murdered. Just his luck to find himself in lust with the woman who was so obsessed with finding the truth about his past that she'd spend her vacation doing so.

He had a bad feeling that the truth she wanted so badly to find was not going to be what she expected. She couldn't see that sometimes the closest people hurt you the most. Maybe he was jumping the gun, but Buster Houston had no reason to lie about Sanford. This was much bigger than a simple lie.

This was going to rock LAPD. The repercussions would be felt all the way to the far sides of gangland.

"You have a question you want to ask, Johnson?"

He snapped out of the trance he'd drifted into. "Yeah…ah, where are we going now?"

"We're going to see if we can find Rivera's widow. If she was whacked out back then and talking nonsense, she should be able to admit that by now. Or, at the very least, explain it. I want to know why she attacked the division her husband loved." She braked for a light and let her gaze settle on his. "I want to know why she isn't dead already if she possessed that kind of information."

A valid point. "You know, Smith, Cornelius is

probably putting a call in to your partner to warn him as we speak."

"Maybe." She moved forward, maneuvering through the traffic. "I guess I'll cross that bridge when I come to it."

Sam had a feeling they were coming to that particular bridge a lot faster than she suspected.

Chapter Eleven

2:00 p.m.

Gloria Rivera lived in a quiet Sherman Oaks neighborhood that had found its place in the ongoing revitalization of once-crumbling communities. The small bungalow sat on a corner lot surrounded by a well-tended yard. In the driveway, a ten-year-old sedan looked a little the worse for wear.

Lisa didn't know Mrs. Rivera very well, but they had met several times during the investigation into her husband's murder. Not once had she mentioned her suspicions to Lisa. It wasn't until afterward, when the case had grown cold and she and Chuck had moved on to one of their numerous other cases that she'd heard Mrs. Rivera had gone to Internal Affairs with her allegations.

Chuck had met with the people from IA and handled the situation. Lisa hadn't been questioned.

Apparently, not enough grounds to pursue the investigation had been found. As far as Lisa had known, that was where it ended. A grieving widow seeking someone to blame.

But could she have been wrong about that? Could there have been more, and she just didn't know about it? That would mean her partner had left her out of the loop on some of the details.

Innocent until proven guilty. Even the most heinous criminals got that benefit of the doubt. Why wouldn't her partner, her division, be worthy of the same?

"I'll do the talking," she reminded Johnson. She didn't need him taking off on his own agenda. She was the one with the badge, even if the investigation was unofficial.

"I'll do the listening," he said, with far more humility than she knew him to possess.

The impulse to tell him what she thought of his patronizing almost got the better of her, but she managed to resist the temptation.

A jungle-gym decorated in brilliant primary colors dominated the side yard. Two kids…who'd lost their father. She swallowed back the sickening sensation that accompanied the thought.

Lisa pressed the doorbell and waited. Canned laughter and the familiar antics of a kids' program blared from a television set inside. Good sign. Somebody was most likely home.

The wood door opened and a thirtyish Hispanic woman peered through the screen door first at Sam then at Lisa. She hesitated for a moment, then said, "I remember you."

"Mrs. Rivera, I'm Detective Lisa Smith. I have a few questions for you if you don't mind."

Another of those troubled hesitations and uncertain glances, first at the man standing next to Lisa then at her. "What kind of questions? What's this about, Detective?"

Shouting from inside signaled two or more children were not happy with each other. The indignant cries for "Mom" confirmed the theory.

"Excuse me," Mrs. Rivera said before rushing off to calm the storm.

A few moments later she returned to the door. "What do you want?" The surprise was gone, only annoyance and maybe some amount of suspicion remained.

"Mrs. Rivera, there are a couple of things unclear about the statement you gave to Internal Affairs three years ago. I'd like to review your statement with you. See if we can't resolve the questions."

"There's nothing to resolve," she snapped, both hands settling on her hips. "My husband was murdered by one of you." Fury glittered in her eyes. "Maybe you didn't get your hands dirty by actually pulling the trigger, but one of you ordered his execution. I don't care what anyone says. That's the truth."

Lisa carefully schooled her reaction. She couldn't let the woman see the shock or the disbelief. "Ma'am, I'm sorry if you've had a difficult time with making yourself understood, but that's why I'm here now. I'd like to change that, if you have the time to discuss the matter now."

Hesitation lingered in her eyes. "All my friends say I should just let it go. But I can't. I have to live with that every day. Knowing that his own people killed him and nobody cares." She unlocked the screen door and stepped back. "Come in."

When Mrs. Rivera had settled the children for the second time, she returned to the living room where Lisa and Johnson waited. She sat down directly across from Lisa and folded her hands in her lap.

"What do you want to know?"

"Did your husband ever talk about any problems he might be having with one or more gang members?"

A frown furrowed her brow. "No. We didn't really discuss his work that often. But the last couple of months of his life he kept talking about requesting a transfer. He said we'd sell the house and move to Pasadena or some place. Anywhere away from L.A."

"Did he mention to you what was troubling him?" Funny, she didn't remember any discontent in Rivera at work. He'd done his job—quite well, at that—and he'd talked about his kids.

"He said there were things going on that he didn't approve of. He'd been approached to participate, but he refused. It was supposed to be okay except the others started acting funny toward him. Made him feel as if he didn't belong." Tears shone in her eyes as she said the last.

"But he didn't give you any specifics on what he meant by things going on?"

She shook her head. "Just that they were getting paid to look the other way. He didn't talk about it a lot, but I could tell it weighed on his mind."

"He didn't mention any names?"

"No. Sometimes he'd rattled off a few names. They might have been gang members. Nothing specific."

Pain and grief had routed out deep lines at the corners of her eyes. She looked tired, perhaps from playing both mother and father.

"If you were so certain that something was going on in our division, why didn't you push the issue? Why let it go so easily, Mrs. Rivera?" It was clear to Lisa, sitting there face-to-face with the lady, that she was a fighter. She was giving everything she had to raise her children and take care of the home. Her deceased husband's pension and life insurance had evidently allowed her to remain a stay-at-home mother. Why would a fighter give up so easily?

As if she'd suddenly remembered an appointment, Mrs. Rivera stood. "You should go. I've said too much already. What does any of it matter now? My husband is dead. Nothing I do is going to give my children their father back."

Lisa pushed to her feet. Johnson followed suit. "Mrs. Rivera, you don't need to be afraid to speak with me about anything that troubles you."

She searched Lisa's eyes, seemed to hesitate, but then changed her mind. "It took me a while to get up my nerve to go to someone about what I knew after my husband was murdered, and it was a mistake. I got the message," she said quietly. "If this is some sort of trick to see if I'll say any more than what I've just told you, it's not going to work. I won't risk my children's lives like that."

"I can assure you—"

"Go," she insisted. "I can't help you."

Sam touched Lisa's arm. "Come on, let's go."

She didn't want to. She wanted to stay until this woman told her the whole truth. She needed names, dates, incidents.

She needed more than this simmering suspicion.

"Thank you, Mrs. Rivera," she said before leaving.

The widow didn't respond. She closed and locked the door behind them without another word.

Lisa strode to the car, her anger building with each step. At the driver's door she glared at Johnson across the roof of the car. "That doesn't prove anything. It's hearsay. Irrelevant."

"You're right."

With that out of the way, he got into the car and closed the door.

He said nothing else during the trip back to the hotel. She didn't ask him if that was where he wanted to go. Their options were limited. Going back to her place more than absolutely necessary was too risky. But there was one thing that wouldn't wait any longer: it was after two and she was starving. A detour through a drive-through took care of that problem.

Disgust settled heavily in her stomach along with the chicken sandwich. She'd been back in L.A. for more than twenty-four hours and she knew nothing. She was slightly closer to that truth she sought, but not nearly as close as she would like to be. And the closer she got…the more confusing everything seemed.

That she'd been right about Johnson's innocence didn't give her much comfort right now. She needed to know who killed those men if she was going to convince her partner of Johnson's innocence.

And now all this dirty-cop business had come up.

Lisa stuffed another French fry into her mouth. She refused to lend any credence to Sam and Houston's allegations regarding her partner. She would need a lot more than some gang lord's conspiracy theories. Or the suspicions of a man who carried a serious grudge.

She parked in the usual spot, and Johnson marked the windows with his borrowed bar of soap. It seemed inconceivable that something as insignificant as soap drawings would protect their car. But so far it had worked.

The lobby was deserted. Silent as a tomb.

Sam didn't like the fact that the guy who was usually behind the counter was missing. Granted the place wasn't that busy, but to leave the desk unmanned seemed a little peculiar.

As they reached the elevator the hairs on the back of his neck stood on end.

Johnson grasped Lisa's arm, drawing her to a stop. "Something's wrong," he said as he surveyed the empty lobby once more.

"Yeah, I feel it, too. Something's off."

"You stay down here." He inclined his head toward the desk. "Maybe behind the counter. I'll go up to the room and check things out."

"Bad strategy. It's you they want. You lay low behind the desk. I'll go up."

"I'm not having you killed in my stead."

The way he looked at her when he made that statement sent a shiver through her. Her safety being important to him—really important—touched her. She stabbed the call button for the elevator.

"Don't be ridiculous. If there's an ambush waiting for us, you know they're not going to kill me until they know where you are. I'll be perfectly safe."

Sam didn't like letting her go, but she had a point and one of them had to do this. She also had a gun and knew how to use it.

"Behind the counter," she ordered as the elevator doors slid open.

"I'll keep an eye on the elevators and the main entrance," he told her before following her order. "If you're not back in five minutes, I'm coming up."

He didn't give her a chance to argue. He hustled over to the front desk and took a position out of sight.

Lisa stepped into the elevator, and the doors glided shut. Her heart rammed into triple time. She checked her weapon at the small of her back. No need to be nervous. Even if Lil Watts himself were up there, she would be safe until they learned Johnson's location.

She exited the elevator and walked to the door of her room. The keycard in hand, she'd just attempted to insert it when the door burst open.

"Detective Smith."

Three of LAPD's finest from Priority Homicide Division waited in the room.

"What's going on, Jessup?" She looked to the detective she knew best, Bruce Jessup. Not that she knew any of these three particularly well, but Jessup was one she'd worked with before.

"That's what we want to know," Scruggs said from his position behind Jessup.

"Just answer a few questions and everything will be fine, Lisa," Jessup urged.

With the door closed behind her, the taller of the two remaining detectives, Tony Hicks, began the inquisition.

"When did you return from Cozumel?"

"Yesterday," she lied.

"Why are you staying in this hotel?"

Now that she took the time to look around the room she had to wonder the same. "My lover didn't want to go anywhere he might be recognized." That at least was partially true.

"We have two witnesses," Hicks said, "who can place you with Sam Johnson just a few hours ago."

"I don't know what you're talking about," she argued, infusing surprise into her tone, as well as her expression. The idea that these guys could be the dirty detectives Rivera's wife had told her about blinked in her head like a caution light. *Impossible*, part of her argued.

A knock on the door signaled a new arrival. God, she hoped it wasn't Johnson. He'd said he would give her five minutes. Jessup opened the door.

Lisa's jaw dropped when her partner walked into

the room. Somewhere beyond the shock, she was glad it wasn't Johnson.

"What's going on here, Chuck?" Now maybe she'd get some straight answers.

Her partner jerked his head toward the door and the others exited the room. Another rush of tension sent adrenaline charging through her veins.

When the door had closed, Sanford lit into her. "What the hell are you doing, Lisa?"

"I don't know what you mean." She worked hard to keep the expression on her face neutral.

"I knew you were obsessed with this case—with Johnson. But to lie to me about going to Cozumel when you never even left the country, that's just going too far."

Guilt pinged her. She'd let her partner down. Left him in the dark.

"I just needed some time to think."

"You're making a mistake, Lisa," he said. "I wish you wouldn't do this."

For the first time since she'd met Charles Sanford, his words felt like a threat…a warning.

"If I do this, whatever you think *this* is, just what's going to happen?" She didn't back off when his glower darkened.

"Johnson is guilty, if not of murder, of something. I don't know why you're taking up with him like this, but it's a slap in the face to all of us at Homicide.

You'll regret what you're doing. Go take that vacation you lied to me about. That'll do you a hell of a lot more good than this."

He pivoted and headed for the door.

"What about Rivera? Did he regret what he'd done? Is that why he's dead?"

Sanford stopped, turned back to her, and the danger in his eyes stole her breath right out of her lungs.

"This is my final warning. Take that time off… get your head on straight."

After he'd gone, Lisa waited until the count of ten before leaving the room. Gave Sanford and his buddies time to get out of there. If she waited much longer, Johnson would come to check on her. He might run into her partner or one of the others.

She wasn't ready for that to happen yet.

Instead of taking the elevator, she took the stairs. She leaned over the railing and looked and listened. Clear. She took each flight in a near run. As she hit the second-floor landing, the door leading into the corridor burst open.

Her brain barely had time to acknowledge that it was Sam before he dragged her into the corridor.

"You were supposed to stay out of sight," she snapped.

"Yeah, well, I never was any good at following orders."

"We need to get out of here," she told him. She

had a bad feeling that their next visitors might not leave so easily and without the exchange of gunfire.

"I thought I recognized one of Priority Homicide's finest. Did your partner show up?"

The question shouldn't have annoyed her.

"Yes."

"What did he say?"

"He said I was making a mistake and that I should take the vacation I'd lied to him about." More of that infuriating frustration whipped through her. He'd basically threatened her and then he'd acted as if nothing at all untoward had happened.

Johnson hesitated halfway to the elevators on the second floor. "Ask yourself, Smith, why would he track you down like this? What's he really worried about?"

She lifted her chin in defiance of what he wanted her to say, what her mind wouldn't let her pretend away. "I don't know, but whatever it is, it has something to do with you. At this point I figure if I stay with you, the whole thing will go down eventually. Maybe then we'll have some answers."

He guided her to the door behind her, shoved a keycard into the door's lock and opened it. When had they changed rooms?

"We have a different room now?"

He shook his head. "The other room is still ours. We need to get a couple of hours' sleep before night falls and the guardians of the turf come out in full force. I have a feeling we're going to be very popular tonight."

"We're already popular," she muttered.

This room had two queen beds. How nice. He'd made sure they didn't have to sleep together again. She doubted she would sleep, anyway.

He stripped off his shirt and shoes and stretched out across one bed. She kicked off her shoes and crawled onto the other. If she could make her brain stop for just a little while she might actually get some sleep.

What the hell was going on with her partner? How could she have worked with him for five years and missed that something was not as it should be?

This was insane.

What was even crazier was the idea that, as fired up as she was about the visit from her partner tonight, she found herself studying Johnson's form. Long muscular arms. Heavy, lean legs. The remembered feel of him had her tingling in places that had nothing to do with anything but Sam Johnson.

How were they going to figure out this puzzle? They couldn't go to anyone for help. Outside their team there wasn't anyone they could trust.

It was just the two of them, with Lil Watts and his thugs coming at them from one side while law enforcement came from the other. Sanford had to be worried or he wouldn't have bothered keeping track of her whereabouts. That had to be the reason he was having her watched. The notion that he was a cold-blooded killer was ludicrous.

Her eyes started to drift shut, but she fought it. She needed to think, to sort some of this out. She doubted Lil Watts would wait beyond the coming night. He knew Johnson was back. He was likely the one behind the drive-by shooting. He would be anxious to finish this.

If they could just survive one more night, they might be able to get some more answers from Buster Houston. He had offered this deal of luring the dirty cop. But in order to go along with that, she needed more information. She needed facts. Specific data.

Until then, she wouldn't call her partner dirty. Yeah, he was overzealous about Sam Johnson's guilt, but did that make him dirty? He could merely be reacting to her actions.

But that explanation felt less and less likely.

And left her with one major sore spot.

How had she been so blind?

Her gaze settled on Johnson once more. He was the one thing in all this that she'd been right about.

A realization settled heavily onto her just then. It was her responsibility to see that he survived this. She was a cop, Homicide. She wasn't about to allow an innocent civilian to be murdered on her watch. One might say he wasn't so innocent, since he had made no move to stop James Watts from overseeing the execution of the vengeance on those three men. But that had been out of Johnson's hands to a great extent. Watts would have done it with or without Johnson's knowledge. The same way he would use him now, with or without his knowledge.

Johnson needed protecting. Just like his family.

The best way for her to accomplish that goal was to allow him to believe that he was protecting her. He'd keep her close without argument.

With that decision out of the way, she let her lids drift closed.

Tonight was going to be a long one.

Chapter Twelve

Crew territory. Central L.A., Forty-eight Street through Seventy-fifth, Western Avenue to Overhill Drive. Twenty-seven blocks with over 1600 active gang members. And somewhere in this maze of neighborhoods and shops was the headquarters of Lil Watts.

Sam had parked along the curb in a busier section in hopes of avoiding trouble. Smith waited quietly in the passenger seat. That she was here at all spoke volumes about just how much she had decided to trust Sam. He wasn't sure he'd ever be able to adequately repay her.

They had taken the risk and rendezvoused with Anders. Sam hadn't slept at all. Instead, he'd laid out a plan that would, if they were lucky as hell, work. Anders agreed that it was the only way, but

Smith didn't like it. Yet she'd agreed to back him up—to a point.

The only way to get Watts off Sam's back was to kill him or send him to prison, and even the latter was no guarantee he wouldn't order executions from behind bars.

What Sam really needed was a major shake-up involving LAPD and the media. Buster Houston would help keep gangland under control after the shake-up. His influence carried a lot of weight—with everyone but Lil Watts. With Watts out of the way, some sort of peaceable arrangement could be reached once more.

Sam was reasonably sure Watts's ego and confidence were overinflated by his in with the cops. Working directly with the boys in blue, he had no fears. His predecessors would never have formed an alliance with cops. Various gang leaders of the past had at times come to understandings with law enforcement but never an alliance of "you scratch my back and I'll scratch yours" like this one appeared to be. But most of that was speculation at this point. What they needed was evidence.

In reality, all Sam had to go on was the word of Buster Houston. Well, and the odd behavior of Charles Sanford.

Time was short. Sam knew he couldn't possibly expect to last much longer without disappearing completely, and then his family would pay the price. He had to act fast with a plan that, admittedly, posed some major risks to all involved.

He needed to make Lil Watts believe that his cop allies had double-crossed him. Sam also needed Buster Houston to publicly stand up against Watts and his secret alliance that benefited no one but Watts.

Smith had accessed the LAPD system to get anything she could on recent gang activities.

Now, armed with minimal knowledge and Smith's .22, Sam's 9 mm and a high-powered rifle Anders had provided, they were almost ready to put the first phase of their plan into motion. The final piece of information they needed was a location. That would be coming any minute.

Sam's cell phone vibrated. He slid it out of his pocket and checked the display. This was the call he'd been waiting for.

"Johnson."

He listened carefully as the address was rattled off. He knew it wouldn't be repeated. The connection was severed, and he turned to Smith. "Got it."

"So we're ready," she said without making eye contact.

"We're not going to do this your way, Detective," he warned. She could raise all the holy hell she wanted. But the decision had been made. Anders and Colby agreed. Sam would be the one to go in, not her.

"If you go in there," she said, finally meeting his eyes, "you're a dead man."

He shifted his attention forward. "To some, I'm already a dead man."

"Funny."

She had this theory that because she was the cop she was supposed to take the risk. Not going to happen on his watch.

"Let's just do it my way and get it over with," he said, "Debating the issue any longer is just wasted effort."

"Look," she snapped, "*if* there's any truth to these allegations about some of the cops in my division, I want to know it. I can't get that done with you dead." She huffed a breath of frustration. "I need you."

The corners of his mouth tilted before he could stop the reaction. "I'm sorry—" he rested his gaze on hers "—I don't think I heard that last part. Could you repeat that please?"

"Go to hell, Johnson."

The amusement he'd felt temporarily vanished. "I can't allow you to risk your life for me." That was the bottom line.

"Don't flatter yourself. It won't be for you. I need to do this for me. For what I believe in."

"For your brother?" he suggested, searching her face and then her eyes when she finally met his once more.

"Sure." She lifted one shoulder, let it drop. "I'm a cop because of him. But—" she pressed Sam with a look that made it clear just how serious she was "—mainly this is about me doing my job."

His gaze narrowed with the new question that bobbed to the surface of all the other troubling thoughts churning around in his head. "You knew something wasn't right when you went to the Colby Agency." The notion had been kicking around in the back of his head since he'd walked into Victoria Colby-Camp's office and found Smith there. This was the first time he'd gone so far as to say it out loud.

"Yeah. I guess I did."

"It's tough." He watched the pedestrians on the street hurrying to get home, now that darkness was almost upon them. "You want to believe in people, in the system. But sometimes one or both fail you. It's hard to know who or what to trust."

"Whether or not I can trust my partner is still up in the air. But there's one thing you can count on— *you* can trust me."

He turned to look at her, wished he hadn't. He'd been pretending for a long time that she didn't really care about him. That he was just another case. But he'd been lying to himself. He'd seen *this* in her eyes before. Had felt that spark between them.

"I think maybe I can," he admitted.

They might never be totally on the same side, but

he knew he could trust her. She'd earned that acknowledgment the hard way, by risking her life to help him survive this long.

"We should get into position."

She was right. He started the engine and pulled out onto the street. The first step was to find a house or apartment they could use close to ground zero. He couldn't risk driving down the block where Lil Watts maintained his headquarters. After surveying possibilities on all sides of the location, he found a workable location one street over. A four-story building for lease. The front of the building he'd selected faced the back of the house that sat directly across the street from the target, giving Sam a direct view of the front of Watts's headquarters. He and Smith would get into position here while Spencer Anders tailed Sanford to make sure he didn't get in the way and to keep tabs on his whereabouts until this thing went down at noon tomorrow.

After parking in the alley that ran between the building and a long line of abandoned shops, they emerged from the car, keeping a close watch in all directions. He didn't need any of Lil's scouts to spot them. Sam took the duffel with the tools he would need from the backseat. Smith grabbed the case that contained the rifle.

The alley entrance provided the best scenario for breaking and entering. Sam retrieved the necessary tools for picking the lock and had the door open in less than half a minute. Flashlights in hand, they entered the building.

An open center stairwell led upward. On the third floor they moved to the front of the building and found the window with the best view. Since the window sashes were painted shut, he used a glass cutter to remove the glass in the lower sash. Smith assembled the high-powered rifle Anders had sent along.

She handed the rifle to Sam and he checked the target through the night-vision scope. Two of Watts's men loitered on the front porch. Sam could see them as clearly as if they were standing right in front of him. Satisfied with the preparations, he leaned the weapon against the wall next to the window.

"Last chance," he said to her. "It's not too late to change your mind. I can deliver the message."

She shook her head. "We've been over this before. It's this way or no way."

"I guess this is it, then."

She nodded and shoved Sam's 9 mm into her waistband and hung the lanyard around her neck so that her badge was displayed in plain sight against her white blouse. "I'll be back in fifteen minutes max."

When she turned to go, he said, "There's just one thing."

Smith paused, looked back at him. "Yeah? What's that?"

He shouldn't have. Hell, he was a fool to do it, but he couldn't help himself. He grabbed her by the shoulders and kissed her hard on the mouth. She tasted soft and sweet, like the chocolate she'd eaten before they left her house. He hadn't kissed a woman in more than a year and he wanted to kiss her on and on, but that would have to wait until this was over. He wanted to explore this thing between them…if she was willing.

"Be careful." He released her, stepped back.

She nodded jerkily then pivoted and headed for the stairwell.

Sam watched her go until she'd disappeared into the darkness, then he took up his position at the window.

Just don't let her get killed, he prayed.

LISA SAT IN THE CAR a moment before starting the engine. Her heart wouldn't slow its frantic beating. She couldn't catch her breath.

He'd kissed her.

She didn't know whether to whoop for joy that he actually had noticed this thing between them, or to be ticked off that he obviously believed he wouldn't be seeing her again.

That was something she'd have to ask him when she got back. And she was coming back. No way was she letting one of these slimeballs take her life.

She had too much to do.

After driving down the block, she made the turn onto the street where Watts's latest headquarters was reported to be. Anders had reached out to his own private sources and gotten the address when LAPD couldn't. She cut her department some slack; their hands were tied in many ways whereas a civilian could cross lots of lines if he had the means.

This was the place. Fourth house on the right. She pulled over to the curb, took another long, deep breath and got out.

Three black SUVs and one white Caddy lined the curb in front of the ranch-style house. The two guards on the porch had already started down the steps, weapons drawn.

Stay calm. No sudden moves.

The two men started laughing as she crossed the street in their direction.

"Is this a bust, baby?" one of them asked with a snort of derision.

"I need to talk to Lil Watts." She kept her arms hanging loosely at her sides in a nonthreatening manner as she neared their position. She looked each man in the eyes, first the one who'd spoken, then the other.

"You'd have better luck talking to Santa Claus. Now get on outta here," the second man barked, "before we find a better use for you."

"This is official business, gentlemen. Tell him that Detective Charles Sanford sent me." That the last part rolled off her tongue so easily was testament to the idea that all she'd heard the past twenty-four hours had influenced her thinking far more than she'd wanted it to.

A look passed between the two men. The guy who'd made the Santa Claus remark said, "This better be legit." He held out his hand. "Gimme your piece."

"I don't think so." She held her ground, knowing this could be the last damned thing she did.

"Suit yourself. We wouldn't want a member of L.A.'s finest to be put out," he sneered. "But make a move for it and you're dead."

"Fair enough," she allowed.

Her escorts led the way onto the porch. One pounded on the door with his fist and the door opened instantly.

"What?" The man who stood on the threshold glared at the two scouts then at her. "What you want?"

"She says she's got a message from Sanford."

A chill crawled up her spine. She couldn't possibly deny that these guys knew her partner. If that meant what it appeared to, then she'd been one big, dumb fool. Frustration and anger kindled in her belly. How could she have been so damned blind?

The guy on the other side of the threshold jerked his head for her to enter. She walked into the house, and the door slammed behind her. That Sam wouldn't be able to see her any longer made her stomach clench. She was on her own now.

"Sit."

She lowered into the closest chair. Three other men lounged on the sofa, one was cleaning his weapon, the other two were playing cards.

The guy who'd allowed her entrance left the room. She watched the seconds tick by on the wall clock. Nearly a minute and about two hundred thuds of her heart later, he returned.

"This way."

She followed him down a narrow hall and into what might have at one time been a couple of bedrooms at the rear of the house. The dividing wall had been taken out, leaving one wide-open space. Lil Watts was draped on a sectional sofa, a half-naked woman on either side of him. He looked Lisa up and down, then gave the ladies a nudge, and the two left the room. Both gave her the evil eye as they passed.

"You got some nerve walking in here like this." He adjusted the shiny chains around his neck. "What is it Sanford wants now? I told him not to be jerking me around no more. I'm The Man now. I won't be taking no more monkey-do orders from him."

Another of those icy chills went through her. "In that case, I'm afraid you're not going to like this message."

Watts pulled a pearl-handled .40 caliber gun from under the loose cushion next to him. "You sure you wanna deliver it?"

"Hey," she gave him a look that said whoa. "I'm just the messenger. If you don't like the message, tell it to Sanford."

He assessed her a long moment. "Maybe I will. He didn't say nothing about recruiting you. When did that happen? I thought you was one of them goody two-shoes cops that still thinks the world is worth saving."

"I got over it."

He laughed. "Needed a raise in pay, huh? You cops don't get paid squat."

She managed a halfhearted smile. "That's for sure."

"So what the hell does Sanford want?"

"He needs you to meet him at noon tomorrow. Corner of South Western and Vernon. An abandoned place called Soupy's."

Watts sent one eyebrow high up his forehead. "That's a little public, ain't it? We usually do our business in a more private setting."

"You want to call him and verify the time and place?" she asked, her tone impatient. She could not let him see her sweat.

His eyes tapered into assessing slits as if he was weighing her suggestion then he shrugged. "Nah. If that fool wants to meet out in the open like that, then so be it. I ain't the one with nothing to worry about." He cocked his head and studied her a moment longer. "Is this about that fool Johnson? That man's dead. Sanford don't need to be worrying 'bout that. I gave the order. He'll probably be dead before the sun comes up on another day."

Lisa shook her head. "I don't think it's about him." Then she opened her mouth as if she intended to say more, but snapped it shut, blinked twice as if uncertain. "That's all." She turned to the door, but he spoke before she could take the first step.

"You have something else on your mind, *Detective?*"

She shifted back to face him, shook her head. "No."

A frown worked its way across his brow. "I think you do."

The man who'd escorted her to the room stepped closer in an act of intimidation.

"I could get in major trouble for saying anything…. It's just that I have a big problem with what he's got planned for you."

Watts rocketed to his feet, fury contorting his face. "Explain yourself fast or one of my boys'll be cleaning your brains off that wall. How's that for major trouble?"

She held up her hands for him to back off. "Sanford and his boys are finished doing business with you. He's planning a switch to Houston. There's going to be a war and you're going to lose."

Rage blazed in his eyes. "Why should I believe that crap? Sanford knows better than to pull anything like that on me. I got too much on that bastard."

"Maybe that's the problem." She backed up a step, bumped into the other guy. She wanted these two to think she was scared. Truth was, she was pretty damned terrified. "Listen, I wouldn't really care, but it was one of Houston's people that killed my brother. I don't have any desire to do business with him or his Nation."

For three beats she wasn't sure if he'd bought it. Then he said, "You tell Sanford I'll be there. Soupy's. I know the place. If what you say is going down, then maybe me and you can do business directly in the future."

She nodded, would have turned away again but he went on. "You keep this part of our talk to yourself. You take care of me, and I'll be sure you don't ever have to worry about working with Buster Houston."

This time she gave him a real smile. "Works for me."

"Why don't you tell me exactly what Sanford's planning?"

Her tension ratcheted up. She hadn't prepared for this part. She'd just have to wing it.

"COME ON, COME ON," Sam muttered.

She should have been out of there by now.

Two minutes more and he was going over there. If it blew the plan then it would just have to blow it.

A creak behind him had him executing an about face.

"Put down the rifle."

Four men formed a line and moved closer to his position, their weapons leveled on him.

Well, so much for holding up his end of the plan. Lisa was still in there and he wasn't going to be any help at all.

"Put down the weapon!" the leader repeated.

Sam propped the rifle against the wall, considered going for the .22 on the window ledge.

"Don't move or you're dead," the one giving the orders said, settling Sam's indecision. "Get the rifle and the handgun," he said to one of his cohorts.

One of the men stepped forward and took possession of the rifle, holding it gingerly with gloved hands. Another patted Sam down and snagged the .22 on the window ledge, then stepped back into line with his pals.

"Do it," the leader ordered.

Sam braced for the impact of bullets.

But no weapons fired.

Instead, three of the lowlifes rushed him.

He dodged the first punch. Wasn't so lucky with the

second. Before he could get in a blow of his own, one of the men had manacled his arms behind his back.

The next several punches landed in his gut.

He tried his best to block the rest of the blows from registering, but his luck didn't hold out for that, either.

Chapter Thirteen

Lisa's hands were shaking when she got back into
the rental car.

She'd gotten through the meeting without getting
shot or otherwise damaged.

Taking a deep breath, her first since before she'd
gone into that house, she started the engine and
drove away. The one-block drive to reach the
building where Sam waited seemed to take forever
when it was in reality less than a minute.

The side-entrance door stood open, propelling
her senses to a higher level of alert. She'd closed it.
Had Sam decided to go after her?

Damn. That could be disastrous.

She shoved the gearshift into Park and jumped
out of the car. Flashlight. She had to have a flashlight. She ran back to the car, got the flashlight then
sprinted into the building.

The silence had her pulse racing. She wanted to

call out his name, but that could alert anyone who might be prowling around in here. She took the stairs quietly, but rapidly. When she hit the third-floor landing she knew there was trouble. He should have called out to her by then.

Silence.

"Sam?"

She ran the flashlight's beam over the window. No Sam. No weapons. Slowly she swung it back and forth over the floor beyond where she stood.

The light hit the soles of his sneakers first.

Fear charged through her.

"Sam!"

She was on her knees at his side before she'd realized she'd moved. He was breathing. Thank God. She ran the light over the back of his head, his torso, then his legs. No blood, no apparent injuries.

"Sam." She leaned closer to him, directed the flashlight on his face. She grimaced. His face was bloody. Eyes swollen.

A sound echoed from somewhere in the building. She drew her weapon and sent the light over the open space around her. Nothing she could see. When she was satisfied that no one was creeping about on that floor at least, she attempted to rouse him again. She had to get him out of here. Slowly he came awake. She helped him to roll over and then sit up. His lip was cut open. His nose had stopped bleeding and didn't appear to be broken.

"What happened?" she asked as she assisted him to his feet. He was unsteady even with her help. She shifted the beam of light to the area around the window once more. "Where are the weapons and the duffel?"

"The guys who beat the crap out of me took them."

In this neighborhood she wasn't surprised at that. She was, however, a little startled that he'd let someone sneak up on him like that.

They could talk about that later.

"We have to get out of here." She guided him to the stairs, checked with the flashlight to see that the coast was clear, then started downward.

He stumbled but caught himself.

"Careful." She tightened her arm around him.

She didn't relax until she had him in the passenger seat of the car. She raced around the hood and got behind the wheel. Her fingers shook as she twisted the key in the ignition. The faster they got out of here the better.

Flooring the accelerator, she barreled out of the side alley and onto the street. Thankfully there wasn't any traffic. She didn't turn on her headlights until she'd reached the main cross street.

"Do you need a doctor?"

She could only see the surface injuries, and

judging by the way he was holding his gut, there could be far worse things going on.

"No." He groaned, grabbed his ribs.

"Okay, that's it. I'm taking you to the E.R."

"I'm okay," he growled. "Just find a drugstore. I'll tell you what I need."

Her nerves were shot and she lacked the energy to argue with him so she did as he said. She'd hit the Strip before she found a drugstore that was open this late. Parking was a pain in the rear but she managed.

"What do you need?"

"Get me some kind of pain reliever, peroxide and whatever else you think we could use."

She didn't like this. At the academy she'd had basic first aid, but there could be something serious going on that wasn't visible.

"What about your abdomen and chest? You don't feel there's any internal injuries?"

He exhaled a pained breath. "No. Some bruising for sure, but I don't think it's worse than that."

She could sit here and debate with him or she could just trust his judgment. Arguing would only waste time.

"I'll be right back."

She locked the car and hurried inside.

Fighting the urge to grab a basket and run down the aisles, she walked at a leisurely pace. One by one she gathered the items she felt might be needed.

She picked up a couple of energy bars and some bottled water. After reviewing the items she'd selected, she took a moment to compose herself. She noticed the dried blood on her right hand and reminded herself to use her left, then headed for the checkout counter.

"Will that be all?" the clerk asked.

Lisa managed a tight smile. "That's it." She dug through her purse until she found her wallet while the clerk rang up the items. Her debit card in her left hand, she waited for a total.

The television mounted to the wall behind the counter snagged her attention. The sound had been muted, but she didn't need to hear the news bulletin for her brain to register the impact.

Yellow tape, pulsing blue lights, and a news man standing in the foreground while cops swarmed what looked like someone's front yard behind him. The breaking news crawler read: Three male victims pronounced dead after a shootout. An all-points bulletin has been issued for Samuel Johnson, Jr. and a female accomplice.

The concept of what she was seeing didn't fully penetrate the shock swaddling her brain until Sam's picture flashed on the screen.

"You can swipe your card now," the clerk said.

Lisa jerked her attention back to the woman. "I'm sorry." Her hand shaking again, she swiped her card, then entered her PIN number.

The clerk stuck the receipt in the bag and thrust it at her.

Lisa hurried out of the store. The overwhelming sensation of being watched washed over her, but she was certain it was her imagination. She hurried to the car and got behind the wheel. She passed the bag to Sam.

"We have to—"

"Anders just called," he interrupted. "They've issued an APB for me and my female accomplice related to some shootout over on Fiftieth."

"I know." That meant they couldn't go back to the hotel, couldn't go to her place. And definitely couldn't use her credit cards.

Her debit card.

Damn. She'd just used it in the drugstore.

She checked her side mirror then squealed away from the curb. Calm down, she ordered. The last thing she wanted to do was get pulled over for speeding or reckless driving.

"We need a place to hide," she mumbled, talking more to herself than to him. He didn't answer. Every patrol car she passed on the street had her fingers clamping more tightly around the steering wheel. This rental car wasn't in her name, but it was in the Colby Agency's name. Her partner knew a Chicago agency was here working on Sam's case.

Not good. Not good at all.

Her parents were out of town on vacation. Going there would be too risky. But that wouldn't be a problem with the Miller house. The Millers were her parents' best friends. They vacationed together every year. That could work.

"I have an idea."

Sam was too busy trying to open the childproof cap on the pain relievers to question what she'd decided. She took the scenic route through the Hollywood Hills. The Millers had a home overlooking the city; a gorgeous neighborhood and she knew where they hid the spare key. She also knew the code for their security system. Every year she was given strict orders to check on their plants while they were away. The Millers had no children and couldn't tolerate pets. Their plants were their babies. She'd stopped by before leaving for Chicago. This was the perfect place to go now. If any of the neighbors saw her they wouldn't suspect a thing.

Sam seemed to be sleeping by the time she pulled into the Millers' driveway. She parked the rental on the other side of the garage in the spot where the Winnebago usually sat. The rental wouldn't be visible from the street, and Chuck had no reason to think she would come here. As far as she could recall she'd never mentioned the Millers to him.

With the drugstore bag in hand she retrieved the spare key from its hiding place in a magnetic holder beneath the elbow in the gutter downspout. Leaving Sam in the car until she'd opened the door and disarmed the security system, she checked to make sure all was as it should be inside. Then she went back for him.

"I'm not asleep," he muttered as she touched his shoulder. "I'm concentrating." He groaned as he pushed out of the seat. "Trying to block the pain until these pain relievers kick in."

She kept one arm around his waist as she guided him inside, then locked the door and reactivated the security system. "Do you want to go straight to bed after we've cleaned up your face?"

"Hot bath," he said on a grunt. "I think that and about four more of those pills might help."

There was a whirlpool tub in the master bath. She headed in that direction. He leaned against the counter and cleaned up his face with a damp cloth while she prepared the water in the tub. He swore repeatedly as he worked. She winced each time she glanced his way. One eye was swollen almost to the point of being closed. The other wasn't quite so bad but couldn't be called good.

When she'd gotten the hot water to the required level, she stood, bumped the bowl of bath crystals, knocking it into the water. "Damn!" She grabbed it, but it was too late. "Looks like you're going to have a bubble bath," she said wearily.

He tried to smile and grimaced. "No problem. I love bubble baths."

As tired as she was, she laughed. "Whatever. Get in the tub. I'll get you some ice."

On her way to the kitchen, she slowed to admire the gorgeous view from the wall of windows and French doors that extended the length of the back of the house. The pool glistened invitingly beyond those French doors. The furnishings were modern yet elegant. Seemed weird to be hiding from the cops in such a posh environment.

In the kitchen she turned on the news while she prepared an ice bag for Sam's swollen eyes. There wasn't any change in what was being reported on the news about the shooting incident. The whole idea was crazy. They hadn't been anywhere near Fiftieth tonight, and there definitely hadn't been any shoot-outs in the neighborhood they'd visited.

She thought of Sam, out cold lying on the floor of that leased building, and the missing weapons.

That was it. Someone had followed them there and waited for the right moment to take the weapons. She would bet her life that the weapons had been used or planted at the scene of the shootings being reported. Her own partner was framing her. She couldn't be certain that was the case, but her instincts were screaming at her to consider the possibility. It would take some fancy footwork to clear that up. Some stupid part of her still didn't want to believe that her partner was the one…but he was. There was no doubt about it now.

She could get kicked off the force because of him, could go to prison.

Could get dead.

Tomorrow's plan had to work. That was the only way out of this whole mess.

The bottle of blush wine in the refrigerator lured her attention back there when she would have closed the door. She could definitely use a drink. And since the pain reliever wasn't the kind that warned against the use of alcohol in conjunction with it, Sam could have one, too.

With two stemmed glasses in one hand, the bottle and the ice bag in the other, she shuffled back to the master suite. She tucked the bottle under one arm and tapped the door.

"Are you in the tub? Can I come in?"

"Yes on both counts."

A trail of clothes led from the sink to the tub. Jeans…socks…shirt…boxers…and then Sam, neck deep in hot water and bubbles in that huge tub.

She placed the glasses on the deck of the tub, then set the bottle of wine there. "Here." She handed him the bag of ice. "That should help the swelling."

"Thanks." He pressed the bag to the eye that was so painfully swollen. He grimaced at the contact.

"Could you use a glass of wine?"

"No." He looked at her with his good eye. "I want at least three."

"No problem. There's plenty more where this came from." She filled his glass and handed it to him. "The Millers have a great wine cellar."

"How long are they going to be gone?"

"For another week." She poured her own glass of wine and sipped it, relishing the smooth taste and the promise of relaxation.

"We could drink a lot of wine and take a lot of bubble baths in a week."

Another of those real smiles spread across her lips. "You're right. We could."

Deciding that sipping her wine wasn't getting the job done, she downed most of the glass. Then poured another. When she'd polished off the better part of it, she poured Sam another and said, "I think I'll have a shower."

"Leave the wine here," he ordered. "I need it worse than you do."

He was right about that, in part anyway.

The shower was in a smaller room along with the toilet. She badly needed a shower anyway and sitting there amid all that rising steam with images of what Sam Johnson looked like under all those bubbles was more than she could tolerate.

She washed her hair then turned the water to the

hottest setting she could bear. Slowly her muscles started to relax and the worries of the day faded just a little. By the time the water had started to cool, she felt tremendously better. After toweling her hair and drying her body, she donned the plush robe hanging on the back of the door.

"Is it okay to come out?" she called through the door before stepping out into the part of the bathroom where she'd left Sam bathing.

No answer. Maybe he'd already finished his bath and retired to the bedroom.

She cracked the door open and peeked out, didn't see him so she emerged. He'd drained the tub, even rinsed it and found a robe or something to put on since his clothes were still strewn over the floor. She gathered his discarded attire and placed everything in a neat pile on the counter. Then she went in search of him.

Sam had found his way to the kitchen and was preparing a cheese and fruit tray when Lisa surfaced from her long shower. He felt immensely better, but he was going to be as sore as hell come morning.

"You hungry?" he asked her.

"Not really, but considering how much wine I've had I'd better eat something."

They claimed seats at the island and had another glass of wine along with the cheese and grapes.

"Do you think Watts went for our story?"

"I'm certain he did." She glanced at the muted television. "I don't know how this will affect his decision to show. We'll just have to wait and see. Plain old curiosity may bring him to the rendezvous point."

"That's assuming those guys who roughed me up weren't part of Watts's crew and somehow knew what we were up to."

She sighed. "Yeah. I thought about that. But how could they have known?"

"Don't know." He popped a grape into his mouth. "Anders called while you were delivering your message. He said that the guys Houston sent confirmed delivery of the message to Sanford." Sam had touched base with him while Lisa showered to let him know they were safe and to ensure he could still track their location with the microfiber bugs they both wore. Anders had assured him all was a go.

"So Sanford thinks Lil Watts is meeting with a new LAPD contact at noon tomorrow in hopes of trading him in for a better model."

"Right. No matter what happens tonight, I don't think he'll be able to resist putting in an appearance just to see what's going down."

Lisa nibbled on her cheese. "God, I hope so. I'm so tired of all this craziness."

Sam pushed off the stool. "Why don't we take this to the bedroom and relax?"

"Good idea."

By the time they'd transported their booty to the master bedroom, it hit Sam that sharing a bed with Lisa was going to do many things, but relaxing him wasn't one of them.

"Why don't you take this room?" he suggested, "and I'll find another." With a house this big there was bound to be a number of bedrooms.

"No." She set the bottle of wine and the glasses on the bedside table. "I want you with me."

He placed the platter on the table on his side of the king-size bed. "It's a big bed. I think we can manage."

"I think so," she echoed.

Together they pulled the covers back. He groaned, this time with something besides pain, as he settled onto the cool sheets. The bed felt heavenly and the cool sheets reminded him just how tired he was.

"You think we'll find our way out of this?" she asked in a small voice.

She was scared. She would never admit it, but she was.

"Maybe. Yes."

Silence.

"I'm sorry I ever thought you might be involved with those murders. I was wrong." She exhaled a big, weary breath. "About a lot of things."

Knowing it was going to hurt like hell, he rolled to his side so he could look at her. "We were both wrong about a lot of things. We're human. Don't beat yourself up over any of this. You wanted to believe the best in your partner. You couldn't have known what he was doing. Hell, evidently, no one does."

She rolled toward him. "You're right."

Her blond hair was still damp, but the way it fell across her throat made him want to reach out and touch her there. She was so beautiful. Big brown eyes and peach-colored lips that looked more kissable than any he'd ever seen. Tasted that way, too, he acknowledged, remembering that brief kiss they'd shared.

As if she'd been thinking about that moment, too, she said, "I'm glad you kissed me tonight. It was nice."

Nice. Not exactly what he'd been going for.

"I'll try to do better next time." He laughed softly, but his attention was riveted to that mouth, already wishing for the opportunity to do better than "nice."

"You could try to do better now," she offered.

Heat rushed along his limbs, hardening every muscle in his body in an instant. "You talked me into it." He leaned his head closer, pressed his lips to hers.

The kiss was tentative at first. Slow and easy. No need to rush. Not like before. There was no hurry. The fingers of her right hand gingerly touched his jaw, taking care not to delve into damaged territory. The feel of her fingers against his skin set him on fire. He wasn't sure how much of that he could take.

He touched her next. First her throat…then her breast. Together, taking their time, they released the ties of each other's robe. The exploration took his breath away, made him crazy with want for her. She touched him everywhere, tenderly, making him forget all about the pain. Not letting her get ahead of him, he examined every inch of her—could scarcely catch his breath between kisses.

She rolled onto her back and urged him to move on top of her. Their bodies fit together perfectly. They cried out together as he sank slowly, deeply inside her. The heat, the sensations…all of it pushed him closer and closer to an edge he hadn't visited in so long.

They found release together, then collapsed, tangled in a damp, hot heap. Long minutes later, when their respirations had slowed to somewhere near normal, they indulged in more wine and cheese and then the kissing started again. This time the lovemaking was more frantic…more desperate.

And this time they drifted off to sleep wrapped in each other's arms after coming apart so completely that Sam wasn't sure he would ever be the same again.

Chapter Fourteen

Chicago
Friday, June 7, 8:00 a.m.

"If just one thing goes wrong," Victoria warned, "Sam and Lisa could both end up dead. Not to mention Detective Sanford and Lil Watts and his followers."

Jim strove for patience, but it wasn't easy. "I'm very much aware of that, Victoria." If half of what he suspected about Sanford was true, he wasn't particularly worried about whether he ended up dead or not.

His mother crossed to the window that looked out on the park across the street from the brownstone the Equalizers called home. Jim was a little surprised to find Victoria waiting for him when he arrived at work that morning. Especially after the way they'd left things the last time they talked.

Victoria didn't agree with the strategy Johnson,

Anders and Jim had decided upon. She felt there was too much room for error. Too many things could go wrong.

It was the only way.

"I have a contact in California's State Bureau of Investigations," Jim went on when she didn't say more. "He's meeting with LAPD's Internal Affairs this morning to try and get a formal investigation going. We've covered every base possible in an effort to ensure the least amount of collateral damage."

Victoria turned back to him. "Then why can't this sting operation fall under IA's jurisdiction or CBI? Why risk this rogue attempt?"

Jim braced his hands against his desk and fixed the firmest glare he could on his mother. "Because we don't have the luxury of time. IA won't do anything until they have justifiable cause—evidence. The word of a gang lord is hardly that. We have to do this now before anyone involved can cover his tracks."

"It's too dangerous." She crossed her arms over her chest, unconvinced. "I could speak to Lucas. See what he could do to hasten things along."

Lucas Camp, Jim's stepfather, was connected, that was for certain. CIA, Homeland Security, you name it. But time simply wouldn't allow a deviation from the plan already in place.

"Mother," Jim said for emphasis, "there are

hundreds—no thousands—of gang members on those streets. Right now there is a contract on Sam Johnson. It's a miracle he's survived the past forty-eight hours in L.A. I'm not risking his life another night. This has to go down today."

"You know that any taped evidence they collect in this operation won't be admissible in court," she reminded, the wheels in her head working overtime to come up with a way to stop this sting from going down.

"Yes, I know. But what it will do is prove what Charles Sanford has been up to. My guess is he'll be trying to cut a deal so fast IA won't know what hit them."

Victoria closed her eyes a moment, her demeanor uncharacteristically troubled. "There are a dozen things that could go wrong."

"You're right. We've moved Johnson's family to a private safe house. Battles and Call will be working with Anders behind the scenes."

"That's a decision I should have been in on," Victoria reminded, disappointment flashing in her eyes.

Jim straightened. "You mean the way I was in on the decision to brief the Johnson family about Sam's presence in California?"

She didn't respond at first. Jim took that opportunity to say something he'd been holding back for a while now. "You're going to have to let me make my own mistakes, Victoria. It's the only way I can move on with my future."

Victoria walked to his desk, held his gaze with those dark eyes. "Even when I know the consequences are grave?"

"Even when you know I'll fail," he confirmed. "This is my life now. You have to allow me to live it."

She reached for her purse and squared her shoulders. "I suppose there's nothing else I can say."

"Not about this operation, no."

"I'll urge my investigators to cooperate fully with Spencer since change at the eleventh hour would only work against us all. But understand that I disagree wholly with this operation. Sometimes playing by the rules *is* the best way to get the job done."

Victoria walked out of his office showing the same determination she'd had when she'd entered. Nothing he had said had altered her opinion of the situation one iota.

Was she right? Could he be risking too much? He and Anders had gone over the strategy for this operation a dozen times. This was the only way to force Sanford's hand. Johnson and Smith agreed. There simply was no alternative. Every minute brought the possibility of death closer to Sam Johnson. He was living on borrowed time.

It was all or nothing.

Jim just wished that Victoria had more faith in him. This didn't have to be a contest about who was the better strategist or who had the most experience. This whole thing felt like a war of blood against blood, Colby against Colby.

The Equalizers were off to a great start. He needed Victoria to recognize that and to respect it.

To respect him as an equal.

Chapter Fifteen

South Western Avenue, Los Angeles
11:00 a.m.

"It's the only way," Sam argued.

Lisa had to walk away. She couldn't listen to any more of this. Sam Johnson was intent on getting himself killed. The man would not listen to reason.

They'd taken up their position at Soupy's, an out-of-business soup kitchen that had served the community for more than a decade before being abandoned because of the growing gang-related activities in the area.

Anders threw his hands up, as disgusted with Johnson as Lisa was. "Okay, man, it's your call."

Jeff Battles and Brett Call were playing lookout on the roof of the dry cleaner across the street. Jim Colby's contact at the California Bureau of Investigations was standing by as unofficial backup. They couldn't risk any official involvement for fear that a leak to LAPD would tip off Sanford. Most of the cops on the force were damned good men and women, but, like Lisa, no one would want to believe Sanford had crossed over to the dark side. Someone would tip him off out of respect.

Considering they were basically on their own, the danger to all involved was multiplied many times over, but there was no help for it. Even if they dared risk involving other cops or anyone from CBI, another gun was the last thing they were going to need; paramedics and maybe a miracle, considering Sam Johnson's inflexible attitude.

She had spent the morning with Anders and Sam rigging the place for video and audio surveillance. Whatever went down in here today would be recorded, so there would be no changing of stories.

The down side to that was that none of the recorded material would be admissible in court *unless* one participant in the conversation and/or activities had consented. Sam wanted to be that someone, putting himself directly in the line of fire.

Lisa wanted to shake him. Actually she wanted to punch him. She closed her eyes and recalled the way they'd made love last night. Every touch… every whispered word had claimed a place in her heart. How the hell could she let him do this?

If he'd been planning to get himself killed, he

had no business making her fall in love with him. Damn it!

"It's time," Anders said.

Final preparations had to be made.

Lisa took a deep breath and did what she had to do.

She and Anders had rigged a surveillance cubicle from the walk-in cooler that was more a hot box than a cooler since there was no electricity. They'd drilled holes leading into the main rooms of the establishment and run video and audio feeds to each. Their weapons were already inside the makeshift safe room. Since cell phones wouldn't work in the cooler, Anders had engineered a landline by tying in to the phone line used by the restaurant across the alley. The restaurant didn't open until four so there wouldn't be any problem with keeping that line open between them and Battles and Call. Vernon Street flanked Soupy's on the other side. The CBI contact had taken a position in a surveillance van on the other side of Vernon.

Sam would stay out of sight in a janitor's closet in a corridor just off the main room. He would enter the scene after the others were on-site while Lisa and Anders monitored the equipment and called in backup if needed.

All three wore body armor, which made for some major perspiration issues...not counting the way her heart and pulse were racing with worry for Sam.

One wrong move, one misunderstanding could cause this thing to turn into a blood bath. But then, she'd done something similar last night and had been just as adamant that Sam allow her to do what had to be done. She had no room to complain today. But she did just the same.

Sam's face was pretty battered, he had matching shiners, but most of the swelling had gone down thanks to the ice. He was sore as hell. He didn't have to say so, the grimace he made with every move told the tale all on its own.

Lisa walked up to Sam, braced her hands on her hips and gave him a glare that said just how ticked off she was. "Try not to get yourself killed, will ya?"

A smile tugged at the corners of his mouth and he winced. "I'll see what I can do."

She started to turn away, since she knew Anders was waiting, but she hesitated. "He's my partner, you know," she said to Sam. "It really should be me out here."

Sam shook his head. "Nope. This is my problem. I'm going to fix it. I want this over so…" That gray gaze caressed hers with a tender look. "So I can get on with my life."

It was stupid, she knew, but she couldn't stop herself. She grabbed him by the ears and pulled his mouth down to hers. The kiss was soft in deference to his sore lips and lasted all of ten seconds, but every moment touched her in a way nothing else ever had.

She drew back, searched his eyes one last time, then walked away. Anders waited for her in the kitchen.

"Ladies first." He gestured to the cooler door.

Unable to speak for fear of letting her foolish emotions show, she jerked the door open and went inside. Anders had set up battery-operated lanterns. She had to give the man credit, he knew how to set up an op in the most challenging of situations.

He closed the cooler door and dropped the steel bar into place that would prevent anyone from being able to open the door from the outside. Lisa tucked her communications earpiece into place.

The players could show up at any time even though they had a half hour before the arranged meeting time.

Lisa watched on the monitor as Sam disappeared into the closet.

"I've got two dark SUVs arriving," Battles related via the communications link.

Lisa braced.

"SUVs are moving on," Battles confirmed. From his position on that rooftop he could see trouble coming from quite a distance.

She made a conscious effort to relax, focused on keeping the tension at bay. She had to be ready for anything and at the same time thinking clearly and calmly. Some tension was good, but too much could screw up the best training.

"We have movement on Vernon," Call said, the words filtering across the link. "It's the same two black SUVs," he verified.

"They've parked at your Twenty," Battles confirmed the stop in front of Soupy's. "Four subjects emerging from each vehicle. Eight total. They'll be inside in five…four…three…the door is opening… they're inside."

"We have the subjects on our monitors," Anders said quietly. That was another handy thing about the cooler—soundproof.

"Lil Watts is present and accounted for," Lisa confirmed for all listening, including the CBI contact who was tied in to their communications link. Sam's visual was limited from his position. Keeping him up to speed audibly was essential.

Watts ordered three of his men to move to the rear of the building, which meant the kitchen. One was sent back out to cover the sidewalk. The others stayed inside with Watts. He wasn't about to be caught without a number of bodyguards, all armed for war.

"We have movement in the alley," Battles stated. "Three—no four subjects."

More of that bad tension rippled through Lisa.

"I have visual confirmation on Sanford." This from Call.

Lisa had been telling herself all night that she was prepared for this, but the reality that her partner was indeed dirty shocked her all over again.

She'd worked with him for five years. Respected and admired him. Not once had she seen anything out of him that wasn't by the book. And here she stood waiting to watch him meet with the man who committed heinous crimes on his orders. She wasn't sure she would ever get accustomed to the idea.

"It's 'bout time," Watts groused as he watched out the window, evidently catching sight of Sanford and his pals.

The four men entered what had once been a dining room. Sanford, Hernandez, Wallingsford and Edmonds. All veteran detectives in Priority Homicide.

Unbelievable.

"What the hell's this about, Watts?" Sanford demanded. He looked around, expecting to find whoever Watts was supposed to meet.

Watts went toe to toe with him. "What you asking me for? You're the one who set up this party."

Lisa watched realization dawn on Sanford's face. "What the hell are you talking about?"

"Your partner said you wanted to meet," Watts sneered. "She said you had plans to switch your loyalty to the other side and I ain't having none of that."

Sanford glanced around the room. "She's playing you, you idiot. She's probably here somewhere taping this whole damned thing."

"She was pretty convincing, dog," Watts warned. "I think maybe I rather believe her than believe you."

"Shut up," Sanford commanded. He jerked his head as a signal to his cohorts. The three detectives fanned out, moving into the other parts of the building looking for Lisa and Sam no doubt.

The door to the cooler jerked a couple of times, but the would-be-intruder moved on, evidently assuming it was locked and empty.

Lisa and Anders exchanged a look.

"You been talking to Buster?" Watts demanded of Sanford. "Your partner says you made a deal with him."

"I said shut up," Sanford ordered.

"You hear that?" Watts said to one of his cronies. "He wants me to shut up."

Movement in the corridor caused Lisa's breath to catch. Sam entered the room from the side corridor. Weapons were swung in his direction.

"Why don't you tell him the truth, Sanford," Sam suggested. "You may think he's just a dumb punk, but he's pretty smart."

Watts glared at Sanford. "What the hell is he doing here?" He looked at the men on either side of him. "He shouldn't even still be alive. Somebody's falling behind on their work."

Lisa wanted to go out there. As if sensing her anticipation, Anders moved up beside her. "Let's just stay calm and focused."

"You've been made, Sanford," Sam said to Lisa's partner. "And you're all going down with him," he said with a glance at each detective as they reentered the room.

"This is your mess," Sanford said to Watts. "You clean it up."

"You," Watts snarled at Sam, "are a dead man."

"So everyone keeps saying," he muttered.

Watts pulled out his .40 caliber and shoved it against Sam's chest. "If a man wants something done right he just has to do it himself."

Lisa grabbed her weapon and started for the door.

Anders grabbed her arm. "Not yet."

"Don't trouble yourself," Lisa heard Sanford say, and went back to the monitor. "He and Smith are both going down for murder. Their prints were found on the murder weapons at the scene of a shooting last evening. I'll just take Johnson into custody and that'll be the end of that."

"Are you crazy?" Watts demanded. "I want this bastard dead. For good. I'm sick of him showing up.

My uncle was stupid enough to make a deal with him. I don't do business with fools like him."

"Just calm down, Watts," Sanford urged. "We can handle this. Whatever's going on, it's contained in this building. Johnson tried to set us both up. But we don't have to worry. He's a killer." Sanford stared at Sam as he said this. "It's time he did the time for his crimes."

Lisa's pulse raced. This could go so wrong any second. The whole game was being held together by a single thread—Sam Johnson.

"Actually," Sam said, "it's you who needs to do time, Detective Sanford." Sam gestured to Watts. "Tell him how you've been using him to do your dirty work. When you wanted someone out of the way, you ordered Watts to have some of his people do it so the deed would be written off as more gang violence. All you had to do was look the other way when Watts had business of his own to carry out without the worry of being caught and prosecuted. Seemed like a fair deal for everybody."

Sanford laughed, the sound grated on Lisa's nerves.

"You're speculating, Johnson. You should know by now that the only thing that counts is evidence. And you don't have a shred of evidence to support what you're alleging. So let's cut to the chase." He nodded, and Hernandez stepped forward. "You have the right to remain silent...."

Hernandez jerked Sam's hands behind his back to restrain him with nylon cuffs.

"Ask Buster," Sam said to Watts, ignoring Hernandez. "He has pictures to back up his stories. Sanford is playing you. Three cops in as many years." Sam shook his head. "Somebody's going to have to pay for real, eventually. He's staging the battlefield for a war and you're going to be the first casualty."

Sanford backhanded him. "Shut. Up."

Lisa turned to Anders then. "That's it. I'm going out there before this thing gets out of control."

"Let him go."

Everyone in the room pivoted to stare at the man standing in the entrance. Lisa's jaw dropped.

Buster Houston.

"What the hell is he doing here?" she murmured.

"Beats the hell out of me," Anders said, just as stunned.

"Clear the room, Watts," Buster commanded. "Just you, me, Johnson and Sanford. We're going to set the record straight."

Watts pointed his finger in the older man's face. "I got nothing to say to you, old man. Your people killed my uncle and you did nothing about it. I could have my vengeance right now with you showing up here like this. You must be going foolish for sure. If you had respected my uncle the way he respected you this thing would not have happened."

Houston stared at him for a second that turned into five. "When we're finished here, if you still feel I betrayed your uncle, then you can put a bullet in my skull and no one will retaliate. You have my word."

No less than a dozen—including those belonging to the three men who had followed Houston inside— weapons had leveled on targets. For ten or so trauma-filled seconds Lisa was certain Watts wouldn't do as Houston asked. Then, to her amazement, one slight flicker of his hand and the room cleared. Except for Hernandez, Edmonds and Wallingsford.

"No way am I sending my detectives out of this room," Sanford said. "We all stay."

Lisa leaned closer to the monitor, didn't want to miss a single facial expression.

When Watts didn't argue, Houston turned to Sanford. "You are a disgrace to your department. You are a disgrace to us all. And you are finished."

Lisa tensed. "Anders…" This was about to blow.

"Give it another minute," he urged as they watched the drama unfold.

Sanford laughed long and loud. "And just who the hell gave you the right to judge me, old man?"

"James Watts," Houston said. "You had him killed for your own selfish reasons, and for that you're going to pay."

Lil Watts looked from Houston to Sanford. "What's he talking 'bout?"

"He's a crazy old man who has outlived his purpose." Sanford pressed the barrel of his weapon to Houston's forehead. "But I can fix that right now."

"Don't you want to see the pictures?" Sam piped up, his expression a little frantic.

Lisa strained to see if that was panic on his face.

Watts demanded, "What pictures?" His voice was thick with suspicion.

Houston indicated his jacket pocket. "See for yourself," he said to Watts.

Sanford pivoted, swung his weapon toward Watts. Sam charged him.

The first shot exploded in the room.

"Now," Anders said as he headed for the door two steps in front of Lisa.

The silence that followed was even more deafening than the sound of bullets flying.

All four detectives and nearly a dozen gangsters faced off in the dilapidated dining room. The variety of weapons would have fascinated any arms dealer. Sam had Sanford pinned to the floor. Nobody moved.

Lisa and Anders stood on the fringes of the deadly standoff, weapons leveled on no one in particular.

Sam jerked Sanford's weapon out of his hand and got to his feet. Sanford scrambled up right next to him, glowering at him with murder in his eyes.

"So," Sam said as he looked around, the confiscated weapon hanging at his side, "how many are going to die here today?"

When no one answered, he went on, "Just so you know, this whole reality show has been recorded for the viewing pleasure of Internal Affairs and the District Attorney's office. We can all kill each other, or I can have some volunteers for plea bargains. What's it gonna be, boys?"

Wallingsford backed away a couple of steps and lowered his weapon. "I want a lawyer."

"Keep your mouth shut, you idiot!" Sanford shouted.

Hernandez lowered his weapon. "I want a deal."

Lisa felt a smile stretch across her lips. It was working.

"They're bluffing!" Sanford screamed.

"No." Lisa stepped forward, garnering herself some wary glances with her abrupt move. "We're not bluffing. At least three detectives are dead and there's no way to know how many others because of you," she said to Sanford. "You're the worst kind of scumbag. You even kill your own."

The move was so sudden and she was so angry that Lisa didn't see it coming. Sanford grabbed Hernandez's arm, swinging his weapon upward and jamming the man's finger against the trigger.

The sound exploded in the air. The bullet plowed into Lisa's chest, pitching her backward in a kind of slow motion. She slammed against the floor. Other weapons fired…but she couldn't see what was happening. She couldn't breathe…couldn't move.

And then Sam was on his knees next to her. "Lisa. God, are you okay?"

The air rushed into her lungs. She gasped. Coughed.

Her hands went to her chest. No blood. Relief flooded her.

"You're okay," Sam urged, pulling her up to lean against his chest. "The body armor," he reminded. "You're okay. God, you're okay."

She turned her head to see what the others were doing…but she couldn't see for all the people.

A uniformed man was suddenly hovering over her. Paramedic, she realized.

"Let's have a look, Detective Smith."

Things got a little confusing after that. But the one thing that Lisa could hang on to was Sam. He never left her side.

Chapter Sixteen

Monday, July 25, 5:05 p.m.
Chicago

Sam closed the file on his own case.

It was finished.

Detectives Wallingsford and Hernandez had spilled their guts, and Sanford was going up the river for a very long time. Watts and Houston had managed plea bargains. Considering no one had died that day, the District Attorney's office was in a very giving mood.

Sam's family was safe and life was back to normal for him. In most ways, that is.

There were still a few questions where his future was concerned.

But considering he hadn't heard from Lisa in more than two weeks, he wasn't so sure if he even had anything other than this job to look forward to.

He shoved the file into a drawer and railed at

himself for all the self-pity. He had his family. He had his life back. Business was booming here at the home of the Equalizers. And he did love his work.

Might as well call it a day. He pushed out of his chair and went to the window. His gaze landed on Jim Colby sitting on the front step. Things were still a little tense between him and his mother. Sam wanted to tell the man that life was short and he shouldn't drag this thing out.

Looked like he wouldn't have to.

A car parked at the street and the driver emerged. Victoria Colby-Camp.

A smile tugged at Sam's mouth. Oh, to be a fly on the step next to Jim.

Sam turned away from the window. Maybe he'd hang around and see how things turned out.

He wouldn't mind another happy ending.

"Victoria." Jim started to stand.

"Keep your seat," she insisted as she approached.

He watched her, this strong, independent woman who had survived hell on earth and still came out fighting. He loved her. The admission shook him a little. But it was true. He loved his mother fiercely.

Somehow they had to find neutral territory again.

She sat down on the step beside him. The image of her sitting on that stone step with her tailored suit and perfectly coiffed hair was something one didn't see every day, but that was Victoria. She set her own style, her own rhythm.

"It's time we ended this standoff."

He was all for that. "We could've done that weeks ago, if you'd chosen to be reasonable."

She cleared her throat delicately. "Reason isn't the issue, Jim."

Here they went again. "Yes, it is."

"Even Tasha—"

"Tasha isn't taking sides," he clarified before she could go there. He and his wife had had a long talk about her position on the matter. "She loves both of us and doesn't want to be put in the middle. Just because she doesn't argue with your point of view doesn't mean she agrees 100 percent, any more than she does with mine."

"You know I only want the best for you. I've waited a very long time to see you happy."

The reminder made his gut clench. "I know that. But we have to learn to respect each other's boundaries."

She laughed softly. "You know what this sounds like, don't you? It's like we're living all the things we missed, the rebellious years of adolescence, the growing pains of early adulthood, all in one big complicated lump of frustrating episodes."

Her vulnerable sincerity as much as her words made him smile. "I think you're right. That's how it feels. I need my space and you want to protect me, like I was sixteen instead of twenty-eight."

"I'm sorry, Jim." She sighed, the sound heavy-hearted. "I've overstepped my bounds repeatedly and I'm not sure how to make it right."

"Mother."

She faced him, her dark eyes too bright.

"Maybe the fact that I had a problem saying this out loud has been part of the problem, but *I love you.*" His throat tightened with emotion. "Deep down I've always loved you even when I thought I hated you. I know you want the best for me. That you want to protect me. But you don't need to be afraid for me. You need to trust me to be the man you believe I can be."

A smile trembled across her lips. "Well said, son. I think that's exactly what I need to do."

They hugged, something they didn't do enough.

And that was the end of the standoff. No more Colby versus Colby. From now on, they would stand together as equals. Unstoppable forces. The Colby Agency and the Equalizers.

"Excuse me."

Jim looked up, as did Victoria.

Lisa Smith stood on the walkway. "I'm sorry to interrupt."

Jim stood, extended his hand. "No problem. How have you been?"

She smiled. "I've been good."

Victoria dabbed at her eyes and produced a smile. "What brings you to Chicago, Lisa?"

As if his mother didn't know. Jim kept that thought to himself.

"Is Sam here?" Lisa asked, her expression hopeful.

Jim hitched a thumb toward the door. "You're in luck. He's still hanging around. Probably waiting to hear if Victoria and I worked things out."

Lisa looked from him to Victoria and back. "Well…did you?"

"We did," Victoria assured her. "We found that place we've been looking for." She looked up at Jim, her face beaming. "Common ground."

"That's great. Really great." Lisa gestured to the door. "I'll give Sam the good news." Lisa flashed a smile for Jim and his mother, then hurried up the steps and into the office.

Connie Gardner looked up from her computer. "We're closed," she said grumpily.

Biting back a chuckle, Lisa assured her, "Yeah, I know. I'm here to see Sam."

"He's in his office," Connie said without looking up again from her work.

When Lisa hesitated, the receptionist gestured to a hall beyond her desk and to the left. "His office is the second door on the left."

"Thanks." Lisa took a deep breath and headed that way. She hesitated outside his closed door and smoothed her palms over her skirt. She'd fretted over what she would wear today as if she'd been dressing for senior prom.

It was silly, she knew, but she just couldn't help herself.

She squared her shoulders and knocked.

The door opened and Sam was standing there. His mouth opened, but the words didn't come for a second.

"Lisa."

"May I come in?"

"Oh…yeah." He stepped back, opened the door wider. "I was just packing up for the day."

"I would have been here sooner, but my flight was delayed."

Sam looked confused. He indicated a chair in front of his desk. "Please have a seat."

She didn't want to sit. She wanted to throw her arms around him and kiss him…she wanted to sweep his desk clean and make love to him right there.

Clearing her mind, she recalled the script she'd mentally written.

"I'm actually looking for a job."

He looked surprised. "Oh. So you're giving up police work?"

She dropped her purse into the chair he'd offered. "I was hoping the Equalizers needed another associate."

"You want to work here?" He pointed to the floor, his expression shifting from surprised to shocked.

She nodded. "I'm looking for an apartment, too. If you have any suggestions, that would be great."

"You're moving here? To Chicago?"

Lisa had to smile. Obviously her revelation had startled him to the point he was having trouble thinking straight. She hoped that was a good thing.

"Do you have a problem with that?"

He shook his head adamantly. "No. No way. I'm thrilled to hear it."

"Good." She couldn't take it anymore. She reached for him, flattened her palms on that muscular chest. "Because I'm looking for a long-term relationship, too."

The shock on his face melted into a goofy, satisfied smile. "I was sure hoping you'd say that."

She moved in closer, lifted her arms up around his neck. "I had to work things out, Sam. Had to make sure I didn't leave any loose ends back in L.A."

"I understand." His arms went around her. "As you recall, I had a few of those I had to take care of myself."

Now, that was something she wouldn't be soon forgetting.

"So, do you think your boss would be interested in a former homicide detective?"

"I'm sure he will be very interested." Sam pulled her more firmly against him. "And I have this great place with space to spare so you won't be needing an apartment."

"What about the long-term relationship thing?" It was all or nothing. She wasn't wasting any more time.

"How does forever sound?"

"Forever is good."

He kissed her lips, just the softest brush of his.

"Then you got it," he murmured.

She went up on tiptoe and kissed him the way she'd been dying to since the last time they kissed. This was worth all the hell they had gone through. Worth the world.

Nothing could stop them now.

* * * * *

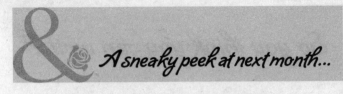

By Request

RELIVE THE ROMANCE WITH THE BEST OF THE BEST

My wish list for next month's titles...

In stores from 19th October 2012:

☐ Sultry Nights — Abby Green, Annie West
& Cathy Williams

☐ Miracle Christmas — Amy Andrews,
Shirley Jump & Cara Colter

3 stories in each book - only £5.99!

In stores from 2nd November 2012:

☐ The Garrisons: Cassie, Adam & Brooke —
Brenda Jackson, Emilie Rose
& Catherine Mann

Available at WHSmith, Tesco, Asda, Eason, Amazon and Apple

Just can't wait?

1012/05